BOOKS BY KRISTIE COOK

— SOUL SAVERS SERIES —
www.SOULSAVERSSERIES.com

Promise
Purpose
Devotion
Power
Genesis: A Soul Savers Novella
Wrath

— THE BOOK OF PHOENIX SERIES —
www.THEBOOKOFPHOENIX.com

The Space Between
The Space Beyond
The Space Within (July 2014)

FIND THE AUTHOR AT
www.KRISTIECOOK.com

To Nicole,
Nice to meet you at
Book Con 2014!
Enjoy!
Kristie Cook

HEARTS BREAK, SOULS
SHATTER, LOVE LIES IN
THE SPACE BEYOND

THE
SPACE
BEYOND

BESTSELLING AUTHOR
OF THE *SOUL SAVERS* SERIES

KRISTIE COOK

PART TWO IN THE BOOK OF PHOENIX

ACKNOWLEDGEMENTS

Thank you to my Maker and His Son, who have blessed me with everything I could ever ask for, including the ability to write and tell stories.

I also couldn't have done this without my amazing family. The Man and the Boys, I love you more than any words could ever express, and I thank you for putting up with this crazy woman who hears voices. Many thanks go to my parents, too, who gave me a foundation from which to grow.

My business partner, publisher, and best friend Chrissi Jackson deserves an award for not kicking me to the curb several times. Thank you for all that you do to make these words become an actual book people can read. Much appreciation to Tammi Swartz, who along with Chrissi, keeps some organization to the chaos of my life.

Thank you to Regina at Mae I Design & Photography for the amazing covers for this series, and to the fabulous models, too; to Jen Trammell and Kristen Yard, thank you for your keen eyes and grammatical finesse; and to Nadège Richards for the beautiful interiors.

My beta readers are the bomb (they even gave me a sweatshirt that says so!). Thank you to Stacey Nixon, Julie Bromley, Inga Kupp-Silberg, Jessie de Schepper, Claire Downs, Debbie Poole, Marissa Feidelbaum, Christina Silcox, and Heather Wakefield for your valuable feedback. Also much thanks to the above, as well as the rest of my amazing street team, Kristie's Warriors, for all of your support: Jeana Todd, Lisa Reeves, Rebecca Roth, Chloe Billingham, Josephine Militello, Christina Madison, Kate Wilson, Char Wilcoxson, Jill Cruz, Zee Hayat, Kelly Victorine, Lisa Ammari, Megan Elworthy, Michele Luker,

Mindy Janicke, Katherine Murphy, Jenny Finnigan, and Annmarie Spiby.

Thank you to April Padgett and Mindy Rasmussen for your help with the Southern-isms, and to my Facebook fans for helping me name Lake Haven and Mystic Springs.

And then there is you, dear reader, without whom, my books would be sitting on dusty hard drives, never to see the light of day. Because of you, I have the best job in the world for me. So thank you so much for giving my books a try and continuing to read them. Thank you for your recommendations and your reviews that mean so incredibly much, whether you are a blogger telling thousands of followers or someone telling a few friends. Thank you for your ongoing support and all that you do, not only for me, but for all authors. You mean all the worlds to me.

TO THE SURVIVORS
BE BRAVE

CHAPTER 1

Jeric SEA-GREEN EYES. Caramel-colored curls. Tip of a pink tongue swiping over full lips. Small body with curves in all the right places. Skin the color of dark honey that tasted just as sweet. The vision of my Twin Flame filled my mind several seconds before her physical self would fill the doorway. I couldn't tell you which was happier to see her—my soul or my dick. Both swelled to greet her.

I pulled my headphones off and tossed them on the night-stand as she closed the door to the room we shared at the Phoenix manor behind her. We'd been here for over a month, since the night we caught a ride with a trucker to meet our fate here in Tampa. Well, specifically, at the Gate in the bottom of Tampa Bay, where our souls were Forged together. The manor overlooked the Bay, appearing to be an old, abandoned hotel that most people ignored.

"I thought I'd find you in here," Leni said as she sauntered toward the bed where I sat. "Hiding again?"

I shrugged, blowing off her concern. "My training was cut short today."

"Mm-hmm," she affirmed as she bent over and placed her hands on the foot of the bed. My eyes drifted to her cleavage automatically, and I swore she flexed or squeezed or did something to make her tits practically pop out of the low-cut, green t-shirt she wore. I swallowed and forced my eyes to hers. "Not hiding at all?"

I gave her my best smile. Her eyes glazed for a brief moment, the distraction I'd hoped for. "Not from you."

She walked her hands closer to me until she had to raise a knee onto the bed. "But...?"

My distraction hadn't worked. She knew me too well and wouldn't let this go. Still, I didn't finish her sentence, but only held her eyes as she slowly crawled across the bed toward me.

"You *are* hiding from everyone else," she finished. I didn't need to answer. She already knew the truth. In the several weeks since we'd been here, I still hadn't grown used to certain things— things she didn't have to deal with like I did. Such as being able to hear again and constantly being surrounded by a whole tribe of Guardians. She leaned back, as though preparing to retreat. "Should I go then? Give you that alone time you need so much?"

I loved the sound of her voice, even as it dripped with sarcasm. But sometimes even *her* voice became too much. After eight years of complete and utter silence and living on my own nearly as long, even Leni—my other half and the woman and soul I loved more than life itself—could be a little overwhelming. I would never tell her that, though. I wasn't stupid. And especially not now, when both my soul and body ached for her so badly.

Like lightning, I reached out, grabbed her wrists, and pulled her to me. She let out a squeal and a giggle, and her green eyes lit up with anticipation the closer they came to mine.

"I need you more than I need alone time," I said, my voice already husky with desire.

She glanced at my lips, and my eyes lingered on hers until I couldn't wait another millisecond to taste them. Soft, silky, wet, and inviting. Her mouth opened slightly, giving permission for me to enter, and I slid my tongue in to meet hers. She straddled my lap and crushed her boobs against my chest as she deepened the kiss. I placed one hand on the small of her back and slid the other up to the nape of her neck and into the mass of curls.

"It's almost time for our shift at the Gate," she whispered when I gently tugged her head back, giving me access to her throat. I groaned against her neck, gave it a quick kiss, and then reluctantly pulled away.

She knew what I needed, and making out wasn't it, which was why she'd stopped us. She rolled off of me, and we slid down until we lay together in each other's arms, our mouths and our minds silent. Our hearts beat together in a rhythm that grew slower as we relaxed into each other. Leni's eyes drifted closed, and mine did, too, as our souls found each other and melded together. We languished in that state—our souls as one yet still in our bodies—the most peaceful existence possible. At least, on this world called Earth.

Right now, it was just us, as one. No me or her. No them. No physical or mental training, no past lives to force into memory or evil enemies to worry about. We didn't even have to think or feel, if we didn't want to, although it felt pretty damn great. Everything simply passed between us, within us, a slow swirl of thoughts and emotions mixing together. The Zen of everything and nothing at the same time that took me, *us*, away from the rest of the world, from the insanity our lives had become since the night we crossed paths in Italy only a couple of months ago.

The only thing better was a physical orgasm at the same time our astral selves collided and climaxed.

But that was on the other end of the spectrum between total peace and the most fucking exciting thing ever. And right now, we needed the peace. *I* needed the peace. When I'd been deaf, it had been easy to block out the rest of the world. Since my hearing had returned with the Forging, along with all kinds of special abilities, escape wasn't so easy to find, not even when we projected.

Pushing our souls out of our bodies no longer automatically meant privacy and intimacy as it had in the beginning. In fact, it was almost as rare to be able to let our souls drift together in that other realm as it was to have alone time in the physical one. Knowing what I did now, I kind of wished we hadn't mastered projecting without sex or controlling our souls so quickly. Now there were expectations, like guarding the Gate, and no dyads did that alone, especially newly Forged ones like us. Otherwise, sitting at the bottom of Tampa Bay could have been as peaceful as melding with Leni was right now.

Until our phones both beeped with text messages.

"Ignore it." I sent the feeling through our combined souls, the way we communicated when together like this.

The phones chirped again. Leni moved us to hover over mine to read the message from Mira:

"Jacquelena and Jeremicah to meeting room C ASAP."

"Sorry, hun," Leni said. "But at least she's asking for both of us."

Mira, who I'd thought had been my grandmother in this life cycle, had known and guided my soul longer than this physical body had been alive. Her soul's name was Mirangela, and when I was Micah, I'd known her as Angela. Now that Leni and I had made it to the Gate and our souls were Forged together again, Mira's role in my life was technically complete. When she was around the manor and had time, however, she tried to help me remember more about my past lives so I could use that knowledge in this one. Thank God she wasn't here often because the life lessons she wanted me to remember—the ones that mattered—consisted of the storms, which made for shitty memories. And so far, all I'd been able to remember was this life, the one before it, and the one before that, when the soul that Leni and I had shared was ripped in half.

Summoning both of us meant Mira probably didn't intend to work on my memory recall, but that didn't necessarily mean whatever she had planned was good. At least Leni would be by my side. Her presence always made all the crazy shit around here more tolerable.

Our soul pulled into two and we returned to our bodies, and then headed downstairs from our eighth-floor room in the hotel part of the manor. Meeting room C was located behind the area where the hotel's lobby used to be. With a conference table and eight chairs, it was one of the smaller rooms where groups of Guardians discussed missions ... or planned Call of Duty campaign strategies. Although we weren't exactly normal humans, we spent our downtime trying to maintain some sense of normalcy from our old lives.

Already seated were Mira and Theo, Leni's Guide this time and last, and Uri and Melinda, two of our healers who'd helped protect our bodies while we were trying to get to the Gate. Mira and Theo had been Guardians in past lives, but this time they'd chosen the easier path of being Guides so they could grow to old age for once. Mira, plump with gray hair and glasses, was in her seventies, and Theo, tall and thin with silver hair and an olive skin tone, was in his eighties. Both were much stronger than they looked. Still, as Guides, they were not equal to Guardians.

"You both look well," Melinda said, eyeing Leni and me as we entered the room and sat down across from the others. Her brown hair was pulled back in its usual braid, keeping it out of one of the oldest faces in the manor, besides those of the Guides. She and Uri, a short, blond man who was her other half, were in their thirties and the oldest of the Guardians at our Gate. They'd only lived as long as they had because they were healers and rarely went on missions, although they were forced to fight the Lakari when necessary. The Guardians didn't really have a hierarchy, but because of their age and time here, Melinda and Uri were the closest we had to leaders.

"Looking well and ready to serve their roles," Uri said, and I looked at him for meaning.

"Let's wait for Brock and Asia before we start," Mira said.

Not a minute later, the other two Guardians, the pair who'd helped us fight the Lakari and led us to the manor that first night, entered the room. Once we'd managed to beat the Lakari, get to the Gate, become Forged, and then healed, Leni and I had felt an instant connection with Brock and Asia that we felt with none of the other Guardians here. Perhaps it was because they'd been Forged only a couple of months before us when the most recent before them had been over a year. We spent most of our time with them.

Brock's body, about as tall as mine with a similar build that came from countless hours in the gym, filled the doorway first, his dark hair hanging over his brown eyes that surveyed the room. As though he seemed to approve, he motioned his hand, and the wispy Asia followed him in, her dark eyes also calculating. They stopped at the only empty chairs, and Asia cocked her head at the others, her silver hair swinging over her shoulder. She changed her hair color like she changed clothes, but not from a box. Just something she could do, apparently. When we first met, it had been short and white-blond.

"What's going on?" she asked, not one to hem and haw.

"Why don't you take a seat?" Mira offered, and she waited for Brock and Asia to sit before continuing. "This won't take long. We have a few things to share with the four of you. Melinda and Uri wanted a couple of Guides to sit in on this chat, and since Theo and I were here today, we thought now was as good of a time as ever."

Leni took my hand under the table. I shared her anxiety. Low at the moment, but Mira's tone set us on edge.

Melinda leaned forward, resting her forearms on the wooden conference table. "Can we see your marks?"

I wasn't the only one who hesitated, but after a silent moment, we all lifted our arms above the table.

"Have you noticed anything different about your marks from the other Guardians'?" Uri asked.

My brows pushed together.

"I've never noticed anyone else's marks," Leni said. Exactly.

"Exactly," Uri echoed my thoughts. "Because they're on our necks or heads. Out of sight."

The four of us on this side of the table each shifted in our chairs.

"Why are we different?" Asia asked.

Uri and Melinda glanced at each other, then exchanged another look with Mira and Theo. Theo nodded.

"Mira and I are simply Guides, and we only know what's been passed down to us by other Guides," he said, "but from what we know and what many of the Guardians are saying, your marks are different because your souls are different. We all believe you're part of the Sacred Seven."

We stared at him silently.

"And ... what's the Sacred Seven?" I asked when no one else did.

"We're not entirely sure," Mira said, "but—"

"Wait," Brock said, holding a hand up. "What do you mean you're not entirely sure? How do you say something like that and not know what it is?"

"Details have been lost over the centuries," Theo said. "We try to keep records to help future Guides and Guardians, but they're always destroyed in some manner or another. The only thing we know for sure is that the Seven are called sacred for a reason. You're the elite. The leaders of the Phoenix Guardians."

"And Jacquelena and Jeremicah are the leaders of the Seven," Uri added.

Crickets, again, as we all absorbed this. Then questions started flying.

"Whoa, whoa, whoa," Melinda finally said, raising her voice over the rest of us. We all quieted. "Like we said, we don't know what it all means."

"Since you don't know much, how do you know we're them?" I demanded. The others backed me.

"We *feel* it," Uri said. He pounded a fist against his chest. "All of the Guardians feel a respect for you at the soul level. We know at our very cores that you are supposed to lead us."

What the hell was he talking about?

"This makes no sense," Leni said. "How could nobody remember more? How could *we* not remember something like this?"

"That's always the question, isn't it?" Melinda muttered as she sat back in her chair. "Memories are always wiped. Any recordings are lost. Any time we try so much as to leave clues for ourselves, we don't remember that we did half the time and can't make sense of them the other half. It's as if the universe is against the possibility of us actually knowing everything we need to know."

"Maybe it is," Mira said. "Every lifetime, no matter how high in the world echelons we've gone, is a chance to grow and learn."

"We can't possibly know everything anyway," Uri added. "Only the Maker knows. We do our best to figure out what we can, but our meager human brains are not capable of understanding everything. It's a waste of time to try."

"So what does this mean for us?" Asia asked. "If nobody knows the answers, does it really mean anything at all?"

Theo leaned forward now. "It means when the time comes, you four will be expected to lead. Especially you, Jeric and Leni."

A prickle ran down my spine. After eight years of being a loner, I hadn't even figured out how to live in a world with other people. And they expected me to lead? Hell no.

"We wanted to tell you now so you can be prepared," Uri said. "You won't be staying here long to guard the Gate. As soon as you're ready, you should be out in the world, doing missions, helping the Broken and Lost. And if and when crisis hits, you'll be experienced to handle it."

"More and more Guardians are talking about you and the Sacred Seven, which is why we thought we better tell you ourselves," Melinda said. "You were bound to hear it from someone."

"So ... that's it?" Brock asked. "You drop this bomb in our laps and leave it at that?"

"Well, we're hoping you remember more," Mira said. "We're hoping that as the elite of all the Phoenix, you'll be able to recall past lives more clearly. That you'll work on trying to remember more diligently so we can all possibly learn what you know." She gave me a pointed look. I resisted the urge to flip her off.

"Who are the other three?" Asia asked. "If there are supposed to be seven, where are the others?"

"Good question," Melinda said. "And it's most likely there are five others. Five pairs. Because an odd number of individuals wouldn't make sense when we're all dyads."

"Do the names Nathayden and Rebethannah ring any bells?" Uri asked. I began to shake my head, but Leni squeezed my thigh.

"They do sound a tiny bit familiar," she said.

"Yeah," Asia agreed, "but it's really vague. Are we supposed to know them?"

Uri opened his hands, palms up. "Maybe. The Guides said they'd heard about the pair from previous Guides. It seems that you all were close in past lives on Earth. They might be another pair from the Seven."

"But they're not here on Earth right now?" Leni asked.

Mira shook her head. "They haven't been for several life-times. At least, not together. We Guides only learn of Guardian souls alighting on Earth when both halves arrive. Our role is to bring the two parts together, so when there is only one half here, we can't do that. We don't even know about their existence here unless Guardians on a mission might find them."

"There's rumor that since you're here and the four of you have been Forged that it means something," Melinda said.

"Like what?" I demanded.

"Like something major with the Gates or the Phoenix," she said. "They're only saying that because none of you have been here in nearly a century and now two pairs are. It's just a rumor, like pretty much everything else. If the Sacred Seven belong here on Earth, then there's really no reason we should be overly excited that two pairs have returned."

"But if you *could* remember something, anything ... it'd help us all," Uri added. "Perhaps help this whole world."

Shit. No pressure there. Assholes. Did they really think we could just go back to our rooms, flip a switch, and remember everything about all of our past lives? All hundreds or even thousands of them? How the hell did we get put into this position? I mentally laughed at myself. I supposed if I could remember, we'd know how we got to be a part of this Seven, and maybe how to get ourselves out of it. There was one thing I knew for sure—if leading the Phoenix meant putting Leni's life in danger, I wasn't doing it.

The Guides and the healers left us with that bomb, as Brock had put it. We all had guard duty soon, so we headed back to our rooms. I sulked the whole way and needed Leni's soul mixed with mine more than ever.

We'd barely settled into the perfect state when we were called. Our soul rose from our bodies as one, then drifted into two clouds of light. One took form as Leni, curls and curves and all, and the other took my form. Although our souls remained connected, we could move as two separate entities. We left our bodies safely in our bed, our physical arms still encircling each other, and floated through the window and outside, where Brock and Asia waited. Or at least their astral selves did, only misty-light forms, like Leni and me. We flew out over the water.

"How you doing, bro?" Brock asked as our souls dove into the water by the island with the single weeping willow tree that marked the Gate.

Only a few Lakari, what we'd called Shadowmen until we learned better, had been nearby, their black souls floating like dirty mist over the water. Not enough to take us on—our Light would shatter their Darkness easily—but that could change at any time. Thus, our need to guard the Gate below. They wanted in ... from somewhere beyond this world.

"Pretty fucked up," I muttered. Of course, nobody truly spoke. The energy of our thoughts carried to each other like vibrations through our souls.

"Yeah, no shit," Brock agreed.

"It kind of explains some things," Leni mused.

"Yeah, like how we feel a connection with each other," Asia agreed. "Brock and I knew you guys as soon as we saw you. Your souls anyway. We recognized them."

"That could just be because we've spent a lot of lives together," Leni said. "Unc—I mean, Theo told us how some souls draw to each other over several lifetimes even when they're not Twin Flames. Some best friends always seem to find each other over and over. And some families have that deep connection, too."

Something rippled through us with her last words—a mix of hope and sadness.

"Yeah, something like that," Asia said. "But—"

She was cut off by the Gate suddenly glowing a bright white through the sand. The light rose around us, creating a solid wall, and then a hole began to yawn open.

Leni's eyes widened along with the hole. "Whoa. What's going on?"

"Enyxa's trying to open it!" Brock nearly yelled, and he responded faster than the rest of us, blasting his light toward the Gate to close the gaping hole before any of Enyxa's Lakari could pass through.

"No," Leni said, shaking her head. She moved closer to the cylindrical wall of light. "It's something else."

I felt it, too, but how could Leni know it was anything different?

"You don't have enough experience to know anything," Brock barked, and I momentarily wanted to punch him for talking to us like that, even if he was right.

"It *is* different, though," Asia said. Like Leni, she seemed drawn to the hole that refused to close. It wasn't black as it usually was the few times I'd seen someone trying to open the Gate from the other side. Colors swirled inside it now, hypnotizing, like the walls in the Space Between the last time we were there.

"Stay back!" I said as Leni moved even closer, tugging at my soul to follow.

"Asia, NO—" Brock's form flew at her, but he was too late.

Leni had lifted a hand toward the hole, and Asia reached out for her. Both of them were sucked inside, and the hole closed up.

"What the hell?" I yelled as I flew at the Gate's wall to no avail. The hole wouldn't reopen. Pain shattered through me as my soul felt Leni's absence, and darkness began to cloud my vision. Brock and I both stood there, in too much shock to think straight. "What do we do?"

Brock didn't answer.

"What the fuck do we do?" I yelled at him as I tried to push away the agony engulfing me. "Brock!"

He still stared at the Gate, which remained lit like a beacon in the water.

"Broderick!"

"I ... I don't know. Nothing like this—"

I didn't hear the rest. Something flew out of the Gate and crashed into me, sending me soaring through the water until I skidded against the sandy bottom of the bay. Everything around me went dark, and all I could think was Dark Souls. Lakari. They'd passed through the Gate. I immediately went into fight mode.

"Dude!" Leni's voice stopped me. "Were you seriously going to hit me?"

The light of our souls immediately swirled together, erasing the pain before I'd even registered that it had been hér form the Gate had spit back out. I didn't have to ask if she was okay. I could feel it.

"Damn, you gave me a scare," I silently said to only her.

I glanced over to Brock, whose form was no longer discernable as just his. Asia had apparently returned, as well.

"What the hell?" he yelled a moment later, his form jumping away from hers. "You know better!"

Leni removed her light from mine. "It's my fault. It was me. I … I *felt* something."

Brock waved his fists in the air like a crazed old man. "You can't be doing shit like that."

I stepped forward. "Dude, don't talk—"

The full force of his energy turned on me. "Do you know what that would do to us? To all of us, since Asia was pulled in, too? We're lucky they came back. If they didn't …"

"We know," Leni said. "We'd all go Dark. I'm sorry, but I couldn't help it. I felt a … a *connection.* Something—someone was in there."

Brock's form stiffened. "What the hell is someone doing in the Gate?"

"He wasn't *in* the Gate," Leni said. "I don't think. It felt like somewhere … beyond. But he was reaching out for us, or for this world, or something."

"Reaching out?" Brock repeated, sounding confused. "But why? Trying to talk to you?"

Asia shook her head. "No, it was more urgent than that. He had the desperation of a soul that's been Separated."

"I think … I think he thought we could help him," Leni added. "But the Gate threw us back here before we could really know."

Brock rubbed his head. "Well, it's a good thing it did. Otherwise, we'd all be in his situation: Separated, desperate, and going Dark."

Losing Leni had become my worst nightmare, and the thought of her soul going Dark scared the shit out of me. I melded more closely with her.

"At least you're back," I murmured to her. "Nothing else matters."

Her soul gave mine a squeeze, but a tremor rippled through us. "A lot more matters, Jeric. Souls like that guy's need to be helped. Even if we are part of the so-called Sacred Seven, we're not the center of the universe."

"Well, you're the center of *my* universe. And I can't imagine a universe without you. I will always make keeping us together my first priority, and everyone else can deal with it or fuck off."

CHAPTER 2

Leni MY BODY WOULDN'T stop trembling, although I was physically fine. After our shift at the Gate was over and the next group of Guardians arrived to relieve us, our essences returned to our perfectly safe bodies back in our room. No more words had been exchanged before then. Brock and Asia had some kind of private conversation going on between the two of them the rest of our time on duty, but Jeric and I had no idea what to think of what had happened. I had nothing to share with him except the extreme feeling of desperation that still haunted me.

Everything had happened so fast. The hole had widened, something or some*one* tugged at my heart with a crazy kind of need, and the next thing I knew, my soul was no longer with Jeric's. I saw nothing but white blankness. I heard only deafening silence. Nothing touched me. We hadn't entered the Space Between or the Beyond. And before anything registered more than this overwhelming emotion of despair, I was back with Jeric, who was about to blast me with a powerful punch of his energy.

Now, he enveloped me in his arms under the covers, trying to stop my quaking.

"Are you sure what you felt wasn't from our souls being apart?" Jeric asked, his voice soft near my ear. "It certainly didn't feel good."

"I don't know. I mean, yeah, that was part of the horrible feeling, but there was something more. Something not *us*. And not Asia, either. That guy ..."

"You felt his presence. I get it. But the pain part—"

"The pain was his, too. Some of it anyway. It was similar to what I felt with your absence, but not the same. I don't know how to describe it, Jeric. But I'm sure there's something wrong with him." I pulled back enough to look up at him, into his deep blue eyes. "Maybe it will happen again when we're at the Gate, and we can find out who he is and what's wrong with him."

"We don't have guard duty for several days." One side of his mouth pulled down as I once again shared the feeling of absolute misery from inside the Gate.

"We have to do something," I said.

He nodded. "I'll see if anyone wants to trade shifts. Just promise me that you won't leave me like that again."

"I promise."

Jeric had no luck over the next few days in finding anyone to give up their shifts for us. Guarding the Gate wasn't normally exciting like it had been that day, but it also wasn't normally so draining. In fact, spending time out of body and near the Gate usually energized and strengthened Guardians. We normally returned to our bodies feeling renewed and on a natural high. So although shifts could be kind of boring, depending on who you shared the shift with, nobody gave their turn up readily.

Like a lingering heaviness in my heart, the guy's desperation haunted me.

After combat training a couple of days later, I caught Asia walking down the hall by herself. I hurried up to her, checked again to make sure no one was around, and whispered to her, "We have to do something. About the soul in the Gate."

Her eyes cut sideways to me, and she sighed. "What can we do?"

"Have you been back to the Gate?"

She shook her head, her silvery-lilac hair swinging over her shoulders. "We're on the same schedule as you."

"What if the guy tries again, and we're not there?"

Asia lifted her tiny shoulder in a shrug. "Then maybe someone else will help him."

"I feel like he wants *us*, though. Like maybe we know him." I gnawed on my lip for a moment, and then blurted out what I'd been thinking. "Maybe he's part of the Sacred Seven. Maybe he's the Nathayden they were talking about."

She spun on her combat-booted heel, stopping us in our tracks, and put a pale fist on her miniskirt-clad hip. She leaned toward me, her dark eyes in slits, and for such a pixie of a thing, she could be intimidating.

"You're the leader, Leni. You tell me," she snipped. "Aren't you supposed to be the Light for the rest of us? They were right the other day. Trying to remember our pasts is the best thing any of us can do right now, especially you and Jeric, the oh-so-precious pair."

"Excuse me?"

She froze with her mouth partly open, and then slowly closed it, along with her eyes. "I'm sorry. I shouldn't have said that. Just having one of those days. Brock and I had a—never mind." She paused again, seeming to collect herself, although her words still came out sharply. "Look, there's nothing we can do for that guy. Not now. That could have been some kind of strange fluke, and there's too much we don't know, like what the guy's problem even is. We don't know if he's on this world and near another Gate at, oh, say SeaTac or Tokyo, or if he's on the other side of the damn universe. Unless and until we learn anything else, there's nothing we *can* do."

She spun again and stalked away, leaving me with my mouth hanging open. Were she and Brock having problems? Or did something else entirely have her panties in a bunch?

"LENI, YOU'RE NOT letting your mind go," Uncle Theo, er, I mean, Theo accused.

Calling him "uncle" had been a hard habit to break, but he wasn't my real uncle, and I was still pissed at him for all the lies he'd told me and for how he'd abandoned me as soon as I'd met Jeric. He was really Theodethan, although he still preferred to be called Theo. He'd been my Guide in both this lifetime and last, when Jacey had known him as Pops. Although the "uncle" part often still slipped, I mostly wanted to call him "Douchebag," especially when he kept things from me as he was doing right now. Which was why I couldn't concentrate and "let my mind go" to drift back to past life cycles.

"I'm sorry. I'm too distracted, I know," I said as my finger spun the bracelets on my wrist.

Another bad habit to break was squelching my true feelings. I'd become better about being my real self, especially when I was with Jeric who knew me better than I knew myself, but it was harder around those I still viewed as "authority." Or maybe it was Theo's elderly status that got to me. Because, in reality, I had much more authority than he did.

I was a Phoenix Guardian. A soldier. A warrior. Theo was merely a Guide. Jeric's and my souls had reached one of the highest echelons—the point where they'd become One. We'd practically been angels before Enyxa, ruler of the Dark worlds, had invaded our world and Separated our soul, making us Twin Flames. At least both of our halves had made it to the Space

Between and chosen to come here to Earth so we could eventually find each other. It took us two tries—Jacey and Micah hadn't quite reached the Gate to be Forged—but we'd made it. Otherwise, if Enyxa had sent us to two different worlds after splitting us ... I shuddered at the thought of going Dark.

Brock and Asia remembered that world, too, and had been just as lucky as us. I'd been wondering if this Nathayden and Rebethannah hadn't experienced our same luck. I just wished I could remember them, especially after what happened at the Gate the other day. My soul still hurt from what I'd felt, and I hated the thought of anyone being so desperate. That was one of my distractions.

"You're still thinking about your parents," Theo said. That was another distraction.

And the real reason I was in this room with him.

I rose from my seat in the generic office the Guides shared when they were at the manor and not out in the world, guiding other souls. I hadn't stopped thinking about my parents, and since Theo had known them, I'd snagged a few moments with him, hoping to learn something new. He thought I'd wanted his help with remembering other lives. He was wrong.

I strode over to the window. The room was part of the main offices of the old hotel the building had once been. To outsiders, it still looked like an abandoned hotel. To us members of the Phoenix, the hotel was ugly and dilapidated on the outside, but the interior retained the simple elegance it once had, although a three-story mansion sat in the middle of it. According to rumor, the best history we had, the mansion had been here first, built by a member of the Phoenix, but the property was later sold and the hotel replaced the home. When the Phoenix regained ownership, the magic of the Guardians (one of those things human minds can never fully comprehend) returned the mansion to existence where the hotel lobby and ballrooms had been.

Only we could see the mansion, though, which was the heart of the Guardians' living quarters. Jeric and I could have chosen a bedroom in it, but we'd chosen a hotel room instead, as far from the center of activity as possible, on the top floor of the eight-story building. Brock and Asia were up there, too. We must have all known in some part of our souls that we weren't like the other Guardians, and instinctively set ourselves apart.

As far as I knew, my Airstream camper was still parked at the RV park near the Florida-Georgia line. Melinda said they'd ensured the lot rent was covered for several more months, and my truck had been taken care of, too. Both waited for my return, although I had no idea when that would be. The only times Jeric and I had been able to leave the manor was when we were in our astral forms. Our physical bodies hadn't left since the night we arrived and almost died. At first, it was so Melinda, Uri, and the other healing Guardians could do their thing and help us physically recover. For the last few weeks, however, we'd been in training. Jeric and I were both growing antsy to get away from this place, at least for a while, but that would mean taking on our own mission, which I wasn't sure we were ready for yet.

The office was on the first floor and had an unappealing view of the crumbling asphalt of the parking lot. But that's not what my eyes really saw anyway. My vision filled with the memory of my parents: my mother with her light Creole skin, dark eyes, and frizzy, black hair smoothed back into a tight bun, and my father, with his Italian olive-toned skin and green eyes just like mine. I used to think he looked like a younger version of his uncle, Theo, but now that I knew the truth, I didn't think Theo looked anything like us. He may have been Italian, but his skin tone was lighter than Daddy's and his eyes were hazel, almost brown.

"How could my own parents forget I ever existed so easily?" I asked as I continued staring out the window, my back to him.

"You can't blame them," Theo said for the hundredth time. "They don't know any differently any more."

"But that's what I don't get. You've said before that there can be a connection between souls. Not just between Twin Flames, but between other souls, too. Like soul mates and siblings and parents."

"Yes, a connection can exist. Not nearly as strong as Twin Flames or even true soul mates, but yes, connected souls are often drawn to each other. They can be parents or siblings, but that kind of draw is stronger, a connection made before conception of the physical body. More often, connected souls find each other later in life, what humans call best friends. What's the term you told me once? BFFs?"

I ignored his obvious reminder of our past relationship, which had been close—before he left me to fend off the Lakari on my own. "So if my soul had been drawn to my parents' at conception, then we could have that deep connection. Why would they forget about me? How?"

A hand dropped on my shoulder and pressure forced me to turn. Theo stood in front of me, his forehead and mouth drawn down in concern. "Little bird, you need to be honest with yourself. Do you believe your parents are Twin Flames for each other? Or even soul mates?"

I didn't have to think about their relationship for long to know the answer. "They never seemed very close to each other."

In fact, I often thought their marriage was one of convenience. My mom didn't want to be the single, black mother left to struggle on her own to raise a mixed-race child as my grandmother had. My father was always the type to do the right thing, especially for those he was responsible for. Did Mama even love my father and he love her? They showed little affection toward each other, although the words were always there. Of course, Mama kept her feelings behind a mask, so maybe they were more loving behind closed doors. Oh, who was I fooling? They certainly did not have the kind of bond Jeric and I did or any of the other dyads here.

"They're *not* close," Theo confirmed. "They have no lasting bond. They're two souls who came together for other reasons than being made for each other, as many souls do, especially in this world. It is a temporary connection. Do you honestly feel your soul's link to theirs is any stronger than that? Do you truly believe, deep down, that your souls go back together beyond this lifetime? What does your instinct tell you?"

I gnawed on my lip, not wanting to think about that question too hard while standing here in front of Theo. Already my heart tightened and my eyes began to burn at the answer that I felt deep down, but didn't know whether to believe. I inhaled a deep breath and blew out the anxiety that threatened below the surface.

"Let's just forget about them like they forgot about us," I said with an exaggerated sigh. He needed to see that I'd moved on, even if I really hadn't. "If you *do* have one of those permanent connections with another soul, you feel it, right? Like you do with your Twin Flame, just not quite as strong?"

"Yes. Do you feel it with Asia and Brock?"

"I do. It wasn't immediate like it was with Jeric, but something deep inside me—"

"Your soul," Theo suggested.

"Right. I *feel* a bond with them. Like we've known each other forever in one way, except I don't feel like I really know them at all."

"It's your soul recognizing the connection when your brain does not. Yet. You don't necessarily recognize the people—the entire package—they are now, but you do at the soul level."

"Yes," I agreed. That was exactly how I felt with them. And they weren't the only ones. "And that's something that would remain even when the world or universe or angels or whatever are trying to erase the relationship, right?"

Theo's eyes scrunched, and he tilted his head. "What do you mean, little bird?"

I suppressed the need to roll my eyes at the nickname. How could he not see things had changed between us?

"You and Mira said the universe makes things happen so we can serve our roles as Guardians. Things like all evidence of our existences disappearing. People forgetting we were ever in their lives. And by universe, I'm imagining angels."

He nodded. "That's how we understand things."

"So whatever it is the angels do," I continued, "these soul connections are stronger, right? That's why we feel something with Brock and Asia, because it goes beyond this current lifetime?"

"Correct. That kind of bond is at the soul's level, not the physical level. You'll know it when you see such a soul. In fact, because you are more in tune with your own soul now, you'd feel the connection even more strongly than you did before, even when the physical world denies your part in it."

My throat tightened at his words. Or maybe at how easily he said them, as if it were no big deal that the world denied your existence. Even your own parents. Ugh. I couldn't push that from my mind.

"Leni," Theo said, his narrowed eyes trained on me, "are you still thinking of your parents?"

"No," I answered, probably a little too quickly. "I'm just trying to understand it all because of Brock and Asia and—" I paused, choosing my words carefully. "—and what you all said about Nathayden and Rebethannah. I was wondering if we'd recognize them if we ever saw them."

Theo's eyes had tightened infinitesimally at the mention of the dyad's names before he pivoted toward his desk. He cleared his throat as he sat down. "Yes, you would most likely know them, at least at a soulful level. Of course, if you could remember from other life cycles, you'd recognize them easier and faster."

A dismissal and an assignment all rolled into one sentence.

"I'll work on it," I muttered as I made my way to the door. I knew everyone was right about that being a priority, and trust me, I *wanted* to remember. There was nothing like having glimpses of yourself across time and being unable to clearly recall it all. I only wished everyone could agree on the best way to do so.

Mira thought the most painful memories would be easiest to recall since they'd be imbedded deeper, and she thought it also most effective because they contained the life lessons that would make us better Guardians and achieve more in this lifetime. Anything else we remembered was superfluous in her eyes. She tried to convince us that focusing on the pain in our hearts and souls would lead us to the pain from our past lives, but all it did was remind us of the horrible things we'd been through in this life. I hated when Jeric had sessions with her, because he had enough pain in this lifetime and Micah's that Mira drew out too easily, making him rehash it all every time.

Theo, on the other hand, believed we suppressed painful memories, and they would be the hardest to recall. He believed in the gradual-then-suddenly theory that we'd slowly regain glimpses of our past lives if we tried to focus on certain triggers, and then, suddenly, one day we'd remember it all. He suggested looking at pictures or bringing out heirlooms of past eras, but it hadn't done much for me. He figured it was just a matter of finding the right trigger.

"Have you been using the Book?" Theo asked as I opened the door. He referred to the Book of Phoenix, the journal where Jacey had written down her and Micah's story to help us remember things faster this time around.

"I write in it, yes," I said as I paused in the doorway.

"Keep doing so. It has more answers than you realize. It belonged to Jacquelena in previous lives, you know."

I looked over my shoulder at him. Why hadn't he mentioned this before? But his glasses were on as he focused intently on a paper in front of him. I shook my head and closed the door behind me. There was nothing in the Book from previous Jacquelenas except Jacey's story, and I'd read it a thousand times already. If there was anything to glean from her writings, we already had. And I'd jotted down things from time to time since being here at the Phoenix manor, like the few bits and pieces I remembered from the cycle before Jacey, when Jeric and I were One soul—but it's not like the Book suddenly began filling in all of the blanks.

Then again ... Theo wasn't the first one to tell me the Book was more than a journal. The Keeper in the Space Between had said there was more to the Book than I knew.

Hmm...

Several Guardians mingled in the outer offices, and I pushed past them, feeling Jeric's presence just outside. Neither of us had taken the opportunity to get to know too many of the others; only Brock and Asia and a couple of other dyad pairs who we'd been assigned to Gate duty with. I honestly didn't know who permanently belonged at our Gate and who didn't, because people were constantly coming and going. Some went out and returned from missions. Some were visiting from other Gates around the world, while our own were out traveling, too. And we knew there were some we'd yet to meet who'd been on missions since before Jeric and I had even crossed paths in Italy. According to Melinda, there were seven Gates on Earth with over a thousand Guardians at any given time. Considering population of Earth, that was a miniscule number, but I found it hard to believe so many of these people were scattered about the planet as complete unknowns to the regular world.

"Hey, babe," Jeric said, snagging my hand as soon as I stepped outside. He'd obviously been waiting for me, and rather impatiently since he tugged me so hard, I nearly fell into his arms. After he gave me a quick kiss, I pulled back to get a good look at him and gauge his needs.

His blond hair had grown out a bit since we'd been here, and it was at its usual level of disheveled-ness, rather than being a complete mess standing on end as if he'd been pulling it. And he wore a big smile with dimples that made my thighs clench, and the grin reached all the way to his bright blue eyes. I couldn't help but return the smile. He was in a good mood, which meant Mira had gone easy on him this time ... or had ditched him again.

"Good news. We got a shift," he said as he entangled his fingers with mine and pulled me toward the stairwell. "It starts in ten."

I hurried alongside him although his strides were much longer than mine. "With Brock and Asia?"

"Nope. Beggars can't be choosers. We're filling in for a pair who had to take off for something going on up in Atlanta. We're with Mat and Kel."

I snorted and looked up at Jeric. "Can you behave?"

He shrugged. "No problem. I'm secure in my manhood. As long as they don't try anything. Not that I'd blame them with this bod."

I slid my arm around his waist and squeezed. "This bod is mine."

"Damn straight."

I giggled at the double entendre.

CHAPTER 3

Jeric "OH, THIS SHOULD be interesting," Mat said as soon as Leni and I met him and Kel near the water for our shift a few minutes later, the golden light of the afternoon sun reflecting off the bay's surface and through their translucent forms. His voice sounded even more feminine than usual in his astral state. Probably because his soul was in its more natural condition—or was it *her* soul I should say? Even his essence took on more of a female shape.

We'd met Mat and Kel one of the first nights we were allowed out of the recovery room after being Forged, when Brock and Asia were showing us around the grounds of the Phoenix manor. Mat was shorter and thinner, cut like a skateboarder, with long, brown hair that only emphasized his feminine looks. Kel was taller, with a buzz cut, and a body more like Brock's and mine. We'd come through the mansion Leni and I had argued over so many times, and out the large wooden doors that led to the grassy lawn with the oak trees I'd seen in my dreams. Beyond the lawn was the water, and there I'd stopped short with my mouth hanging open. Mat and Kel had been standing by the shore, kissing under the moonlight. Or, at least, I assumed they were. I had to look away as soon as my brain caught up with my eyes. I'd done some kinky shit in my life, but watching two guys make out? No thanks. Not my thing. At. All.

To be honest, I was surprised to see a gay couple as dyads. Leni and I hadn't been told much at that point, but we'd learned that each Twin Flame pair had what we humans would describe as a masculine side and a feminine one, two halves of a whole soul, although the differentiation was more complex than that. So at the time, I'd assumed that meant each dyad pair consisted of a dude and a chick. Obviously, I assumed wrong.

According to Brock, who gave us the low-down, Mat's soul's name was Matoria, and she was the feminine half with Kelverich, the masculine side. In other words, she usually took a female body, and he took a male one. When Matoria came to Earth for this life cycle, her soul found its home in a male fetus. Brock said her soul had almost gone Dark because her so-called Christian parents disowned Mat because he had the hots for guys. After being on the streets for a while, Mat finally found Kel—who'd had no interest in men until he met Mat. Total wig out at first that Brock said included a fist-fight, but once they remembered who they were and reached the Gate, it all made sense, and they were just as much together as Leni and me or any other dyad couple. I'd heard we had a lesbian couple at our Gate, too, but they'd been out on a mission for weeks, and we hadn't met them yet. Not that I gave a shit before about who loved who—Leni's concern about my potential behavior came because I loved pussy, and I wouldn't stand down from an argument that it was the best thing God gave man—but I now had a whole different perspective about homosexuality.

What grated on my nerves were guys like Mat who tried too hard to be the funny flamer, and they only came off as assholes. So it wasn't the words or the girlish lilt that got to me, but the snide tone that promised more of the same for the entire shift.

"Yeah, quite interesting," I muttered.

A sigh from Leni rippled through our soul. It wasn't for me or my sarcasm, though. She'd picked up on Mat's snark factor, too.

"This shift won't do us any good," she said so only I could hear as we traveled to the Gate.

"Too late to back out now," I told her, then I gave her a mental squeeze and added, "We'll just have to make it worth our time after."

A vision of her naked body trembling as she straddled me played in our minds. Sex in this state made everything else worth it.

"Do you ever think of anything else?" she teased.

"Only when I'm forced to."

Conversation was nonexistent with Mat and Kel, the silence broken only by the Guardians who we relieved as they gave their report of no activity. The Lakari seemed to have grown quiet lately. Brock thought Enyxa was up to something. I couldn't help but think it had something to do with what happened to Leni and Asia the other day. I secretly hoped Leni was right about this shift, because as much as she wanted a repeat of the events of the other day, I didn't. Especially without Brock and Asia here. No activity at all would be perfect.

Nothing ever went my way.

The Gate remained dim for the majority of our shift, and I thought my wish would come true, until it lit up like a spotlight shining from the sandy floor of the bay up toward the surface. Any marine life that had been swimming or drifting around scattered, leaving only the light and us. Above the water, however, Dark souls hovered. I could feel them like an icy trickle on the nape of my neck as they waited eagerly for the possibility of their comrades to join them and strengthen their numbers.

A small pinprick showed in the light of the gate, and as it grew open, Leni's anticipation washed through us. We both hesitated, watching and waiting to see if this was like the other day or a more normal hole being ripped open by Enyxa or her Lakari. Mat and Kel, of course, went into immediate action, as they were trained to do. Light shot out of them in streaks as they tried to plug the hole before any Lakari could pass through.

"Come on, we gotta get it closed!" Kel yelled as he and Mat used their light to tighten the hole back up.

Still, Leni and I watched and waited.

"Wake up, bitches," Mat said, "and get to work!"

"They're coming," Kel bit through gritted teeth.

A dark shadow began filling the hole and pushing its way through. Leni and I snapped out of it and attacked, thrusting our light into its darkness. The Lakari was almost through, though, with many more pushing on it from the other side. Dark souls wanting in to take over the Earth. As if this world needed any more Darkness in it. Leni and I used all of our strength to shove back as Mat and Kel worked to close the hole.

"Fuck," Kel muttered, his voice strained by his effort. "Destroy them, damn it."

Leni threw herself into me, combining our forces. We soared at the Lakari and shattered it into pieces. The bits flew back into the hole just as Kel and Mat finally closed it up. As soon as the Gate fell dark, Mat flew at me.

"You need to step the hell up," he yelled into my face.

Although we weren't in our physical bodies, I bowed up. "What the fuck does that mean?"

"You had your thumbs up your asses, just staring at the bitches," Kel said, sidling up behind his partner.

"We've heard nothing but how great you're supposed to be, how you're such a strong warrior and leader, but you're nothing but a fucking pussy," Mat snapped.

Before I could respond, Leni soared toward me and bumped against my form, making me stagger back. Her essence seeped into mine. I immediately calmed when it did.

"Leave it alone," she whispered as her soul stroked mine.

I swallowed down my retaliation, but I couldn't so easily dismiss their words and the meaning behind them. Everyone else had been tiptoeing around this, but they all felt the same way, I knew. They were waiting for me—and Leni, too—to become the leaders they thought we were. As if there were a fucking switch we could throw and bam! *Here we are, bitches!*

Maybe that had happened in past life cycles, but not this one. I didn't see how anyone could do that, though. How do you so quickly and easily say, "Screw everything I know about this world and the people in it—they were just means to this end"? I couldn't do it. I couldn't believe the accident that killed my sister and parents was simply a convenient way to remove them from my life. How messed up is that? And what about Micah's Marine brothers? They had their own lives, people who loved them, things they cared about. What happened to all these people's souls? They just moved on to another world, completely forgetting who was left behind here? That sucked.

"Erm ... that's not how I understand it," Leni said, interrupting my thoughts that, of course, she felt, considering we were basically one entity at the moment. "Those souls had their own purpose and their own paths. It wasn't all about you. Besides, you may be with them again." She paused, and a twinge of hurt ran through us. "I don't know about my parents and me, but you had a different relationship with your sister and your parents. A closer one. Maybe that wasn't the first time you'd been together as a family. Maybe that connection will bring you together again."

I mentally grunted. "Yeah, well, it won't be in this lifetime, will it? And *this* is the life I'm in now. Everyone wants us to forget that—to forget everything about ourselves until now."

Not that life had been a fairy tale before meeting Leni. In fact, it had pretty much sucked ass. I'd lost my family and my hearing right when things were going so perfectly. I became a loner. Even when I was with all those girls, I was alone, in my own silent world. Before the accident, there was talk of our band hitting it big, and I thrived on that attention. I lost that thrill, though. Fighting and modeling never brought it back. Yeah, life sucked before I met Leni, but damn, it had been *my* life.

"We're *people*," I said aloud so Mat and Kel could hear, separating myself from Leni and turning to them. "Earthlings. Whatever the hell you want to call us. We have a life. A *recent* past. We're more than Guardians, and we're not the people we were in the past, so deal with it."

"Yeah, you just keep thinking that, buddy, and we're all screwed," Kel muttered.

I shrugged. "We are who we are now, and if you don't like that, you can fuck off."

Mat's essence darted through the water until he was in my face. Again. "Get off your self-righteous high horse and do what you're supposed to do, *Jeremicah.* You chose this, remember? We all did in the Space Between. So buck up and be the leader everyone needs. Or, at least, do your god-damned job so the rest of us can do ours and maybe actually live a while longer. You keep this up, and you'll get us all killed. Including your own Flame."

I stared at Mat's form, seething.

"Kel, call your bitch off," I growled.

Mat glared at me for a moment longer, then sauntered back to Kel. "No need, babe. I said my piece."

I turned away from them, and Leni came up to me. I needed her to back off, too, though. I could imagine my heart racing in my physical body, and the need to punch something was overwhelming. I didn't want to hurt her. What made me angrier than anything was that Mat was right. I chose this life to be a Guardian, and part of that choice was taking my rightful place as Leni's protector. I couldn't imagine not being by her side and keeping her safe. But part of *that* was being the leader with her that we were meant to be.

And fuck. How do you reconcile who you thought you were for the past 23 years with something like that?

CHAPTER 4

Leni   OUR SHIFT WITH Kel and Mat couldn't have been more disastrous. Jeric grew even moodier, and I became even more anxious. Maybe we'd needed to hear their words— the only ones with guts enough to say them—but we still didn't know what to do to change things. We spent a lot of time in our room the next few weeks, only coming out for combat training and Gate duty, admittedly avoiding more confrontation now that we knew what everyone truly felt. Unfortunately, the guy in the Gate never reached out for us again, and no significant memories had returned.

"The music from the last eight years sucks major duck dicks," Jeric said as he threw down his headphones on the bed.

I shrugged. "There were some good songs. Wait. Ducks have dicks?"

"I think I've heard them all already. And yes. They're fucking disgusting."

I shook my head, at the fact that he actually knew what duck's penises looked like and at the theory that he'd listened to every song made since he'd lost his hearing. I could almost believe it, because he'd been listening to music every chance he had, making up for lost time. After the first couple of weeks, I enjoyed it because he'd learned the words and sang along. Lately, though, he only scowled. Maybe because he found that most of it sucked, as he'd just put it, or, just as likely, because he'd been in a bad mood and nothing was bringing him out of it. Not even music.

"Of course, maybe if you danced for me, it would sound a lot better," he said as he trailed his fingers over my hip.

I laughed. "Even when you're pissy you're horny?"

He smiled and moved his fingers to my chin. "Leni. Whenever I'm with you, I'm horny. Hell, I don't even have to be with you. I just have to think about you. You make my mind live in the gutter, imagining all the dirty things I want to do to you." He leaned in closer and brushed his lips against mine. As if I didn't already have goose bumps crawling all over my skin. "But I like to watch you move. Your body does this thing that's ... *mesmerizing.* Takes the rest of the world away. And that makes me less *pissy,* as you say."

Heat rose into my cheeks as my gaze dropped to the bed and the Book between us. While he'd been listening to music, I'd been trying to find answers this Book was supposed to provide us. I'd been thinking about what Melinda and the others had said about Guardians trying to leave clues for reincarnated selves, and I wondered if the Book held such clues. If so, I hadn't discovered them yet. I'd let my mind wander, hoping to remember any little thing from our past lives, and when I did, I sketched it in the Book. Except, I wasn't the artist in this dyad pair, and my sketches were lacking. As in lacking anything recognizable. When Jeric's hand reached out and turned the journal at a different angle, I realized he was studying my drawings. I snatched the Book away and shut it.

"How about that dance?" I suggested.

He looked at the Book and back at me, the Book, me, and he grinned. "Okay."

I knew I wasn't off the hook. He'd ask me about the pictures a four-year-old could have drawn better later. If we projected, though, I could simply share my snatches of memories with him, and he wouldn't have to look at my pathetic artwork. Even better, I could get him to remember along with me, and besides smell, sounds were known memory triggers—like music.

"I have an idea," I said, and I grabbed the iPod. Although my account had been closed when the rest of my life disappeared from the world, the Guardians set us up with new ones. I scrolled through the music genres until I found what I was looking for, and then docked the iPod on the speaker.

I stepped away from the bed, and when the music started playing, I began doing the jitterbug. Within a minute, Jeric was off the bed and swing-dancing with me as if we were old pros. He picked me up, swung me upside down, around his back, and back to my feet, then pulled me up against his hard chest. When I looked up at him and his eyes locked on mine, our world disappeared.

We no longer stood in our hotel room at the manor, but on a makeshift dance floor in a dark and smoky room, with ragtime music playing as other couples danced and laughed. Jeric and I continued dancing as if nothing had changed. When the music stopped, I spun into his arms. I noticed for the first time how the beaded fringe of my black dress flew out as I turned, and how Jeric wore a white suit jacket. And although I knew it was him, his hair was dark and so were his eyes.

I know this. The memory returned full blast. Mick. That had been Jeremicah's name then. We were in a speakeasy in Seattle in the 1920s, our last cycle on Earth until Jacey and Micah. One of our last life cycles anywhere as two souls.

"Elle," Jeric—er, Mick said to me, "let's get a drink and find Nat and Betsy." Elle. Right. That had been my name, and I'd had a black bob, china-doll skin, and blue eyes that never looked quite right for the makeup trends of the era. We'd been Mick and Elle. "If they don't have any news, we'll go another set. I promise."

I'd loved to dance then, too.

Mick handed me a drink at the same time a man's hand clamped onto his shoulder.

"You were right, my man. They're going by Ana and Erick, and they're holed up at a joint right up the street." This man was Nat, I immediately knew. Nat and Betsy were ... Nathayden and Rebethannah. This was a memory with them in it! "They've Bonded, and the Lakari surround them."

"Sorry, doll," Mick said to me, "looks like our fun must wait."

He took my hand, and Nat took the hand of another female. As Mick tugged me toward the dark corridor that led out of the secret bar, I looked over my shoulder and staggered. I froze. I looked at Nat again, with his brown hair and eyes the color of coal, and then at his girl. Betsy. Black hair and big blue eyes that caused something deep inside me to clench like a vise. My heart contracted then swelled, overflowing with emotion for them and especially her. I couldn't tell if I was me, Leni, or me, Elle, at the moment because I felt like I *knew* this girl, right now, as though if I saw her in a crowded room, I'd recognize her immediately even knowing she'd look completely different in my time. The connection traversed over generations and planes and worlds. The connection with Nat felt similar to what we had with Brock and Asia, but what I felt with this girl, this soul, was so much stronger.

"Your sister's coming, don't worry," Mick said as he pulled me back into the past. I didn't understand.

"My sister?"

"Betsy's right there. Come on," he said impatiently. "Anastasia and Broderick need us."

Anastasia and Broderick. Ana and Erick then.

The memory began to fade out. I vaguely remembered helping Anastasia and Broderick get to the Gate so they could be Forged. My mind moved on, picking up pieces of memories of the six of us enjoying the party of the roaring twenties while serving our duties as Guardians. We'd had a lot of fun then, many good times ... but then a dark moment.

Lakari surrounding a soul, trying to take it. Mick and I led the charge with Nat and Betsy and Ana and Erick right behind us. We shattered the Lakari's darkness, but they were numerous and strong. Instead of disappearing into mist or tiny birds or anything else, the pieces melded back together and hovered over the soul they wanted so badly, like vultures waiting for a dying animal to take its last breath. As we formed to charge again, a group of Lakari flew at us. Mick and I were in the front and would be the first ones hit. We braced for it. But Nat and Betsy flipped over our heads. Protected us.

"Help the soul," Nat yelled, but Mick and I were already headed for the body the Lakari had surrounded. We were in our own physical bodies, not projected, so I couldn't actually see the soul, but I could feel it as it tried to float away from its corporeal self. I could feel the Darkness that already permeated it. Little Light remained. It must have been Darkening over several lifetimes and was now almost consumed by it. This was our last chance to save it, and if we didn't hurry, this soul would be lost forever to Enyxa.

We weren't even half way to the guy when a young woman's scream spun me around. Hundreds of Lakari had appeared from nowhere and dove at Betsy.

"NO!" Nat yelled as he jumped in front of her. But he was too late. There were too many. Betsy collapsed under the pressure. Nat went down almost immediately after. Mick and I hadn't even taken three more steps before their physical bodies died. We had to rush them to the Gate for their souls to reach the Space Between before the Lakari took them.

"My *sister*," I'd sobbed, and the memory faded to black, followed quickly by others.

The six of us again, but on another world, though it was similar to Earth. Like fanning through a stack of snapshots, we jumped from memory to memory, lifetime to lifetime, and world to world. The majority of our lives had been spent on Earth, and most other worlds we'd been on were fairly similar to Earth with water and land, trees and sky, animals and beings that were much like humans. The colors and the shapes differed, but not too drastically. Sometimes our skin had more of a green or purple tint to it because of the color of the water; sometimes it was practically clear because we lived underground and had never seen sun. In some places, sandy desert stretched out for as far as the eye could see, and in others, water covered nearly the entire planet. The biggest difference, however, was when the six of us became three.

We spent only two very short lifetimes as one soul, on two different worlds in the second-to-highest echelon. I remembered the last one—the one before we'd been split and returned to Earth—even before Jeric and I had been Forged. For some reason, my memory insisted on dwelling there, on focusing on that world with its pink trees and glass spires that tickled the teal sky. I hated this memory. Not the bliss of being One, of course, or of the peace that pervaded the world. Enyxa's Darkness had invaded and destroyed everything. Even in our higher state of light and love, we couldn't fight off the millions of Lakari she'd sent. Not when Enyxa herself came through and Darkened everything. Weakened our souls. Tore us in two so we were once again Jeremicah and Jacquelena but never quite the same after living as One. My soul still felt the excruciating pain of being ripped apart, severed, left to die as only a half.

But this time as we relived the memory, I saw more clearly beyond Jeremicah and me. I saw what Enyxa did to the other souls who were closest to us. I watched as she yanked the soul out of a body and tore it in half, tossing the two pieces away as if they were garbage—the soul that became Broderick and Anastasia once again.

"We have to get to the Gate and the Space Between," Broderick's soul said. "We have to hurry!"

Jeremicah's soul, its edges raw where it should be connected to mine, tugged at me. As I followed, I couldn't help but watch the scene we were escaping. Horror filled me as I watched Enyxa attack the other soul nearby. I gagged as she pushed her Darkness into the body, a black hand that emerged with a bright light clasped in it. The light of the soul twisted and turned, and I swore I could hear its shrieks as it fought for freedom. Enyxa, nothing more than blackness in a near humanoid shape, growled like a beast, angered at this one's fight. With a ferociousness no one should ever witness, let alone feel, she tore that soul in half. My mind screamed as I watched one piece float to the ground—the half I knew was Rebethannah. The other half never fell. Enyxa didn't discard it. The light of Rebethannah followed the Dark mist of Enyxa as she floated away.

What did she do with him? To them?

I wanted to go after them.

"Come on, Jacquelena," Jeremicah's soul called to me. "Hurry! We have to get to the Space Between together or we won't survive."

The memory disappeared. No strangely colored world overcome with darkness. No pieces of our souls lying about. No inkling of what happened to Rebethannah and Nathayden. Only the vague memory of her chasing after him, trying to help him.

A scream lodged in my throat, and I clawed at my neck as though trying to get it out while my consciousness fully returned to the present, where I sat on the floor of our hotel room in the Phoenix manor, my hands at my throat. Jeric sat next to me like a statue. Based on his shocked expression and wide eyes, he must have remembered everything, too.

I crawled into his lap, and his arms slowly fell around me and eventually tightened. We held each other, rocking back and forth, as our minds tried to make sense of the past and what—if anything—it all might mean for our present.

After several minutes, once our heart rates settled, Jeric nudged me off his lap and reached for the Book of Phoenix. He flipped through the pages until he came to a blank one. If he even noticed my crappy pictures, he didn't say anything. His mind seemed to be focused on something else. He picked up the pencil that had been sitting in the groove between the pages and began sketching his own drawings.

The pencil dashed over the page so quickly, I barely caught the image before Jeric turned the page and went to work on a new sketch. He repeated this several times, as if in a daze, and within minutes, he'd filled half a dozen pages with images of men. After he finished the last one, he flipped back to the first, and we both studied the rudimentary portrait. Jeric had some artistic talent, but nothing like Jacey. Still he was better than me (now), and as he filled in more details, the face became clearer.

"His eyes were darker then," I said, and Jeric nodded while rubbing the pencil lead over the page, darkening the irises.

Once that version looked more complete, he turned to the next page. This guy had lighter eyes, but dark hair, and I recognized him just as I had the first. We went through each one, Jeric bringing the drawings to life as best as his talent allowed, and I offered little details as they came to mind.

"He had a mole on his left jaw that time, remember?"

"You forgot the cowlick right over the middle of his forehead."

"Be sure to add the *doofa*. He only took it off for bed back then." The word came out as if I used it every day. At one time, I had, and Jeric knew exactly what I was talking about. He drew what was a sort of hat that stretched over our long heads and protected the sensitive ridges along the back.

"Make the ears and nose pointier. We looked kind of like elves then. And we had no eyebrows or eyelashes, remember?"

By the time we were done, the sun was setting and we had several drawings of Nathayden in his various forms. We assumed they represented his lifetimes before he and Rebethannah had become One, most spent here on Earth, but some not. They were all vaguely familiar, except the last one. If only we could remember all of these lives, and the hundreds or thousands of others we'd lived, in the same detail as the memory of our

Separation. Maybe Mira was right—painful memories, unfortunately, had a way of bubbling up on their own no matter how hard we tried to suppress them.

"Now what?" I asked when Jeric finally dropped the pencil and shook out his hand.

"No idea. I just had the urge to draw these, like if I didn't, he'd disappear completely from my memory."

I nodded with total understanding. Now that we'd experienced that deluge of memories, I felt like many of them were already slipping away. More specifically, those that included Nathayden ... which were most of them.

"What about Rebethannah?" I asked. "Should we draw her?"

Jeric stared at the Book for a long moment, then dropped it and practically jumped to his feet as though it had sprouted legs and teeth.

He rolled his neck and shoulders, as though to play it off, then rubbed his stomach. "Not right now. I'm not feeling it like I did with him. And if I don't eat something soon, my stomach will devour itself."

As if in answer, my own stomach growled with hunger. We hadn't eaten since breakfast.

Although a former hotel, the manor didn't offer room service unless you were sick or injured and confined to bed by order of the healers, so we had no choice but to freshen up and head down to the dining room, where we found Brock and Asia taking their seats. After filling our plates at the buffet, we sat down with them and told them everything we remembered.

"Wow. You're one of Theo's cases of gradually then suddenly," Asia said. "I can't believe you remembered *all* of that at once."

"Well, not everything. Not by a long shot. There were tons more holes left open than filled," I said. "It was like what Melinda and Uri and the Guides said, though. Both of you were in all of these memories, always in our lives. So were Nathayden and

Rebethannah. We remember them pretty clearly. At least, we remember the connection we had with them."

Although now that we were in the present, I didn't feel it as strongly, especially the link to Betsy. The gut feeling was fading with the memories.

"Shit. I wish we could remember more," Brock said before taking a bite of his hamburger.

"Music," Jeric suggested. "That's what worked for us, anyway. Leni put on some old jazz and big band from the roaring twenties, and it took us back."

"We tried that," Brock said. "Didn't work."

"Actually," Asia corrected, "we only listened to Billie Holiday and Nat King Cole. Maybe we should try something older."

"Hmm ..." Brock seemed to consider this. "You're right. You're so damn smart."

He leaned in for a kiss, but Asia shouldered him away.

"I'm eating, dork," she said around a mouthful of food.

If that had been Jeric, I would have taken the kiss anyway, at least on the cheek. Asia and Brock seemed to have a different relationship from ours, though. Although they tended to joke around a lot, I thought they did it to hide a lot of hurt. I sensed pain—recent pain—in them that they didn't share with the rest of the world. I wondered if that had anything to do with what had Asia on edge a couple of weeks ago when I had tried to talk to her in the corridor. She'd started to mention something with her and Brock, but had clammed up right away. Maybe some day she'd come to trust me enough to share, but until then, it wasn't my place to pry.

I pushed my food around on my plate, tracing the image of a phoenix on the dish with a strand of spaghetti, while gnawing on my lip as I considered something.

"I have another idea," I finally said. "Jeric and I have this old journal that our Guides left for us to help us remember."

"The Book of Phoenix?" Asia interrupted. "We found it, too. It helped us come here and to the Gate."

Jeric looked at me sideways. We hadn't known this.

"Was your last life written in it?" Jeric asked.

"No," Brock said. "Nothing to tell from ours. But yours was."

"You read Jacey's journal?" I asked, and although I usually had a hard time thinking of her as actually me, this made me squirm. There were some pretty private moments detailed in the entries.

"Sorry," Asia said, catching on to my discomfort, "but we had to. It saved us. Our souls."

I grabbed my glass and took a drink of water, washing away the weird embarrassment.

"So anyway," I said, pushing on, "Theo said something about how Jacquelena had owned the Book in the past, before Jacey. I thought maybe it's something where we've left clues for ourselves, like they'd mentioned that day when they told us about the Sacred Seven."

"Oh," Asia crooned. "I like this idea. Did you find anything?"

I frowned. "Well, no. I was hoping maybe if you guys looked at it, you'd remember something from the past. Maybe figure out any clues."

"We know that thing by heart," Brock said. "Studied it inside and out until Theo said he needed it back for you guys. If there was anything, I'm sure we would have noticed."

"We've added some things," Jeric said. "Some drawings of Nathayden and other stuff. Maybe those will at least help you remember something."

"You should borrow it for the night and see if it helps," I suggested.

After we finished eating, they followed us to our room and took the Book back to their own room. The next day, they came back with a few of their own memories.

"Just more flashes, mostly," Asia said as we ate breakfast at the same table where we'd eaten dinner last night, in the same seats. "But we do remember more about Nathayden and Rebethannah now. Nathayden, especially. I mean, we remember her there all the time, too, but not as clearly. You know what I mean?"

I kind of did, but it had been the opposite for me. I'd remembered her more clearly than him.

"Do you remember when we were all Separated by Enyxa?" I asked, lowering my voice because it was such a sad memory. "Do you remember what happened to them?"

Brock and Asia looked at each other, communicating silently.

"Not really," Brock finally said. "We remember trying to get our Separated souls to the Space Between together so we wouldn't permanently lose each other."

"I vaguely remember seeing Enyxa attack us," Asia said. "You first, then us, then she went after ... ugh, I can't remember their name when they were One, but the body Nathayden and Rebethannah were in."

"And the agony. I remember that clearly," Brock muttered.

"You didn't see what Enyxa did with them?" Jeric asked, and he told him what we remembered of Enyxa carrying Nathayden off and Rebethannah chasing after them. Neither Brock nor Asia remembered that part, so they didn't know what happened to the two halves either.

"They haven't been here on Earth, so nobody's heard word of them since," I added when he was done.

"Maybe they were able to escape and get to the Space Between," Asia suggested.

"Yeah. They're strong. Surely they made it," Brock said. "They're probably together and chose to go somewhere different than Earth. Somewhere safer. Hell, maybe they got lucky, and they're still on their first cycle since the Separation."

Nice thought, but I highly doubted the idea. Guardians didn't have easy lives, even on the quieter worlds. We didn't live to old age unless we became Guides, and that was a decision we had to make in the Space Between, right after our last life ended and before our next life began. In other words, at a time when you're wanting another chance to beat Enyxa and her Lakari. Guardians, especially at our level, rarely made that kind of decision.

I didn't think Nathayden and Rebethannah would give up their roles as warriors. However, from what I understood from the Keeper, time passed differently in the Space Between than it did on physical worlds. So perhaps time passed differently between worlds. I wanted to believe those souls who had always been closest to us were in a good place. A better place than Earth. And that they were together and able to enjoy life. I liked Brock's theory for that reason.

When Jeric and I were in our room later that night, though, all hopes for that were dashed. I crawled into bed and set the Book of Phoenix on my lap to study it once again. It fell open to the last drawing Jeric had done of Nathayden. And scrawled onto the opposite page in a barely legible hand that neither of us recognized were two words:

Save Rebethannah.

CHAPTER 5

Jeric "I CALLED BROCK and Asia," Leni said in the morning, and I scowled although she couldn't see me as I stood under the shower. She was somewhere on the other side of the curtain since I couldn't talk her into joining me. She'd already been in and out before I'd even awoken. Talking through any kind of barrier, even as thin as the plastic sheet between us now, usually felt surreal, but at the moment, I felt a hair of nostalgia for when I could take a shower in peace. "We have to figure out what to do, Jeric."

She must have sensed my displeasure. Wouldn't have been hard—we'd already talked the subject to death last night after finding the mysterious message in the Book. The damn thing freaked me out. It wasn't the first time random messages had appeared. The words "You know the rest. Remember." were still imprinted several pages back, trying to get Leni to remember that she was Jacey and I was Micah, but that didn't mean I jumped with joy over this time. Funny how the logical part of me knew I *should* believe the magical note, because when I hadn't believed any of this before, Leni and I had almost been killed. I'd promised to be more open-minded about things, and I'd accepted quite a bit of shit that I'd never have believed before—I had my hearing back, for God's sake. But what the hell were we supposed to do with this message? *Save Rebethannah?* How were we supposed to do that if we didn't even know who or where she was?

Leni had an idea of what we were supposed to do, and that's what had me on edge more than anything. She wanted to share the idea with Brock and Asia, and after what the healers and the Guides had told us, Brock and Asia would follow us.

I didn't want to lead them—or anyone.

I placed my hands against the shower wall and let the hot water pour over my head and down my back for several more seconds, loosening the tense muscles of my neck and shoulders, before reluctantly twisting the knob to the off position. When I jerked the curtain open, I about jumped out of my skin at the sight of Leni. She'd been silent for the last couple of minutes, so I'd thought she'd left the bathroom. She sat on the closed toilet, though, and reached behind her for a towel. She stood up to hand it to me, and I couldn't control myself, especially as her sea green gaze raked down my naked body and lingered at my junk. It came to attention with no thought of my own. When her eyes came back to mine, her brow jutted upward as she pressed the towel against my chest.

"They're on their way right now," she said, before turning and sauntering out of the bathroom, her perfect ass swaying as she pulled the door closed behind her.

Damn. The girl would be the death of me. Or at least of my dick. It wasn't used to not getting its way every single time. But the manor was only so big, and no matter where they'd been, it wouldn't take long for Brock and Asia to get here. I could be easily satisfied in that short time, but that wouldn't be cool for Leni, so I talked myself down as I dried off so I'd be able to throw my jeans on.

Living at the manor was what I'd imagined college being like. Most Guardians were young with only the healers lasting past their twenties, and we lived in rooms in the mansion or the hotel with communal meals in a dining hall, classes, and meetings and such. We even had a gym for physical training and Guides who were sometimes like professors. Only, we roomed with our other halves rather than typical same-sex roommates. At least there was that. By the time I emerged from the bathroom, dried and dressed, Leni already had our bed made and dorm-like room straightened up. Just in time because there was a knock on the door.

I sat on my side of the bed, up against the padded head-board left over from when this place was an actual hotel, while Leni swished Brock and Asia inside. She then circled to her side of the bed and plopped the Book in the center, opened to the message. Brock and Asia each took a corner at the foot of the bed, sat, and leaned over to study the two simple words and their complex meaning.

"Did you write them?" I asked with the smallest bit of hope. Leni had dismissed this idea, and I had to agree it made no sense.

"Of course not," Asia said.

"It has to be from Nathayden, right?" Leni asked as she leaned against the headboard next to me. There was a noticeable space between us, though, showing that we weren't on the same page with this. Actually, if it were up to me, there would be no page. I'd tear it out and burn it and go on as though we'd never seen the stupid message. As wrong as I knew that was, I didn't want us involved. We weren't ready. Leni and I were newbs at this whole Guardian thing.

Brock and Asia straightened up after closely inspecting the two words that had mysteriously appeared kind of like the phoenix marks on our arms. Brock scratched his head, and then he shrugged.

"No idea. Who else could it be from?" he asked.

"My only other idea was the Keeper," Leni said. "But it doesn't feel right."

"Who's the Keeper?" Asia asked.

Leni and I both cocked our heads at the same time.

"She means the Keeper of the Space Between," I clarified.

Brock and Asia exchanged a look that seemed pretty meaningful, but then again, maybe I was reading too much into it. An old habit left over from being deaf for so long.

"What is it?" Leni asked. Had she noticed the silent communication, too?

"I didn't have anyone called a Keeper when I was there," Brock said. "Did you, Asia?"

She shook her head. "No. I've told you all about it. There was just a bodiless voice surrounding me, telling me my options."

"Wait," Leni said, "you two weren't at the Space Between together?"

"No," Brock said. "You were?"

"Well, yeah," Leni said. "Wow. You guys got lucky then, to come to the same world at the same time."

Asia shrugged. "The Space Between is weird. From what I've heard, it's different for everybody and from life to life ... or death to death, however you want to put it."

"I know it changes," Leni said, "but you really didn't have a Keeper? Someone who explained everything and your choices?"

Asia shook her head. "Just the voice."

"I had a guy, but he didn't call himself the Keeper," Brock said.

Asia's mouth twisted, and her wide eyes narrowed as she appeared to be considering something. "You know what I think? I think the voice—or your Keeper—or whoever is supposedly divulging secrets is really a manifestation from our own souls, telling us what we already know deep down. I mean, it's not like we get *real* answers. Like, don't you wonder more about what there is besides the different worlds our souls can go to?"

Leni leaned forward, and I could feel her interest spark. "Yes! Like, is there a Heaven and a Hell or just other worlds?"

"Right," Asia said. "As high up on the echelon as we had gone, almost to the level right below the angels or spirits or whatever you want to call them, shouldn't we know more about those things? But we don't—Brock and I don't, anyway. We have all these fat holes in the memories of our past lives and the other worlds we've been on. And we remember *nothing* beyond what we experience in physical forms. Like, the Space Between, for example. It's always different, and we never remember it every time we go. Don't you think that's weird?"

I rubbed the back of my neck. "You think we're just talking to ourselves in the Space Between?"

"Not exactly," Brock answered. "Just the remembering part. We think our souls remember everything we know while we're in the Space Between, but as soon as we move on to the next life, we forget it all."

Asia nodded. "There's someone or some force, like a higher power or the angels, guiding us to the decision for our next life, but we don't think they give us any answers we don't already know."

"Huh," Leni said as she leaned back against the headboard and rested her chin on the back of her hand. "So, if that's true, and we're really only helping ourselves even in the Space Between, then it's probably true that we've left clues for our future selves." She paused as she thought harder on this idea, and then her excitement grew again. "And I think we did that with the Book! My gut's telling me that we've used the Book in the past for many things, like discovering our missions. That would explain why the Lakari would want it—so we wouldn't discover our own secrets before they killed us."

She paused for a moment, staring at her hands as her fingers tapped a rhythm on the blanket, and I already knew her next thought. I had to control myself from clamping my hand over her mouth to keep her from saying it, as though that would prevent the thought from already being a reality. Because remembering our pasts was kind of fun, like solving a weird mystery, but what she was thinking took us to a whole different level. One I wasn't ready for.

"I have this strong feeling the guy in the Gate who'd sounded so desperate was Nathayden. And I think ... saving Rebethannah is our first mission."

She lifted her head to look at us. I turned mine to stare at the wall, my jaw clenching. She already knew my feelings on this theory.

"What do you guys think?" she asked when nobody said anything.

My eyes cut to Brock and Asia, who shared another look, but they didn't hold back this time. Asia reached out and laid her hand on Leni's knee.

"You tell us," she said to my other half. "We remembered last night that this has always been your thing, like your super power—you lead us to the souls we're supposed to help."

The hair on the back of my neck rose, and I jumped to my feet as though the bed itself had caused the feeling. But what I felt came from inside, and no matter how much I wanted to deny it, to make it go away, to pretend it didn't exist, I couldn't. The truth is the truth, and what Asia just said was no doubt a truth. I knew it in my gut, or in my soul, as everyone else would say. Leni—or Jacquelena, to be more accurate—was our light, showing us the way. Theo and Mira had emphasized this when we'd been Forged at the Gate. Not just mine, but everybody's. I hadn't fully understood what that meant at the time, but it was starting to make more sense.

Didn't mean I liked it.

"No," I said, unable to form the words I wanted to say. "Just ... no. Not yet."

"Jeric—" Leni started, and I spun on her.

"Can you really say you feel ready to do this?" I demanded, leaning over her on the bed. "Do you even know what you're doing?"

Leni stared at me for a moment, opening her mouth then closing it like a carp as she considered my question.

"Yes," she finally said, and when I lifted my brow and sucked in a breath to argue, she held a hand up. "It's not knowledge to be gained, Jeric. I don't have to learn this. It's intuition. Instinct. My soul talking to me. I know how that sounds, but look at our lives now. Look at what we *do* know and tell me that relying on our instinct, on our *souls* that have existed for eons compared to our measly human brains, isn't what we're supposed to do. *That's* the lesson we're supposed to learn more than any others. Am I right?"

She turned back to Brock and Asia, who both nodded.

"So we're just supposed to cut off our brains and all logic?" I snapped.

"Don't be ridiculous," Asia said with a sigh. "You just have to let your brain catch up to what you already know in your soul."

I glared at each of them in turn, not sure why this bothered me so much. I'd practically vowed to trust Leni and her intuition, to accept her as our light to lead the way. And I knew deep down that she'd be right—that her soul would know exactly what we're supposed to do. The "normal" side of me, the Jeric I'd been for the last twenty-three years, however, bristled at the thought of going out and being some kind of supernatural-like ninja, helping people who probably didn't even know they needed to be helped. How were we supposed to do that anyway?

"So you think your *soul* will lead us right to whoever Rebethannah is now?" I demanded. "And you really think that's our mission?"

Leni pressed her lips together and dropped her gaze to the blanket again. "I don't know yet," she nearly whispered, but then she lifted her eyes to me and raised her voice. "But it's time to find out."

We argued about it some more until Asia finally suggested we talk to Melinda and Uri or to some other Guardians since we didn't really know the protocol for missions yet anyway. I hoped they'd be too busy for a day or two so we could think through this further, maybe gather more information and figure out if we were really supposed to find Rebethannah. No such luck. Life was definitely a woman with her mood swings, and right now, she was a bitch. Melinda and Uri invited us down right away, and a few minutes later, we were all gathered in the same meeting room C where they'd told us we were part of the Sacred Seven—which, by the way, we still had no recollection of. Mira and Theo were also in there. Leni and I glanced at each other as we took our seats across the table from them.

"This was good timing," Theo said. "Mira and I were about to leave the manor for a while and were going to call you to say goodbye."

"Where are you going?" Leni asked, curiosity getting the best of her when she'd been acting like she didn't care about them the whole time we'd been here.

"We have a pair of Twin Flames to help," Mira explained. "We'll be out of touch for a while. They're older than you two were when you needed us, so we should only be gone for a few months. But it could take longer to bring them together."

Theo lifted his clasped hands to rest on the table. His eyes were full of warmth as he looked at Leni. "We wanted you to know first that we believe in you. That we know you—all of you—are ready to serve your roles for the Guardians."

His eyes traveled from face to face, but lingered on mine the longest.

"It's time for you to go out on missions," Mira clarified, and I wondered if she and Leni were conspiring against me. All of them, actually.

"What a coincidence," Leni said. "That's what we wanted to talk about. How, exactly, do missions work?"

Melinda leaned forward in her chair and folded her hands together on top of the table. "You go out into the world, and your souls will lead you to your target—a soul that's very close to going Dark."

"And how do we know?" Brock asked.

"There are usually Lakari nearby," she said, "shadowing the person with their Dark presence, sometimes even influencing their decisions. Usually they wait for the body to die to take the soul, but they're known to murder, especially if it serves another purpose for Enyxa."

"And they're all Broken?" Leni asked. "Separated Twin Flames?"

Uri shook his head. "Not necessarily. Some are single souls who are almost completely Dark. Besides Broken Twin Flames, they're the souls the Lakari are interested in, and the ones you must help, if you can."

"You may find a Broken or Lost soul, though," Melinda said. "And if you do, if you get any indication at all, you need to help it. Broken Twin Flames go Dark faster than other souls because of the pain and despair they feel. It only takes them two or three lives before it's too late. Lost souls go even faster, because their other half, whether a Twin Flame or their soul mate, has already gone Dark."

"So how do we help them?" Asia asked.

"If they're not Broken or Lost, you keep the Lakari in check," Uri replied. "They feed off of souls that are tainted with Darkness, especially when the physical body is dying, but that doesn't mean they'll get the soul in the end. We always have free will, so it's up to the soul itself. But the Lakari try to give them more Darkness, pulling the soul their way."

"Like they did with you, Jeric," Leni said. "Right before we were Forged."

"Yes," Mira confirmed.

"If the soul is Dark enough, it may deny the Light and choose to go with the Lakari, and there's nothing you can do about that," Uri continued. "But if the Lakari attack, or try to take souls against their will, then you can act. Then you can fight them."

"That's it?" Brock asked, and I understood his disappointment. All of the build-up of our powers and everything, and all we had to do was scare off the Lakari, maybe fight once in a while?

"That's it for most souls, but your greatest concern is always the Broken and the Lost," Melinda said. "That's who you need to search for and to help. They're definitely more difficult because you have to try to convince them that there's a reason for their misery. If they're on their third or more life since their Separation, they won't take as much convincing. They'll be desperate and pretty Dark. It may take a few weeks or months, but eventually, they'll do whatever it takes and will agree to come here with you. And then we escort their soul to the Gate so they can meet their other half or at least find solace in the Space Between."

"Okay," Leni said, a little too cheerfully for my liking, "so how do we get a mission?"

"If we know of a Broken soul and don't have dyads available, we'll assign a mission to those who are here on Gate duty," Melinda said. "But usually, you go out and discover your own mission. You, Jacquelena, are supposed to be especially adept at that."

"Damn it," I muttered. Were they all in on the conspiracy against me? I'd stayed quiet through all of this, letting them clear the air, while hoping the whole time Melinda and Uri would say only more experienced Guardians went out on missions. I knew deep down that didn't make sense, since "experienced" was a relative term here. Guardians were lucky to survive three or four missions in a life.

"That's what I needed to hear," Leni said. "We think we have our first mission."

"This really was perfect timing," Theo said. "We were just telling Melinda and Uri that it was time for you to leave the manor and seek out your first one."

"We're not ready, though," I growled, no longer able to hold it back. If I had my way, we'd never be ready. Because missions meant danger and danger meant Leni's life would be at risk and just the thought of that killed me. I relived Jacey's death every night in my dreams. I would not watch her die again.

"You are," Theo insisted. "But you will only believe it once you are out there, living the life of a Guardian. You won't have a choice but to be ready to fight—or to die."

"Exactly," I muttered. "So we're supposed to go out there and find a soul when we don't even know where or who it is?"

"It's not too difficult to find the single souls on the verge of Darkness, especially in this day and age," Mira said.

She meant those souls who had repeatedly refused to acknowledge their soul mate or their soul mate had refused to acknowledge them. Or they've gone to different worlds, and may never be on the same one at the same time. After several life cycles of never finding the soul created especially for theirs, despair and depression set in, worsening with each life, until the soul becomes completely hopeless. That's when they're at risk of choosing to go Dark permanently, which was when the Lakari could conquer and take the soul to Enyxa. See—I'd learned a lot. Still didn't mean I felt ready to put it all into practice.

"You have Leni's camper, so you already have a place to live," Mira continued, taking their argument in a different direction. "That's one thing you don't need to worry about. And if you need to travel, you can take the camper with you. A perfect set-up for Guardians."

She was appealing to my logical side. She knew me too well. More than I cared for. It aggravated me even more.

"We don't think you'll need to, though," Uri said. "According to recent Guardian reports, there seems to be Lakari activity in Lake Haven, the town where Leni's camper sits right now."

I stood with such force, my chair fell backwards, and I leaned over the table, right in front of Mira and Theo.

"You're putting Leni's—and my—life at risk because it's *convenient?*" I seethed.

Mira glared back at me. "*You* may have brought them to the soul they're swarming."

The accusation—and the feeling of responsibility—tightened my throat. "Only because you disappeared with no answers or instructions! If it's anyone's fault, it's yours and Theo's. And anyone else who refused to help us out."

That last bit had been for everyone else in the room, who had all known Leni and I had been struggling and could have used their help. Supposedly nobody was allowed to give it—we had to figure out everything on our own because that would somehow make us better Guardians. Funny how we were supposed to help other souls avoid exactly what we were forced to face on our own.

"You can't live here forever, Jeric," Mira said. "It's time you do your job."

"We'll do it when we're prepared!" I barked as I leaned closer. I had to give her props for not moving away or even flinching.

"You will never be fully prepared as long as you don't *believe*," she bit back. "That's the only place you're lacking, Jeremicah. Believing is your fuel for everything. Melinda and Uri can heal you because they *believe* they can. They trust in themselves, in their former selves, in everything they know in their souls. Our warriors fight so well because they *believe* they can. They are faster and stronger because they always have been, in every life, just as you always have been. When you fought the Lakari on your way here, you *believed* in your abilities. You believed in Leni's ability to jump over their heads and run up the side of a building. You believed she could break the glass and the two of you could jump from eight stories high because you'd done it before, countless times. It's been proven to you over and over. You only have to trust in what you already know in your soul."

My nostrils flared as I glared at her, refusing to admit she was right about it all. Believing in all this mumbo-jumbo, crazy-ass, supernatural, sci-fi shit wasn't exactly easy.

"Jeric, we can do this." Leni had risen to her feet next to me, and her small hand gripped mine. "We *need* to do it."

My jaw popped as I clenched it, but I kept any further fuming to myself. Didn't she get that she was all I cared about? Okay, maybe not *all* I cared about—I wasn't that much of a douche. But she was definitely all I needed. To have her safe by my side or in my arms was more important to me than anything.

"And I'm going with or without you," she added. I suppressed a growl.

"So are we," Asia said. "We'll figure it out, Jeric. We're strong, remember? The strongest of them all."

"You'll have each other," Melinda said. "When you find Lakari swarming, take up residence and make yourselves a part of the community where they're hunting. You may need to get to know the people so you can find out who's going Dark, especially if Leni's senses don't pick it up right away."

"And be careful with small towns," Uri warned. "They make things more difficult. It's always best for one pair to go in first, while the other hangs back for a while. If the Lakari suspect an influx of Guardians in the area, they might jump the gun and swoop in on the soul before you even know who it is."

"We can do this," Leni said confidently.

"I still don't like it," I muttered.

Leni squeezed my hand again. "We chose this, remember? It's time to step up and make ourselves useful. And like I said, I'm doing it with or without you … but I'd much rather with you."

I cut my eyes down to her and huffed my breath through my nose like a bull. The woman was stubborn. And a pain in my ass. And would always get her way when it came to me. No fuckin' way would I let her go out on her own.

"Remember to *believe*, Jeremiah," Mira called after me as we headed for the door.

I'd remember. I really had no choice now, did I? I had to believe in our abilities if I was going to keep Leni from getting herself killed. The silver lining: At least we were getting away from everyone's stupid expectations and judgmental glares here at the manor.

CHAPTER 6

Leni AS WE PREPARED to leave the manor for the first time in months, the only thing that had me doubting this decision was that the mission pulled us away from the Gate ... and possibly from Nathayden. We were setting out to hopefully find Rebethannah, but what if she was near here, and that's why Nathayden contacted us, and now we were traveling hundreds of miles away? What if she was in the Gate, too? For all we knew, she wasn't even on our world.

I didn't know if my instinct told me one way or the other. Not something I'd admit to Jeric, especially not right now, because when needed, my intuition had been loud and clear for us. I didn't have that strong pull right now that told me what to do. Options bounced around in my mind, but I didn't know if my preference was by instinct or mere desire. I wanted to get away from the manor. I wanted to prove to myself and to Jeric—and to everyone else—that we were ready to be the warriors and the leaders we were meant to be. I *wanted* to do a mission more than I'd wanted almost anything since we'd been here. I just hoped this strong desire was truly my intuition.

And I hoped we'd somehow be able to help Rebethannah and Nathayden.

"You really *believe* we know what we're doing?" Jeric asked as we packed our few belongings, the sarcasm dripping over Mira's favorite word.

"Of course," I said, sounding more confident than I felt. I still had it—the ability to mask my true feelings. Jeric stopped shoving clothes into his bag and eyed me. Okay, so hiding feelings from him was basically impossible, since he could pretty much feel them, too. He turned toward me and placed his hands on his hips.

"Don't lie to me," he growled.

"We can do this," I said.

He took a step toward me, and I backed away from his predatory advance. Another step had him right in front of me again, and another of my own steps backward had me pressed against the wall. Each of his hands landed on the wall next to my face, and he leaned his head in so close, I could see every speck of indigo in his royal blue eyes. His warm breath fell on my lips, followed by his gaze. His eyes slowly lifted to mine.

"I will follow you into the dark," he said, his voice low and edgy. "I will do anything for you, babe. Just know that if anything happens to you, it will destroy me."

"Jeric," I murmured as I placed my palms on his narrow hips and slid them up to his chest, where I fisted his shirt in my hands and pulled him even closer, "if you can't believe in anything else, at least believe in *us*."

His eyes bore into mine as he considered my meaning, then his gaze dropped to my lips again before sliding back up. When his eyes reached mine, he nodded slightly. Then he crushed his mouth against me, taking me under with a kiss full of urgency and passion and life itself. I parted my lips, his tongue thrust inside, and I met it with my own. My hands released his shirt and slid up his pronounced pecs to his tense shoulders and neck and into his hair, while one of his slid down my side, over my hip and to my thigh. He hitched my leg up, and I wrapped both around his waist as he pressed his erection against me and ground his hips. I had to lean my head away to catch a breath, and his lips traveled south, over my chin, down my neck, and to my collarbone, while his pelvis continued grinding out a rhythm. When he hit just the right spot, I moaned with pleasure.

"I believe in us," Jeric panted against my chest. "More than I believe in anything in this world. I *really* believe in us when we're naked, though."

He thrust against me again, but harder this time, as though we were already naked, and I cried out more loudly. His hands grasped my waist, and his fingers dug into my hips as he stepped away from the wall with my legs still wrapped around him. He turned and leaned forward, and we crashed onto the bed. Our hands desperately tugged at our clothes while our mouths refused to separate unless absolutely necessary. My top was off and his shirt was on the floor and his jeans fly undone when both of our phones rang with a text message. Jeric moaned into my mouth before we extricated ourselves to find our phones.

Brock: "Ride's here."

"We can believe in us as soon as we're settled into the camper," I promised Jeric before giving him one more lingering kiss. His fingers caressed the bare skin over my ribs before pulling the cup of my bra down so that my breast sprang free. He wrapped his mouth around the tip and swirled his tongue around my nipple before drawing it between his teeth so that it stood hard and tight, making me ache for more.

"I'll hold you to that," he said huskily before tucking my boob back into my bra and grasping my hand to pull me to my feet. His hand cupped an ass cheek and squeezed. "Because I'm going to believe you in every way I can, including ways you've never been believed before until the whole damn RV park knows just how hard I can believe."

"That's all I ask for," I teased with his own double entendre.

He threw my top at me. "Put this on before I say fuck them and believe you right here and now."

"Admit it," I said with a smile as I pulled the shirt over my head, "you're glad to be getting away."

He admitted no such thing, but I could feel his relief as though it were my own. What happened to his Marine brothers and Jacey when he was Micah and then with his sister and parents earlier in this life had really screwed him up. Although I hadn't recalled everything from our past lives, I was certain Jeremicah had always been more cautious than me. Always someone who wanted to gather as much intelligence as possible and then analyze it from every angle before moving forward. But at some point, armed with his data and my intuition, he'd make a decision and recruit whatever comrades we had at the time. He enjoyed strategizing with them, and then leading us where we needed to go. He also always loved celebrating victories with them. Now, he wanted nothing to do with anyone but me. He was scared. And now I knew of what.

The realization hit me like a smack in the forehead: His life as Micah hadn't started it all. It wasn't what happened to Jacey or his sister in this life that sparked his fear. It went back further, to our Separation in the life before. When our single Bonded soul had been ripped from our body and torn into two. When we became Twin Flames. He *did* believe in us, and that's what he was so afraid of losing.

I swallowed the lump in my throat and blinked away the sting in my eyes as I retrieved our things from the bathroom. I had to take a few deep breaths before returning to his side. We tossed the rest of our belongings into our bags and hurried downstairs where Brock and Asia already waited in a newer model yellow Camaro. Asia hopped out of the front seat when she saw us and climbed into the back. When I squeezed in after her, I immediately knew Jeric would have never fit back here.

"You brought the Book, right?" Asia asked as Brock put the car into gear.

I patted the bag on my lap. "Of course."

With that, Brock slammed on the gas pedal, and we took off, out of Tampa and toward the Georgia state line.

"So we agree that our mission is to find Rebethannah?" I asked once we were on I-75.

"Brock and I were talking about it while waiting on you guys. Since you already have your camper set up in Lake Haven, maybe you guys can go into town and see if there really are Lakari hanging around there while we find a place to stay."

"Good idea. We'll probably need a few days to settle in and figure things out," I said.

"And Lake Haven's a small town, right?" Asia asked. "Which means we'll need to hang back anyway."

"I don't get that," I said. "How are you supposed to help if you're not right there?"

"Oh, we won't be far," Asia promised. "Trust me. Besides, that's only if we have to stay at Lake Haven, which we might not. Maybe the Guardians were wrong or the Lakari have moved on by now."

"If we're lucky," Jeric muttered, his first contribution to the conversation.

"We're the best of the best," Brock said. "Don't worry so much, man. As corny as Mira made it sound, she was right about believing. Any special gifts and inhuman abilities are already there—you just have to trust in them. And believe yourself."

Jeric snorted, and I suppressed my own laughter at the euphemism we'd been using earlier. Brock took it the wrong way, though.

"Dude, it's in your hands," he said, and this time neither of us could hold back the laugh. This only frustrated him more, and he huffed out a breath. "Fine. Believe whatever the hell you want. But at some point, you'll see that I'm right. When your life's on the line, you'll be believing me so hard you'll be screaming my name."

"That'll *never* happen," Jeric choked out, and both of us howled with laughter.

Asia eyed us with bewilderment, and Brock scowled.

"Screw you both," he muttered, and Jeric and I lost any control we'd had.

We spent the rest of the drive trying to convince Brock that we weren't laughing at him nor saying we'd never trust him. Eventually, we had to let them both in on our silly little joke before we lost them completely as comrades.

"Ahhh, I get it," Brock said with exaggerated enthusiasm. "And by the way, Jeric, believe you to hell and back."

"Fuck you, too, dude," Jeric replied.

When we pulled into the small RV park and I saw my old red truck parked next to my Airstream, nostalgia hit me hard. Life had been so confusing when we'd been here, but in a way, so much simpler. We'd discovered each other on several different levels and even had our first fight here. So much had happened in the two days we'd been stranded at this campground. Now, we were entirely different people.

Brock and Asia didn't hang around after dropping us off, and we hadn't even reached the door to my camper when a white cat streaked over and rubbed against my legs.

"Ghost?" I asked with disbelief as I picked up the cat and nuzzled my face against his soft fur. "I can't believe you're still here."

"He looks to be well fed," Jeric pointed out as he opened the camper door.

As soon as we walked in, the nostalgia disappeared, replaced by content. This was home. More "home" than anywhere else we had anymore, because neither of us really felt at home at the manor. Jeric had only stayed in this camper a few nights with me, but I could feel his appreciation for the sense of familiarity, too. Seeing my tie-dyed curtains and multicolored collection of pillows, the funky décor all over the interior, I realized I wasn't really an *entirely* different person. I was still me, just ... more.

Jeric dropped our bags in the middle of the floor, grabbed my wrists, and pulled me into him.

"Now?" he asked, his lips already against my neck.

I giggled. "I said when we're settled. We need to go into town, get some groceries, maybe even scope things out and see if there are any Lakari around."

He lifted his head to eye me and must have seen I was serious because he groaned. "You're killing me, babe. I haven't stopped thinking about you since my shower this morning."

My lips twisted in a smirk. "I call your bullshit. If you'd been thinking about me, you wouldn't have gotten so pissy with everyone."

"I got so *pissy* with everyone, which, by the way, I hate that word. Girls get pissy. Not dudes. But I lost my cool because I *was* thinking about you. Just in a different way. But the other way is always in the back of my mind, too." His eyes lit up again, and I didn't have to wonder what he was thinking about this very moment. I debated giving in, but decided it wouldn't kill either of us to wait. Patience only came with practice.

"The sooner we go, the sooner we can get back so you can believe me all night long."

He must have liked the sound of this, because he reluctantly gave in, and we made a list for the store. When we headed out, my truck started up right away, and I gave her a pat on the dashboard.

"Good to see you, too, girl," I said. Jeric quirked an eyebrow, but I ignored him.

When we'd been here before, my truck had been in the mechanic's bay at the truck stop across the two-lane highway, so we'd never made it into the nearby town of Lake Haven. The diner, bar, and convenience store had provided our sustenance. So although we'd seen people around the RV park and over at the bar, I didn't expect anyone would remember two strangers who'd spent a couple of days outside of town a few months ago.

I forgot about dancing the bull and the fight that came after. Well, not a fight really, since Jeric had one-hit the dude and knocked him out before carrying me over his shoulder out the door. Apparently, we'd made an impression, although they probably only remembered our faces. Any details of our actual existences had been wiped out.

"Hey," said almost everyone whose paths we crossed after we parked on Central Street and walked around a little. They all gave us a welcome smile. The younger people, anyway, and all of the men. Some of the older women, all dressed up with lipstick and everything, smiled, but their grins weren't very welcoming. Guess they heard about my dance and didn't approve. I didn't care what they thought. Except hearts like that were easy prey for Lakari. Maybe one of these old uppity women was their target.

"Have you seen any Lakari?" Jeric asked.

"I don't feel them specifically, but I do feel a lot of Darkness. Don't you?"

He answered with a harrumph while I glanced around the businesses lining Central Street, which intersected with 1st Street, the other main drag. It was the middle of a weekday, so activity was probably at its peak. There was one dude down the street, standing in the doorway of a business, who didn't seem to fit in. A little squirrely looking. When I saw that the business was an insurance agency, though, I dismissed him.

"If they're here, they'll probably be out at night," I said. "That seems to be their preferred time of day. So I guess that's when we come out, too, to see where they gather."

"You promised *me* tonight," Jeric reminded me as he took my hand.

"I know," I said with a smile. "We need to get our bearings better anyway. Get to know some people and everything."

"We'll start that tomorrow." He steered me into the doorway of a diner. "Let's grab something to eat so we're not shopping hungry."

The mom-and-pop diner was exactly as you'd expect in a small Southern town. Booths that were probably manufactured in 1974 lined the outside wall and tables with lots of character and mismatched chairs sat in the center. Lunch hour had come and gone, so only a few people lingered at the tables. Along the inside wall that separated the kitchen from the dining room was a buffet that was empty at the moment. The fragrance of fried chicken and ham and beans drifted from the kitchen, though.

"Grab a seat wherever ya'll want," a female voice called from the kitchen.

Jeric and I sat down in a booth in front of a window that provided a great view of the center of town.

"Sweet tea?" the same voice asked, though nearer and not quite as loud now. A woman, late thirties or early forties, had come out and stood at the counter between the buffet and the cash register. Her pale blue eyes scoured us, as though determining with a hard stare if we were good people or not. Her blond hair was pulled into a clip on the back of her head.

"Water, please," I said. I hated tea.

"And for you?" the woman asked. Her expression changed when she looked at Jeric—I swore her eyes glazed over.

"Coke, please," he said.

"What kind?" she asked.

Jeric gave me a questioning glance.

"Everything's Coke in the South," I explained. "Thought you knew that. Didn't you live in Florida?"

My time in Georgia had taught me a lot. That and Mama had been from Louisiana.

"The farther south you go in Florida, the more north the culture," Jeric said. "And most parts of Miami are more Cuban or Haitian or Dominican than American."

"What kind of Coke?" the woman asked again.

"Oh, uh, just make it a sweet téa," Jeric answered.

"Alrighty then. Your menu's on the table, and our special of the day is chicken-fried steak, gravy, mashed potatoes, corn, and collard greens."

I pulled the paper menu from its slot between the metal napkin dispenser and the salt and pepper shakers. Traditional Southern offerings had my mouth watering, and I couldn't decide.

"Are ya'll ready to order?" asked another female voice, though this one was younger and right in front of our table.

When I looked up, I gasped.

"Hey," the redhead said with a smile as she placed our drinks on the table. "I know ya'll! You finally came back, huh?"

She looked over at Jeric and blushed, proving that she remembered more than just our faces. How could that be when the rest of the world who'd known us before the Forging had forgotten we existed? Was it because of the timing of when she'd met us—while we were in transition, so to speak? Or something else entirely?

But it wasn't the familiarity of Bethany's face or the fact that she'd brought Jeric to her place when he was drunk or even that she remembered us that left me speechless. It was something about the girl herself. About her soul. Once again, as I had the very first day we met in the RV park's office, I felt a faint twinge of recognition, but that wasn't what got to me either. Maybe our souls had met in the past, but the feeling was so weak that I was more inclined to believe that she simply reminded me of someone I'd known from a dance camp or something. Although, I had to admit, the feeling was actually stronger now than it had been last time. Maybe there was more to our mutual pasts, but still, I could barely think about that.

The sadness, the despair, the *Darkness* that tainted her soul mesmerized me. I'd felt a blanket of Darkness outside, but now it all seemed concentrated into her perfectly curved little body.

"You okay?" she asked me, her blue eyes darkening with concern.

I blinked.

"Are *you?*" I blurted. "I mean ... no, you're not. You're not okay at all, are you?"

"*Leni,*" Jeric snapped in a harsh whisper. "What's wrong with you?"

I blinked again and looked at him, then back at Bethany, then back at him. He raised his brow with a question. I closed my eyes briefly and inhaled a long breath. When I opened them, he and Bethany still stared at me, her eyes wide.

"I'm, uh, I'm sorry," I stammered. "I just ... felt ..."

"It's okay," she said, and she smiled, although I didn't know if it was Southern charm or real relief that brought it on. "It's been a long day and it's not even two, so yeah, I'm kind of draggin'. Liz'beth, the gal who took your drink order, she's an empath, too, and knew it right away like you just did. She does it all the time—knows my feelin's and moods and all, ya know—so I'm kinda used to it."

I gave her a weak smile and nodded stupidly. Empath? I didn't even know they existed outside of books and movies, but I did know what I felt was more than Bethany's current feelings and mood. What I felt went deeper. Lasted longer. Maybe even across lifetimes.

"So ya'll need more time?" she asked as she tapped her pen against her order pad.

"Um ..." I looked to Jeric. Before she'd walked up, I'd been telling him how everything sounded good, and seeing that I was speechless, he ordered a fried chicken platter for me and the daily special for himself.

I couldn't tear my eyes off Bethany as she wrote our order down. Something glinted in the side of her nose—a piercing. I didn't remember that from before. She also had new ink that peeked out from the collar of her gray t-shirt, which said "Memaw's Diner" across the front in cracked blue lettering.

Another tattoo showed from under her sleeve on her upper arm. She'd been dressed so skimpily the last two times I saw her, surely I would have noticed the tats. Or would I have? I hadn't exactly been so enthralled with her before.

She glanced at me when Jeric finished, and her brows pushed together for the briefest of moments, and for some reason, the expression made my heart stutter. Then I came to my senses: she gave me that look because I'd been staring. She was already headed for the kitchen when I snapped out of it.

"You all right?" Jeric asked when I looked back at him.

I shook my head, as though a haze had been filling it and doing so would clear it out. I leaned over the table and whispered, "I can *feel* something in her, and between her and the Darkness in this town, I think we do need to stay here for a while. It may even be her the Lakari are here for."

Jeric raised a single eyebrow, glanced toward the kitchen, then back at me. "Would it really be that easy?"

I shrugged. "Doesn't matter if it's easy or hard if I'm right, does it?"

Jeric studied my face for a moment, and then nodded. "True. But we should observe for a while, make sure it's her."

Jeric and his need for observation and knowing all the facts. "I *feel* it, Jeric."

"I get it, babe. I don't doubt you do. But we just got into town. Maybe she's not the only one with a hurting soul. Maybe someone else is worse off. Closer to going Dark. Maybe there aren't even Lakari here."

The longer we were here, though, the more sure I felt about the Darkness hovering—both over the town and in this girl. If my instincts were right, it really had been this easy. Of course, I wasn't exactly confident in my instincts yet, but I could always hope the Book would help us out.

A few minutes later, Bethany placed our food in front of us, and again, I couldn't tear my gaze from her face. From her eyes, especially. As though they really were windows to the soul.

"Let me know if ya'll need anything," she said, but she stood there, with me staring at her and her staring at Jeric until it became extremely awkward. Then she blurted out, "Weren't you deaf?"

I finally tore my eyes away from her and looked at Jeric, who shared my same momentary panic. We hadn't planned for this. We hadn't expected anyone to remember we existed, let alone details like Jeric's hearing.

"Hearing aid," I quickly replied.

"Surgery," Jeric said at the same time. Another moment of awkwardness passed. Then he looked away from me and gave Bethany his most winning smile. "I had an operation, and they implanted a special kind of hearing aid."

Bethany gazed at him for a long moment, then at me, and then scrunched her brows.

"Um, okay then. That's really awesome," she said with false excitement before turning away again. She must have been only curious, but didn't really care. Or maybe we'd weirded her out too much for her to second-guess us.

I looked down at my plate and wrinkled my nose. "You got me collard greens?"

"Oh, crap. Sorry, babe, I forgot. Hey, Bethany?" Jeric called, and the girl turned around.

She wore an expectant smile as she returned to our table, although it didn't reach her eyes.

"I don't go by Bethany anymore. Too many bad memories go with it," she said, and she tapped a fingernail against her name-tag. The "thany" part had been blacked out with a permanent marker, and painted on top with what looked like white nail polish was a simple X. "It's Bex now."

The way she said it—her tone, the glint in her eyes, how her lips quivered with more of a smirk than a friendly smile—felt like a freightliner slamming into me. Memories of me as Jacey with her best friend Bex flooded over me, and my body trembled with the realization. She was Bex. *That* Bex, one and the same. She'd been murdered last time, but she hadn't been completely Dark, so the Lakari hadn't taken her soul. But from what I felt from her now, they just might be able to this time. I wondered how many lifetimes she'd been like this.

And then another thought occurred to me that made me practically jump out of my seat. I slammed back into it before making an ass of myself with some kind of nonsense she'd never understand, but not before knocking my plate and drink across the table and onto the floor ... which resulted in me making an ass of myself after all.

"Ohmagosh," Bex squealed. "Are you okay?"

My mouth was too dry to speak, but somehow I forced out a grunt that sounded like "yeah."

"I need to clean this up, but I'll get you a new order in." She hurried off, probably completely freaked by my behavior.

But I couldn't help it.

"Jeric." I clawed excitedly at his hand, trying to grab it.

"What was that all about?"

"It's her, Jeric. I'm almost positive."

"Who? Bex?"

"Yeah. *Jacey's* Bex. And not just that ... Jeric, I had this thought that she might even be Rebethannah."

CHAPTER 7

Bex

"BUTTER MY BUTT and call me a biscuit, I can't believe that just happened," Elizabeth said as I stomped into the kitchen. "You okay?"

"I'm fine," I muttered. My hands gripped the bus tray as I called out to the cook, "Aunt Faye, we need another fried chicken platter. Green beans instead of collard greens."

Aunt Faye wasn't my aunt—she was Elizabeth's and they owned the diner together—but we all called her Aunt Faye anyway. Memaw's Diner was opened decades ago by Aunt Faye's actual memaw, and the building itself had been in their family since it was built in the 1800s. The place was definitely haunted, but what just happened was no ghost. That chick was off her flippin' rocker. And no *bless her heart* added to that. Not in my head, anyway. I didn't give a shit about her heart or anything else at the moment.

As I pushed my way through the swinging door, I wished I could shoot arrows out of my eyes at the girl. Instead, I remembered Grams' words I heard every morning for years before walking out the door: "Don't forget to put on your smile, the mos import'nt thang you can wear." Of course, if I walked out the door with nothing but a smile, she would have eaten her words, God rest her soul, but that was the Southern way. So I grinned ear to ear as I headed for the mess on the floor in front of the table with Mr. Hawtness and his nutters girlfriend.

Even now, she wouldn't stop staring at me.

Weirdo. I hadn't blamed her when she thought I'd messed with her boyfriend that one time, and I actually thought she was pretty cool in a daring kind of way when I saw her dance on the mechanical bull out at Sullivan's Bar at the truck stop. She'd seemed pretty normal then. Now? She freaked me out. Why did she keep staring at me? I swear, there was hunger in her eyes, as if she wanted to devour me rather than the food she'd pretty much thrown on the floor. Were they wanting a threesome or something? Is that what was up?

Wow. That was new for me, and I'd done some pretty kinky shit. Girls weren't exactly my thing, although if I did do a girl, I guess I'd do her. She was gorgeous, with big green eyes, smooth skin that was a bronze I'd kill for, and light brown curls that fell past her shoulders. A little curvier than mine, her body was pretty hot, too. And him? Yeah, I'd taken advantage of his drunken state before for a reason—talk about a body to die for, and those blue eyes and dimples melted bones—but I'd never been rejected by a guy before, especially not a drunk one. If she hadn't made my day go from bad to worse, maybe I would have considered a roll in the hay with both of them. Or maybe not. Damn. I was going to hell just thinking about it.

"Here, let me help you." Crazy girl was on her knees next to me, reaching her hands out to scoop the pile of chicken, taters and gravy, greens, and broken plate.

I moved my arm in front of her, blocking her hands. The last thing Elizabeth and Aunt Faye needed was a lawsuit because she cut her hands open. Yankee out-of-towners would be all over that shit.

"Oh, no, I'll take care of it," I insisted. "You just sit down and don't worry your pretty little head over it. Your food will be out in a minute."

The bus tray was pulled away, though, as a new pair of jean-clad legs knelt down beside me.

"I got this," said a familiar male voice that made my belly quiver and my throat tighten even though I hadn't heard it in years. "Go get her food."

My eyes slowly lifted, taking in the jeans that strained across thick thigh muscles, the wide belt buckle at the narrow waist, the Stu's Bait and Tackle tan t-shirt that stretched over pecs, shoulders, and biceps that had been smaller when the shirt was bought, and up to full lips spread into a smile and hazel eyes framed by dark lashes longer than Sissy's fake ones staring at me from under a red baseball cap. As if I didn't have a thing for guys in baseball caps. As if I hadn't once had a thing for this particular guy. As if I'd thought my day couldn't get any crappier.

"Go on now," Ty Daniels insisted. "You're lettin' her food get cold."

Without a word, I stood and strode for the kitchen, and not because crazy girl's plate was ready yet or because I was following Ty's orders, but because I needed a moment. Lots of moments.

"What the hell is he doin' back?" I seethed out loud as soon as the kitchen door swung closed. I leaned against the wall and stomped my foot. Yeah, I actually stomped my foot. And my hands formed fists at my sides. My eyes stung, but with tears of anger and frustration. *I will not cry over him. I will not cry over him.*

"Oh, baby girl, I meant to tell ya," Elizabeth said as she wrapped her arms around me. She'd been my boss for years, as well as a friend—as good a friend as a boss could be. Since Grams died two months ago, she'd kind of taken on a mama role because my own mama had run out years ago. Well, she'd found a way to wiggle herself back into our lives recently, but she hadn't been a real mama to me since … since I was born, really. Grams, God rest her soul, pretty much raised my sister and me the best she could. "I heard he came in over-night."

How had I not noticed? He lived next door to me. Was he staying somewhere else? Of course, I'd left home before the butt-crack of dawn this morning, so his trailer was probably still dark. It didn't matter. I drew in a deep breath and forced my heart to slow to normal.

"It's okay," I said through another breath. "I'm not gonna let him get to me. I'm over him. His loss. I've moved on."

"That's my girl," Elizabeth said as she gave me another squeeze before letting me go. She lifted my chin with her knuckles and scrutinized my face.

"I'm serious, Liz'beth. I'm done with him." And I was. Ty Daniels was no longer a prickly thistle stuck to my heart.

Having grown up in the same trailer park, we'd known each other for as long as we could both remember. There'd been those couple of years Mama had moved us away, but as soon as we came back, Ty was knocking on the door, ready to play, no questions asked. That's what I'd liked about him. We'd been buddies for years, and then in high school, it became something more. But he was never right for me and I wasn't right for him, which he pretty much told me right after his graduation and right before he took off for the Army. He left me back home to finish my own schooling a year later, never sending word, even when he went off to Afghanistan. It took me a while to realize he was right. Ty Daniels wasn't good for me. He wasn't The One I was sure was out there, somewhere, looking for me.

So why did I have to react to him the way I had? If only my body would realize just how bad he is ... and forget just how *good* he is.

"The big stuff's all cleaned up, but I need a mop to get the rest," Ty said as he came into the kitchen with the bus tray under one arm.

Elizabeth gave him a warm smile and took the container from him. "Thanks, Ty, but you don't need to do that. You don't work here anymore, remember? In fact, it's been some time since you did."

"Yes, ma'am, but I never forgot what you taught me. Never ignore a pretty girl's needs." His eyes cut over to me as one corner of his mouth lifted in a grin.

I snorted and rolled my eyes before taking the plate Aunt Faye had just placed on the counter. I'd rather put up with crazy girl than Ty and how my body betrayed me around him. My damn belly quivered with that one crooked smile. Quivered! But even with the threat of going to hell hanging over my head, a threesome with these guys would be much better for me than anything with Ty Daniels. They'd be on their way again afterward, and so would Ty, but only he would leave me with another broken heart.

Ty took a seat at a two-top table, and although Elizabeth waited on him, I was completely and fully aware of his presence. I'd barely even noticed when Mr. Hawtness and his girlfriend scooted out, although I did notice the nice tip they left me. I half expected a note to meet them at their camper, but there was none. Maybe I'd misread their intentions. Thank God and baby Jesus. The girl's craziness had been enough to deal with when it came to those two. And with Sissy's phone message she'd left here during this morning's breakfast rush, then Ty's sudden appearance, I really didn't need anything more added to my plate today, thank you very much.

"Bethany, sweetheart," Ty said after Elizabeth had cleared his table and disappeared into the kitchen. I'd been too busy wiping tables and checking condiments to notice we were the only two left in the dining room.

"Don't call me that," I said, and it came out harsher than I intended. The "sweetheart" part made my knees weak, which annoyed the crap out of me, and the "Bethany" part was like nails on a chalkboard. He was one of those bad memories tied to that name, but only a minor one. Mostly I hated it because it reminded me of the daddy I'd never really known, who'd given the name to me, and my mama, who used it against me every chance she got. I was sure she blamed me for his not being with us anymore. The way she used to draw out my name but cut it short at the same time—*Bettttth'neeee*—because she was too trashed to say it right still made my skin crawl. I'd gotten over it for a while—suppressed the memories, a fancy head doctor would probably say—until she called two months ago. That's when I decided to never go by that name again. Unfortunately, in a small town, it was hard to get people who knew you all your life to change their ways. "It's Bex now. And if you call me Bethany again, I'll punch you in the nose."

Ty chuckled. "I miss your feistiness." He paused, and not until I turned to face him and he could look into my eyes, did he add more quietly, "I miss all of you, sweetheart."

Oh, dear Lord. Don't fall for it. DON'T fall for it.

I strode over to his table and stood across from him. I placed my hands on the edge and leaned forward. "You left me."

He nodded. "I know. And I was stupid for it."

"No, you weren't. You were right."

"I was wrong, boo. Totally wrong."

I gritted my teeth at his term of endearment. "Ty, it took me a long time to get over the hurt—"

"I'm so sorry, Beth—Bex." His hand reached out for mine, but I moved before he could grasp it.

"Don't be. It sucked, and I hated you for a long time, but it was the best thing for me."

"Don't say that, sweetheart. Please don't say that."

I stood up and shrugged, even though my heart was pounding painfully against my ribs. Saying this all out loud was much harder than I thought it would be, but he didn't need to know that. "Why not? It's the truth. You made me realize we weren't right for each other. We never were and never will be."

"I don't believe that. Not anymore." He stood and reached for my hands again. I stepped backwards, and something in his eyes seemed to crack with the rejection. "I came back for you. For us."

I swallowed against the lump that had formed in my throat. "Well," I said, my voice barely more than a whisper, "you shouldn't have. It's over, Ty. There is no us."

"Be-ex, please, boo."

My eyes closed for a brief moment before I opened them to look into his. I had to clench my jaw and make my spine like a steel rod to say my next words. "Don't beg, Ty. You're not a dog."

He stared at me for a long moment as multiple emotions passed through his expressive eyes. Then he pulled his cap down further over his forehead, threw some money on the table, and strode out the door. I stood there for a moment, trying to pull myself together. Hopefully, that was the end of the suck for the day. I'd had enough, and I needed it all to follow him out that door. But if it did, it blew right back in with the next person to walk through. Sissy.

"Ty Daniels?" she asked as she looked over her shoulder at the old, beat-up, black Ford truck leaving the parking lot. She turned back to me with her dark brows raised over big blue eyes that were just like mine. Her raven hair was pulled back in a clip, and she wore little makeup, revealing the purple half-moons under her eyes. I couldn't believe she was out in public like this— that wasn't the Sissy I knew. She looked as exhausted as I felt. She may have been younger than me, but she'd always had an old soul, and right now, no way did she look only nineteen years old.

"Yeah, he's back home, but don't worry. I sent him packin', at least from me. You look like hell." My sisterly way of trying to change the subject.

She didn't take my eggin', though. "He's probably the best thing for ya, sis. You probably shouldn't let him go a second time."

My eyes narrowed at her as she stepped to the table nearest the door and hesitantly sat down. She'd seen the hot mess I'd been when Ty left. She'd claimed to hate him as much as I had.

She looked up at me and rolled her eyes at my expression. "Oh, come on, sis. Settlin' down with Ty is a lot better than you runnin' around and gettin' it on with a different guy every month. Aren't you tired of that yet?"

My nostrils flared as I blew out an angry breath before yanking out the seat in front of her and dropping into it hard. I crossed my arms on the table and leaned toward her.

"I do *not* get it on with a different guy every month! Quit makin' me sound like a two-bit whore!"

She only stared at me with her brow raised again.

"Four guys, Sissy. I've been with four guys since Ty left me three years ago."

She still stared silently. I squirmed and leaned back.

"Okay, maybe it was five. That's still a long shot from one a month."

"And is that countin' the carnie from Atlanta?"

"I didn't get it on with him! We made out a little, but that's all. He kissed like a fish attacking a worm on a hook." I shuddered at the memory.

"Still another man. And what about the surfer from Daytona? The cowboy whose truck broke down on the way to the PBR finals? Oh, and let's not forget Punk Roberts."

I sighed. If she counted them, her list could go on, but I'd actually slept with Punk. I really thought he'd been The One. He'd graduated as Michael Roberts several years before me and went off to become a nearly famous rock star. No doubt he would be there one of these days. He'd come home for a break for a couple of months, and we'd hit it off right away. I'd never told Sissy because she would have talked me out of it immediately, but I'd been ready to pack my bags and hit the road with him, glad to say goodbye to this Podunk town forever. Until I found out he'd succumbed to the typical rocker lifestyle on the road, fueled by drugs that hyped him up and more that forced him to sleep. I'd had enough of that bullshit in my twenty years at the time. I wasn't about to go there with him.

Sissy fell silent, and when I looked up at her, sadness filled her eyes. She reached out for my hands and took them into hers.

"I'm sorry, Be—Bex." That was the first time she'd called me that, so she must have meant it. "I didn't come here to pick on you. I'm just worried about you, is all. And I know you hate Ty for what he did to you, but maybe you can find it in your heart to love him again."

The problem was I'd never stopped loving him. But only as a friend. He'd been the rock in my life, but now I couldn't count on him anymore. Maybe that was it—I couldn't trust him. And if there's no trust, there's no relationship.

"So you knew he was comin' back home and you didn't tell me?" I asked, bitterness filling my voice. I yanked my hands away from her. "Left Mama's side and came all the way here to convince me to take him back? Did he put you up to this?"

Sissy pressed her hand to her chest and shook her head. "I had no idea he was back, I pinky swear. I just saw him and thought he'd be good for you. He's always been a good friend to us, and we kinda need that right now." She folded her hands on the table and dropped her gaze as she picked at her fingernails. "But no, there's somethin' else. Did you get my message this mornin'?"

"Yeah, Liz'beth told me. I was goin' to call you back before I went to my *other* job."

Sissy's face lifted, looking even more exhausted than she had before, and I felt bad for my jab at her. Sorta bad. I thought she sometimes forgot who was working her ass off to support us and pay for at least some of Mama's medical bills. Someone had to do it after all, and sometimes she became quite the martyr, never letting *me* forget who does the caretaking of Mama.

"You need to see her," Sissy said, her voice soft and quivery.

"I've got no need to."

"Beth ..." She sighed. "Bex ... she only has a few more weeks. Maybe a month or two, but the doctors reckon it'll be shorter."

I stared at her for a long moment, and then looked away, out the window, although my mind barely registered the trucks and cars passing by on Central Street. It was trying to process everything that Sissy's words meant, but failed.

"She's your mama," my baby sister reminded me.

"We may have came out of her hooha, but she's never been a mama," I whispered. Sissy was only eighteen months younger than me, but she may as well have been five years sometimes. She'd been younger enough to not remember a lot, and I'd sheltered her from most of the rest. And, I'd admit, she had a bigger and more forgiving heart than I did.

"Don't be like this. Not now. Mama needs you, just to see you again, to say her apologies and goodbyes, so she can go peacefully."

My heart squeezed, and my throat suddenly felt like a peach pit had lodged in it. I didn't know that she deserved to go peacefully, but I also knew that was a shitty thing to think.

"I don't think seeing her will give either of us peace," I managed to say.

Sissy reached for my hands again and grasped them firmly. "*I* need you to do this. If you can't bring yourself to do it for her or for yourself, then at least do it for me."

My gaze came back to Sissy's face and her pleading eyes. My heart contracted again. I'd always done everything I could for her, but I didn't know if I could do this.

"I don't know when my next day off is," I said. "Working three jobs doesn't really give me time to drive all the way to Orlando, you know."

Sissy closed her eyes and inhaled a long breath that caused her ample chest to lift—at least Mama had given us something to work with. Our looks and figures came from her. Of course, they hadn't really been her gift, since she had no say in the matter. That was all God's doing.

Apparently, Sissy's calming method didn't work. She stood up and glared at me with her hands on her hips. "Where's your common decency? Your mama is dying! Maybe you should make your family a priority for once!"

I jumped to my feet, too, knocking my chair over. "Oh, hell no! Don't you pull that one on me. The only reason I work three jobs is for you and that bitch who's done nothing but hurt us and leave *us* for dead. You really think she'd give two shits if the tables were turned?"

Sissy huffed out a breath then stomped for the door. As soon as she grasped the handle to pull, she looked over her shoulder at me. "Well, in a few weeks, she'll never be able to hurt you again. And for that matter, I'll be outta your hair, too."

I stared after her as she left with my mouth hanging open.

"You tryin' to catch flies?" Elizabeth asked behind me. I snapped my jaw shut and went back to work cleaning tables and checking condiments.

Elizabeth stepped behind the register and flipped through the lunch tickets. "She's right, you know."

I let out a low growl. "I don't need it from you, too."

"I know how you feel about your mama, including that you're torn right now on what to do. Which means you *know* what's right, but you just don't wanna do it."

She crossed her arms over her chest and tilted her head, daring me to call her a liar.

"There's been a dark energy around this place for months," she said.

"Maybe it's Papaw Willy angry at your music again," I half-joked, trying to relieve the tension. Papaw Willy was the original owner of the building and one of the ghosts that hung around to mess with us. That's what Elizabeth thought, anyway. We'd all witnessed a few bizarre happenings that convinced us *someone* was around who shouldn't be, but only Elizabeth could feel his presence and put a name to him. He tended to throw his fits when Elizabeth played her heavy metal rock.

"It's definitely not Papaw Willy. I don't know what's causin' it, but it's heavy and full of sorrow. And I'm sure any of us showing some extra love and forgiveness wouldn't be a bad thing. Maybe give a little light to the blackness hanging over us."

I had no idea what she spoke about and figured she was just trying to take a different angle to talk me into doing the right thing. The dinner shift distracted me well enough, at least until afterward, when I went into the bathroom to clean it. A little, red plastic dinosaur sat on the edge of the sink, left by one of the kids who'd been in earlier, and it taunted me with its reminder of childhood. I picked it up, turned it around in my hands, and blinked back the tears that threatened.

Why couldn't we have had a normal childhood? A normal mama who cared about us and provided for us instead of making us live on the streets because she was too proud to face her own mama, but not too proud to make her daughters sleep in abandoned cars? Someone who loved us for who we were and noticed that Sissy would want the Dollar Store makeup and I would have been excited for a little, red plastic dinosaur? She didn't notice at all, or, more likely, she didn't care. Her gifts for us came from her grabbing whatever she could quickly stuff into her bag or pocket when no one was looking. Always stupid stuff like fancy scarves—we lived in the hellpit of Nowhere, Florida!— or sparkly pins. What were we supposed to do with those? Would they somehow make our third-hand, grimy clothes look newer and nicer?

Didn't matter. Everything she gave us always disappeared anyway. She blamed thieves until I was old enough to watch her exchange the items for little bags of white powder or brown pill bottles of something that made her sleep for a full day or longer. When I cried about it, she misunderstood my pain. It wasn't the pretty but useless presents I missed when she sold them for drugs. It was my mama I missed.

I squeezed my eyes shut and didn't open them again until I'd pushed the memories aside. The bathroom window had darkened since I'd been in here, and nightfall meant time to change and head to my other job. I gave the sink another quick wipe, grabbed the dinosaur for the lost-and-found box up front, and removed the trash bag to take out back. One job down, one to go, and then maybe I could relax a moment and figure out what I was going to do about Mama.

Throughout my hours at Sullivan's, the truck-stop bar, I still couldn't decide if going to see Mama was really the right thing. Every time I imagined seeing her face, I wanted to throw something at it. I wanted to hurt her, to make her feel everything she'd put Sissy and me and Grams and the rest of her family through.

As I walked home from Sullivan's through the RV side of the park to our side, where the permanent trailers sat, the lights on the silver Airstream caught me by surprise. It had been dark for months, and I'd already forgotten that couple had returned. I turned away from my usual path that crossed in front of it, afraid they might be outside, and passed between two other campers and into the clump of trees that separated the two sides. My heart stuttered when I saw a large figure sitting on the steps of my trailer house, but then relaxed when I recognized him.

I exhaled a tired breath. "What are you doing here, Ty?"

I didn't have the energy to deal with him again. He grasped a brown bottle in one hand and held another up to me.

"I wanted to apologize. I didn't know everything goin' on with you and Sissy. Thought you could use a friend."

Tears pricked my eyes at the kindness. I took the peace offering, sat on the step below him between his legs, and took a long pull on the cold beer. He wrapped a strong arm, thicker with muscle than it used to be, across my chest and pulled me backwards. I leaned my head against his hard stomach.

"Thank you," I whispered.

"I'm here for you now, boo," he murmured as he finger-combed my hair away from my face. "However you need me, I'm here."

And the thought of how badly I needed him right now should have scared me. Instead, against my better judgment, I took him up on his offer and let him be my friend. He did what he'd done so many times before: held me while I cried over my mama.

CHAPTER 8

Bex

I COULDN'T BELIEVE I was doing this. My heart pounded a beat hard enough for a Godsmack song as the elevator rose, racing with the thought of what was about to come, as well as with the memory of my first elevator ride. It had been in a fancy hotel in some big city I didn't know then and couldn't remember now. Mama had smiled at Sissy's and my excitement, chattering on about how beautiful the hotel was as it raced by through the glass walls. Her hands shook so bad, though, I'd thought she'd been scared.

When we reached our floor way up high, she led us down a corridor that smelled good, like expensive soap, to a door that a strange man answered. I didn't like the look he gave us as he ushered Sissy and me through a door in his room to another room exactly like his but with two beds instead of one. Mama told us to watch TV and be good while she visited with her new friend. They closed the door, and we had to turn the volume on the TV way up to drown out the man's icky noises coming from the other side of the adjoining door. It lasted all night, except for a while when Mama came to see us, wearing the hotel's robe. We got room service—our first meal in a week that hadn't come from a McDonald's dumpster—and slept in real beds, and Mama got her drug money. At the time, I didn't know that's what it was, but I knew she suddenly had a wad of cash in her purse, we still didn't eat again for two days and went back to the car to sleep, and she'd stopped shaking.

My stomach squeezed at the memory, and I forced myself not to retch.

Maybe I should have taken Ty up on his offer to come with me. Nah. I needed to do this alone. And I needed somebody to stay on my side, to not see her in her weakened state, but to remember her like I always had: a selfish druggie who'd abandoned her young daughters. I'd see Ty tonight. Elizabeth had given me the entire day off, and I hadn't been on Sullivan's schedule. I had a few things to do for Uncle Troy when I got back, but after that, Ty had promised me dinner. I kept telling him it wasn't a date—reminding myself as much as him—and he insisted he was still just being a friend. He said I'd need it after today, and he couldn't have been more right.

The elevator dinged when it reached the fifth floor and the doors slid open. I stood frozen, staring out at the corridor in front of me, glad no one else was in here to push me out. Forcing the lump in my throat down with a hard swallow, I wiped my hands on my miniskirt, and wobbling on the heels I usually had no problem walking in, I took a step forward at the same time the doors began to slide shut. My breath caught, and I jumped backwards. The doors came to a close, and the elevator began moving downward without me pushing a button. Maybe this was a sign that I shouldn't be here. Nothing good could come of it. In fact, there was a strong possibility I'd put Mama out of her misery early, and I'd be hauled off to jail.

By the time the elevator reached the ground floor again, I was prepared to walk out the hospital doors, to my car and get the hell out of here. When the doors parted, though, Sissy stood on the other side, wearing yoga pants and a tank top.

Her eyes popped wide open. "Betha—Bex! You came!"

She rushed inside the elevator and swallowed me into a hug.

"Did you already see Mama? I wish you woulda told me you were comin'. I woulda been there to provide support and all. I ran out to grab somethin' to eat, though, but I s'pose she told you that already." She pulled away and punched the 5 button before quickly retreating to my side as more people stepped on board. "Do you mind comin' back up? Did you get to talk to the doctors? I know Dr. Hayes really wanted to chat with both of us at the same time."

My head swam. My palms started sweating again as we rose. My stomach once again threatened to toss my measly breakfast.

There was no point in lying to her. Mama's face when she saw me would give away that I hadn't been there yet. My voice came out sounding like a toad's croak. "Um ... I couldn't remember the room number. I haven't seen her yet."

Sissy took a closer look at me, and her brows drew together. "Oh, bless your heart, look at you. I can't tell if you're scared or want to puke."

A little bit of both, actually.

"Don't you worry," she said as she slid her hand up and down my upper arm. "You'll be fine. And it's the right thing to do, Bex. Besides, she's a whole different person now. Too weak to be a bitch, bless her heart."

The smartly dressed woman standing in front of us glanced over her shoulder with a look of disdain. I wondered if she'd be so disapproving if she knew everything our mother had put us through. Of course, nobody but I knew about everything, not even Sissy.

The elevator emptied as we made our way up, and by the time we reached the fifth floor, I was glad to have my sister by my side. She took my hand and led me out of the box and down the hall. We stopped at the closed door of room 532 and paused as I inhaled a deep breath full of the nasty odors of disinfectant, bleach, and sickness. I blew it out slowly. Sissy watched me closely until I nodded that I was ready. As ready as I'd ever be, anyway.

Except I'd never be ready for the sight that greeted me.

The thing lying in the hospital bed looked nothing like my mama. In fact, it barely looked human at all. The top of the bed was raised, and a low-watt lamp behind the bed was on, haloing the head that was barely more than a skull. She'd once had a full head of scarlet red hair like mine and the same bright complexion covered in freckles. We'd inherited our blue eyes from our daddy, but her brown ones had the same wide shape. They did at one time, anyway. She'd been a looker way back when. Even before she'd left us, I'd seen the drugs taking their toll on her. I just hadn't imagined it would be this bad. She looked ninety, and she wasn't even forty yet.

Her brown eyes turned to me, still appearing large but only because the sockets were sunken. There was no roundness to her face at all, only gray, mottled skin pulled tight over sharp cheekbones, framed by patches of thinning, dull-red hair that looked brittle enough to break if a brush even touched it. Recognition flickered in her eyes, and her thin lips parted in a crooked O, showing her few remaining teeth that looked too large for her mouth because the gums had receded so much. She lifted a bony hand off the bed a few inches, the tube leading under her skin following, and I was surprised she even had the strength for that because she seemed to have barely any muscles left on her bones.

"Beth'nee," she whispered hoarsely. "You came."

Sissy gave my hand a squeeze, then gently pushed me forward. I about fell face first because my feet remained glued in place. I'd wanted to be angry. I'd wanted to yell at her, to tell her once and for all how badly she had hurt us, how much she had made us suffer. I'd wanted to throw a classic hissy fit that I felt completely entitled to. In fact, the only way I'd been able to talk myself into coming today was by thinking that this was my last chance to tell her exactly how I felt. And once again, she was robbing me of that satisfaction. How could I yell at this skeleton?

"It's okay," Mama said. "I know you hate me. And I prolly look scarier than a hellhound on Halloween. I'm just pleased as pie that you came at all."

She paused to draw in a breath that rattled through her lungs as though pebbles filled them. She didn't look scary, though. Not as scary as she did when she went through withdrawals and took her problems out on us. She looked weak and vulnerable and sad. Very sad.

I glanced around the typical hospital room, noting that no one occupied the other bed. At least she had the privacy of a single room without the cost. A chair sat next to each bed. An adjustable table stood next to Mama's, rather than over it. A meal of soup, Jell-O, and juice was on top, looking barely touched.

"Um ..." I swallowed against my tight throat and tried to make conversation. I wasn't really sure what to say, though. "Did I interrupt your lunch?"

"Oh, no, I'm done. I ate until I was fuller than a tick on a hound."

Sissy walked over to the table, examined the contents and looked back at Mama. "You didn't eat a thing, Mama. You need more than that."

She pushed the table closer to Mama's bed, sat on the side, and picked up the spoon. She scooped out some green Jell-O and brought it to Mama's mouth. Mama rolled her eyes at me while parting her lips in compliance. The chords in her neck strained as she swallowed, and I wondered if she was actually still hungry but didn't have enough energy to feed herself. Which meant she probably needed help with other necessities, like going to pee and cleaning herself.

No wonder Sissy spent so much time here. She probably had even more to do when Mama wasn't in the hospital. Sissy had pretty much moved into her one-bedroom apartment to care for her up until a week ago, when they put her back in the hospital.

We'd had a big fight a while ago about how I needed Sissy to help out with the bills, but then she showed me how much a home nurse would cost. I'd had to bite back the words I'd wanted to say and gave in. Now I understood better. Mama needed full-time help, and not just someone to bring her a meal every now and then and do her wash. I could have never helped Mama like this. Not because I hated her, but because it just wasn't in me. I'd rather work three jobs and let Sissy handle this part. I knew what it was like to take care of a helpless child, but a helpless adult was a different story.

"I remember when it was me feeding you," Mama said.

And that one statement brought me back to life.

Renewed anger jolted through me, and I nearly jumped at her.

"Oh, hell no! You have no right to say that!" I nearly screamed. "*I* fed her. *I* made sure she had food, and *I* made sure it got in her stomach while you lay on the couch all drugged out. And I was only three years old!"

Tears stung my eyes, and my body trembled. I couldn't believe she'd even gone there!

"Bex," Sissy hissed.

Mama placed a hand on hers, stilling it from bringing another bite to her mouth. "No, she's right. She's right about me, and she's right to be angry. I deserve it. I was talking about you, Beth'nee. When I used to feed you. Peaches were your favorite. And ice cream. Boy, did you love ice cream."

She wheezed another breath then began coughing. My mouth slammed shut and my anger deflated.

"I was a good mama once, but you don't remember that," she eventually continued. "You were just a wee thing. When your daddy died, God rest his soul, a piece of me died with him. I tried to escape the pain with drugs. The doctors prescribed them at first. Ain't that a hoot?"

I didn't find it a hoot at all, especially as she broke into another coughing fit. What kind of doctors prescribed drugs to a pregnant woman with a one-year-old?

"The doctors started it twenty years ago, and now they're tryin' to fix it," she continued. "I reckon they're a little late, though."

Sissy looked over at me with an expression full of warning. Apparently, Mama didn't know how right she was.

"Speakin' of doctors," Sissy said, probably wanting to change the subject, "has Dr. Hayes been to see you yet?"

I swore Mama's face lit up at the name. "Oh, he's a looker, ain't he? I know how you like him, Sis. No, he's not been in yet, lucky you."

Sissy's face flushed. Interesting. She hadn't mentioned anything about this Dr. Hayes to me.

"He wants to *talk* to us," Sissy said. "That's why I asked. I was hopin' we hadn't missed him already."

"Mmm …" was all Mama said, and then her eyes closed, her head rolled to the side, and her mouth fell slightly open.

My breath caught and my heart raced as I watched closely for her chest to rise, because she looked deader than a doornail. Panic swept through me. There was still so much to be said. We needed more time! Why hadn't I come sooner? Done more? Been the better person? How could I be so stubborn? So selfish? My hand flew to my mouth as a sob threatened its way up. But then I saw her chest move. Her breaths came slowly, but they did still come. I could finally take my own breath.

I guess I didn't want her dead as badly as I thought I did.

Sissy rose and took my hand and led me out of the room, the first I'd moved since arriving. She pulled the heavy door behind her, ensuring it closed quietly.

"I don't know how long she'll sleep," she said. "Sometimes it's only for a few minutes, and others it's for hours. You're not gonna go, are you?"

I pushed my hands into the front pockets of my miniskirt while watching her face that filled with hope. "You said the doctor wanted to talk to us, right?"

She smiled and nodded, then headed down the hall for the nurse's station. I stayed by Mama's door, leaned against the wall with one ankle crossed over the other, and let my head fall back to stare at the ceiling. My mind and emotions were all over the place, and I needed to see which way was up. How could I still love this person I hated so much? I didn't think I had, but couldn't deny it now. Not with the way I'd reacted when I thought she'd died right before my eyes. After treating us worse than dogs and leaving us on Grams' doorstep with not another word until two months ago, how could I possibly still love her?

Because she was my mama. That's why.

"You must be Bethany," said a male voice that sent a shock through my nerves.

I came to immediate attention, stood up straight, and opened my mouth to correct him, but nothing came out. My stomach did this crazy-ass flip-flop thing I'd never felt before. My heart made its own gymnastics move in my chest. When he lifted a brow and gave me a model-like smile, I had to squeeze my thighs tight because I thought my panties would fall right down to my four-inch heels, soakin' wet and steamin'. Holy. Shit. Dark hair and silvery green eyes like the color of Spanish moss, a tanned complexion, and enough scruff around his square jaw and chin to make me wonder what that would feel like against my cheek ... okay, against my thighs. This was one sexy specimen of a man. And he didn't look much older than me. Well, maybe by four or five years. Still acceptable.

"Dr. Mason Hayes," the man said, thrusting his hand out.

Oh. My. God. Sissy had been holding out on me big time! And I guess I was off on his age: he had to have been a little older than I thought to be a doctor. I noticed for the first time he was dressed in scrubs. I decided right there and then that I had a bigger weakness for a man in scrubs than I did for ball caps.

"Um ..." I had to clear my throat, which suddenly felt like sandpaper. "Yeah, I'm Bethany, but I go by Bex."

My hand could barely hold still as I reached out to shake his. As soon as he wrapped his quite larger hand around mine, my knees nearly buckled and I almost fell off my stiletto heels. His voice had been nothing on my nerves compared to his touch. I felt electrified. In a good way. A *damn* good way. His mouth moved, but I couldn't hear his words as blood rushed in my ears before dropping southward. I wanted to have this man's baby. I wanted to start right now.

A pinch on the back of my arm snapped me out of it.

"What are you doing?" Sissy hissed in my ear.

Dr. Hayes was still grinning at me, and I was still shaking his hand, and I didn't know what her problem was ... except, oh yeah, she'd been way down the hall when our hands had first met and here she was by my side. How long had I been holding him prisoner? Embarrassed, I yanked my hand away and gave him a stupid grin.

"I'm so sorry," I said. "I guess I'm just glad to finally meet you."

Good heavens, was my hand sweaty or what? I tried to discreetly wipe it on my skirt. I hoped he hadn't noticed, but that was a hope in vain. How could he not? Gross.

Sissy gave me a hard stare, and I lifted my brows, trying to look innocent. Her eyes tightened before she turned to Dr. Hayes.

"I was just havin' the nurses page you," she said, her voice sweet as honey. "We must have been thinkin' the same thing. I see you met my sister?"

"I'm making my rounds, yes. Found her here studying the ceiling as if Michelangelo had painted it. One look and I knew you two had to be related." Dr. Hayes' eyes hadn't left my face, and a renewed thrill ran through me.

Sissy cleared her throat. "You said you wanted to talk to us?"

His weight shifted back to his heels, and he finally slid his eyes away from me to Sissy. "Did you tell her what I told you?"

Sissy bit her lip, which she did when she was upset, and stared at the floor. "A few weeks to a month or so. Yes, I told her."

"And the rest?"

My gaze cut over to Sissy, who stood next to me, facing the doctor but still not looking at him. She hadn't told me more, but I hadn't exactly given her the chance to, either. She shifted her weight, and her hands fidgeted with the hem of her tank top.

"What's the rest?" I asked.

When she didn't answer, I turned back toward Dr. Hotty. He cocked his head as his gaze bounced between Sissy and me.

"You don't know much at all, do you?" he asked.

Now my turn to squirm. Guilt washed over me for the first time for ignoring Mama's condition. I'd been so angry that she'd finally reached out to us only because she needed something that I hadn't taken the time or energy to learn exactly what was wrong with her. Sissy tried to tell me all the time, but I only pretended to listen. And somehow, Dr. Hotty figured this out in less than a minute. I could tell by the look in his eye that it was news to him, so it hadn't been Sissy or Mama ratting out our family secrets.

"Um ..." I stammered again. "I've been working crazy hours and live a couple hours away ... and ..."

And what? *I didn't really care about my mama?* I couldn't say that. Especially not after seeing her.

Dr. Hotty nodded. "Sissy and your mom told me you're the supporter. But you need to come up to speed. We're at a big turning point in our treatment. Can I, uh ..." He scratched at the scruff on his jaw and squinted his eyes. "Can I take you down for some coffee? There's a lot to tell you."

I glanced at Sissy and back at him. Like I could say no.

"Yeah, sure. Is Mama gonna be okay up here alone? What if she wakes up?"

Sissy elbowed me in the ribs for suddenly caring. "There are nurses here, you know."

Or maybe for being stupid.

"Oh. Duh." I let out an embarrassed laugh.

"Maybe you should stay up here, Sissy," Dr. Hayes suggested. "So if she does wake up, you can tell her Bex is coming back. I know she'd hate to think she slept through your visit. She'd never forgive herself."

Disappointment flashed in Sissy's eyes, and I recognized that look. I'd done something again, but I didn't know what. She placed a hand on my upper arm and gave me a shove toward the doctor. A little bit harder than necessary, if you asked me.

"Of course. Ya'll go on and catch up. Hopefully, she'll actually listen to *you*, Dr. Hayes." Sissy threw another eye-dagger at me before spinning on her heel and returning to Mama's room.

The doctor swept his arm out in an "after you" gesture, and we headed for the elevator. His arm that was closest to me remained raised behind me the whole time, and I imagined his hand near the small of my back. Just the thought of it gave me shivers. He was a perfect gentleman, though. He bought me coffee and everything.

"What kind of work do you do?" he asked as we sat at a two-top in the nearly empty cafeteria.

Heat began to rise into my cheeks, but I pushed it away. I was not going to be embarrassed, even around this highly educated, beautiful person with the professional career.

"I'm a waitress at one place, tend bar at another, and do my uncle's bookkeeping and other office stuff," I answered with as much pride as I could muster.

Dr. Hayes eyed me. "*Three* jobs?"

I put on my best smile. "I do what I have to do, doctor. We have bills to pay. One of them is yours."

He returned my smile and leaned forward in his chair. "I'm sorry. I didn't mean to offend you. Actually, I admire a woman with a strong work ethic. Which one do you like the most?"

I pulled back with mild surprise. Nobody had ever asked me that, and I'd never really considered it. "Well, I like working for my uncle the least, but he gives us free lot rent, so I kinda have no choice there. The diner and the bar both have their goods and bads."

With a little encouragement from him, I told him all about Elizabeth and the diner, and the craziness that could break out at the bar. The doctor was very easy to talk to and now I understood why both Mama and Sissy were smitten with him. I was pretty smitten myself. Well, beyond smitten, to be honest. He seemed so genuine, as if he honestly cared about everything I was gabbing on about. Then there were his eyes that completely mesmerized me, making me forget when and where we were.

"I really hate to cut you off, Bex," Dr. Hayes said after a while, "but I need to get back to my rounds, and we still need to discuss your mother's condition. Did you know she gave you power of attorney, and you have authority to make all of her health decisions?"

I blinked at him as several thoughts ran through my mind, from embarrassment for spending so much time talking about my stupid jobs instead of Mama, to wondering why the heck she'd picked me for this.

"I'm assuming you didn't know," Dr. Hayes said after a moment of silence.

"Um, no." I shook my head. "We've never been close. And it's not something I ever thought about."

He gave me a kind smile. "It's time you start thinking about it. Your mother's very ill."

"I'm sorry." I cleared my throat and picked at my skirt at the same time. "I, uh, well, I don't even really understand what she has. It seems like every time I turn around, Sissy's talkin' about something new Mama's come down with."

He clasped his hands on the table. "That's basically how it is. Your mother has several things going on at once. She's given me her history of drug and alcohol abuse, so it's no wonder. When they say that shit'll kill you, they're not kidding."

I looked up at him, slightly thrown to hear a man in his position swear, even if he was young and talking to someone younger with ink and piercings. "She's really dying?"

He frowned. "Yes and no. She's not well at all. In her current condition, if we did nothing more, she has a few weeks, maybe a month or two. There are some things we can do differently that could possibly give her much longer, maybe even years. Then again ..." The corner of his mouth quirked. "You never know what karma or the universe itself has in store for any of us. Life—and death—have a way of surprising even us doctors."

His beautiful eyes bore into me with that statement, making me think he was talking about more than Mama's life. I lifted my hand to my throat as I continued to stare back at him for longer than was probably acceptable. When the moment became uncomfortable, I dropped my hand and my eyes and cleared my throat.

"So, um, what are these things she suffers from?" I asked as I looked back up at him.

"To start with, she has rhabdomyolysis, hepatitis C, and cirrhosis of the liver."

I stared at him blankly. Did he just switch to talking in Greek or something?

"Can you say that again in a way lil ol' waitress me can understand?"

"Sorry. Basically, her skeletal muscles have deteriorated, she's severely malnourished with several mineral deficiencies, and her liver is failing. Among other things. Her heart and lungs aren't doing well, which is the most immediate problem. If we could improve those, we could probably get her on a liver transplant list."

"And how do we do that?"

"Drug therapy. She needs certain medicines—"

"But wouldn't those be bad for her liver, too?"

He eyed me with obvious appreciation. I wasn't as stupid as I looked or even sometimes acted. In fact, I'd once had my own dreams of going to college. I'd never had the opportunity to decide what I wanted to be when I grew up, though, because life had other plans for me, like raising my little sister, and now keeping Mama alive.

"Yes, they could damage her liver further, but if the goal's to get her a new one anyway, the risk is worth it."

I nodded. "Okay, then why isn't she on the meds already? Or is she?"

He sucked in his upper lip and glanced at the clock on the wall behind me. It hadn't been the first time. I was tying him up when he had other patients to tend to.

"You should probably talk to your mother and sister about that," he said. "The medicines … they aren't cheap. In fact, they're pretty damn expensive. And there's no guarantee they'll work, and if they do, that she'll get a transplant."

I swallowed hard as I stared at him. "So you're sayin' we're too poor to save her life."

CHAPTER 9

Bex

DR. HAYES CRINGED at my statement. He looked at the clock again and grabbed our empty coffee cups. "There's a lot more to talk about—programs and things that can help—but I selfishly used up our time trying to get to know you better. When can I see you again?" His eyes widened for a moment, and he pressed his lips together as though fighting a grin. "I mean, when can we finish this discussion?"

"I don't know, honestly," I said as we stood and headed for the elevator. "I have double shifts at the diner and the bar for the next three days. Or is it four? I don't remember. I have to run the office for Uncle Troy on the weekends ..."

The elevator doors opened and we both walked on silently. He reached over to push the button as a woman and a young girl joined us. They got off on the third floor.

"Can I call you?" Dr. Hayes asked once we were alone again.

My head about jerked off my neck I turned it so fast, my eyes wide.

"To discuss your mother, of course."

Of course. How stupid of me to think this doctor—a flippin' *doctor*—would be interested in me.

"I don't have a phone," I admitted.

"You don't have a phone?" he repeated as if he didn't understand the words, as if I was the one speaking Greek now.

"It broke, and it was kind of a waste to replace it. I'm always at the diner, the bar, or the RV park, so everyone knows where to find me. Sissy needs the other one we have." I didn't explain that my phone broke the day Mama first called because I threw it at the wall, nor did I admit that we couldn't afford a second phone and line anymore.

"Can you call me?" He patted his chest and ass, as though looking for something but realizing he didn't have pockets in his scrubs. "Guess I don't have a card on me, but Sissy has my number."

The elevator door slid open on the fifth floor, and we both stepped out.

"Yeah, sure, but I don't know when."

He placed a hand on my shoulder, sending another electric jolt through me. His eyes filled with concern and sadness. "We don't have long, Bex."

I gave him a nod. "I know. I'll call as soon as I'm at a phone and have a few minutes."

He turned right down the hall to finish his rounds, and I turned left for Mama's room. She was awake again and smiled when I entered the room.

"You came back," she rasped.

I gave her an awkward smile. "Didn't Sissy tell you I was?"

"She said she wasn't sure."

I threw a look at my sister, but she paid no attention to me, not even a glance. She sat in the pink reclining chair next to Mama's bed with her arms and legs crossed, the top leg swinging up and down, and a scowl on her face. I wondered what had crawled up her ass and died.

"Sissy, don't forget the most important thing to wear," Mama said, and Grams' words made us all fall silent. Mama's head rolled to the side and she stared off with eyes glistening. After a minute or so, she sniffed. "She died too young, and I never got to make my amends with her. Ain't that how life is? As soon as you see what you got and lost, it's too late. Ya can't count on havin' someday to make it right. You gotta do it now." She rolled her head back to look at me. "That's why I'm so glad you came, Bex. I want no more regrets with you."

I pressed my lips together, stuck on the fact that she'd called me Bex. Sissy must have told her, and she'd made the effort to show that she'd respect my desire. I pulled the chair from the vacant side of the room to Mama's bed, opposite from where Sissy sat.

"How was your visit with Dr. Studmuffin?" Mama asked. The heat rising in my face must have shown because she let out this weird sounding raspy noise that I thought was a laugh. "Oh, looks like someone else is smitten with him."

"Who in their right mind wouldn't be?" I blurted, glad to have something silly and not awkward to talk about. "And I swear, by the way he was lookin' at me and some of the things he said—he kept slippin' up in the way he said things like he was trippin' over his own tongue."

Mama's smile reached her eyes. "You can't blame him. Any man with a lick of taste would be fallin' all over you. You're beautiful and strong, just how I always knew you'd be. Both my girls are."

Sissy suddenly sprang from her chair and ran out of the room. What the hell was wrong with her?

"I'm not too fond of that thing in your nose, though," Mama continued. "Or those tattoos. Why would you do that to your beautiful body? If God wanted us to look like that, we woulda been born that way."

And just like that, tension filled the room again. Who was she to judge and talk about what God wanted? God wanted mothers to take care of their children or He wouldn't have given us to her!

"Or maybe God gave us a blank canvas so we could express our individuality," I said with as little edge as I could muster.

Mama's head tilted, and I thought she was going to nod off again. I kind of hoped she would because I was ready to get out of here.

"I never thought about it like that," she said as her eyes came back to me. "We really don't know everything God wants or thinks, do we?"

I blinked and my mouth parted, though I had no words to say. Mama smiled again.

"I've been thinkin' a lot about God and life and what-not," she said. "Not much else to do now, is there? And I don't know why He gave me two such beautiful and smart girls knowing I'd screw it all up. I never deserved you two. I finally realized that when I took ya'll back to my mama's. She didn't deserve to have all that dumped on her, either, but I didn't know what else to do. All ya'll deserved the goodness of each other without me ruin't it all." She sighed then hacked then sighed again. "Married at sixteen, a mama at seventeen, and a widow at eighteen. By twenty-five, I was a proper screw-up, wasn't I? And now at thirty-eight, my grave's been dug and I'm dyin' like an old woman."

She closed her eyes and fell silent. I dropped my head into my hands, leaned my elbows on the armrests and closed my own eyes. I'd never thought about her life like that. I knew she'd married young and had me when she was practically a babe herself. God knows how many times Grams talked about Mama tryin' to grow up too fast. But I'd never really considered what it must have been like to be only eighteen with a toddler and a baby on the way and to have to bury your husband who was barely more than a child himself. I'd always thought her weak and pathetic for not being the super-hero single mom, for not moving on like other widows did, at least enough to take care of her children properly. Not once had I stopped to put myself in her shoes—like actually in *her* shoes with *her* experiences and tragedies, rather than lumping her in with the other mamas who struggled and made it when she didn't.

Was her youth an excuse to pick drugs over her own children? I wouldn't go that far. She'd chosen to have a family and take on that responsibility, even if she hadn't planned on doing it by herself. But at twenty-one, I was three years older than she'd been when the doctors prescribed her first sleeping pill, and if someone much older and wiser and licensed to know better offered me a temporary escape from my reality, I'd probably take it, too. I didn't have two little ones depending on me while dealing with the worst thing that could ever happen. I couldn't even imagine it. So how could I judge so harshly the path she'd gone down?

Probably because deeply etched into the backs of my eyelids was the memory of her shoving a needle into her arm not ten minutes before dumping Sissy and me at the door of Grams' front office, and then she drove off with some asshole loser, never to be seen again. She was twenty-seven by then. Old enough to know better.

I pushed myself to my feet. I needed to get out of here. Too many memories and raw emotions—some I'd never felt before— threatened to brew a storm worse than a Cat 5 hurricane. Mama didn't need that in her condition, and nobody else deserved to have to clean up the damage afterwards.

"I need to get home," I said. "I've got books to tend for Uncle Troy and work early in the morning."

"I'm so sorry it turned out like this, baby girl," Mama said, and she gave me a sad smile. "But I'm happier than a pig in slop that I got to see you at least one more time."

I moved one step toward her bed, but stopped, unable to propel myself any closer. "I'll be back as soon as I can. Got things to discuss with the doctor and all, but I don't know when. It's not easy finagling a whole day off."

"Whenever you can is just fine. I'll be right here. Don't think I'll be goin' anywhere soon."

I couldn't bring myself to hug or kiss her yet, but I did think about grabbing her hand for a moment before leaving. It looked so small and weak, though, I was afraid I'd crush it. So I gave her an awkward wave and an even more awkward smile as I said goodbye.

Sissy had apparently been waiting out in the hall for me, and as soon as I came out, she grabbed my arm and practically dragged me down the corridor toward the elevator. She didn't push the down button, though, and when I went to hit it myself, she blocked me.

"What bee's in your bonnet?" I hissed.

"Have a nice chat with the doctor?" she snapped.

I pulled back and crossed my arms over my chest. "Yeah, I did. We have a lot more to talk about, too. Things you haven't bothered to tell me."

"Well, isn't that precious. I'm surprised Mama even came up at all. Was that before or after he was trippin' all over his tongue? And exactly where was that tongue at the time?"

"Sissy Anne Waters! You watch your mouth." I moved closer to her so our chests were nearly bumping and dropped my voice. "He was nothing but a professional. Because that's what he is. If you're all worried that I hiked up my skirt to give him a ride, don't be. He's not that kind of man. But it's good to know you think I'm that kind of girl."

I reached around her and jabbed the down arrow.

"Go take care of Mama," I said.

"Beth ... Bex, I'm sorry."

My jaw clenched. "Go on and take care of Mama. Ya'll can be sorry together."

Thankfully, the elevator opened then. I stepped on and slammed my finger into the button to close the doors in case she tried to follow me. Before I could break down, a couple got on at the fourth floor. I lifted my chin and smiled for them and kept wearing that all-important fashion accessory until I reached my car inside the parking garage. I crossed my arms on the roof and dropped my head onto them as I breathed in car fumes rather than clean air to clear my head. I couldn't wait to get out of the city.

The sound of a car door shutting a few slots down made me look up. A man with the palest face and blackest eyes I'd ever seen returned my gaze as he rounded the rear of a late model sedan. He wore a black hoodie with the hood up, covering his hair, but the way he moved triggered a vague memory. Did I know him from somewhere?

"Everything okay?" he asked, and his voice, too, rang with the slightest hint of familiarity. He continued walking my way, which made sense because it was the way out, but fear rose in my chest. When Elizabeth said she felt a dark aura, this was how I imagined that feeling. He grinned, baring sharp, crooked teeth, as he moved closer. My heart stuttered and then took off in a gallop.

"Bex," a male voice rang out from behind me.

The pale man seemed to shrink, all confidence in his stride gone. Not daring to turn my back on him, I looked over my shoulder out of the corner of my eye. Dr. Hayes jogged toward me. My heart had a totally different yet equally dramatic reaction to him, but at least I felt like I could breathe again. When my gaze returned to the white-skinned creep, he was gone. I hadn't seen any movement. I glanced up and down the aisle, but he was nowhere to be seen.

"I thought I'd missed you," Dr. Hayes said, and I turned fully to him as he walked the last few steps. His brows scrunched together when he saw my face, and I might have melted a little at the concern in his eyes. "Are you okay?"

"Um, yeah." I put on my smile. "I thought I saw something, but I guess I was imagining things. It's been a long day."

"I, uh …" He paused and broke eye contact with me, and it was all I could do to not beg him to look back at me. To mesmerize me with those eyes like he had earlier. He finally did return his gaze to me, accompanied by a grin that once again had my thighs clenching. *I will not hike up my skirt. I will not hike up my skirt and offer him a ride.* Only because I didn't want to give Sissy the satisfaction of being right. At the moment, I so wanted to be that kind of girl. "So, this is completely against hospital rules, and I've been fighting with myself for the last hour, but I can't help it. I have no shame, and I'm a selfish bastard."

He paused, and I opened my mouth to ask him what the hell he was talking about.

"Can I take you to dinner?" he blurted.

Whoa, nelly. I was not expecting that. I tilted my head. "You mean so we can finish our discussion about Mama, right?"

"Yes, of course," he said in a rush, and I tried not to be disappointed. How could I get my hopes up that he'd actually asked me out on a date? But then he added, "That and I can't fathom the thought of not seeing you again. Even for a day."

I gulped. I might have died a little, too. I know my heart was ready to jump out of my chest and serve itself up on a platter for this beautiful man who'd walked straight out of my dreams. Like almost literally. One of my recurring dreams was of a man as charming and as hot as Dr. Hayes here, who said things that knocked my socks off like he just did. The dreams I had of The One—my soul mate, my true love, the man I knew was out there looking for me just as much as I was looking for him. Could Dr. Hayes be The One?

I wasn't about to go there yet, but, ohmahgosh, what if he was?

"I ... uh ..." I stammered, trying to answer him because he'd been looking at me so expectantly after putting himself out there. "You mean right now?"

He flinched, and I immediately felt foolish for asking like that, but then he put his hands on his hips, right where his scrubs hung low, and gave a small shrug.

"Yeah, right now. I know it's a little early for dinner, call it a late lunch if you want, but I'm starving, and you have a long drive home, and I don't want you on the roads late. Can you stick around the area for another hour or so and allow me the pleasure of buying you dinner?" He took a step closer to me so we were only inches apart, sending my heart into overdrive. Then his gaze dropped to my lips and lingered there long enough for the need to lick them to become overwhelming. I thought I heard his breath hitch when my tongue involuntarily slid out and over, providing the moisture my lips suddenly lacked. He lifted his eyes to mine, and when he spoke, his voice came soft and smooth, like butter on bread fresh out of the oven. "I know it's asking a lot, but like I said, I'm selfish. If you have to go, I understand, but if you can stay, you'd make me a very happy man. And I'd make sure to return that favor."

Whoa. Was that not full of promise or what? And I already knew he could deliver. Just asking me out, saying those words made me giddy.

My mind tried to run through what I still needed to do today, but couldn't move past the first thing of Uncle Troy's books. Well, those could be done any time, like later tonight.

"Okay," I said. "I s'pose I could eat now."

I was actually starving since I hadn't eaten since before leaving home this morning. The talk of eating made the hunger pangs more noticeable.

"What do you like? Would steak be okay?" he asked.

Wow. I hadn't had steak in months. Not since we'd had them as a special at Memaw's and Aunt Faye had accidentally over-cooked an order and let me eat it.

"Sounds delicious," I said, hoping he didn't hear my stomach growl.

"Great! There's a Ruth's Chris down the street. I'll meet you there in ten minutes. I need to change." He gestured toward his scrubs, and my eyes, acting on their own because apparently my brain had lost all connection to my body parts, followed his hands and skimmed down to the drawstring of his pants. The top had shifted up a bit over his muscles, revealing a strip of skin and a thin line of dark hair that led down, under his waistband. My mouth went dry. I almost pleaded for him to leave the scrubs on until *I* could take them off.

"See you in a few," I said before anything else came out on its own. I fumbled to open my door, forgetting that I'd locked it since I was in the city. Dr. Hayes took my keys and opened it for me. I slid inside, and he dropped the keys into my waiting hand. "Thank you, Dr. Hayes."

He groaned, then leaned down between the door and me, once again impossibly close. "Bex, you're killing me. I can't be a doctor taking his patient's next-of-kin on a date."

What? Was he bowing out now? I stared straight ahead, too scared to turn toward him.

"Call me Mason."

"As you wish ... Mason."

"Mmm ... Say it again."

Unable to help it—did I mention I'd lost all control over my body?—I turned my head toward him. He was insanely close, just as I'd feared.

"Say it again," he said huskily. "What you just said."

Um ... "As you wish, Mason," I whispered.

His mouth pulled into a wide grin, revealing perfectly straight, white teeth, and his green eyes lit up like I'd just given him the greatest gift ever.

"I could listen to you say that all day, every day," he said. "And I will have you saying it again." He winked, then bounced up to his full height and stepped away from the door. "See you in ten."

Damn. Did I have time to stop at a Wal-Mart and buy some new panties? Mine were definitely ruined.

I pulled into the restaurant parking lot a few minutes later and sat in my car, waiting on him and debating on leaving. I couldn't see this—whatever it was between us—being anything more than sexual, and I really didn't have time for that right now. I didn't have time for anything at all, to be honest. Not with Mama and three jobs and everything else. But what if The One came along, and I ignored him because I was so wrapped up in my shitty life? That's what kept me in that parking lot, waiting: the thought that maybe, just maybe Dr. Mason Hayes was my soul mate. How would I ever know if I didn't spend at least an hour having dinner or lunch or whatever with him?

A clawing sound at my window startled the bejesus out of me. Mason, now wearing khakis and a dark purple Polo, pulled my door open and held out his hand. Warmth traveled through me as soon as I touched it. He only let go after he closed and locked my car door, and that was so he could place his hand on the small of my back as he led me to the restaurant's entrance. Once we were inside, I almost turned around and left. I didn't know what a Ruth's Chris was, but it was obviously way fancier than anywhere I'd ever been. My self-confidence took a severe nosedive into the shallow end of a knee-high pond. When I saw the prices on the menu, I had to clench my jaw to keep my mouth from falling open. One steak dinner was more than I made in five days of tips. Maybe I needed to reconsider where I worked.

"Tell me about yourself," Mason said after giving the waitress our order. He hadn't asked me what I wanted, but I couldn't imagine anything being bad here. Everything on the menu made my mouth water.

"What do you mean?" I asked.

"I want to know everything there is to know about you," he said, leaning over the shiny, dark wood table.

I glanced around the empty dining room. We were their first customers of the evening, probably because it wasn't quite evening yet. You wouldn't know it from inside, though. Heavy crimson-colored drapes covered the windows, and the interior lighting was turned low. An employee moved from table to table, lighting little candles inside the hurricane lanterns. Needing something to do with my hands, I picked up my napkin and laid it out on my lap.

I didn't know where to start. He thought he wanted to know everything, but he really didn't. Nobody wanted to know the ugliness of my childhood.

"Start with your favorite color," Mason suggested when I still hadn't responded. I smiled gratefully.

"Hot pink," I said easily. "I'm kind of your girly girl, but not really."

"A typical Southern girly girl?" he asked with a teasing lilt. "Sweet, dressed up, and always wearing a smile while holding a shotgun on her lap as she drives her pickup through the mud?"

I laughed. "Yes and no. I like pink and black lace. My favorite outfit is a sweet little halter top and cut off shorts with cowboy boots ... but I also like miniskirts and heels."

His leg brushed against mine under the table. "Like you're wearing right now."

I laughed again, and it sounded more like a giggle. How embarrassing.

"I definitely noticed," he said, his voice low. "Those sexy legs stretched out as you leaned against the wall were the first things I noticed."

"And then what?" I teased as I propped my arms on the table.

His gaze traveled over my face and down, lingering on my chest before coming back up. "Your eyes, of course. But your lips were right after that."

Again, I couldn't help but lick them. How come I had that undeniable urge every time he focused on my lips?

"Really?" I drawled, enjoying the look on his face. Like he wanted to devour me.

"I couldn't wait to hear what they had to say."

I smiled.

"Or to see that."

My grin grew while my face heated. I was thankful for the low light because a red face on a redhead wasn't very attractive.

"Tell me more," he urged.

"Well, I don't have a truck, as you know, but I'm not afraid to play in the mud. And I also love to dance."

"Two-step?"

I groaned. "Not unless you held a gun to my head. Here's where I stop being the typical Southern, small-town girl you think you have pegged: I hate country music."

He laughed and leaned back in his seat. "Hate it? All of it?"

"Well, there are a few modern bands I can tolerate, but yeah, pretty much hate it all."

"So what kind of music pleases those ears of yours?"

"I like some hard rock like Avenged Sevenfold and Godsmack. And what Sissy calls weird stuff like Foo Fighters and Vampire Weekend."

"Mutemath?"

"Hell, yeah!" I clamped my hand over my mouth and looked around, relieved we were still the only ones in the room.

He laughed then leaned forward again, a new playfulness in his eyes. "I have tickets to next Monday's show. I've seen them before, and they're wicked awesome live. Especially their drummer."

"Ohmagosh, I'm so jealous! I've seen the videos. I'd do anything to see that in person."

"Anything?"

I narrowed my eyes. What was he getting at?

"I have two tickets, and my brother couldn't get the night off, after all. Shame for me to go by myself."

I gulped. I obviously didn't mean *anything*, but the only things I wouldn't do in exchange for any kind of payment—monetary or otherwise—I'd gladly do with him anyway.

"What do you have in mind?"

He gave me a slow smile. "Another date? I already know this hour with you isn't going to make me happy enough. I need more."

I wanted to give him more, too. Except ... I frowned. "I don't know when I'll get another night off."

"Maybe you can work out next Monday? Surely your bosses will understand. It's *Mutemath.*"

I laughed. "Liz'beth might, but Sullivan's? They'd think I was asking for tutoring or something like that. Then again ..." I trailed off as I considered it. Sullivan's was closed Mondays. Not a chance I would be on that schedule. And Elizabeth might be willing to let me off after breakfast shift that morning, especially if I promised to see Mama while I was here. Driving home that late was a problem, though, and if I stayed at Mama's apartment with Sissy, that meant needing the next morning off, too. "I'll have to see if I can work things out."

"Tell me what to do to make it happen, and it's done. Anything."

"Anything?" I teased.

"Anything," he said flatly.

The waitress arrived with our food before I could make any suggestions that I'd never expect him to actually do. The subject changed to other favorites, then to birthdays, stories from school—college for him and high school for me—and other light topics. We skimmed over family and barely touched on any history. He only told me that he grew up in a suburb of Philadelphia, graduated high school at sixteen, and put himself through college and med school. He came down here for his residency, and the brother he'd mentioned was a fraternity brother. He made no mention of any real kin, and since he already knew more than I'd ever choose to tell him about my family, I didn't press for details. I understood everyone had family secrets, and since we'd just met, I had no right to ask his.

We never did finish our conversation about Mama.

"I hate the idea of you driving by yourself this far, in this car, and with no phone," Mason said when we'd returned to my car. He took my keys from me again to open the door.

"I'll be fine."

"I still don't like it. Is there at least some way you can call me when you get home? Just so I know that you made it?"

I did still have books to do in the park office. "Yeah, I could. If I had your number."

He fished his wallet out of his back pocket and withdrew a business card from it. When I slid it from his fingers, I couldn't help but think about how close it had been to his perfectly sculpted ass (scrubs leave little to the imagination).

"Be safe," he said before leaning down toward me. His lips barely touched my forehead when I leaned my head back to look up at him, causing them to skirt down my nose. His kiss landed on the tip, but when he pulled slightly back, he was staring at my lips again. "You're seriously trying to kill me, aren't you?"

"Would you die happy?"

"Only after this."

His mouth skimmed over mine, but I didn't let him go so easily. I grasped his bottom lip between both of mine, and next thing I knew, he had me pressed against the car with his hips, his hands framing my face, and his tongue exploring my mouth. Holy. Fuck. He was hot, smart, a damn doctor, and the best kisser I'd ever known. By a long shot, which was saying a hell of a lot. He kissed me like he was doing some of kind of delicate but urgent procedure with his lips to my mouth. My belly dropped. Chills swept over my skin. My thighs trembled, and my toes curled within thirty seconds of his lips touching mine. I had to push him away because I swore I was about to have an orgasm.

"Go," he ordered, his voice husky and his eyes a stormy gray with desire as he stepped backwards. "Go before we get arrested for public indecency."

I chuckled giddily. "You think I'd—"

"Not you. Me. I don't have the self-control to be decent with you a second longer."

CHAPTER 10

WITH MY MIND replaying the events of the day, the two-hour drive flew by. Once I turned into the trailer park a little before sundown, I barely remembered the drive at all, which was a little scary, because it was like I was there and then suddenly here. I could have run someone off the road and not even noticed. My car's clock showed 7:42 and I still had work to do, so I parked my car at home and made a beeline for the office.

Sissy and I'd been helping Grams out with her RV and trailer parks since Mama dropped us off when I was nine and Sissy was eight years old. At first, we helped clean up the grounds, but Grams brought us in to help in the office when we started high school. My Uncle Troy, Mama's big brother, took over the business after Grams passed. Sissy quit to take care of Mama, but I thought also to get away from our uncle. He was a lot less pleasant to work for. Less pleasant as in he was a total asshole.

He blamed Mama for Grams' death, because she'd died of a heart attack less than a week after The Call. He said her heart couldn't take the shock of Mama suddenly reappearing in all our lives. Maybe he was right. He often took his frustration with Mama out on Sissy and me, starting by forcing us to move out of the apartment adjacent to the office where we'd lived with

Grams for twelve years. He gave us free lot rent for the trailer Grams had given Mama and Daddy when they got married, so at least we had a home right there. I tried not to complain too much. Even though we still had to pay utilities, the free rent saved me over three hundred bucks a month.

By the time I finished the month's closeout of the books, Grams' grandfather clock in the apartment where Uncle Troy lived now had chimed in nine o'clock. Before I left, I wanted to check a few things out about Mama on the Internet, and this was my only access to a computer. That's when I remembered to call Mason.

"I'm here," I said as soon as he answered, maybe a little too excitedly at the sound of his voice.

"Do you have any idea how close I was to jumping in the car and heading that way to make sure you weren't in the ditch or something?" He paused with only the sound of a deep breath coming through from his end. "What took you so long?"

"Sorry, but I'm not used to having to check in with anyone."

Another moment of silence. "Shit. I'm sorry. I don't mean to sound like a douchebag. It's just that I haven't stopped thinking of you or that smile of yours or those … lips since the moment you left. I hate not being able to call you, even just to hear your voice."

"Well, you can hear it now. Just don't ask me to sing. I can't carry a tune in a bucket."

"So talk to me. About anything."

I rolled the office chair a bit to the right to grab a pen and paper. "I'm so glad you said that, because we didn't talk about Mama at all."

Was that a groan from him? "You want to talk about work, huh?"

Oh. I hadn't considered that. He was home, likely chilled out for the night, so his work was probably the last thing he wanted to discuss.

"I'm teasing," he said. "Let's talk about your mother."

"Thank you. I wanted to look some things up but I can't remember all the medical mumbo jumbo you were rattlin' off earlier."

"Does this mean you have a computer? Email?" A new interest lit up his voice.

"Computer, sometimes. Email, no. And no, no Facebook or Twitterin' for me. Enough people around here know my business better than I do, so why bother posting it? It'd take the fun out of hearing their gossip. Besides, I'm on my uncle's computer at the office."

"You're at work?"

"Yep. So see, you aren't the only one sort of not working right now. So what was it you said Mama has?"

He patiently went over her many illnesses and disorders with me, spelling each one out so I could write them down. He also gave me the names of the drug treatments he could give her and the government and social programs that could help with the costs. A knock at the office door interrupted us just as we'd moved on to other subjects, such as how much we both enjoyed dinner, and I glanced out the window at the figure illuminated by the floodlight, holding a plate of food in one hand and two beers in the other.

Oh, shit.

"Mason, I gotta go."

"Is everything okay?"

I sighed. "I hope so. I mean, yeah, it's fine. Just something with a friend."

"Call me soon?"

Another knock on the door. My heart sank with guilt.

"When I can. I really gotta go." And I pretty much hung up on him.

I rushed to the door and threw it open. "I'm so sorry, Ty!"

"Figured I'd find you here when I saw you pull up, but you never came over." He held the plate toward me. "As promised, I brought you dinner."

A grilled hamburger on a bun and potato salad filled the plate. He'd made the burger exactly as I liked it—no ketchup, mustard, and sweet pickle chips. It'd been several hours since filling myself to the gills with the heavenly steak and potato, but I had little desire to eat again. I'd already screwed up, though, and didn't want to hurt Ty's feelings, so I took the plate and a beer and motioned him to sit across the desk from me as I sat back down.

"How'd it go?" he asked. "You seem better than I thought you'd be. I was 'fraid you'd be half-drunk before you even got home."

"It wasn't as bad as I expected," I admitted around a small bite of lukewarm burger I had in my mouth. I pulled on my beer to wash it down, then pushed the potato salad around my plate with the plastic fork he'd brought. The salad definitely came from Memaw's, which meant it was homemade by Aunt Faye. I used to live on the stuff, to the point that I could barely stand it anymore. Even if I'd been starving, I wouldn't have been able to stomach it. "It was ... weird, ya know? I wanted to hate her, even tried to pick a couple of fights. But she's so sick, Ty. I ... I didn't know what to think or feel anymore."

I told him how bad she looked and how she'd fallen asleep in an instant and I'd thought she'd died right there and then. I told him about meeting with Dr. Hayes—leaving out the part about dinner or the sex-in-a-kiss—and explained as best as I could about Mama's condition. I showed him the page of notes in front of me.

"You trust this doctor already?" Ty asked skeptically.

For some reason, maybe because I went on a date and kissed said doctor, the remark felt like a jab.

"He's her doctor, so, yeah, I do. He seemed to really care about her." The words came out harsher than I intended, and I didn't tell him that I never actually saw him interact with Mama. In fact, I didn't realize that until now. Mama and Sissy didn't have any complaints at all about him—in fact, just the opposite—so surely he was good with her. He sounded completely caring and concerned when he talked to me, and he really wanted to help her get better with new treatments. "Why *wouldn't* I trust him?"

Ty held his hands up. "Whoa, now. Settle them horses. I'm just sayin' that maybe you should think about getting a second opinion. I mean, if ya'll really want to see if her life can be saved, ya know?"

I relaxed, feeling silly about getting so protective over Dr. Hayes when Ty had no clue what my personal feelings were for Mason. He was trying to be the friend he'd promised to be.

"Sorry," I said as I dropped my head into my hands and massaged my temples. "Feelin' a little stressed out here."

The sound of a chair scraping on the linoleum was followed by two footsteps and then warm hands on my shoulders. Ty squeezed and kneaded the tension away, massaging a path from my neck to the middle of my back. When he went lower, it felt a little too intimate for comfort. Especially after my time with Mason, as short as it was. I coughed and moved back in the chair so he couldn't reach me anymore.

"Yeah, you're probably right about that second opinion. But first, I need to see what I can find out about all these things she has." I pushed the plate still covered with potato salad and more than half the burger to the side and pulled the keyboard in front of me. "Thanks for dinner. Sorry I wasn't very hungry, though."

Ty took the hint. He gave my shoulders a final squeeze and planted a kiss on the top of my head. "Don't forget to get your beauty rest."

I spun the office chair around. "Ty Daniels! What's that supposed to mean?"

He laughed. "Nothing, boo. Just tryin' to wake you up." He leaned down and put his hands on the armrests of my chair, placing his face only inches from mine. I thought he might try for more than a kiss on the head, and I panicked at the thought. It wouldn't have been the first time I'd kissed two guys in one day, but I really wasn't up for it now. Especially with Ty. "You're always beautiful, sweetheart. But I'm worried about you. Do you ever sleep? Relax? Have fun?"

I blew out a sigh, and he must not have liked my hamburger breath, because he pushed away and straightened up.

"No time for such nonsense," I said, even though I'd at least had an hour today of nothing but fun and could possibly be going to a concert in less than a week. For some reason, I just couldn't bring myself to tell Ty about all of that. Well, I knew the reason—Ty himself. He was a fighter, and knowing he had competition would only make him push harder.

"Bex," he said, and I craned my neck back to look up at his face. "I seen some things while I was gone. Stop taking life so seriously and enjoy it while you can. You never know when your last day is." He tweaked my chin, kissed me on the head again and strode for the door. "I'm here if you need anything. I won't leave you again."

But then he did just that. Strode out the door and left me in the dark office. Of course, he'd only be a hundred yards away in the trailer where he grew up, left by his daddy who'd passed away right before Ty graduated high school. His mama had died in a car wreck when we were six, right before my mama took Sissy and me away. Poor Ty. Except for an aunt who'd moved north before he was even born and whom he barely knew, he was all alone. Maybe that's why he'd come back for me—the only family he had. He'd left me to get away from it all, and maybe that's what he'd needed to realize where his home still was. If only I could be for him what he wanted me to be. But I didn't think anything could convince me that we were right for each other. That he was my soul mate. I just didn't feel it anymore.

Now Dr. Mason Hayes? I dared to hope that maybe he *was* The One. After all, I'd never felt anything before like I did with him. As I made my way across the trailer park after a little Internet research, I tried to imagine a life with the sexy doctor. Being a doctor's wife, with a big home and beautiful children and fancy cars and no jobs except volunteer work to help homeless kids. My imagination apparently wasn't creative enough, though, because I couldn't see it clearly. Not with *me* as part of the picture, with my pierced nose and tats and my poor, small-town upbringing.

Sadness washed over me, along with a heavy feeling of darkness. It had been a long, tough day with a whirlwind of emotions, but this feeling I had now was different. A deep sense of gloom that didn't come from only one hard day, but from a lifetime of them, and the kind that never went away. Something felt seriously wrong. Elizabeth's warning yesterday was getting to me, but she was the empath, not me. I couldn't possibly be feeling what I was. I clasped my hand over the back of my neck where the hairs began to rise and looked up. There must have been no moon tonight because the sky was pitch black. So dark, I suddenly felt cold and shivered. Not until I was inside did I wonder why I couldn't see the stars either. As I crashed into bed for a few hours of sleep before I had to open the diner, the last thing I saw was a nearly full moon shining through my curtains, high above the trees.

Where had it been just a few minutes ago?

"I THINK YOU'RE downin' more coffee than the customers," Elizabeth said the next day as we wrapped up the breakfast rush and prepared for the lunch crowd at noon.

"I didn't sleep a wink last night," I said as I poured my fourth cup of the day.

"You felt it, too, didn't you?" she asked. "Don't have to be an empath to feel it anymore. Somethin's going on in this town, and it's only gonna get worse. I'm half fixin' to pack up and get out while I can."

My brow raised as I leaned against the counter and sipped my coffee. "It's that bad?"

"It's not good, baby girl. But the sick part of me wants to stick around and watch it go down." She turned her full gaze on me. "You, though, oughta high-tail it outta here, hun. You already have more darkness in you than any one person should have, 'specially at your age."

I rolled my eyes. She was always telling me that I needed help. She thought I'd been through way too much for someone to handle on her own. Sure, I screwed up sometimes, but for the most part, I thought I handled things just fine. I (usually) did the right thing and went to church every Sunday like a good, God-fearing Southern girl. Yeah, life had been crappy, but I was turning out all right, I thought. Any darkness she sensed in me was only temporary. Once I found me a good man—the one I knew was out there specifically for me—it would be gone. Not that I thought I, or any woman, needed a good man to be happy or that all my problems would miraculously disappear when I met The One. Far from it. But I held onto the belief that when you had true love, when you shared life and all its foulness with your soul mate, all those problems were a little easier to shoulder.

After meeting Mason yesterday, things were already looking brighter.

"So are you gonna tell me how it went yesterday or not?" Elizabeth asked. "There's somethin' different about you, but I haven't figured it out yet. Can't even tell if it's good or bad, but it feels like both."

"Mmmm ..." I teased, pretending she'd get no more than that. She narrowed her eyes, so I spilled everything, from my time with Mama and how that went to my dinner with Mason.

"I'm not sure I like this doctor," she said when I finished.

"You don't even know him, so you can't say that."

"I know that he's gotta be at least thirty, don't he? To your twenty-one?"

I frowned. When I'd thought of him being older than me, I hadn't *really* thought about the age difference. "He finished high school two years early, and he doesn't look that old."

"If he's been through med school and everything it takes to be your mama's doctor, he's too old for my baby girl."

I let out a harrumph. "I'm not *your* baby girl, and I'm not a baby at all. And age is only a thing if you make it a thing."

"And if I meet him and don't like him, I *will* be making it a thing," she promised. Not that she really had much say, but at least she cared.

"So can I ask a huge favor and have next Monday's dinner shift off? And Tuesday's morning shift, too?"

Elizabeth looked up from the ketchup bottles she was filling. "You never ask for a day off."

"I know."

She squinted at me. "What for?"

"I'm goin' to see Mama again. See how the new meds work out for her." I sucked my bottom lip, then added very quietly, "And going to a concert with Mason."

"I don't like it. Mark my words, girl. But who am I to stop you?"

I tried not to jump with glee. "Well, you are my boss. You *could* stop me."

"But I'm not goin' to. I'll just hope that he either makes you very happy and that helps lighten this cloud over us, or that you'll realize quickly he's an asshole preying on girls way too young for him."

When she put it like that, I had to wonder about Mason. How could someone with his brains, his wit and charm, and his looks be single? And why wouldn't he want to be with someone closer to his age and status? Our differences—age, income class, education, upbringing, everything—were painfully obvious. But then I thought of our chemistry. And that's something you have no control over.

"I'm pretty sure he hadn't been standing behind the Coke machine, waiting for some young chick to come along so he could take advantage of her. If that's all he was after, he would have been all over Sissy long ago."

"That's the only reason I haven't decided to make you work triple shifts for the next three weeks until you forget about him."

I threw my arms around her, making her spill ketchup. "Thanks, Liz'beth. I owe you."

"Nah, you don't. You deserve some time off."

"Can I use the phone to make a few calls?"

She pulled her cell phone out of her shirt, where she kept it in her bra, and handed it to me. "Use this one."

I wrapped my hand around the warm metal and glass and headed outside and around back for some privacy. I called Sissy first.

"Dr. Hayes gave me some information that I looked up," I said once she was able to step out of Mama's room. "Is there a reason Mama hasn't started on the meds so maybe she can get a transplant?"

"Yeah, there is. Have you seen the cost?"

"Yeah. It's insane, but—"

"She doesn't want you to have that burden, Bex. She doesn't want *us* drownin' in her medical bills if it don't work and she dies."

"Seriously? She's dying anyway."

"Yeah, well, at a lot cheaper cost."

"Sissy, we can't let her die if that's the only reason."

The other end went silent for a moment. "I didn't think you'd see it that way."

Ouch. But I totally deserved that and couldn't blame her for saying it. "I'm tryin' to forgive her. I'm certainly not gonna let her die over what she did to us."

"Well, what do you want me to do, Bex? Even if I stopped taking care of her and got a job, no way could we afford it."

"Dr. Hayes told me about some government and other programs that could help. If we get the paperwork started, he doesn't have to wait to begin the treatment, and we don't pay anything right away."

"And you really think she can get approved with her history?"

"He said he'd help us."

"Yeah, I'm sure he did," Sissy muttered, and the bitterness came loud and clear.

"What is it with you? Mama says you're smitten with him, but I'd almost think you don't like him."

"Oh, I like him all right. The question is why do you have to? Every single guy, Bex. Do you have to have them all?"

"What?"

"Why can't you just be with Ty and give me a chance for once?"

My breath caught. "Oh. Ma. Gosh. You're more than smitten with Mason, aren't you?"

"*Mason?*" Her voice came out in a whispery shriek. I imagined her standing in the hospital corridor trying not to make a scene while the jealousy flooded her. "You met him once and you're on a first-name basis?"

"Sorry. Dr. Hayes." I couldn't tell her about dinner last night. Not in the frame of mind she was obviously in. She might be pissed off enough to rat him out to his bosses. She was my sister, and I was dying to tell her everything, but that would have to wait. "Sissy, he's way too old for you."

"But not for you?"

"You're practically jail bait to him."

"You're only eighteen months older than me. Not much of a difference when the gap's that big."

"Think about it, hun. At your age, that's a big difference. I'm of legal age in every way. You can't even go to a club."

She huffed out a breath. "Well, I hope you and *Mason* are happy together."

"Sissy, don't be that way."

"I'll stop being this way when you stop taking every guy I ever had a thing for."

"Maybe instead of being mad at me, you should look at yourself and figure out why they *don't* have a thing for you."

Sissy gasped. "Bethany!"

I pressed my fingers to my temple, feeling the heavy pressure returning. "In this case, I mean your age."

"Whatever," she snapped. "I'm sick of fighting with you over guys. Maybe some day you'll finally settle down so everyone else has a chance."

And that was her real reason for her wanting me to take Ty back. She didn't care if we'd be happy together.

"Let's just talk about Mama. I'm gonna call Dr. Hayes and get the paperwork going. Mama needs to start the meds."

"I'll tell her," she said. "No guarantees she'll do it, though."

"Talk her into it. Force her if you have to."

"Only you can do that and only if you can prove she can't make her own decisions."

Oh, yeah. "Why did she do that? Why not give you that authority?"

Sissy sighed. "Because she thought you'd be more objective. That you would listen to her wishes and not try to keep her alive on machines and all because you didn't wanna let her go. She didn't think I could make that same decision."

"Oh." I didn't know what else to say. "Well, this is somethin' that we have to try. I'll call you again when I can."

"Wait, Bex?"

"Yeah?"

"Thanks for doing this for her."

"She's our mama, Sissy." That's all there was to say, and we hung up.

I pulled Mason's card out of my back pocket and dialed his number. His voicemail answered, so I left a message with our decision about Mama and also that I had next Monday off if his offer was still open.

Unfortunately, I had to go back on that. Sullivan's hired the new girl, Leni, which was good in a way because we really needed another waitress who could also help out at the bar. But they wanted me to train her, which meant giving me the crappy shifts until she was ready to take on the busiest nights. Crappy shifts meant suck-ass tips, which meant I couldn't afford to take time off for a concert. I could justify a shift here and there to see Mama, but not several in a row for something unnecessary.

I made it down twice in the following couple of weeks, but at least I got to see Mason at the hospital. We had coffee both times, but didn't have an opportunity for anything more than that. He was a perfect gentleman, too, always pulling away after giving me a quick peck on the head or nose. He said it was because once his lips touched mine, he'd never be able to stop, and he was not going to make me a dirty little secret he snuck into the janitor's closet. But he did insist on giving me a cell phone.

"I want to be able to talk to you whenever I want to," he said when I tried to give it back to him. "Especially since your mother's being discharged, and I don't know when I'll see you."

The meds for Mama's heart and lungs had finally stabilized her, and there wasn't much more they could do at the hospital until she either improved and received a transplant, or she worsened. So they were sending her home.

"We can't exactly talk whenever we want. I still have to work and so do you." I held it out to him.

"I know, but it makes me feel better that at least I know I *can* call you, even if you can't answer. I can leave you voicemails. Sext you, even." He gave me a smile that made me weak.

"Don't you dare."

"Don't worry. I'm a doctor. I'm not that stupid. But know that I'll be thinking about it."

So I ended up with a cell phone that he paid for. Part of me felt weird about it—it's not like he was family helping kin or anything—but part of me appreciated that not only could he call me at a whim, but so could Sissy if something came up with Mama. Sometimes I felt so far away from all of them, but unless I wanted to move down there and hope to find a job that could make up for the ones I had here, there was nothing I could do. And I wasn't exactly ready to do all that anyway. A mere couple of weeks with Mama or Mason wasn't enough to make me pull up and move out.

And then there was Ty.

"Bex, sweetie, you're exhausted," he said one night when I came home to him sitting on my steps again. It had become our thing—every time I had a shift at Sullivan's, he waited for me afterwards to share a beer on my stoop. I dropped in front of him, too tired to argue, and grabbed the beer he had waiting for me. "You need a break."

"Can't afford it." I chugged half the bottle.

"You can afford an afternoon of fun. A day in old Mr. K's field."

I laughed, giddy with exhaustion. "They still party there?"

Mr. K's field included a small lake or big pond, whatever you wanted to call it, and was where everyone went to party. Mr. K had actually passed long before I was old enough to go out there, and his relations that inherited the land lived up north, so they had no idea about what went on down here.

"Everyone's going a week from Saturday. Come out and have some fun for once."

"I gotta work."

"Troy'll give you the day off for me. He likes me." That was true. "A lot more than that doctor you're seeing."

"I'm not seeing the doctor. I don't have time to see *anyone*."

"Well, you sure do spend a lot of time with him, from what I hear. You know you don't fit in that world, Bex. You belong here. With me."

"I'm not fixin' to fit in any world, Ty. Whatever Sissy told ya'll, she's lying because *she* wants to be the one seeing the doctor. She's setting you up."

Ty's hands fell onto my shoulders, and he pulled me backward. I tilted my head to look up at him as he hovered over me. "I don't wanna argue. I just want you to remember that life's about more than work. Come hang out. Jeric and Leni and their city friends are comin'. It'll make things all kinds of interesting."

"Jeric and Leni?"

"Leni from the bar and her boyfriend Jeric. Did you know he's an ex UFC fighter? He's been training me. And did you know he used to be deaf but by some miracle, he's not anymore?"

I nodded, although I didn't know the full story beyond whatever surgery he'd had. During our shifts together at Sullivan's, Leni didn't talk much about herself, but was always asking me questions about me and if I was okay. The girl, bless her heart, was still weird and overly interested in my business.

"Wait," I said as all of Ty's words hit me. "What do you mean he's been training you?"

"To be a cage fighter. My first fight's next week."

I jumped to my feet, spun around and put my hands on my hips. "Ty Daniels! What in God's name are you thinking? You're seriously going to jump into a ring and let someone hit you for the fun of it?"

"Not for the fun of it. For the money." He gave me a grin and cockiness shone in his eyes. "Besides, who said anything about *letting* someone hit me? Jeric hardly ever can, and he was a pro."

"I don't like it. Not one bit." I placed my hand against his cheek. "You're gonna ruin this face of yours."

His expression fell serious, and he clamped his hand over mine. "Glad to know you care."

Oh, crap. He was taking it the wrong way. I slid my hand out from under his and returned it to my hip. "Yeah, well, that face of yours is about the only thing you have goin' for you."

He laughed. "You just wait and see, Bex. I'm gonna be famous and rich, and then you won't care how I look when I can give you the life you've always wanted. That doctor won't have nothin' on me."

I groaned, but before I could say anything, Ty reached out and grabbed my arm.

"Get inside, Bex." His voice was suddenly full of warning, and his gaze was focused on something in the distance, near the highway. I turned to follow it. A man's figure stood on the edge of the road. He appeared to be staring at us, although I couldn't tell for sure because a hood blocked his face. "There's been some weird guys hanging around town, and I think that's one of them. I don't know what they want, but they're creepy as hell. I feel like they're following me all the time, and I don't want them seeing you."

He ushered me inside my own house, then watched out the window until the creep disappeared. The only way I could get Ty to leave, too, was to concede to going to the party if Uncle Troy actually allowed it. My uncle did have a soft spot for Ty since he'd served our country, but I still never believed in a million years he'd give me a day off.

CHAPTER 11

Jeric   I STOOD OUTSIDE Sullivan's, waiting in the dark parking lot for my girl and watching the Shadowmen who leaned against an unlit lamppost at the edge of the lot, near the highway. Pretty much in the same place where they'd jumped me when I'd been carrying Leni out of the bar the first time I saw her dance the bull. When they took human shapes like this pair did at the moment, my mind reverted to calling the Lakari the name Jacey had coined and we had used before we knew exactly what they were. These Shadowmen had an unnatural interest in both the truck stop and the RV and trailer park, always around, at least at night. Sometimes others joined them, but when they sensed Leni and me, and Brock and Asia not far off, they scattered, leaving only these two.

However, the group never left the area. There were at least twelve watching over the town at any given time. Or one divided into twelve human shapes. The Lakari could combine and split like that because they weren't really separate entities. The Dark spirits, controlled by Enyxa, took human form to blend into this world called Earth when they had to. They hadn't attacked anyone yet and hadn't even challenged us Guardians, so my guess was they were weaker than they wanted us to know—so probably fewer in number than they wanted us to know, as well.

"Always here, aren't they?" Leni's voice came from the back door of Sullivan's before her sexy body emerged into the pool of light provided by the security lamp.

"Who the hell are they and what do they want?" Bex asked, stepping outside behind Leni and turning to lock the door. "They're creepy as hell."

"Stuff of nightmares," Leni agreed as she crossed her arms across her stomach, her eyes never leaving the Shadowmen who hadn't budged from their post.

I moved out of the shadows over to the girls. "Exactly why I'll be walking the two of you home."

Leni knew of my presence—we always knew where each other was at any given time—but Bex jumped.

"Ohmagosh, you scared the shit out of me," she exclaimed in her Southern accent that at one time would have been the icing on the cake of the entire hot little package she had to offer. But since Leni, I couldn't even think of another girl like that. It never occurred to me except when I noticed just how much I'd changed. "Good heavens. Liz'beth's got me all worked up and jumpin' at a June bug's shadow."

"I like to think I'm more threatening than a June bug," I said, taking my position between the two girls and sliding my arm around Leni's waist as we began the short journey home.

"I don't know. You ever have one of those massive suckers fly right in your face?" Leni shuddered. "They smack right into you like they're flying drunk."

"I hate those things! But Jeric, trust me, ya'll are worse. You *and* that friend of yours," Bex said, referring to Brock. He and Asia had come into the bar earlier to keep me company while Leni worked. They'd been making occasional appearances, allowing the locals to get used to them being around ... and the Lakari, too. "And Ty's told me all about your fightin'. Do you really have to train him? You're just encouragin' him."

"It's what he wants," I said with a shrug. "I need a job. Besides he's good."

We stopped at the highway to wait for a car to pass. Movement in the corner of my eye came from the place where the Shadowmen had been standing. I looked over my shoulder, where they still stood, but no longer like a couple of loser loiterers. They were in a more attentive stance now, feet shoulder-width apart, hands clasped behind their backs, shoulders squared. Hoods covered their eyes, but I could feel their glares on me. If it remained just the two of them and Leni didn't have to get involved, I would have said to bring it on and taunted them into a fight. I could have used the chance to release some pressure. But I didn't know how close their friends were, and Leni would insist on getting involved. Or, they'd do what they did when Brock and I approached them to ask what they wanted: they disintegrated into smoke without a word. So I simply made sure they knew I knew of their presence, then turned back as we began to cross.

"Is he really?" Bex asked. "Good, I mean? Because I feel like he's tryin' to prove somethin' in the stupidest way possible."

"I wouldn't waste my time or his neck if I didn't think he had a real chance," I said. "He's good, Bex. Better than most at his level. Don't worry your pretty little head over it. That's my job, and I'm honestly not all that worried."

"You better not let anything happen to him," she warned, and although she didn't look physically threatening, I took her seriously.

Ty had told me enough about Southern girls' tempers, especially when it came to protecting their own. They could be sweet as pie and offering up all kinds of Southern hospitality one minute, but as soon as they felt they or someone they love was threatened—as soon as you heard that, "Oh, hell no!"—don't be surprised to find a shotgun in their hands. And they were trained to use them. Leni had a touch of Southern in her from her mama, and I had firsthand experience facing the barrel of her shotgun. Luckily, she didn't shoot me. I didn't know if that luck would hold out with anyone else. I might be a former fighter and a current warrior, but I did not want to piss Bex off.

"It's his choice to get in that cage, and after that, there's not a lot I can do. But when he's not in the fight cage, I'll take good care of him," I promised, and I meant more than ensuring he trained smartly and stayed out of trouble.

Although Leni felt the pull to Bex and was almost sure she was Rebethannah, that didn't mean the Lakari were there for her. They could just as easily be there for Ty, whose unrequited love could be leading him to dark places. Or a number of the people in town who suffered from depression, anxiety, and other ailments that affected the soul … or could come about because of a Dark soul. This town seemed to have more than its share per capita of tragedy and hard times—quite the attraction for the Lakari. Plenty of tainted souls for them to hunt.

Brock, Asia, Leni, and I discussed the Lakari a lot more than I preferred. We couldn't figure out why they hadn't acted yet. We could only guess that they must have been waiting for something. Like a Bonding between soul mates, a re-Bonding of Twin Flames, or, on the flip side and what seemed more likely, the soul they wanted reaching the peak of its hopelessness and doing something irreversibly stupid, like murder or suicide. Since they never attacked, we couldn't figure out who they hunted, if anyone specifically. For now, they seemed content to watch and wait, basking in the bleak mood that hung over the town.

We took advantage of their foot-dragging, learning as much as we could about the people by becoming a part of their community. Maybe our presence kept the Lakari from acting—I could at least hope. If that were the case, I'd be perfectly fine with hanging out in Lake Haven until we all became old and gray and the Lakari grew bored shitless. Not likely, I knew, but I wouldn't have complained.

"So I guess he talked all ya'll into going to your first K-bomb," Bex said as we strode across the sandy area between the highway and the paved path of the RV park.

"K-bomb?" Leni asked curiously. I knew what Bex meant, but kept my mouth shut.

"What we call the big parties on the lake in old Mr. K's field," Bex explained. "They've been having parties there for decades, ever since they closed off the real Lake Haven."

"There's an actual Lake Haven, as in a lake?" Leni asked, her surprise and curiosity leaking over me. We hadn't heard that yet.

"Well, yeah, that's what the town's named after. But it's all shrunk down to a pond and only that because it's spring-fed. They closed it off years ago because at least once every generation, someone died there and always of mysterious causes. It's like the town's skeleton in the closet. Nobody even talks about it anymore." She paused to draw in a breath and waved her hand in the air, dismissing the subject. "So, anyway, Ty said ya'll were goin' to the party Saturday?"

Leni threw me a questioning look, and I cringed. I hadn't brought this up with her yet. She narrowed her eyes.

"I was going to talk to you about it tonight," I said, trying to cover my own ass. She lifted her chin in that *don't you forget it* look girls do.

"Hey, ya'll's camper's that way," Bex said, tossing her head to our right.

"I said I was walking you home. All the way home."

She pointed to a mobile home about sixty yards away. "I live right there. Think I can find my way."

I glanced over my shoulder. The Shadowmen were no longer in the parking lot. I didn't know where they disappeared to, but I did know they hadn't gone far.

"I got it from here," said a male voice in front of us. Ty stepped out of the shadows of trees that separated the RV side of the park from the permanent trailer side.

Bex's breath had caught again, and she blew it out angrily. "Cripes! Ya'll need to stop scaring the damn bejesus outta me."

Ty placed his hand on Bex's back and nodded a thanks to me before he and Bex headed for her place. Leni and I didn't move, though, until we were sure both made it safely inside.

"So what's this about a K-bomb?" she asked once we were home in her camper.

I stuffed my hands into my jeans pockets and leaned back on my heels. "Like Bex said, a party. Ty was telling me about it and asked if we wanted to go. Says it's the best time we'll find around here."

Leni placed her fists on her hips and lifted a brow. "And you really think we need to be looking for a good time?"

I smiled and sauntered over to her. She backed up as far as she could go, and I pinned her with a hand on the counter on each side of her hips. I leaned down and with my lips barely touching her ear, I whispered, "I don't think it would hurt anything. Could be fun."

Her hand slid between us and pressed on my chest. She pushed me away, and her tone came harshly. "We're not here to party, Jeric."

I cocked my head, not expecting this kind of reaction. I thought she'd be a little upset for not discussing it with her first, but angry? Didn't see that coming.

"No shit. I know what we're here for, as much as I hate it. But we're supposed to blend in, get to know the people, find our target. What better way is there than at a party where everyone under thirty will be?"

She glared at me with sharp sea-green eyes. "Why is that important?"

I grinned with a bit of pride at my cleverness. "Because if the Lakari show up, then we know they're after someone young, narrowing our choices down to someone severely depressed, terminally ill … or a pair of Twin Flames. Should be easy to pick out in a young crowd, right? And if they don't show, we've eliminated half the town's population."

She still stared at me, but her eyes softened.

"Besides, people will be drinking and letting their guards down and in a more private place than the bar," I added before she could protest any more. "We can get the scoop on probably anyone we want."

Her head tilted to the side. When she spoke, her tone had lightened, but still held an undertone I didn't quite trust. "So you want to go because you think it will help the mission? Not because you want to party?"

I dropped my chin and looked up at her through my lashes with a slight smile while lowering my own voice. "Is there anything wrong with having a little fun while we're there? Don't we deserve it?"

She blew out an exasperated breath and threw her hands in the air. "I knew it!"

I lifted my head and sighed as well. "You knew what? What's your problem, Leni?"

"My problem," she said as she stepped right up to me and pressed a finger into my chest, "is that you're more worried about having a good time and getting wasted than you are about our mission. And I won't even mention Rebethannah!"

Except she did just mention her. Why do girls do that?

My jaw clenched and my nostrils flared as I kept my temper in check. This was a stupid fight, but I didn't like her accusation.

"What I'm worried about is you and us," I ground out. "You. Us. That's my priority. I will do whatever it takes to keep you safe and keep us—our souls—intact, and if that means being by your side in this mission, then that's where I'll be. And I'm not thinking about getting wasted. I'm thinking about the best and *safest* way for us to find what we're looking for without getting people worked up. And especially without getting the Lakari worked up. A harmless field party sounds like a damn good way to do that. If we happen to enjoy ourselves, so much the better."

She stared at me for a long moment as if she wasn't sure to believe me, which was ridiculous because she could practically read my mind. At the very least, she could feel my emotions, and she had to be feeling my sincerity.

"Will Bex be there?" she asked.

"I think so. Ty's working on it. I know he'll be there for sure. Brock and Asia, too."

She lifted a brow. "Brock and Asia knew about this party before I did?"

I held my hands up, palms out. She seemed to be coming around, and I didn't want her temper flaring again. When I'd finally convinced her to let go and not be afraid to show her emotions, I'd basically freed a wild lion out of its cage—and I'd never get it back in again. She'd rein it in for others, but didn't have to for me. She had a lot more Southern in her than most people knew.

"Let me rephrase that," I said. "Brock was going to talk to Asia about it tonight just like I was going to talk to you. I wasn't lying when I said that. Brock was at the gym with us when Ty was talking about it so he invited them, too."

Her eyes narrowed as she once again studied me. "All right. Fine. I guess we go. Maybe I can finally find out more about Bex."

I let out a slow breath of relief and moved to sit on the futon covered in pillows, the place I'd slept the first night at a lake in Georgia that felt worlds away now. I grabbed Leni's hand on the way and pulled her over with me. Once I sat down, she fell onto the futon next to me with her legs over my lap. She picked up the Book that was always nearby. She studied it at every opportunity, but still hadn't figured out any clues we might have left ourselves. I began to suspect she was wrong for thinking we had. I think she was beginning to doubt the idea herself.

"She's not quite the open book you expected?" I asked as I flipped her shoes off and massaged her feet.

She didn't open the Book yet, instead dropping her head back and sighing with pleasure, immediately turning me on. "Yes and no. She talks about just enough where you feel like she's friendly, but she doesn't really open up. Everyone knows her mama's dying, her sister's taking care of her, and Bex is working like a dog to support them all. There are rumors her mama was a drug addict and abandoned them, but I don't know how true that is. I think she and her sister grew up in this trailer park, though. And I've also heard that after Ty left her for the military, she got a reputation as a slut because she hooked up with so many guys. Beyond that ... she's really good at covering up what's going on inside."

"Like someone else I know," I said pointedly as I squeezed her foot.

"Mmm," she moaned. "Yeah, I guess. But I think she's better than I ever was."

"And you still think she's Rebethannah?"

Leni sighed and laid her head back on an oversized pillow she used as a backrest. "I don't know. Every once in a while, I see this look in her eyes, when she thinks no one is watching and she can let her guard down, and I *feel* it. I feel a connection to her. My soul recognizes hers. But it's so quick, I can't be sure of the feeling. I'm almost positive she was Jacey's Bex—there are too many similarities and too many times I want to say, 'Hey remember that time ...' But she'd think I was whacked out."

I chuckled. "I'm pretty sure she already thinks that."

"Yeah, well, that's why I don't know what to do. I don't know if my soul recognizes her only from Jacey's life, or if the connection is deeper than that. There are so many things that add up to her being Rebethannah, like how she remembered us when the rest of the world forgot us, and maybe it's because we have one of those eternal connections. And then there's her name both times, the fact that my soul met up with hers both times like it was drawn to her, and if she and Nathayden were

Broken, then her history with guys makes sense, too—she's always looking for love. *Both* times."

"It does start to add up," I conceded as I dropped her foot and picked up the other.

"I know, right? I want so badly to try to trigger her past memories, but what if it's not her? And even if it is, or if she's another dyad half we might have known before, she hasn't reconnected with her Twin Flame, so there may be nothing I can do to make her remember. So, yeah, then I look like a bigger ass than I already do."

I'd convinced myself before that Leni had been trying too hard to fit the Bex peg into the Rebethannah hole, but as she got to know the girl more and made these points, I could almost believe we'd found her. I needed more proof, though.

"Maybe this party will be your chance to find out more about her," I said.

"Maybe."

I grabbed her chin playfully and turned her face toward me. "Come on, admit it was a good idea. Saying that we'll go."

She rolled her eyes. "I will do no such thing until we're there. For all I know, you'll end up wasted and we'll have accomplished nothing."

"You could just as easily be the one wasted."

She giggled. "If so, I'll warn you now that I'll probably end up dancing on the picnic table."

I cocked my head and narrowed my eyes. "As long as you keep your clothes on. At least until we get home."

"Yeah, well, I don't think it's me we really need to worry about. I seem to recall you being drunk, or at least buzzed, four of the first five nights we were together. Or was it all five? I don't remember seeing you without a bottle of Jack nearby."

"Leni," I said, dropping my voice and leaning my head against hers so our mouths nearly touched. I lifted my hand to the side of her face and rubbed my thumb over the soft, smooth skin of her cheek. "When will you understand I don't need that shit anymore? I don't want to be numb. As long as you're with me, I want to feel it all. Everything. I don't want to miss a single moment or a single word or a single touch from you. I want to feel every bit of every moment. I want to feel *you*. Fully and completely."

Without closing her eyes so she could look directly into mine, she parted her lips and nipped my bottom one. "I want to feel you, too," she whispered, her breath hot against my lips. "All of you, in me, right now."

She didn't have to ask me twice.

Afterward, our souls drifted together outside of our bodies in that perfect place of just her and me.

Except it wasn't so perfect.

"They always ruin the mood," Leni's soul murmured into mine. I didn't have to ask who she meant. The Lakari's Darkness was tangible and heavy, like swamp muck trying to suffocate from above and suck from below until it swallowed you.

"Let's take care of them," I said with a mental groan.

After enjoying another moment of peace, we pushed our souls through the roof of her camper to do our nightly job. As usual, several Dark spirits hovered over the trailer side of the park, covering the entire area. Their black shadows were like gauze, allowing the moonlight to pass through them like a sheer curtain, so they were spreading themselves thin. If there were more and the Darkness deeper, the people in their homes below would have been miserable. All of their souls would have been at risk. Was Enyxa after everyone here? Or was she simply not showing her hand yet?

"Let's get rid of them and get back," Leni said, not wanting to contemplate Enyxa or her Lakari's intents while out of our bodies.

Staying together as one brightly lit soul, we swooshed and soared through the trailer park, a streak of Light forcing the Darkness away. There weren't enough Lakari to fight us, so they flew off like cowards, knowing our Light could permanently destroy them. When we returned to the roof of Leni's camper, we hovered for a bit, enjoying this special time together that was much more fun and relaxing than any party or bottle of Jack Daniels could ever be, and also ensuring the Darkness didn't return. At least not tonight.

CHAPTER 12

Bex "I HAVE TO admit I'm glad you have to work today," Mason said, and although I couldn't see him, I could imagine the twinkle in his light-green eyes.

"That's not nice," I said as I squeezed the phone between my ear and shoulder and shuffled through the registration cards for each of the RVs and campers in the park. Grams, God rest her soul, had done everything the old-fashioned pen and paper way, and Uncle Troy and I were slowly beginning to computerize things since she passed. Camper registrations hadn't quite made it there yet. "You're always telling me I work too much, and now you're glad that I am?"

"If it means you can't go to a big party without me, yeah, I kind of am. I want to be the one who lets you relax and have fun. I want to be with you when you do. Did I mention I'm a selfish bastard like that?"

I sighed, even though my insides flipped with joy. "For that to happen, we both have to have the day off at the same time."

Mason, it turned out, worked about as many hours as I did. His shifts at the hospital were long, and he rarely took a day off. He said he would for me, but, of course, that was nearly impossible to make happen.

"Take off next weekend, and I promise I will, too," he said.

"Weekends are impossible. Uncle Troy races on Saturdays and is always going out of town for them."

"Friday night, too?"

"I work at Sullivan's then."

"Take it off."

I laughed. "I make more money in tips on Friday nights than I do the rest of the week!"

He groaned. "I'll make it up to you. Whatever you'd make, I'll give you."

My spine pricked. "I am *not* a charity case, Dr. Mason Hayes."

"You're killing me. I swear, you are going to be the death of me."

"We'll figure something out," I promised as movement in the office window caught my eye. Uncle Troy was outside, probably getting ready to load up his stock car for tonight's race somewhere far off from here. Although we had a racetrack right outside town, they only had stock car races twice a year, one for the Fourth of July and one in early August. The rest of the season, Uncle Troy spent weekends traveling around Florida.

"Let's call in sick tomorrow," Mason said. "I'll drive up there tonight, and we can spend the whole day together. Nobody will have to know."

I laughed again. "*Everybody* will know in this town. And I can't lie like that, especially to my own uncle."

"Wait. You've never called in sick?"

"Only once, years ago. Because I *was* sick."

"Huh." He paused. "I didn't take you for being such a good girl."

Now the sound that came out was more like a snort than a laugh. "Don't you worry. I can be bad. Very bad. Just not when it comes to my work. I thought you liked a girl with a strong work ethic."

He sighed. "Yeah, I do. But I don't like when that work ethic gets in the way of me being able to spend time with a beautiful girl."

"Oh, I'm sure there are plenty of beautiful girls you can spend time with," I teased. Sort of. I still didn't get why he was chasing after me when there were a number of gorgeous nurses and lovely doctors falling over their feet for his attention. I knew because I'd seen it firsthand.

"There's only one I'm interested in spending time with," he said flatly.

More movement in the window made me look up. Uncle Troy was headed this way.

"One day. I promise," I said. "But I gotta go."

"When are you coming to see your mother?"

"I don't know, Mason. I have to look at my schedules again." The knob on the door turned. "Seriously, I need to go. Now."

"Call me later," he said, his voice distant because I was already hanging up.

Uncle Troy eyed the phone in my hand before looking up at me. "Talkin' to that damn doctor again?"

"Sure was," I said cheerfully. "Mama's still the same, if you care."

"Not really," he muttered. "Ty Daniels is waiting outside for you."

My eyes flitted toward the window and back to my uncle's face.

"He's at his house," Uncle Troy clarified.

"Well, what's he need that he can't come in here and ask?"

"He needs to show you somethin', and I said that was fine."

I stared at him blankly, not understanding.

He waved his hand at me. "Go on. Take the day off. I'm not sayin' it twice, though."

"Don't you have to go?"

He moved around to my side of the desk. "Nah. No races this weekend." His big hands grabbed the back of my chair and tilted it forward. "Now go, girl, before I change my damn mind."

I stood before I fell out of the seat and moved slowly around the desk, still hesitant. "Ty—"

"Ty Daniels is a good man who fought for his country and would do even more for *you*," Uncle Troy said as he stared me down with brown eyes like Mama's. His round face had softened, though, for once showing concern. "You deserve a good man like him, and you deserve a day off. Today you get both. Ya'll can thank me later."

He shooed his hands at me again. Baffled, I grabbed my purse and went outside, the door banging behind me. Ty's big, black truck sat in front of his house, and he stood on the far side of it, his forearms leaning on the walls of the bed. He wore a white tank undershirt and a red ball cap and even though I couldn't see his lower half, I knew it was clad in jeans and cowboy boots. He also wore the biggest smile I'd seen on his face since he'd come back from the Middle East.

"Told ya," he said as I approached.

"Told me what?"

"That Troy would do this for me."

I sighed and looked down at myself. "I'm not dressed for a party."

"You look fine to me, but you can change if you want." He walked over to this side of the truck, and I was right: jeans and his old worn cowboy boots. "But we don't have to go to the party. I wanna show you somethin' first, then we can do whatever you feel like."

"You seriously got the day off for me?"

"Troy likes me. He likes us. Together. The man is smart."

I raised a brow.

He laughed, his smile sending a blast of warmth through me. "Maybe smart's pushin' it, but I ain't gonna argue with him about this."

"I don't get why he cares so much." Not like he ever did before.

"Probably because he knows you been talkin' to that doctor, and if you go off with him, Troy's left to run this place by himself."

"Ah." I nodded. "Now *that* makes sense. Always lookin' after himself."

"I don't care who he's lookin' after right now because you get a day off. Finally. So do you plan on changing or are you gonna get that pretty ass into my truck as it is? I can't wait a minute longer to show you my surprise."

"Surprise?"

Ty moved over to the passenger door and grasped the handle. "Better make up your mind quick or I'll pick you up and throw you in."

"Okay, okay. One minute." I laughed as I jogged over to my house and hurried inside to change.

I quickly yanked off my t-shirt and replaced it with a button-down halter, then changed from my work jean shorts into my favorite cut-off Daisy Dukes and exchanged my flip-flops for cowboy boots. I pulled the brush through my hair and twisted the dark red locks up in a clip. I put on a little eyeliner and mascara since I hadn't this morning because I thought I'd be working in the office by myself. For a moment, I admittedly thought about blowing off Ty and calling Mason back. But I couldn't do that to my friend. Or to Uncle Troy, who may never give me a day off again if I did. Besides, I was a little intrigued by Ty's surprise.

"Time's up," Ty said as he barreled into my trailer. He found me in the bathroom with a blush brush in my hand. "Oh, for shit's sake. You don't need that crap."

He wrapped his muscular arms around my waist and lifted me off the ground.

"Ty Daniels, put me down!" I squealed as he threw me over his shoulder, but I couldn't suppress the laughter that bubbled up. I couldn't remember the last time I felt like laughing like this. When he began moving, I tossed the brush toward the bathroom counter. It clattered to the floor, but there was nothing I could do as Ty strode outside and dumped me in the passenger seat of his pickup.

"Where we goin'?" I yelled over the music blasting from the speakers after he turned onto the highway, headed into town. Some of my hair loosened from the clip and blew against my cheeks from the wind through the open window. "What's your surprise?"

"If I told you, it wouldn't be a surprise, now would it?" He looked over at me and grinned mischievously. Damn him for being so cute. Did I ever tell him about my thing for guys in ball caps? Must have, because he seemed to use it against me every chance he got. Or maybe it was because he always looked so good in one that started my thing in the first place. I didn't know anymore. At least he wasn't wearing scrubs, too, or I would have been a lost cause.

That thought made me think of Mason, and then I felt guilty because I'd turned him down so many times to work, and here I was, off with another man. Ty and I might have had this friend thing going on right now, but it once had been more than that. I knew he wanted more again. He'd been doing everything right since he arrived home, finagled this day off for me even. Now I felt guilty for thinking of Mason when Ty deserved my undivided attention. At least for today.

"Almost there," Ty said, and I refocused on my surroundings as my arm rode the air current outside the window.

My brows came together when I saw we were on the two-lane road heading north out of town. "I thought you said we weren't going to the party."

"We're not. Not right now anyway. If you want to after this, we can, though."

He slowed down and turned right into a driveway that ended at a little wood-sided cabin nestled among several live oaks dripping with Spanish moss. Back behind the house were some woods and, I knew, beyond that were open fields and a lake.

"But this is Mr. K's place," I said.

"Not anymore." Ty threw the gearshift into park and turned the ignition off before hopping out of the truck. He ducked his head down and smiled at me. "This is my surprise."

I narrowed my eyes as I looked at him, then at our surroundings. I didn't understand.

"Are you comin' or what?" he asked.

I turned for my door and had barely touched the handle when he was already on my side, yanking it open. He grabbed my hand and helped me out, grinning like a four-year-old on Christmas morning. At least, how they showed it on TV, even though I had no experience like that of my own. Ty led me up toward the dark brown house, but stopped several yards in front of it. He stepped behind me and placed his hands over my eyes, then gently pushed me forward a few more steps with his chest and hips.

"Surprise," he whispered, his mouth so close to my ear that goose bumps rose when he spoke, and he lifted his hands.

We still stood in front of the cabin. Nothing had changed.

I tilted my head up and back to look at him.

"It's mine now," he murmured, and his face broke out in the biggest grin of all. My traitor heart fluttered. "All of it."

"What do you mean?"

"I bought Mr. K's place."

I gasped and spun on my heel to face him. "How on earth did you do that?"

He gave an easy shrug. "Saved most of my money while I was in the Army. Made the last part of what I needed the other night in the fight, just in time, too. I closed on it yesterday."

"You bought a house." As the reality of it hit me, I squealed and threw my arms around his neck. "You bought a house, Ty! A real house!"

"Told you I'd get out of that trailer park one of these days," he said as he took my hug for all it was worth. Then he pulled back and stared down into my face, his all serious now. "I've always said I'd get us both out. And I meant it, Bex. I still do."

Something passed across his hazel eyes—something I didn't want to label. But I couldn't deny that he was about to kiss me. So I stepped back and dropped my arms from his neck.

"Can you show me around?" I asked with a heavy dose of enthusiasm. "Can we go inside yet? How much land is it anyway? When do you move in?"

He chuckled at the questions and began answering them as he walked up the front porch and stuck a key in the door. Wow. Ty had bought a house. He was seriously moving out of the trailer park. He was right now throwing open the door to his very own place that wasn't a six-second walk from mine. He'd no longer feel trapped in that rundown shit-hole his daddy had left him with the horrible memories it held, and I'd no longer have to feel guilty when we finished our beers on my front steps after work and I went inside without inviting him in.

So why did I feel like crying? Why did tears leak down my cheeks?

"You okay?" he asked as he stood at the open door, waiting for me.

I gave a breathy laugh and wiped at my face, thankful for waterproof mascara. "Yeah." I walked up the steps and gave him a smile. "I'm just so happy for you."

And that was it, right? That's what it should have been. But if I were being honest with myself, I knew there was more to what I was feeling than that. Nostalgia for our crappy childhoods. Envy that he was getting out. And sadness that he would no longer be sitting on my steps, waiting for me with a cold beer when I came home after a long day and night of double and triple shifts. Even though he wouldn't be far and he'd probably come over the minute I called, I had this weird mix of feelings going on that my best friend was moving away and my childhood sweetheart was moving on. Both had happened years ago when he'd chosen to break up with me before leaving for the Army, but the anger had overwhelmed the bitter-sweetness of what I felt now.

"Bex," Ty said softly from behind me, very close, so close, I could feel his presence against my back even though no parts of us touched. When he shifted, though, we touched completely, his chest against my back, his arms sliding around me, his chin on my shoulder. "I'm only five minutes away. I told you—I'm not leaving you again. And whenever you're ready, this place can be yours, too."

And suddenly, I wanted that. This. The house. The life. Ty. The two of us together. But the feeling was temporary. It *had* to be.

I knew that's what he meant, but I chuckled and stepped away from him. Again. "If Uncle Troy ever kicks me out, I'm sure we'd make great roommates."

He sighed, and I tried to ignore the hurt in it, even when it made my own heart squeeze with the ache for what could have been. I walked across the living room to the door that led out back, onto a wooden deck overlooking the backyard.

"It's beautiful," I whispered.

"It is nice, isn't it?" he asked as he leaned against the railing next to me. "I see lots of beer drinkin' on this porch. Maybe a few bar-b-ques in the backyard. I just need to dig a roasting pit."

"It's so peaceful. Except ..." I listened closely, hearing music in the far distance, and laughed. "Sounds like your first party's already started." I threw a hand over my mouth. "Ohmagosh, Ty, the K-bombs are on your property now! Are you gonna throw them off?"

"Hell, no! I just made sure I never have to bring my own beer again."

I laughed, then nudged him with my shoulder. "You wanna go?"

"To the party?"

I shrugged. "Why not? I haven't been to one in forever, and you deserve to celebrate."

"I do! I won my first fight, and that's only the beginning. This is only the beginning."

I turned to stare at him, tilting my head as I really studied his face. He'd mentioned the fight earlier, but I'd been so preoccupied with the house, I hadn't really tuned into his meaning. Now that he mentioned it again ... I lifted his hat, removing the shadow over his eyes.

"Oh, Ty," I breathed. I dropped his hat and stroked the bruise over his left eye and cheek with the tips of my fingers.

He caught my hand in his. "It only hurts when you touch it. And you should see the other guy." He kissed my palm before letting go. My heart ached even more.

"That's what they all say. That's what you used to always say when you got in fights at school."

He grinned. "But it's true. Especially this time. I won by a landslide, Bex. You shoulda seen me."

My stomach tightened at the thought, even though I used to get a thrill watching him kick someone's ass, usually because whoever it was had made the mistake of calling Sissy and me white trash in Ty's presence.

"Maybe someday," I said vaguely. "Just keep winning, though. Because whoever hurts you will have to deal with me, and I won't fight fair."

He laughed and grabbed my hand again, pulling me inside and toward the front door. "Let's go party."

CHAPTER 13

Bex MR. K'S, OR, I guess, Ty's property stretched back in a long rectangle from the main road from town to a line of trees on the other side of the lake that marked the property line. Down the way a bit and around the corner was a sandy road that usually only the utility companies used. About a hundred yards past that was the lake. We drove the truck over there rather than taking the direct route from the cabin, keeping Ty's purchase a secret, and he parked in the grass with all the other trucks, Jeeps, and a swamp buggy.

The smells of dirt, grass, and roasting meat floated on the air, followed by the sounds of country music punctuated with laughter. Ty leaned over the truck bed and lifted a large, blue cooler out.

"You knew we were comin' all along," I said as I walked over and attempted to grab one of the handles to help him carry it. He twisted away from me, refusing my help.

"I've known you forever, boo," he said. "But even if for some reason you didn't want to come, a cooler of beer can always come in handy."

As we walked toward the lake and the party, lifting our legs high over the tall reeds of grass, I was glad I'd switched to my cowboy boots. The ground squished underfoot, still a bit soggy after the summer rainy season. The music grew louder—Florida Georgia Line playing, one of the few country bands I could tolerate. In fact, I kind of liked this song. Someone must have shot a wild boar because one was dressed out, hanging from a spit over coals in the bar-b-que pit that had been dug way back when, before my time. The smell of smoking wood chips and the thought of succulent pulled pork made my mouth water.

The late summer sun beat down on us, warming my skin in a way I hadn't felt in so long, and I basked in it, even knowing freckles were growing by the second. By the end of the day, I'd be one big freckle from head to toe, but I didn't care. The sun, the music, the smells of roasting boar mixed with coconut sunscreen, whoops and hollers as people greeted us from their folding chairs scattered by the lake's edge, the cold beer Ty was placing in my hand ... I hadn't realized how much I missed it all until now. And by the looks of it, the party had only just begun. The craziness would come later.

My mouth stretched into an uncontrollable smile as the excitement of downhome fun filled me.

I knew everyone there, of course, and bopped around to say hey to them all. Kaylee, a girl from my high school class who was already pregnant with her second kid, offered me some hunch punch—a homemade, redneck cocktail made with fresh fruit and grain alcohol.

"I can't drink it, so you may as well get to enjoy it," she said, rubbing her belly.

I took a cup from her and pulled a small swig. "Ohmagosh, this is the best I ever had."

She frowned as I drew another long swallow. "Don't tease me like that! Josh says the same thing, which is why he makes me make it even when I can't drink none."

"I'll drink for you," I said with a big smile. "Maybe someday, you can return the favor."

She laughed. "You and Ty again? Ya'll finally fixin' to settle down so you can join me as a baby factory?"

I smiled even though my shoulders tensed as though her words were a knife skimming down the nape of my neck. I was only twenty-one. What was this "finally" bullshit? It wasn't the first time the word had reached my ears since showing up here with Ty. Apparently, Uncle Troy and Ty—oh, and Sissy and Elizabeth—weren't the only ones who thought we belonged together. Was I the one being blind as a bat after all? Or just stubborn as a mule? I groaned internally at the stupid clichés. Not just the bat and mule ones, but the cliché of Ty and me together. The best friends growing up, the high school sweethearts who'd thought they wanted something different but were always meant to be together, settling down and having babies and living happily ever after, best friends first but lovers forever. Was that us? Was that supposed to be my life? *Was* Ty The One, and I was in complete denial over it?

"Wouldn't that be somethin'?" I said aloud, as much in reply to my own questions as Kaylee's.

Ty jogged up to me and grabbed my hand. "Come with me."

I downed the rest of the hunch punch and dropped the cup on Kaylee's table as Ty pulled me away. "Where we going?"

"I realized I forgot to bring chairs, and I can't have you sittin' that pretty ass on the damp ground, now can I?"

"So we're leaving to get chairs?" Sounded stupid to me. We just got here.

"Hey, Ty, ya'll takin' off already?" Joe Baker called out. Someone else wolf-whistled.

"Just goin' to get my truck," Ty yelled back.

"Ain't you worried about bringing it out here and the law knowin'?"

"Hell, no! This is my place now." He laughed loudly, and the secret came out of the bag when he gave a brief explanation before taking off in a jog, pulling me with him. With Ty's encouragement, a couple of other guys followed us.

Ty opened the driver's side door of his truck, and I started to pull away to head for the other side, but he tugged me back and in one swift motion, lifted me into his side. When I saw him coming in, too, I scooted over.

"You might wanna hang on, sweetheart. This is gonna get fun."

His hand reached between my legs for the gearshift, making my thighs tremble at his closeness. As soon as he threw the truck into gear and we jolted forward, I grabbed the dashboard with one hand, his thigh with the other, and held on tight. He eased the truck into the field, and it immediately began to sink. Ty flipped on the four-wheel drive, whooped out the window, and stomped on the gas pedal. Tires spun. Mud flew. The truck slid sideways for a moment, and then flew forward.

Of course, he didn't cross the hundred yards to the party in a straight line, but twisted and turned and did donuts in the muddy field. Two other trucks did the same, spraying mud up on each other, everyone laughing uncontrollably, including myself. The adrenaline rush, the twists and turns as Ty made us slide, the screams of laughter surrounding me ... I felt *alive* for the first time in months. Years. Probably since the day he broke up with me.

We'd never been able to go mudding out here before. The town cops and county sheriffs weren't dumb enough to know we didn't party here—they'd done their own fair share of it in their days—but they only came if there was trouble. Tearing up Mr. K's field was considered trouble, and more than once they'd identified the vandals by tire tracks left in the mud. But now we had Ty, and he obviously didn't care.

"It'll all need to be tilled up and worked on anyway," he said between hollers and howls of laughter. "If I ever decide to grow anything on it in the first place. For now, it can be our playground."

He gave me a big grin, squeezed my hand that was still on his thigh, making me tighten my own over the thick muscles of his leg, then slammed the gas again as he spun the steering wheel to the right. The g-force pressed me against his side and sucked a scream out of me that dissolved into laughter. By the time we reached the lake and he turned so the tailgate faced the party, I was practically in his lap and breathless.

"I told you so again," he murmured against my ear while shutting off the ignition.

"What did you tell me now?" I asked, my voice barely more than a whisper as I tried to catch my breath. I wasn't sure now what had me gasping—the thrill of mudding or of Ty's mouth so close to my skin.

"This is where you belong, boo," he answered. "Right here. Nowhere else."

He lifted my hand from his leg, kissed my palm and gave me a wink, all while he slid out of the truck. He strode off before I could respond. Before my spinning mind could come up with *how* to respond. Because all I could think was, "You're right, Ty."

I slid out of the truck and followed him to the back in somewhat of a daze. He'd gone over to retrieve his cooler, and I was still speechless as he brought it back, his biceps and forearms bulging, his chest straining against the tank shirt he wore. I backed up against the tailgate he'd already lowered and was about to jump up when he was suddenly in front of me, his hands on my waist. Our eyes locked as he lifted me, and the hold didn't break as he stood in front of me, between my legs. A numbness must have set in because I didn't feel his hands still on me until his fingers tightened and his thumbs pressed into the sensitive strip of skin between the bottom of my halter and the top of my low-rider shorts. I drew in a sharp breath and finally blinked. I didn't know what must have passed across my face, but it made

Ty's eyes darken and his hands open. He turned away before I could stop him, and my heart sank to my stomach.

"Looks like you could use this," Kaylee said from beside me. I hadn't seen her come up, but she held out the red plastic cup filled with more hunch punch. I took it gratefully and swallowed what tasted like nectar of the gods. Or maybe of Elizabeth's goddesses. I knew I'd eventually regret it, but for now, I had no respect for what tomorrow would bring. At the moment, this *was* where I belonged. *In* this moment. Living life right now because who knew what tomorrow or the next day would bring.

By the time Leni and Jeric showed up later in the afternoon with their friends Brock and Asia, I had a pleasant buzz going. I'd been a little worried some people might be rude to them, but not because they were outsiders. More than one person had brought a new significant other I'd never met before—lovers they'd met at college or while traveling—and they fit in just fine. In fact, you couldn't help but accept them because they were such perfect fits for our friends. They seemed to have the kind of love I wanted so badly.

Being outsiders was only a small part of my concern. There was Jeric with his pierced eyebrow and sleeves of tats and Asia with her silvery-purple hair, heavily lined eyes, and combat boots with her black miniskirt. I'd been given enough flak when I'd pierced my nose and added more ink than any girl in town had, but I still "belonged." My concerns were unwarranted, though. Apparently, word had gotten around that Leni loved cowboy boots as much as any of us and could ride the mechanical bull better than any guy here, and Jeric … well, he was a former UFC fighter. Enough said in a circle of rednecks. Especially when he'd just helped one of our own win his first semi-pro fight.

Like the newly paired lovebirds, they had no troubles fitting in.

Brock and Asia were a little more reserved, though, and tended to stay on the fringes of the group, their gazes constantly sweeping over us, as if they were looking for something.

Or watching over us. I somehow felt that comforting when I probably should have found it weird. Maybe because I'd had plenty to drink.

Late afternoon turned into dusk and as darkness fell, some people called it a day and left, but most of us stayed for the bonfire, a traditional part of a K-bomb. The fire blazed, the smell of hunch punch and a country night and burning oak filled my head, and the music wrapped around me.

"Come on, girl," Leni said after her second cup of punch, "let's dance."

She jumped up on Ty's tailgate and reached down and grabbed my hand. A strange shock traveled through me, kind of like when Mason had first touched me, but different. I looked up at her, confused, but my vision swirled. Eyes. So many different eyes sliding in and out of focus before me. Gray, blue, brown. Light green. Hazel. Back to green. A different green, though, like pictures I'd seen of southern seas. Leni's eyes. Her entire face came back into focus, and I blinked away the blurriness. Damn. How much had I had to drink? She pulled up on my hand and I jumped, joining her in the bed. I immediately forgot about the odd visions and let the music take command of my body.

The headlights on the truck across the way turned on, spotlighting us as we danced, and many catcalls and wolf-whistles rang through the air. Leni was a much better dancer than me, but I could almost keep up. After the second song ended, Jeric retrieved her, and Ty climbed up and danced with me. I'd forgotten what a good dancer he was.

The more the alcohol flowed, the rowdier the party became, but it was all in good fun.

At least until I went into the trees to pee and felt like someone was watching me. As I pulled my shorts back up and turned to look behind me, eyes stared back. They didn't look quite human, though.

"Hey!" I said, trying to scare off whatever kind of animal it was, although my heart beat so loud, my fear could probably be heard. What sounded like a million pairs of little wings flapped against the branches before some kind of flock of black birds rose into the night sky. I couldn't help the scream.

"You okay?" Ty yelled as he ran for me while I stumbled out of the trees. He swept me into his arms and held me tightly as he peered into the darkness.

"Yeah. Just some birds," I panted against him, my heart still racing.

He released one arm from me, but kept the other firmly around my waist as we slowly walked back for the party.

"Damn. Talk about a buzzkill."

Ty chuckled, and I giggled. Well, maybe my buzz wasn't completely gone.

"It's good to see you havin' so much fun," he said.

I slid my arm around his waist and gave him a squeeze. "Thanks for it all."

He pulled me closer, and our steps slowed. "Are you ready to tell me how right I am?"

"About what?"

"About you belonging here."

I stopped walking, and he did, too. We turned toward each other, and he stared at me expectantly, the distant firelight shining in his eyes. Laughter and music carried over the air, but right here around us was completely silent except for the sound of my heartbeat rushing in my ears. The night had grown a little cooler and goose bumps rose on my arms. Or did the chill come from the look in Ty's hazel eyes that had gone from expectancy to desire? No, wait. I'd seen desire in many a man's eyes, and this was different. More emotional. And what I saw in Ty's eyes was what I'd wanted so badly for as long as I could remember. Or, at least, for as long as I could remember since discovering boys weren't so icky after all. The moment Ty had shown me that years ago. And here he was, showing me even more, and with just a simple look of adoration. Of love.

I pushed up onto my toes, placed my hands on each side of his face, softly because I didn't want to hurt him, and answered him so only the two of us could hear. "You were right, Ty. This is where I belong. Right here. With you."

His eyes searched my face for a long moment before his face broke into that huge grin that made my knees weak. Who was I to deny it? Ty Daniels had had my heart for as long as I could remember.

He scooped me into his arms and ran as he carried me to his truck. Quietly, trying not to alert anyone else that we were there, he opened the door and placed me inside. I scooted backwards on the seat until I hit the passenger door as he climbed in over me, pulling the door shut behind him. One of his legs was on the truck floor, the other between me and the seat back. He braced himself with his hands on each side of me, holding himself above me as he waited for confirmation.

"Are you gonna kiss me or what?" I asked, and I didn't have to say it twice.

His mouth crashed down on mine, retaking what was once his, and I was instantly reminded of how much I loved kissing him. Our lips moved like long-lost lovers, slowly but passionately, immediately recalling the exact way the other liked to be stroked and nipped. Memories of kissing him in this very truck, out here in this field or under the big oak on the other side of the lake or even in the school parking lot, flooded through me, bringing tears. My only memories of true happiness were when I was with Ty. My only memories of feeling safe were when I was in his arms. And I felt it all now—happiness, security, and dare I say it, love.

I parted my lips and let his tongue claim me. He lowered himself gently against me, and the full weight of his body pressed against mine as the kiss deepened. I pushed his hat off and ran my hands over his short hair, then down his neck and to his muscular back, feeling the tightness of his shoulders under my fingertips.

"Fuck, Bethany, I've missed you so bad," he murmured against my lips as we both took a breath before I pulled the tank over his head and we dove in again.

He kissed me until my whole body burned and ached for his touch. One of his arms held him up slightly, his hand cradling my head. The other hand hadn't moved from my waist, his fingers digging into my hips as his thumb moved up along my skin to just under my halter, then down, to just below my waistband, making my belly quiver. I shifted underneath him, and without breaking contact because I couldn't stand the thought of missing out on one more second of kissing him, I unbuttoned my halter and opened it enough to feel his skin against mine but not enough for anyone who tried to peek through the window to see anything. Ty pulled back and studied me.

"Are you sure, boo? About this?" he asked, his voice husky and heavy with the same need that pulsed through my veins, throughout my body.

No, I wasn't sure. Not deep down inside. But every part of me ached for him so badly that I knew the only way to find out if I *was* sure was to do it.

"I need you, Ty," I said breathlessly. "I need to feel you to know."

I didn't know if he understood because he hesitated for another moment until I wrapped my arms around his neck and my legs around his waist and pulled him down so he crashed onto me. The weight of him, his hardness between us, pressed against the center seam of my jean shorts, rubbing the sweet spot that made me whimper. He apparently liked that because he smiled as he moved his hips, grinding against me again. I moaned louder. He did it once more, making my back arch, but then he held still, except to lean down and kiss me crazy. When he seemed too busy with my mouth and then my neck to do it again,

I lifted my hips and stroked against him. Now he moaned. We rocked against each other several times, until he lifted himself again to look at me, as if to ask to go further.

I was about to beg for more, when more eyes slid across my vision. Not like in the woods when I peed, but when Leni had touched me. Beautiful eyes of different colors sliding in and out of focus. They once again settled on green, but not Leni's green, and not Ty's hazel that was more brown than green.

Mason.

The light color had to be his. The sick feeling of guilt pitted in my stomach.

But before I could focus on any other thought, someone pounded on the window.

"Ty, you and Bex need to get out of here." Was that Jeric's voice? Why did he sound so ... panicked?

For the first time, I noticed the commotion outside.

"Get out of here!" a male's voice yelled. Not Jeric's this time. Was it Brock's?

"Hurry!" Jeric yelled from right outside the truck again.

Ty and I shared a look, and then I quickly buttoned up my halter as he pushed himself off of me. We couldn't see anything through the steamed-up windows, but the sounds coming from outside made little sense. And also raised the hairs on the back of my neck. Screeching and snapping and the cracking of things breaking.

Ty finally threw the door open. "What the hell?"

I tried to look out but only saw streaks of dark shapes flying by.

"Get Bex home," Jeric yelled. "We got this, Ty, but you two need to get out of here."

"I ain't—" Ty was shoved back into the pickup.

"GO!" Brock yelled. "She's not safe here."

Ty's head snapped toward me, his eyes wide. I scurried over to the passenger side, about to open the door to see for myself, but he already had the engine turned over and was slamming the truck into gear. With one hand on the wheel, he grabbed his shirt with the other and wiped the windshield enough for him to see. It was already starting to clear, though, and I could see blurred shapes of trucks driving away, leaving only Jeric, Leni, Brock, and Asia, who fought some people in black pants and black hoodies. Like those guys who were always hanging out in the truck stop parking lot after Sullivan's had closed.

"We can't leave them to fight those guys!" I said.

"It's their fight," Ty said, "and you heard them. It's not safe for you."

"Like it's safe for *them*?"

He glanced in his rearview mirror, and I looked over my shoulder. The window had cleared enough to see the field now far behind us.

"Jeric and Brock are fighters," Ty said, "and those two girls are holding their own, too."

"Who are they?" I asked, but I didn't really expect an answer. Watching them now, they barely seemed human the way they moved. And I meant the people we knew as much as those we didn't.

A dark shape streaked toward us. A heavy blackness slammed through me. A Darkness like I'd never felt before. As the figure crashed into the back window and exploded into nothing but a mist, the word "demon" came to mind right before I blacked out.

CHAPTER 14

"LENI, GET BEX and Ty! They're in the truck," Asia yelled at me before swinging her fist at a Shadowman's throat.

Jeric and Brock were closer to Ty's black truck than I was, though, and Jeric banged on the window. I sprinted after the Shadowman about to attack him. My shoulder plowed into the Lakari's side, and we rolled head over feet for about ten yards. I jumped up at the same time he did, and he lunged at me. I grabbed his forearm with both hands, gripped tightly, and swung him over my head, twisting my body around with the momentum. He grunted on impact when his back slammed into the ground, but didn't burst into pieces or smoke. His hands clawed at mine, his long, sharp fingernails that belonged on a beast, not a human, digging into my skin. I kicked him in the head. His grip loosened. I stomped on his chest. He disintegrated.

Ty's truck threw two fountains of mud and grass up as he took off out of the field. I watched the taillights for a moment, glad to see they escaped, hoping they weren't followed. They were the last to leave besides us Guardians.

"Leni!" Jeric yelled.

I spun toward him, but it was too late. A Shadowman's fist drove into my temple. Stars shot across my eyes. My vision went sideways as I stumbled and almost fell. I caught his next swing, my hand blocking the blow, but he lifted his knee at the same time, and it nailed me in the ribs. The air flew out of me. I didn't have time to pause, though. Another fist headed for my face. I blocked it with my forearm and swung around to kick him in the kidneys—or whatever they had in their lower backs. It was a tender spot, I knew from past experience. The impact pushed him off-balance. He stumbled, tripped, slowly went down to his knees. I thrust the heel of my hand upwards into his nose. He exploded into dust that sprayed all over me before swirling together and rising to the sky.

There were still six more Shadowmen on the ground, and a cloud of Darkness churning overhead. My body lurched forward as I tried to run to help fight, but I couldn't catch my breath. A sharp pain tore through my side every time I inhaled, like a stitch but much worse. I pressed a hand to the place right below my left boob—damn, did it hurt. I took a few more steps as the others still fought, but my vision wavered in and out of focus. If I could only breathe ...

"Jeric, you guys project," Brock yelled. "We'll cover you!"

Jeric ran for me, his eyes filled with horror, his arms reaching out for me. He caught me just as my knees buckled. We both went to the ground.

"Come on, babe, let's do this the fun way," he said, and we both projected from our bodies.

The light from our souls lit up the field like a spotlight. We soared for the Shadowmen on the ground, making Brock and Asia's job of protecting our bodies easier. Our Light burst holes through them, and their pieces scattered before rising to the others. Once the ones in human form were gone, we flew upwards toward the Dark cloud. We split into two tines, encircling the cloud until we met on the other side, then squeezed inward like a noose. The Dark souls screamed like sirens as we demolished them.

Once they were gone, Jeric's soul filled every nook and cranny of mine, the feeling better than any pain meds human doctors could prescribe.

"You're hurt, aren't you?" His words swirled through us.

"I'll be okay. Just give me a little more time like this."

While Jeric's soul removed the pain, the Bonding would help me heal faster than normal. We watched Brock and Asia carry our bodies to their Camaro. They must have known I was hurt, too, and knew what I needed. They placed me in the back and Asia crawled in with me, then Brock put Jeric in the front passenger seat. They drove us through town and toward the RV park. Jeric and I stayed in our soul forms, letting our bodies tug us along. As we floated through the night, we remained alert for any Lakari. None were nearby, but if they were really interested in someone in Lake Haven, more would be back very soon. We dropped into our bodies right before Brock parked next to my truck so they wouldn't have to carry us again.

"Ow," I gasped as soon as I tried to suck in a deep breath. The pain in my side was no longer like a pick lodged into my ribs as it had been before, but I had a feeling I had more than bad bruises. "I think my rib's broken."

"Let's get you inside, and you two can spend the rest of the night Bonding," Asia said. "You'll feel tons better in the morning, I promise."

Jeric helped me out of the car and wrapped his arm around me, trying to take most of my weight.

"That hurts more," I said, pushing away from him. "I can walk."

He didn't leave my side, though, his arm out, ready to catch me if I fell.

"Come in, guys," I said to Brock and Asia while Jeric unlocked the camper. "We need to talk."

"We can talk about it in the morning," Asia said. "You need to rest."

"I won't be able to until I know what the hell happened." I stepped inside and fell to the futon. The jolt made me gasp again.

Jeric moved some pillows around to prop me up better, and then sat down next to me. Asia sat on the other side of the little dining table so she could see us, and Brock was barely inside, leaning against the cabinet that held the microwave and refrigerator, his arms crossed over his broad chest. The four of us in here at once made my little camper feel like a tin of anchovies.

"Did you guys feel any warning, because I sure didn't," I said. Everyone shook their heads.

"Brock and I were sitting at a picnic table, watching and listening," Asia said. "The last twenty or so people were all gathered around the bon fire. Except Bex and Ty."

"He could have been a very happy man tonight," Jeric muttered. "His truck windows were all steamed up."

"And the Lakari came out of nowhere," Brock said.

Asia tapped her finger against her lip. "I did hear a scream from the woods."

"I did, too," I confirmed. "It was Bex. She came running out of the woods with Ty. She sounded more surprised than scared, though, so I think he might have snuck up on her."

Brock's chin tilted down, and he looked up at us under a wrinkled forehead. "The Lakari came from the woods, too."

I hadn't seen when they arrived, although I'd felt the tingle on the back of my neck. By the time Jeric and I had turned around to see, a dozen of them in human form were sprinting for the party. Brock and Asia had already been yelling at everyone to run while they darted toward the danger.

"So they could have come for Bex and Ty?" I asked.

"They had to have been in his truck for a while by the time the Lakari showed, though," Jeric said. "We can't be sure based on that. Especially since we don't know what shocked her."

"But we know for sure they're hunting someone young and someone at that party," I said. "As far as I know, that's the first time Bex and Ty have really been together for years, if they were steaming up windows. Maybe the Lakari were trying to stop it."

"Why now, though?" Jeric asked. "They used to be together as a couple already. If they were Twin Flames, he wouldn't have been able to leave her."

"Unless … can something block a connection between Twin Flames, like if they're too young or something?" Asia suggested. We all stared at her. "What? It's an idea. A possibility, right? I mean, nobody remembers anything worth remembering, so that could be one of those things."

"Enyxa could have figured something out," Brock said, following the idea further. "And then figured out a way to send Ty off to be killed in Afghanistan before they ever Bonded."

I stared off into space, running this possibility through my mind. Until and unless we were able to remember any reason this couldn't happen, I supposed the idea had potential. It didn't feel right to me, though, in my gut. Not like the theory that Bex was Rebethannah did. Because if she was and Ty was her other half, then wouldn't we recognize his soul, too? And why would Nathayden have sent us a message to save Rebethannah if he was already here? Ty had shown up back in town the same day we had. Of course, I didn't know for sure if Nathayden had sent that message, or if he had, when. We also had no idea where Nathayden was—on this world or another. The two words had appeared magically, without a date stamp or postmark giving a location. How inconvenient.

"Well, we all feel Darkness overhanging both of them," I finally said. "But that would have gone away when he came back, right?"

"Or maybe not until they really got together," Jeric said. "Bex has been pushing him away, keeping him in the friend zone until tonight."

"We can watch for the signs over the next few days," I said. "We should know pretty quickly."

"Maybe," Asia said, "but since everyone's reBonding is different, we may not notice anything. Especially from the outside."

"They'll head for the Gate or get soul-sickness if they don't, like Jacey and Micah," I said.

"Only if they're Guardians. Not if they're regular old Twin Flames. And even if they are, it could take a day or a few weeks for soul-sickness to set in. Sometimes longer."

I tilted my head. "Really? I thought it happened pretty fast."

Asia shrugged. "I just know every dyad's experience is different when they first meet."

"Asia and I didn't get sick at all," Brock said. "And we'd been together, off and on, for a while. We just knew from the journal that we needed to go. Well, Asia knew."

"I think I felt the sickness coming on," she said.

"But there were the phoenix marks on your arms, the word dyad screaming in your head ... all of that. Right?" I asked. "And what do you mean off and on? How could you even be away from each other? Jeric's car exploded into flames when he tried to leave me."

Asia shrugged. "None of that happened with us. We read about those things with Jacey and Micah, but it took us a while to catch on because we weren't like that. But even when we weren't on, we weren't that far from each other ..."

She trailed off, and Brock cleared his throat. "It just wasn't like that for us, okay? We didn't even have the phoenix marks until the day we decided to head for the Gate. That's what made us realize we were like Jacey and Micah. But the point is, everyone's different."

My gaze slid from Asia to Brock. Both of their faces had closed off, putting an end to any more personal stories from them. Jeric picked up my hand and gave it a squeeze. I'd thought before that our relationship felt tighter than theirs. I knew for sure now that it was at least different. Sparks flew immediately for Jeric and me—and Jacey and Micah. We thought that was standard for Twin Flames, but now my perspective changed on everything, including whom the Lakari could be targeting.

"So, Bex and Ty are still possible options," Jeric said, taking us back to the problem at hand. "Did you two find out anything else?"

I hadn't realized how tense Brock had been from that last tangent we'd been on until I watched his shoulders drop a few inches now that we'd moved back to our mission.

"I heard one of the guys—the one who left early—say something about needing to get home to his girlfriend, because she was sick," he said. "Mentioned something about getting test results next week."

"So someone who could be really ill," Jeric said. "Except she has a boyfriend, so probably not going Dark."

Asia snorted. "That doesn't mean anything. There are a gazillion unhappy relationships in this world. Millions of married people who are severely depressed. Millions more getting the shit beat out of them by people who say they love them."

Jeric scowled at Asia's point. He knew this truth too well.

"So she's a possibility," I said, pushing on. "We need to find out who she is."

"There was also a lot of talk about the new people, and not us," Asia said. "I guess a few of the old high school crowd were back in town with new partners. A couple of them seemed pretty tight, too. Could be Twin Flames meeting up ... or soul mates."

"More possibilities then." I blew out a frustrated sigh—we still had no clear answers—and whimpered at the pain. The conversation had distracted me for a while, and I'd nearly forgotten about my injuries.

Jeric jumped to his feet. "That's it. Bedtime for you, babe. You need some Bonding action."

Brock chuckled and reached his hand out for Asia. "That's our cue. You two have fun with that."

"Feel better, Leni," Asia said as her other half tugged her out of the camper.

"I'll be fine." I fought a grimace as I stood up.

Jeric locked up the camper as I headed back to the bedroom and crawled into bed. A few minutes later, he climbed in next to me, and we scooted and wiggled until we were comfortable and I could breathe without pain. Then we projected and Bonded throughout the night. A couple of Lakari had already shown up, staying in spirit form over the trailer park. They sure did have an interest in this side of town. Ty and Bex had to be their target. Right? But who were they to each other? And to us? Anything at all? Or ... nothing?

I felt almost completely new the next day. At least, my body did, but my mind still reeled with all of the possibilities.

"You gave me a real scare last night," Jeric said as he sat at our picnic table next to me with a cup of coffee in hand. He kissed my temple. "That's exactly why I don't like the idea of you fighting. Of us being here at all, doing this ... thing that we do."

I cupped my hand over his cheek. "But this *is* what we do, Jeric. This is our choice and our reason for even existing. Please don't try to take me away from it."

He sighed. "Doesn't mean I like it."

He leaned in and kissed me on the lips, then slid his hand over my back and rested his chin on my shoulder. As usual, I had the Book of Phoenix in front of me. Too distracted last night, I hadn't even thought about checking it, but I was dying to look this morning. Several days ago I'd had what I thought to be a clever idea to write a note to Nathayden in the Book, hoping that he might be able to answer me. Right below the words "Save Rebethannah," I'd written, "Who are you? Are you on Earth or another world?"

I checked the page morning, noon, and night for an answer. So far, there had been none. With a deep breath (that didn't hurt), I opened the journal and flipped to the page.

And there was still no answer.

CHAPTER 15

I AM SO going to hell. I sat in church the morning after the party with a pounding headache, a queasy stomach, and those words echoing through my head. Everyone who had been at the party sat silently in pews, some hiding secretive smiles behind their hands and others looking as green as I felt. At least, everyone who still went to church, which was almost all of us. We were born and raised to fear God, and boy was I fearing him now. I think the preacher always knew when there was a K-bomb—word traveled like fire in this town, so it was definitely possible—because every Sunday after a big party, his sermons focused on immoral deeds, imbibing in the devil's brew, and living in sin. He basically preached for over an hour how much we were all heathens.

Not only the drinking, or the dancing, or how far I'd gone with Ty when I shouldn't have even kissed him, or thinking of Mason *while* kissing Ty had convinced me of my afterlife destination. The last image I remembered from the night—the demon that I still swore up and down that I saw—made it clear. It was after me. I *felt* it. The demon had come for me because ... because ...

My stomach lurched. Oh, crap, I was about to toss my cookies. I bolted from the pew and ran for the ladies' room with my hand over my mouth. Half the congregation broke into stifled laughter.

Several minutes later, I pressed my face against the somewhat-cool car window while I tried to drive myself home, wishing I could die while promising that I'd never, ever, ever drink hunch punch or anything else ever again. Relief washed over me when I pulled into the trailer park without puking a second time. Uncle Troy had seen me leave church early. I only hoped he got the message that I was in no shape to work.

I stumbled up the steps and into my trailer and barely made it to my bed in the back room before collapsing. Never had hunch punch or any alcohol affected me so badly. I couldn't remember the last time I'd had a hangover like this, if ever. If I hadn't known the people I was with, I'd reckon someone had drugged me, but that wasn't some nightclub in the city, and Ty had stuck too close to me for anyone to dare.

I groaned as I rolled onto my back and stared at the ceiling, thinking about Ty. He'd apparently brought me inside and left me here because I woke up this morning in my own bed, still wearing the same clothes except my boots. He'd taken those off, but nothing more. There was no evidence at all that he'd slept here, too. I sure hoped he hadn't. I'd let things go way too far last night, and now remorse added to all the icky feelings tumbling in my gut. I'd never wanted to lead him on, and last night I'd done just that.

But even now, I couldn't help but think that maybe he was right. That I needed to get the idea of Mason, being with a doctor, leaving this town and lifestyle behind, out of my head, because this was where I belonged. This was home. Perhaps I even needed to forget the idea of there being someone out there who was my soul mate. Maybe The One didn't exist. Maybe Ty was the best I'd ever get, and truth be told, he wasn't all that bad.

If I could trust that he wouldn't leave me again.

Something deep inside me stirred, though, letting me know that The One *was* out there. Or maybe right in front of my face. Either way, my soul knew he *did* exist. Somewhere.

Without standing up, I managed to wriggle and worm my way out of my maxi dress, and I lay on top of my covers in only my bra and panties and fell asleep. Visions of men danced through my head. Lots of them. But they weren't hot, lucky-me sex dreams I had. Just a variety of faces, their appearances very different, yet something felt *the same* about them. As if they were all the same man, even when they had different hair and eye colors, different styles like they came from more than one era. And with each one, I felt a strong connection. I thought, *He's The One.* Every single time. When I drifted awake, the last face floating behind my eyelids showed a tan complexion, sharp cheekbones and jaw, buzzed hair, and light eyes, either gray or light green.

Voices in my trailer brought me awake, and I figured my subconscious had intertwined the last face with reality because Mason Hayes was in my house.

Wait. Mason Hayes was in my house? What the fuck?

"Found her," he said.

My eyes opened. Mason stood over me, with Sissy in the doorway right behind him. I shot straight up, realized I was practically naked and yanked the covers around me. My head swam, my vision blurred, and I almost crashed back down on my bed, but Mason caught me and laid me down gently. Even with the frown that puckered his brow, he was so damn hot.

"You're so damn hot," he said, echoing my thoughts, and my face flushed. The corners of his lips quivered. "Yes, in that way, too, but I mean your skin. You have a fever."

"Nah, just a sunburn." I struggled to sit up, but he refused to let me.

"I'm a doctor. I can tell the difference between a sunburn and a fever."

My eyes scrunched. "You think I'm sick? I thought it was a hangover."

"So you did go to the K-bomb," Sissy said, a twinge of jealousy lacing her tone.

Oh, crap. I looked at her and back at Mason, my lip tugging to the side with guilt. "Um ... yeah."

His light green gaze swept over my face, and he shook his head while smiling. "Well, I hope you had fun, because you aren't going anywhere for at least a day." He stood up and towered over me. "I'll be back in a few. But you might want to put something on. Once I get back, I won't be going anywhere, either."

He strode out of the room and a few seconds later, the screen door slammed shut. I bolted upright again.

"What the hell is he doing here?" I demanded of my sister. I couldn't believe she'd brought *him* to our house. Our little two-bedroom, thirty-year-old tin can of a trailer house.

"I was going to ask you the same thing!"

"*Me?* You brought him here! And what are you doing here anyway?"

She placed a hand on her shorts-clad hip. "I needed a break so thought I'd come home and see my sister. He, uh ..." She paused and glanced out my window. "He followed me, I guess."

I looked out the window, too, and watched a newer model, black sedan leave the trailer park, turning for town. Sissy's old beater sat outside next to mine.

"To see me?" I asked, unable to mask my awe.

She snorted. "Well, definitely not to see me. He hasn't even called to see how Mama's doing, until this morning. I told him well enough for Mama's neighbor to hang out and take care of her while I came to see you. I think he was really calling to fish for info, you know, since he followed me and all."

I leaned back against the wall and pulled my knees to my chest. "How's Mama doing? If I'd have known Uncle Troy was going to give me the afternoon off yesterday, I woulda come to see you guys."

"You woulda come to see *Dr. Hayes*," she corrected me. She crawled on the bed on all fours until she reached the other side and sat next to me.

"I woulda seen you and Mama ... first."

"Well, you're not missin' anything. She's the same. No better, no worse. Her other doctors say it'll take time for the new meds to make a big enough difference. Time she doesn't really have." She leaned against me and rested her head on my shoulder. Her next words weighed heavily with grief. "I don't think she's gonna make it, Bex."

I hung my arm over her shoulder and pulled her closer. "Think positively, Sissy. And pray. Hard. She needs as much prayin' on her behalf as we can do."

She nodded and sniffed and pulled away. "Good heavens, Bex, you really are burnin' up."

I snorted. "I still think it's just a sunburn, but if Dr. Hotstuff's gonna take care of me, I ain't gonna stop him."

Sissy tilted her head. "Didn't you just go to the K-bomb with Ty?"

"Yeah. So?"

"And weren't you gettin' it on with him in his truck?"

"Good night, word sure gets around fast."

"Yeah, Kaylee called me, all excited. So are you gettin' back together with him or what?"

I sighed. "I don't know, Sissy. It had felt so right last night, and even a little bit this morning, even though I haven't seen him at all. But ... I just can't. I can't let him in like that again. Ty is toxic for me."

Sissy rolled her eyes. "Don't be so dramatic. Ty screwed up by leavin' you, and he knows it now. Doesn't everyone deserve a second chance? If you gave Mama one, surely he deserves one."

I scowled at her. She made an excellent point. And part of me did want to give Ty a second chance. But another part of me thrilled at the sound of tires crunching on sandy gravel outside—

without the loud sound of a truck engine accompanying it. I glanced out the window. Ty's big black truck still sat over at his house, not moving at all today. And Mason's sleek and shiny black car came to a stop behind mine.

"Quick! Throw me some clothes!" I commanded Sissy.

She jumped up and yanked open a dresser drawer, and then threw an old, paint-stained t-shirt and cut-off sweats at me. I didn't have time to complain or choose something better, so I hurried into them right before Mason walked inside. Peeking from my bed down the hallway and into the living room, I watched as he dropped some shopping bags on the kitchen counters and then turned in a circle, taking the place in. I sagged back against the wall and closed my eyes. How embarrassing.

Even more embarrassing was when my stomach heaved again, and I had to run for the bathroom. Then the chills came on, and at some point, I stopped being self-conscious because I was too sick to care.

Mason stayed and took care of me. As in, stayed the night and the next day and that night, too. Sissy had gone back to Mama's Monday morning after sleeping on the couch because she gave up her bed for Mason. I think she was keeping an eye on us, making sure he stayed in her room at the other end of the trailer from mine. So precious of her to care about my virtue. But one night on our old lumpy couch with its scratchy, plaid upholstery was enough for her. Besides, she needed to get back to Mama and her caretaking duties.

"You look a lot better," Mason said Tuesday morning when I finally emerged from my room and after giving my teeth a much needed scrubbing.

"I can't believe you're still here." I made it as far as the couch, where I lay on my side, curled in a ball. I hadn't checked yet but I should have had a six-pack, the way my abs ached from all the barfing.

"I took off a few days to see you."

"Too bad I was sick the whole time."

He rose from his seat at the tiny kitchen table and came over to the couch. He lifted my upper body, sat down, and then laid me back down so my head was on his thigh.

"I can't say that was my top choice of how to spend time with you, but it was better than nothing," he said as he brushed the straggly hairs away from my face. Good heavens, I needed a shower. How he could stand to be so close was beyond me. "But I have another day, so you're not sick for the *whole* time."

"I *can* say that if anyone was to take care of me, you'd be my top choice." When he grinned cockily, I added, "Because you are a doctor, after all."

He laughed. "Geez, and I thought you meant because of my great looks or my fantastic bedside manner."

"Hmm ... yeah, maybe those, too."

He laughed again, and I smiled, enjoying the sound.

"So I don't have to worry about this Ty dude who stopped by?" he asked, and my body tensed. "Or do I?"

"He's, uh, an old friend. My best friend, besides Sissy. He's been friends with us both since we were little." Could I say friend any more times? Who was I trying to convince—Mason or me?

"Yet you never mentioned this *best* friend to me before." He twirled his finger in my hair, and I couldn't tell from his voice if he was teasing or serious. I guess that did sound a little worrisome, from his point of view. I'd be a little suspicious, too, if he had a female best friend that he'd failed to mention to me. Who he happened to have gone steady with and possibly been in love with for several years. Who still lived next door ... at least for the time being. I mean, it's not like Mason and I were dating, but we'd talked enough, set the stage enough, that something like this probably should have been brought up. And since it hadn't, well, I knew it looked like I was hiding something. Maybe because I was. Mason chuckled. "I'll try not to be jealous, although I may not have been able to help it when he came by to check on you."

"Ty came by?" And here I'd been wondering the whole time I was sick why he hadn't bothered. Why he'd dumped my passed-out self in my bed and never returned. Wasn't like him.

"Yesterday morning. He said he'd been sick and wanted to apologize for his disappearing act. He wanted to see you, but I insisted that he not wake you up. I might have pulled the doctor card. He looked pretty pissed off, so I'm thinking you did tell him about me."

Oh, shit. My head swam again and my stomach clenched, but not from feeling ill. Not physically ill, anyway. I imagined the scene of Ty showing up and finding Mason here after the night we had together, and then being shooed off like a pesky ant by the very guy Ty knew was trying to steal me away from him .... Damn, it couldn't have been good. I needed to talk to Ty, but I honestly didn't know what to say to him. I didn't know what to do about Mason right now, either.

I liked him here with me. I liked how he'd taken care of me. I liked the bright pink flowers that stood in a vase on the night-stand next to my bed—flowers he'd brought me. He'd held my hair back, doctored me until the fever broke, made me suck on ice cubes and then sip water to ensure I didn't dehydrate. When I could finally hold anything down last night, he made me broth and crackers. And not once did he try anything or give a hint that he did it all for any other reason than he simply cared.

My heart was torn.

"So," Mason said, the tone of his voice changed, lighter and more cheerful, when I didn't respond, "what should we do today?"

"Mmm ..." I groaned. "Lie here and do nothing?"

"You don't want to at least watch movies? Play a game or something? Feel up to a walk?"

I groaned again. We were definitely not going for a walk. His car being here for two days now was surely the town's gossip of the week. They probably had me pregnant, even though I hadn't had sex with anyone for months, and Mason and I hadn't even kissed since that first night we met. No need to take the chances of having to face anyone, especially Ty. Oh, dear God and sweet baby Jesus. Two days ago the gossip had been Ty and me, even reaching Sissy's ears. And now Mason and me, and since they surely assumed I was knocked up, they'd probably already gone on to whose baby it was and which one would be raising it. Sissy was going to love this. Elizabeth was surely hating it.

"Crap. I need to call Liz'beth and Sullivan's," I said.

"Done."

I rolled on my back and looked up at him. "Done?"

"Sissy called them both yesterday morning. I called Memaw's again today, just to be sure they knew you wouldn't be in again. The woman on the phone didn't sound happy, but I don't think it had anything to do with your absence."

Yep, Elizabeth was hating the gossip ... and Mason. "Liz'beth tries to fill my grams' shoes. She doesn't know you so she doesn't trust you."

"I should meet her, then. As soon as she meets me, she'll fall in love, just like all the women do."

"Good heavens. Arrogant much?"

He gave me a grin. "You know I'm quite charming."

I couldn't argue with that.

"If you want to meet her, go on in, but I'm not going anywhere. You're probably going stir crazy, though, aren't you?"

"Not at all. Especially now that you're up and speaking in more than grunts."

"There's that charm again."

He laughed then tweaked my chin between his thumb and fingers. "You know I tease you because I adore you."

Heat flushed my face, and I cleared my throat. "So, um, anyway, if you want to go home, I'll be fine. I'll be up and at 'em again tomorrow."

"Which is exactly why I'm staying. I have you all to myself for what? At least twenty-four hours?"

I glanced at the clock on the stove. Not exactly twenty-four hours, but we did have one day together, and one night, and I'd never had a day and night after being sick that was so amazingly perfect. Mason treated me like a princess, continuing to take care of me because I was still a little weak, almost babying me sometimes. We did what I wanted to do, and he didn't lift a brow when I gave him the list of chick-flick, rom-com movies I asked him to get from the rental box in front of the park office. He sat on the couch with me, seeming perfectly content to simply be there while we ate ice cream and watched movies. We played a few hands of gin rummy, and he didn't get too upset when I beat him the first time, and didn't act like an ass when he beat me the second hand. And when my energy was drained and I was ready for bed, I awkwardly took his hand and led him back to my room. He lay down with me and held me, but we did nothing more than talk until I zonked out.

I had to get back to work the next morning, even though he begged me not to.

"You need another day of rest," he insisted.

"I need the money more."

He scowled, not liking that answer. "We have to figure something else out for you, Bex. You're taking so long to recover because your body's exhausted. You can't work as much as you do."

I didn't point out that I got sick after partying all day and night, and probably from kissing Ty, who'd also been sick. Of course, Mason did have a point about how long it had taken me to recover. Ty had apparently been better after twenty-four hours, but it'd taken me more than twice as long. I still didn't feel quite up to par.

"I'm going to look into a few things for you and your sister and your mother," he said as he walked me out to the car. "I hate this, Bex. I hate you working so much. I hate being so far away."

He leaned down and gave me a kiss goodbye, the first one since I'd practically jumped him in the parking lot of the steak house. My toes curled again.

"I'll see you soon, precious," he said as he pressed his forehead to mine.

"Precious?" I asked skeptically.

"Yes. You should know that you're quite precious to me." He kissed the tip of my nose and headed for his car.

As I slid into mine, I heard a door slam. Not a car door, and not my house door. It came from the trailer next to mine. Ty's. I shut my car door, leaned back in my seat and closed my eyes. My heart ached for what I knew I needed to do.

In my search for The One, I'd never had this problem before. Two men I cared about. Two *delicious* men who cared about me. But I obviously couldn't be with both, and I needed to make a decision before I led one of them on any further than I already had. This decision would be one of the hardest I'd ever had to make, because I had strong feelings for both, but I knew deep down which one was right for me.

And it killed me to have to break the other man's heart. I could only hope mine wouldn't be broken in return.

CHAPTER 16

Bex

WHEN I CAME home from work that night, no Ty sat on my steps waiting for me. He must have moved his few belongings out of his trailer while I worked, because not even his truck sat outside. I tried calling him and left messages, but he never returned them. Mason's presence while I was sick must have really hurt Ty, and I felt horrible about it all, but didn't know what to do when he refused to acknowledge I even existed. If I could have taken a break to sit at his house and wait for him, I would have, but my couple of days off had cost me too much. I needed every hour, every tip I could get to make up for it. The more time that went by, the worse I felt. Elizabeth kept telling me to take care of it because she felt the darkness over town growing even stronger, and apparently, that was entirely my fault. Maybe it was because my heart was breaking all over again.

Finally, between breakfast and lunch on Friday, she practically kicked me out the door to find Ty and talk to him. But I couldn't find him. He wasn't at his new place and not at the trailer picking up anything he'd left behind. He wasn't at the only gym in town, but I found Jeric at the silver Airstream, and he said Ty had gone to Gainesville for a few days. Well then. That was that. There were two things in Gainesville that I knew about: his other best friend who still hadn't graduated college and probably never would; and college parties and beer. Oh, and girls.

I didn't cry, though. I knew this would happen. I knew he'd eventually leave me, and I'd promised myself I'd never cry over Ty Daniels again. I couldn't be the girl he wanted and needed, and that's why I'd made the decision I had. But my heart still felt heavy. He could have at least given me the chance to talk to him about it and try to be friends.

On my way back to Memaw's, Sullivan's called and said they didn't need me to work that night. They'd accidentally scheduled too many bartenders and since they gave me more shifts than anyone, they had to give someone else the opportunity to work. I supposed it was only fair, but with the money I'd already lost earlier in the week, losing the tips, especially on a Friday night, would hurt. Feeling completely bummed, I called Mason as soon as Elizabeth sent me home right after the last lunch guest left.

"Come down here," Mason said. "I know your mom would like to see you, and she's not the only one."

I sighed. "I can't afford the gas."

"If you have enough to get here, I'll fill your tank."

"Mason—"

"Don't argue with me, Bex. Let me do one little thing for you. What else are you going to do? Sit at home alone and mope? There are people here who care about you."

I guess those were the magic words, because I packed an overnight bag, left Uncle Troy a note to say I'd be in the office by noon, and drove down to Orlando. I spent some time with Mama and Sissy at Mama's shitty little apartment that smelled like stale cigarette smoke and urine.

"Maybe we should move her back home," I said to Sissy once we stepped outside while Mama slept. My nose involuntarily wrinkled as I looked over the second-floor railing at the so-called courtyard below. It was nothing more than patches of crabgrass and sand, littered by the wind with bottles, wrappers, and plastic bags. Perhaps a few needles and syringes, too. Graffiti decorated many doors and walls, on a background of faded pink paint that had probably come out of the can when I was in the first grade. Most windows to the other apartments were covered with sheets or blankets instead of curtains, half of them falling down in one corner.

I turned to my sister, who stared at me with round eyes and her brows raised to her hairline. "You'd really let her move in to the trailer?"

"Believe me, it's not my favorite idea," I said, hating it wholeheartedly, to be honest, "but it's technically her trailer, and I never thought I'd say it was better than anywhere, but it's definitely better than here. And getting you guys out of here would save us a few hundred dollars a month in rent."

"The government pays her rent here."

The government did cover most of Mama's rent since it was Section 8 housing, but not all, and there were utilities, too. Sissy tended to forget these things, but I didn't want to argue about it now. "Still, it would be easier, wouldn't it?"

"Not really. Her doctors are here. If something happens …" Sissy trailed off. "Besides, she's already got the county here helpin' her out, and we'd have to start the paperwork and everything all over at home. And with doctors visits, we'd be spending a lot of money on gas, and I'm sure the oxygen deliveries would be more expensive since it's so out of the way …"

"Okay, okay, I get it." She had a point with those extra costs, and I almost sighed with relief for a variety of reasons—mostly that I didn't want the stress of coming home after multiple shifts to feeling obligated to help Sissy take care of Mama. But I hated being so far away, and I hated this place where they lived. As soon as Mason called when he was done at the hospital, I was more than ready to skedaddle.

"Are you sure you don't want to stay here tonight?" Sissy asked, and I had to suppress a shudder. "I don't like you driving all the way home. It'll be dark soon."

"I'll be fine," I said, not exactly lying to her. I just didn't give her the whole truth. "Uncle Troy's expecting me tomorrow."

"You could leave early enough in the morning."

"Yeah, I could," I said even as I hugged her goodbye. "Tell Mama bye. I'll be back when I can."

Sissy squeezed me hard. As I walked away, I told myself not to look back because I didn't think I could bear the look I imagined on her face. I really didn't want to leave her in this hellhole. She kept it clean and sanitary inside, but the whole building gave me the willies and no amount of bleach and ammonia could cover the grime and odors trapped in the walls. When I reached my car, I couldn't help but look up at Mama's apartment on the second floor. Sissy still stood outside the door, but she wasn't alone. Some guy, about our age, was leaning against the railing, and her laugh—the giddy one she used only with guys she liked—carried down to me.

Well, then. Guess she'd be okay.

I'd barely turned off the ignition after parking at the restaurant Mason told me to meet him at when he yanked my door open and pulled me out of my seat. He held me at arm's length for a moment as his eyes skidded appreciatively down from my face to my toes and back up, lingering on my lips until I smiled.

"I missed you terribly," he said before grasping my face in his hands and crushing his mouth on mine. The welcome kiss didn't last long enough for my liking, so when he tried to pull away, I dug my fingers into his thick, dark hair and tugged him back. Once my knees began to quake, I finally let him free. He slid his tongue over his lips. "Mmm ... that's what I call a sweet hello."

I smiled and gave a little shrug. "I might have missed you a little, too."

He slid his arm around my waist and pulled me up against his side, and then we headed for the restaurant doors. A rush of noise hit us when we entered, and I could have kissed him again for bringing me to a bar-grill kind of place rather than another fancy steak house. It was happy hour on Friday, so a large crowd packed the bar area, and Mason took my hand to lead me through it. We stopped at a six-top bar table, and Mason began introductions. Three guys, three women, all older than me and dressed smartly for business, though their top few buttons were undone and their ties loosened in a display of freedom for the weekend. When Mason took two beers out of the bucket on the table, I realized these weren't mere acquaintances. Good heavens, he was introducing me to his friends!

I wanted to return to the steak house. At least we were alone there. These people wanted to talk, the girls especially. They practically attacked me with all kinds of questions, particularly where I was from (because, being Yanks, they adored my accent) and what I "did" (as if I "did" one particular thing).

"So you're putting yourself through school while bartending and waiting tables?" one of them asked as her professionally manicured fingers twirled the straw of her Cosmo. Her tone sounded genuinely curious ... and genuinely presumptuous so it was barely even a question. I didn't have a chance to answer before she added, "What are you getting your degree in?"

"Um ..." I blinked, trying to control the swirl of emotions running through me that made it impossible to think. *A master's in none-of-your-fucking-business*, I wanted to say, but these were Mason's friends. I'm sure I was embarrassment enough without making it worse for him by letting my Southern redneck show even more.

"Bex's future plans are on hold right now," Mason answered for me as he turned toward us girls. I didn't think he was listening, absorbed in his own conversation with the guys. He took my hand and squeezed it. "Unlike you, Natalie, she's too smart to spend five years in school on a degree she'll never use. How are things at Bloomingdale's, anyway?"

Natalie narrowed her eyes for a moment, then put on a fake smile that would have made my Grams proud and launched into a ramble about her "private clients." I couldn't figure out what she did for them, except to bring them clothes and accessories and sometimes even food to the fitting rooms. She sounded like a glorified sales clerk, if you asked me. Still, judging by the designer clothes and the jewelry she wore, and how her hair was perfectly styled, she made a ton more money than I did.

"Sorry about Natalie," Mason said later as he walked me to my car. "I think she grew up in a country club and has no clue of the real world."

I simply nodded.

"Everyone else was nice, though, right?"

"Yeah, sure," I said as I focused my attention on unlocking my car door. He grasped the handle before I could and pulled it open, then turned me to look at him.

"What's wrong?" he asked, the space between his eyebrows creasing.

"Nothing," I said, putting on my most important accessory. "What now?"

"That smile doesn't fool me." He grasped my chin and ran his thumb over my bottom lip. "Did something happen?"

I sighed, but didn't let go of my smile. "It's really nothing. I didn't fit in, is all. But it's over, and I'm fine. It's just you and me, now, right?"

He chuckled. "To tell you the truth, I don't really fit in with them, either. I've just known most of them since I moved down here, so they're kind of friends by default. Haven't had time to make others." He leaned in and brushed his lips over mine. "And yeah, just you and me now. Do you want to go somewhere else?"

"I don't really know where there is to go."

He left his hand against my face as he considered this. "There are plenty of places around here, but let's take your car back to my place so we don't have to caravan around town. Follow me?"

I nodded, and he gave me another kiss as though he were saying goodbye for a week rather than a few minutes. I followed him to a large, upscale condominium complex, and then toward the back. Finally, he stopped and stuck his hand out the window, waving me forward. I pulled up next to him and rolled down my window.

"Park in space 66," he said, pointing at the one to the front of my right bumper. "I'll take the visitor's spot."

I parked and slid out of the driver's seat, then reached to the backseat for my overnight bag.

"Now that's what I call a view," Mason said from behind me, and I jerked upward, hitting my head on the doorjamb. I yelped, and he swept me into his arms. "Oh, precious, I'm so sorry."

He peppered kisses all over my face.

"I'll live," I said, giggling at his overreaction. "I happen to know this hot doctor who will take good care of me if it's serious."

"Damn right," he murmured as he used his body to push me backward, up against my car, where he proceeded to give me another bone-melting kiss. "Let's take your stuff inside, then we can decide where to go."

He grabbed my bag from me, locked and shut my car door, then took my hand and led me up the stairs to his third-floor unit. I'd never seen a home so immaculate and ... *boring*. Gray walls, black, boxy furniture, white tile floors, glass and marble tables, but no knickknacks, no snapshots on the walls or end tables, nothing that made it feel like a *home*. Not even a throw pillow, for heaven's sake. Mama's hospital room had been homier than this. The only "adornment" on the walls was the one in the dining room covered in a floor-to-ceiling mirror—as if reflecting the barren room made it any more interesting.

"Do you *live* here?" I asked as I walked past the bright white kitchen that looked like it had never been used and into the open dining room/living room area. Not a single thing said this was Mason's place—not a hat, a set of keys, a phone charger cord, nothing.

"Most people would say I live at the hospital," he said, "but I do hang out here once in a while. I'm usually unconscious, though."

"What about your brother?" No evidence he even existed.

Mason shifted his weight from one foot to the other. "Fraternity brother. And he went back north last week. We didn't make good roommates."

Something sounded a little off, but I still wasn't ready to pry into his business. If he wanted me to know, he'd tell me. Or when things got really serious—like a proposal—he'd have to fess up then. Whoa nelly, did I really just go there? Nothing like getting a little ahead of myself.

Mason set my bag on the floor next to him, glanced at it, puckered his mouth as though he sucked a lemon, and picked it back up. He nodded to the door on the right side of the living room.

"Guest room," he said, and then he tilted his head toward the door on the left side of the room. "My room."

He was asking me to pick where I wanted to sleep tonight! I lifted a corner of my mouth, walked over to the guest room, and opened the door. More gray walls, a black bedspread, and white furniture made it as plain and stark as the rest of the condo. Nothing to show that anyone had been living here a week ago. I sauntered over to the bed, sat down and bounced a few times.

"I guess this will do," I said when Mason stood in the door.

I watched his face carefully, keeping my own straight. His eyes tightened in the slightest way before he set my bag down on a chair that appeared to belong with the dining room set.

"Do you need to freshen up?" he asked, his voice hesitant.

I couldn't help the burst of laughter. He'd been acting so gentlemanly and now this?

He smiled. "I mean before we go out."

"Oh." Why was he acting so weird? So formal and uptight?

I kicked off my shoes and moved backward on the bed. His eyes never left me. I leaned forward onto my knees and hands. He still stared, crossing his arms over his chest.

"What if I said I'm ready for bed?" I asked.

"I'd say you're lame," he replied. "And a liar."

I pursed my lips together, trying not to smile. "What if I mean I'm ready to *play* in bed?" His eyes grew the size of sliced pickles, the reaction I wanted. I sprang to my feet and jumped on the bed. "Like this."

He watched me jump a few times, open and closed his mouth, and blew out a breath. Then without warning, he lunged for me. I leapt out of his way, laughing hysterically and still jumping. He reached again, and I hopped back. He threw one of the pillows at me, and I caught it. With a devious look in his eyes, he grabbed the other pillow and jumped to his feet. We both swung at the same time, and we both ducked simultaneously, too, dodging the hits. I swung again and the momentum of the pillow took me down with it. Mason's pillow hit me on the ass, knocking me over. I grabbed for his legs and pulled him down with me. We both crashed to the mattress, unable to breathe through the fits of laughter.

Panting, I tried to roll to my back under Mason's weight. He shifted just enough so I could, and when I landed, I stared straight up into those mesmerizing, silvery-green eyes. He braced himself on his elbows over me, his gaze sliding over my face until it reached my lips, where it once again became stuck.

"Do you really want to go out again?" I asked, my voice low and hoarse from the squeals and laughter.

His eyes came back up to mine. "Only if you want to. I didn't want you to think I only wanted you to come here because I expected something."

"Mason," I said, quietly but firmly. He ceased all movement, even his breathing, as he stared down into my eyes. "I *am* expecting something. In fact, I'm expecting quite a lot."

He studied me for a moment, then a slow smile stretched across his face. "A lot, huh?"

He ducked down and swept his lips over mine.

"A. Lot." I confirmed.

"Is that a challenge?"

"Are you up for it?"

He didn't answer me with words, but with actions. Lots of actions. On my lips, my chin, my neck, my collarbone, and everywhere further south. He kissed me, caressed me, stroked me, and performed all kinds of beautiful acts until he left me screaming and panting his name at the same time, my hands clawing into the bed. And then he hovered over me, tribal tattoos on his bare chest and a savage look in his eye, right before he thrust into me and had me screaming all over again until we climaxed together. He collapsed on top of me, still shuddering.

"Did that meet your expectations?" he asked after a few minutes, when both of us were able to breathe again. He shifted to the side of me, removing his full weight from my body, but leaving his arm draped across my chest.

"Mmm ... it was good," I said, running my fingernails lightly over his back.

He lifted his head to look at me, his eyes glazed and the corners of his mouth turned up. "It was more than good. Admit it."

My eyes rolled up to the ceiling as I pretended to consider this. His hand slid down my side, over my hip and across my thigh until his fingers tickled my center. I was still so sensitive, my pelvis jumped at the light touch.

"Okay, okay, it met my expectations."

"Only met?" He tickled me again.

My muscles clenched. "You keep that up, and I'll be expecting more. Right now."

I lifted his hand with my own and returned it to my stomach.

"Because it was so good," he said lazily. "Say it. Say I far exceeded your expectations."

I giggled, but when I looked back into his eyes, I couldn't be sure if he was teasing or not.

"You have no clue just how far you exceeded them," I said. He gave me an approving smile. "But ... that only means I'll be expecting more. Very soon."

His grin grew. "You can count on it."

He dropped his head next to me, and the weight of his arm grew heavier.

"Mason," I said, "you do know I have no desire to sleep in here, right?"

"Thank God," he muttered, but he didn't move. Not for a while anyway. We both lay on the guest bed, still on top of the covers, Mason dozing while I stared at the ceiling. For the first time ever, I didn't feel guilty about what just happened. Every other time, no matter who I was with or how good it was or how long we'd been together, something about it felt wrong. Or if not exactly wrong, at least neutral. No feeling at all. But this ... with Mason ... this felt right. Extremely right.

That's when I began to seriously consider he was The One.

After his little catnap, he carried me into his room. Still no belongings out, no photos, no personalization at all. A nice, neat, clean place to lay his head was all it was. By the time we were done, though, the room looked as though a tornado hit with blankets and pillows everywhere. We rolled up in a sheet and passed out from sheer exhaustion.

I awoke to the fragrance of bacon cooking, and my mouth watered immediately. My stomach growled. I'd been too anxious to eat much of the bar-food appetizers last night, my insides twisted in knots while we were with Mason's friends, and I'd certainly burnt all those calories after we came home. When I sat up, I gasped at how clean his room was already. He'd even properly arranged me in the bed where I belonged, rather than the upside-down, diagonal position we'd slept in. My bag sat on a chair identical to the one in the guest room. After a quick brush of my teeth and pat down of my hair, I threw on the pajama shorts and tank I'd brought and walked out to the kitchen. The clock showed 7:45. I had a couple of hours before I had to leave to get back to the office.

"I didn't think you actually cooked here," I said as I hopped up onto the counter. Mason gave me a strange look. Well, more specifically, he gave my ass on his counter a look, probably because a little café table sat in front of the kitchen window, but I wanted to be here, right next to him. He made no complaint, though, and handed me a cup of coffee.

"That's part of my plan," he said. "If I didn't like you, I could have easily sent you on your way, and you wouldn't have thought twice about no breakfast."

"So since you're cooking for me, that means you like me?" I asked as I watched him over my coffee cup.

His head turned to face me, and he leveled me with those stunning eyes. I didn't think I'd ever get used to them. "I more than like you, beautiful Bex. If it were up to me, I'd be cooking you breakfast every morning."

My heart stuttered. What was he getting at with that kind of statement? His cell phone rang at that precise moment. He glanced at the screen, then snatched it up. He'd barely left the kitchen when he jogged back in again.

"On my way," he said, and he dropped the phone on the counter while reaching for the spatula. "Emergency. I need to go. Can you finish up here?"

Already turning for the doorway, he swung the spatula toward me, but it hit the carton of eggs. The whole kit-and-kaboodle tumbled to the floor with a bunch of splats as the eggshells broke. A great, gooey mess spread across the shiny white tiles.

"Son of a bitch, mother fucking bastards!" he barked, loud enough to make me cringe. "God damn it!"

I stared at him for a moment, shocked, and then jumped down from the counter, careful to avoid the smashed eggs. My heart pounding from the outburst, I pressed my hands on his chest. "Go. I got this. Don't worry about it."

"*Shit.* I'm sorry." He sighed.

"I said don't worry about it. Go on. You have an emergency, remember?"

He glanced at the mess on the floor. "You don't mind?"

"No. Now go." I shoved him out of the kitchen.

He was dressed in scrubs in two minutes and flying out the door. I mopped up the eggs, finished the bacon and made myself some toast to go with it. Then I cleaned the kitchen up before heading to the guest room. I figured I should toss the bedspread in the wash, but when I opened the door, he already had that room cleaned to perfection, too.

"Bit of a neat freak," I muttered as I padded back to his room.

Once I was dressed and had my bag on my shoulder, I stood in the entranceway by the kitchen, unsure of what to do. He lived in a nice area, but I'd noticed last night that he'd had both the doorknob and the bolt locks fastened. I sent him a text, although I didn't expect an answer. As I was about to walk out, planning to lock only the knob from the inside, I received a text back:

"Spare key in the junk drawer. I want you to have it."

I opened a few drawers and found what I assumed to be the junk drawer, but I couldn't help but laugh. If there was any junk in it, it was hidden between the orderly rows of containers holding rubber bands, batteries, pens, and other small items. Even his junk drawer was perfectly organized.

As I left, I wondered how he could stand to stay in my trailer the few days he had. I figured it was because he was a doctor that he kept things, even his home, practically sterile.

"I miss you," Mason texted a few hours later, although I didn't see it until I locked up the park office at precisely six o'clock. "Come back."

An hour after that text, had come another: "I found a piece of eggshell on the floor."

I didn't know what that was supposed to mean. Some kind of euphemism?

"Oh. Oops," I texted back as I walked home. My phone rang almost immediately.

"Oops?" Mason asked.

"Oops about the eggshell."

"That's all you can say?" His voice did not sound at all like he missed me. More like a father's to a misbehaving child. "You promised you'd clean it all up."

"Hey, you knocked it over. The whole damn carton. Sorry if I missed a piece. Anal much? And is this really what you've been thinking about my visit?"

Silence came from the other end, then a sigh. "I'm sorry. Yeah, I can be anal. Raw eggs can contain salmonella, and being a doctor makes me a little germaphobic."

I opened my front door. "Well, I'm not a doctor but I have been working at a diner since I was fourteen, and I know all about food safety. I'm sorry if I missed a piece on that white tile of yours, but I can guarantee it was bleached with the rest of the floor."

"Bex, I'm sorry for snapping at you. It's been a long day and not a good one."

"Your emergency?"

"Yeah. Doesn't look good."

"I'm sorry," I said softly. "I wish I could make you feel better."

"Come back."

I chuckled as I sat on the couch in front of the window and looked at the sky turning peach and pink. "I wish I could. But I gotta work again tomorrow, and I'm not about to become a two-hour commuter."

"I miss you," he said. "I miss those plump, sweet lips of yours."

We talked for a good long while until both of our batteries were dying, and even then, it was hard to hang up.

"*Please* come see me. I'll pay for your gas," he said the next day, and I had to give in. I'd barely been able to concentrate on work because I'd been thinking about him all day.

For the next few weeks, I drove down to see him every couple of days, stopping in to see Mama and Sissy only about half the times, though, because I didn't want them knowing exactly how often I was making the trip. It was irresponsible, but I didn't care. I had way too many responsibilities for my age, and if I wanted to be a little carefree, I would.

A couple of times a week became every time I didn't have to work at Sullivan's, which was becoming more frequent. Although the locals were drinking as heavy as ever, business from the truckers was slacking off. They seemed to be avoiding the truck stop all together. Elizabeth blamed it on the dark cloud hanging over the area, although I didn't see it. Sunny skies as always for this time of year. Leni offered to give up a few of her shifts, saying she didn't need them, but I didn't want her to lose her job. Ever since the K-bomb, she and I had become closer, and she was about the only thing that made working at Sullivan's worth it. The locals didn't exactly tip well.

"Move in with me," Mason said one morning before I had to make the drive home.

"What about my jobs?"

"Screw them. Get a job here. You could work one job here and make more money than you do at all three in Lake Haven. And you don't have to pay rent or utilities or anything. Not even food."

"Mason, I can't live off of you."

"Why not? I *want* you to."

I sighed. The offer was seriously tempting. The more time I spent in Orlando, the more I realized that I could be making tons more money there. Plus, it'd save a bunch of time and gas, and I'd be a lot closer to Sissy and Mama, who'd made little improvement.

But move in with Dr. Mason Hayes?

I really liked him, maybe even loved him, but I just wasn't sure if I was ready to make that leap. Especially those mornings when I'd awake from a haunting dream of a man calling for me. He had eyes kind of like Mason's, but they seemed lighter in my dream. More like gray than green. And his voice was even sexier, but sad, almost desperate sounding, to the point where I couldn't understand what he said. But I somehow knew he called for me, troubling me the entire day after.

"Move in with me, Bex," Mason said again a week after the first time. "You know you want to. You know it makes total sense. And ..." He paused for a moment before gushing, "And I love you. I want to be with you every day. I want to wake up to your precious face every morning and hold you in my arms every night as I fall asleep. I love you, Bex."

Oh, shit. That was my undoing. I couldn't help but say the words back.

"So you'll move in with me?"

"Let me think about it," I said.

I didn't have to think about it long. When Memaw's burnt down from a grease fire, I was pretty much screwed here anyway. I felt horrible for Elizabeth and Aunt Faye and wished there was something I could do for them, but they decided to keep the insurance money instead of rebuilding, leaving me high and dry ... and on my way to Orlando.

Once the decision was made, my heart did a strange little leap. I could only reckon that meant I was doing the right thing. That I belonged with Dr. Mason Hayes. That he was The One.

CHAPTER 17

Leni "I CAN'T BELIEVE you're moving down there," I said as I grabbed a sheet of newspaper and a ceramic angel from Bex's shelf. "I hate saying goodbye when we were just becoming good friends."

"Aw, I know." She gave me a look full of sympathy. "I know it's not easy around here, but it's not like I'm movin' across the country. Ya'll can come see us in Orlando any time. Mason has a guest room, so you don't even have to splurge for a motel."

"Sullivan's won't be the same, though," I said. Not that I planned on staying there much longer. The job had been a way to get to know Bex better and to catch any gossip from town, but, sensing the Shadowmen growing restless, I wouldn't need the job much longer—one way or another, I had a feeling we'd be learning who their target was soon. On a different note, or maybe not, I also had a feeling Bex was making a huge mistake moving in with this Mason guy. "Are you sure you want to take everything?"

Bex looked around the trailer, which even in its prime hadn't been exactly luxurious and now was out-right rundown. The floors were soft in places. Water stains marked the ceiling. Duct tape held the mauve carpet in place. More duct tape, the kind that came in different colors and in this case hot pink, also held many other items together, including the refrigerator door handle. The furniture appeared to be as old as Bex herself. She kept the place clean, but no amount of scrubbing would make the aged surfaces shine.

I could understand *why* she was excited about moving away from here. She'd opened up to me enough that I knew she wanted nothing more than to escape this world where she'd grown up. I just wasn't sure about how she was doing it.

"I don't trust my Uncle Troy," Bex said as she ran tape over the bottom of an empty box. I was surprised it wasn't hot pink, too. "He was madder than a hornet when I told him I was quittin' and finally gettin' out of here. He said he'd give me a month, and I'd better be back, or he'd rent this place out."

"At least he gave you a month," I said. "In case things don't work out."

She stopped what she was doing, and her shoulders sank. "Oh, Leni, they *have* to work out. I'm giving up everything for this chance to finally be happy. I'll be close to Mama, and Mason's even going to get her a home nurse so Sissy can have some time off, and she and I can spend more time together. Mama's doing a little better, so that's a good sign. Who knows? Maybe this was what she needed to make her realize what she has in Sissy and me. Maybe all of this happened—her illness and everything—to bring us all together."

Handing her the figurines I'd wrapped so far, I studied her face. Her eyes were bright with hope, and I had a feeling this was the first time in a long time she'd felt such a thing as hope. I pushed back the frown wanting to claim my face and returned her smile.

"I really feel like he could be The One, Leni," Bex continued. "He's so sweet and gentlemanly and kind. And so generous. He's always saying he's a selfish bastard, but he's wrong. Nobody's ever been so concerned about me and what I want and need. He got Mama the help she needs, too, even going out on a limb by signing some papers. I just can't imagine anyone more perfect."

I tilted my head, sensing an opportunity. "Do you think Mason's your soul mate? Do you believe in them?"

She grinned. "I do believe in them! I think we each have someone we're supposed to be with, you know? The problem is finding them in this big world, and I don't think everyone's lucky enough to do that. In fact, judgin' by the divorce rate, I think most people end up hookin' up with the wrong person more often than not."

"It's a shame, don't you think?"

"Yeah, it is," she said with a sigh.

"I definitely know Jeric's mine. I feel it in here." I pressed my hand against my chest, watching Bex carefully. Something flickered across her face, but too quickly for me to understand. I hedged further. "In fact, I feel like our connection goes even deeper. Have you ever heard of Twin Flames?"

Her expression definitely changed, her eyes showing a note of familiarity. "Hmm ... I think I've heard of them. Liz'beth must have mentioned them once."

"From what I've read, they're even more connected than soul mates because they actually used to be the same soul, but it's been split in two. The two halves are always searching for each other, sometimes finding each other right away, sometimes not. Sometimes it takes lifetimes."

"Like more than one lifetime?" Bex asked, skepticism lacing her tone. "As in reincarnation?"

"Yeah, crazy, huh? And really sad, too, if they never find each other. I can't imagine how horrible that would be. It must make a person desperate." I couldn't help but hold my breath as I waited for her response.

She rolled her eyes and snorted. "Sounds like bull-honky to me. I don't believe in reincarnation. Preacher says only Jesus overcame death and lived again, and the only way for us to live forever is through Jesus, and that means in heaven. Thinkin' anything else will give us a one-way ticket straight to hell." Her eyes narrowed, and she tilted her head as she looked at me. "You don't believe you and Jeric are these Twin Flames, do you? Or in reincarnation?"

I gave a nonchalant shrug. "Who really knows what comes after this life?"

"Preacher seems to. Says it's all spelled out in the Bible. God's Word and all. Came straight from The Man Himself."

I knew it was probably pointless to push it any further, but I thought maybe planting the seed in Bex's mind could at least make her think about it more ... and maybe ignite some kind of memory, or, if anything, the tiniest bit of recognition at the soul level. *If* she was Rebethannah, anyway, and until I could prove my intuition right, that was still a big, fat if.

"Right," I agreed. "But wouldn't God have to put everything in terms we lowly humans could relate to? And back then, when they knew so little about this world, let alone anything about the universe, they could only comprehend so much. Like, maybe God said he created worlds—lots of them, all with people—but back then, they thought this was the only world. That everything revolved around this planet, right? So they'd write that he created earth, just one, because that was the extent of their understanding. Then, of course, there's the fact that words had different meanings then than they do now."

"Yeah, yeah. I've heard people argue about the Bible being translated lots of times, too, so meanings probably changed. But if those were God's people doin' the translatin', then they had to have done it right. Right? And usually the people arguin' are the ones who want to pick and choose which parts to follow."

I snickered at her last statement. "Yeah, I guess you have a point there. I'm just saying that maybe we don't really *get* the Bible or God or any of the religions, really. Like you said, we can't compare ourselves to God, so how can we say we know everything at His level?"

She hesitated, and then gave her own shrug. "All I know is what I've been taught all these years, and it's enough to put the fear of God in me. But you can believe whatever you want. I'm the last person who has any right to get all judgy. I just know I've done enough to be sent to hell as it is, and there's no need to make things worse by second-guessin' God."

I had to give her props for holding steadfast in her beliefs, but I kind of wanted to shake her until her mind—and her soul—opened up to hear what I was trying to tell her. If I knew for sure she was Rebethannah and a good shaking would wake her up, I might have even done it. But I didn't know, and all I could do was hope that maybe she'd find herself thinking about the little seed I'd planted and it would grow into an actual memory for her. Again—*if* my instinct was right and she was Rebethannah.

But I had to give one more stab, from a different angle.

"I'm totally changing the subject here—"

She giggled nervously. "Yeah, we're gettin' a little deep, aren't we?"

Not as deep as I'd preferred, but I'd pushed in that direction too far already. "Let's talk about boys again."

"Oh, now that's more my speed," she said with a real laugh.

"Do you know anyone named Nathan or Aiden or even Nathayden? Anything that sounds like that?"

"Um … no. Don't think so. Why? A new boy now? I thought you said Jeric was your soul mate."

"No, not for me. Just a name I overheard recently. But I don't know if I heard it right, and I hadn't met anyone around here with a name anything like that."

She paused and seemed to consider something. "Well, Mason kind of sounds like Nathan, right? And his last name is Hayes. I'm sure lots of people are talking about him, now that word's out I'm movin' away. A bunch of the old gossipin' women are expectin' me to start showing any day now. Nobody believes I'm not pregnant!"

She carried on about the town's rumors, but I tuned her out, thinking about Mason's name. Excitement of a new thought fluttered in my gut. I wished I could think about it harder, but it would have to wait.

"And, goin' back to your question about Mason," Bex continued, coming full circle, "I think he *is* my soul mate. He's too perfect for me."

"Well, then, maybe this was all meant to be," I said as I reached over and patted her knee before grabbing another sheet of newspaper.

A picture in the paper caught my eye—and my breath. I read the caption, then glanced up at the dateline. I gnawed on my bottom lip for a second.

"Mind if I keep this page?" I asked, already folding it neatly.

"Find something interesting?"

I stuffed the folded paper into the back pocket of my jeans shorts. "Maybe. I want to read the article later."

"Sure, take it. It's not like we don't have enough. I think Mason collected every spare issue of the Orlando papers he could find. If we run out, I can have him bring more. He's coming up later to help move all these boxes." She clapped her hands together. "Ya'll should come over! Brock and Asia, too. We can have one last cookout here, and all ya'll can finally meet Mason."

I glanced out the window to where Ty's truck used to sit when he lived here. "Ty's fighting today. If he wins, like Jeric expects he will, we'll probably already have plans."

Jeric had wanted me to come to the fight, which I always did when they were out of town because the separation was too much for our souls—and Jeric's comfort level for my safety. But this fight was in Misty Springs, only one town over, and I'd already promised Bex I'd help her pack. And I'd much rather pack than watch a couple of grown guys beat each other up for fun. We had enough real fighting with real bad guys in our life. Besides, I couldn't pass up this opportunity for some quiet one-on-one time with this soul. I'd hoped to feel a stronger connection than I'd been able to make so far.

Bex's shoulders sank, and she looked out the window towards Ty's old place, too. "Guess he wouldn't want Mason and me there for his celebration."

I studied the angel figurine—Bex had quite the collection, and this one was painted solid black, which seemed odd to me— as I turned it over in my hands. "Have you talked to him yet?"

She sighed. "He refuses to have a thing to do with me. Won't take my calls or return them. I swear he has a camera out, watching for when I head to his place so he can disappear. Probably just has people ratting me out when they spot me comin'. Everyone's on his side, of course, blamin' me for breakin' his heart so bad. They forget that he did it to me first."

"He'll come around," I said, though I wasn't sure about that. I hadn't seen much of Ty myself, but Jeric said he was in bad shape, taking out his anger in the practice ring and the cages. "I'm sure, in the end, he wants you to be happy. If Mason does that for you better than he ever could, he'll see that you two really don't belong together as anything more than friends. Then he'll find his own perfect mate."

"I hope so," she whispered. "I want him to be happy. I just know I'm not the one to do it."

She sniffled before rearranging the box to fit the rest of her angel collection. We finished packing it in silence.

"Wow," Bex suddenly breathed as I handed her the last one. I looked up at her. "I just had this crazy feeling of déjà vu. Like you and me have done this before."

I froze. She laughed and shook herself.

"Liz'beth loves when that happens," she said. "Says we'd probably known each other in a past life and done something similar." She laughed nervously. "More of that reincarnation crap. Anyway, it's such a weird feeling, ya know?"

My heart skipped a beat. I did know. I knew about the feeling, and I knew Elizabeth was right, regardless of Bex's beliefs in reincarnation. We *had* known each other in a past life, and we *had* done something similar. At the end of their freshman year in the dorms, Jacey had helped *her* Bex pack up her room while Bex cursed out another guy she'd broken up with. I was convinced this Bethany sitting next to me hadn't chosen to go by Bex by coincidence. I knew that much. It was the part of whether she was Rebethannah or not where I wished I could be more certain. My instinct whispered that she was, but I still didn't know if I could trust it.

A few minutes later, I sensed Jeric approaching, and I felt his good mood. Ty must have won. About ten minutes later, Bex glanced out the window again.

"There's your truck. Jeric just pulled in," she said as she stood and looked around at the room that was nothing but bare walls and lonely furniture now. "Good timing, too. Looks like we're about done here. Thanks so much for your help, Leni. I can't believe Sissy ditched me."

Jeric knocked on the door a few minutes later. I'd felt him coming over, but was surprised he'd bothered.

"Did he win? Is he okay?" Bex asked as soon as she opened the door.

Jeric grinned, showing his dimples. I didn't know if I'd ever get used to the combination of his piercing blue eyes that could be threatening in themselves, his muscular body with all its ink, and those sweet, boyish dimples when he smiled like that.

"He's fine," Jeric said, but his smile faltered. "Physically anyway. Knocked the other guy out again."

Bex nodded and beamed, though I recognized the falseness of it. "That's good."

"Your sister showed up," Jeric said as he eyed her.

Bex's eyebrows shot up. "*Sissy?* She went to Ty's fight?"

"Yeah. I was almost afraid you'd come with her. That could have been a deadly distraction, so thanks for being here."

"You're welcome," she muttered. "I can't believe her. She did that instead of coming here to help me pack. This is half her shit, too!"

Jeric cocked his head. "It might be a good thing. For both of them."

I understood fully what he meant, feeling it from him, but I didn't know if Bex did. Something seemed to dawn in her eyes, though.

"So I guess all ya'll will be celebrating together," she said.

"Actually, Ty and Sissy stayed over in Misty Springs to celebrate with a bunch of their friends. I think they wanted to rub it in to the people over there," Jeric said.

Bex snorted. "Not surprised. They've always been a rival, thinkin' they're better than us and everything." She looked at Jeric and then me, her eyes bright again. "So then ya'll can have a cookout with Mason and me, right?"

Jeric and I exchanged a look, and I nodded. After the discussion Bex and I had just had, I wanted nothing more at the moment than to meet this Mason, especially with the revelation that Mason Hayes did kind of sound like it could be a version of Nathayden.

Jeric rubbed his hand over his head. "I'd already asked Brock and Asia to come over."

"Bex," I said, "why don't you and Mason come over to our place? Your stuff is already packed up, and there's no reason to dirty anything."

She grinned. "Perfect!"

Jeric and I left to make a trip to the grocery store, then clean up and prepare for our guests. He enjoyed the normalcy of planning for our first little dinner party—if you called grilling burgers in the fire pit of our campsite, chips, and beer on the picnic table outside a dinner party. I liked the idea, too, but was even happier that we'd all have the chance to spend time with Bex and Mason.

"Do you still think she's Rebethannah?" Asia asked as we formed hamburger patties inside while Brock and Jeric started the coals outside. Bex had called to say Mason was still thirty minutes away.

"Have you changed your mind?" I asked.

"Nope," Asia said matter-of-factly, shaking her head. Her hair, now a deep violet color, swished over her shoulders. "I don't feel it. But you're the one who's supposed to know long before the rest of us. Remember?"

I scooped up a handful of meat and rolled it around between my palms. "I do still think she was Bex in my past life. And I know for a fact that Bex didn't meet her Twin Flame before she died. She was always searching, though. Just like this one."

"Yeah, I get it," Asia said. "You think she's going Dark. You think the Lakari are here for her. You keep saying that, but we haven't seen a shred of proof of it. In fact, when I saw her at the bar the other night—her last night there?—she was happy, Leni. She practically glowed. I don't think that's how a soul going Dark looks."

I groaned while pressing a patty into shape. "I know. That's what keeps throwing me off. But then I wonder if it's her Darkness that's getting in our way of knowing for sure. And if she is Rebethannah, I can't help but wonder if Nathayden's somewhere else, on a different world, and that's why she's Dark. And why she keeps searching, and why he was trying to reach out to us."

"Or maybe she's one of those souls who hasn't found and Bonded with her soul mate yet," Asia countered. "You have to consider she's not a half of anything. And Nathayden ... we haven't learned anything about him at all. Did you ever get an answer in the Book?"

I frowned and shook my head. "Nothing at all. And as far as we know, nothing exciting's happened at the Gate, either."

"Then he could be anywhere, Leni. He could be on this world alone, or he could be somewhere else completely. He could be with Rebethannah this very minute."

"Yeah, he could be," I admitted as I glanced out the window toward the trailer park. "But I had an idea today when Bex and I were talking. There's a chance we might know tonight when we finally meet this Mason dude."

I told her about our conversation and suggested the possibility that Mason could be Nathayden.

Asia's pixie nose crinkled. "Now that's one option I'm sure is wrong. That makes the least sense of anything. If both of their souls were here, the Guides would have known. The Lakari would be all over them if they'd Bonded. Hell, their Bond would be so strong right now, we wouldn't be having this conversation. We'd know without a doubt."

"You're the one who said everyone's different."

"Yeah, but how long did you say they've been seeing each other? A couple of months, right?"

"I'm not sure when it actually started, but yeah, at least that long, I think."

"I don't think any dyads have gone that long without being attacked or getting soul-sickness."

I looked out the window again, watching Jeric and Brock play with the fire, and sighed. "You're probably right. I'm just so frustrated. I *feel* like we're this close"—I held my finger and thumb within millimeters of each other—"to our answers, yet worlds away from them, too."

As Asia had said, we had no evidence of anything. We were barely better off than the day we'd come to Lake Haven. We didn't even know for sure that the Lakari were after Bex, which meant we were failing in all three of our missions: identifying whom the Lakari hunted, finding Rebethannah, and helping Nathayden. Theo had told me repeatedly to follow my intuition, that it was my soul talking to me, but so far, my soul was just as confused as my brain. And the damn Book hadn't helped us one bit.

"I do think you're about to learn something," she said, lifting her chin toward the window. Bex had come through the trees with a tall, dark, and handsome guy by her side. "I think meeting this Mason will give us answers. They may not be the ones you want, but at least you'll know."

I nodded and put on my smile, though my insides didn't feel so confident. After we washed our hands, I grabbed the plate of raw burgers and followed Asia outside.

On closer inspection, Mason wasn't as handsome as I'd expected or thought he'd been from a distance. At least, not to me, but in my eyes, nobody compared to Jeric. The doctor had more of a pretty-boy face with light-green eyes many might find gorgeous, but I found unnerving. As Bex made introductions, grinning the whole time like a schoolgirl with her first real crush, Mason seemed nice enough. I couldn't help but notice, though, that he appeared to size up Jeric and Brock, even as he joked with them. When it came time to shake my hand, something passed between us, but so quickly, I couldn't identify it.

And I felt absolutely nothing from his soul.

Bex, on the other hand, obviously felt everything. She'd seemed happy with Ty at the party in the field, but only now did I see that had been a ruse. Or maybe it had been the alcohol. She definitely had a connection with Ty, but it wasn't deep and he did nothing for her compared to Mason. She really did glow around him. Her smile appeared genuine, reaching her eyes—no, coming through her eyes and reaching her mouth. She laughed giddily at his jokes, and when she wasn't close enough to touch him, her hand twitched or her leg bounced, as though she ached to be close enough again.

"He's definitely not Nathayden," Brock said after the lovebirds had left. Asia must have told him my lame theory—my hope that had now been squashed. The two of them sat in lawn chairs, and Jeric and I sat backwards on the picnic table bench on the other side of the fire pit. Small flames licked the remainder of the wood in the pit, and the burning coals cast an orange glow on everyone's faces.

"No, he's not," I agreed, my heart sinking with the admission. Jeric slid his arm over my shoulders, trying to relieve the frustration he felt from me.

"He seemed great, though," Asia said. "You can't deny how happy he makes her."

I leaned forward, put my elbow on my knee, and rested my chin in my hand. Was he all that great? Or did he only *seem* great on the outside but had something going on inside? Or was I reading way too much into him? I stared into the fire, as if the flames could provide answers.

"Yeah. If she were in danger of going Dark, I'd say that guy brought her out of it," Brock said.

"Which means he'd be her soul mate, right?" Jeric asked.

"Could be," Asia said. "If they were split souls and reBonded, the Lakari would surely be on the attack by now. They're obviously not. I don't even feel their presence."

I did. As we'd expected, the Lakari had returned after the party, and they still maintained a presence. The Dark ones weren't as close as usual at the moment, but I felt them somewhere nearby. Still, they certainly weren't riled up and trying to stop a pair of Twin Flames from Bonding.

"So if they're soul mates, it's a simple matter that each of their souls were made for the other, and they found each other this time around," Brock said. "They probably have several cycles to go before they become One. If they ever get there. In other words, not our concern."

"And she's definitely not Rebethannah," Asia added. "No way can a split soul feel the way she obviously does about someone who's not her Twin Flame."

This fact disappointed me the most—because it was so spot on. If there was any proof Bex was not Rebethannah, this was it.

Which meant my instinct about her had been completely wrong. Even just this afternoon, I'd been fairly sure she was Rebethannah, but I knew better now. I couldn't trust my intuition after all. And how was I supposed to do my job for Jeric and everyone else if my instinct was broken?

"At least we know that much now so we can focus on who *is* going Dark around here," Brock said. "My bet's still on Ty."

We'd discussed the possibility of Ty being our mission before, but I didn't feel it. Not then, not now. Ty was heartbroken, yes, but I didn't think he was at risk of going Dark. Not any more than several other people in this town, including Elizabeth. In fact, my bet would be more on her than Ty. But I didn't say any of this aloud.

I remained stuck on Bex. And on Mason. I stared at the fire, trying to work through exactly what I felt in my soul. There was *something*. Something about him, maybe. Definitely something about her. She may not have been Rebethannah, but I still felt a connection to her. I needed to figure out why.

And speaking of someone on the verge of going Dark, I could almost believe it to be Mason. Yes, he seemed to make Bex happy, and he appeared to be happy with her. But appearances could be deceiving. Something lay under his surface, and it definitely didn't feel like Light. If he lived in this town, I'd say with near certainty he was the Lakari's target.

My soul pricked on this idea, and I thought maybe I was on to something. I needed to find out more, though, before I could suggest this new theory to the others. Especially since my instinct had been so far off already.

"I'm sorry, babe," Jeric said later, after Brock and Asia had left. "I know you thought there was more to Bex."

"I still do," I said quietly. "Something's off, Jeric. I can't pinpoint what it is, but I *feel* it."

Ghost strode up and rubbed against my legs. "Mrow," he said.

I picked him up and held him against me as I petted him. He purred appreciatively. "Do you know, Ghost?"

"Mrow," he repeated.

I sighed. "Well, if you do have the answers, you're no help because I don't speak Cat."

I set him in my lap and stroked his back while tilting my head to lean on Jeric's shoulder.

"What do you think we should do?" he asked. "I'm here for *you*, babe. I'm perfectly fine doing what we're doing, but I know I'm supposed to trust you and your instincts. And I'm trying. So tell me what you think we should do."

I snorted. "I'm beginning to wonder if my instincts are worthy of your trust, and I don't know what to do. But we can't dismiss Bex so quickly, Jeric. And I don't think we should blow off Mason, either. As much as it looks like he's good for her, I ..." I lifted my hands, palms up. "I don't buy it. There's still something about them that we need to figure out."

CHAPTER 18

BORED OUTTA MY mind. I'd been in Orlando for over a week and hadn't done much more than play house. Mason worked a lot more hours than I'd realized, and he was hardly ever home. I cleaned all day to meet his perfectionist standards and fixed him dinner, and he gave me an hour or so of attention before either crashing after a double-shift or returning to the hospital for another. For someone used to working every waking hour, I was close to losin' my marbles.

Before I'd even unpacked, I'd gone out and applied for jobs at every restaurant and bar in a ten-mile radius. Nobody talked to me, just gave me applications to fill out, so I'd hit them all in three days. I'd thought it would be easy to find something with my experience, especially with the holidays and tourist season coming up, but either everyone else in Orlando was looking for work, too, or these nicer places simply took more time to make decisions. I was sure if I walked into a honkytonk, they'd hire me on the spot if they had an opening, but I wanted the big tips that you don't get at a hole-in-the-wall beer shack.

"Why don't you try something different?" Mason had asked over dinner last night. "There's a ton of hotels in this city, and your work at the RV office would probably count as experience."

I used my fork to press designs into my mashed potatoes. "I don't know about that."

"How different could it be? It's customer service and assigning rooms to people, just like assigning RV sites, right? And you have tons of customer service experience, too." He shoved a bite of meatloaf in his mouth and chewed it. "Or, there must be an office job for you somewhere."

I looked at him with an eyebrow raised. "Who's going to hire me for an office job? Or for a hotel front desk, for that matter? I have a piercing in my nose and ink in lots of places."

He frowned. "Take the piercing out. Cover the tats with clothes, like I do. You should have probably thought about those things before you got them. Think ahead next time, Bex."

My eyes widened, then I blinked.

"I *did* think ahead and knew I'd never want a stuffy-ass job where I couldn't be myself," I snapped. I stood up and snatched his plate, not caring if he was done eating or not, stacked it with mine and carried them into the kitchen. I couldn't help but add, "Or a stuffy-ass boyfriend, for that matter."

I began rinsing off the dishes until Mason came behind me and took them from my hands. "Let me do them."

"No. I need something to do."

He pressed his body against mine and his mouth to my ear. "You're going to break something, Bex."

I eased my grip on the glass plate, but didn't let go. He remained behind me, his arms wrapped around me as we did the dishes together, his erection growing as it rubbed against my ass the whole time.

"I have plenty for you to do now," he said when we finished cleaning the kitchen.

His gaze slid slowly down my body, clad in a sundress and not much else. In a lightning flash move, he had me backed against the counter and his hand under my dress and in my panties. He stroked me with his finger before sliding it inside me, our eyes locked the whole time, even as I gasped and convulsed. Just as quickly, he removed his hand, making me want for more.

"Take off your dress," he ordered.

Ah. I smiled. We were doing this again. Pretty much since I'd moved in, he'd taken a dominant role in the bedroom. I didn't mind. It was kind of fun, actually.

I glanced at the window with the open curtains.

"I said to take off your dress," he said. "Now what do you say?"

"Um ... the neighbors?" I offered, although I knew that wasn't the answer he was looking for.

He narrowed his eyes. "Fuck them. If they want to watch, let them. Now. Take off your dress, Bex."

He'd been in a kinky mood. Being on the top floor, however, I doubted too many people could see in anyway.

"As you wish, Mason." I pulled the straps off each shoulder, then reached behind me to unzip the back. He watched me closely, hunger in his eyes, as my breasts sprang free from the tight top and the dress dropped and pooled at my feet. He licked his lips as his gaze landed at my panties.

"Turn around. Slowly."

I kicked my dress to the side and did as he said. I may have jutted my ass out a little as I looked over my shoulder at him.

"Damn, Bex, you look good in a thong. Turn back around," he said while he began unbuttoning his shirt.

When I did, I stepped forward to help him, but he shook his head, already done. He slid his shirt off and then his undershirt. I reached out to touch his chiseled chest, wanting to lick his ink, but he grabbed my wrist and yanked my arm down.

"On your knees," he said.

I looked at him with a smile playing on my lips.

"On your knees," he ordered again.

"As you wish, Mason," I said as I dropped to my knees.

He smiled down at me and brought my hand to the bulge in his pants, making me rub it.

"Release my cock," he said, and I undid his buckle and the button and pulled down his pants and boxer-briefs together so that he sprang out at my face. His fingers brushed across my lips, then slid inside, and I sucked them for a moment before he used them to open my mouth wider. At the same time, his other hand clasped the back of my head and pulled me closer to him, so I had no choice but to wrap my lips around him and take him in. "Fuck me with your mouth, Bex."

And hearing him moan, feeling him tremble, knowing I was making him lose control now, that I could bring him to this ... it made being a little submissive worth it. His returning of the favor made it worth it, too. When he was satisfied, he lifted me up to the counter, not complaining now about my ass being on it, and played with my tits before dropping to his own knees and spreading my legs wide. I couldn't help but look at the window, gazing at our reflection and wondering if anyone else was watching, too. Just in case, I did everything to make it a great show, especially when he sprawled me on my stomach across the café table right in front of the window as he entered me from behind and pounded until he collapsed on top of me, both of us trembling.

"I love you exactly as you are," he whispered in my ear afterward, sending an aftershock down my spine.

My days may have been boring as hell, but sex with Mason made up for it all.

Now, I sat on the couch at Mason's immaculate condo, the remote in one hand, and my other one rubbing between my legs, teasing myself while I wished he was home. I thought about making a mess just so I could have something to do by cleaning it up. Daytime TV bored me. Arts and crafts were never my thing, and what would have been the point? Mason had thrown a bit of a hissy fit when he saw some of my things out, decorating this place and making it look more like a home. Turned out, it was a silly matter—he said he felt like my angels were staring at him, making him feel guilty for even touching me in an inappropriate way. Even so, *if* I were to bother making something with my own two hands and he threw another fit, I'd probably punch him.

I tossed the remote on the coffee table and glanced at the clock for the sixtieth time in an hour. Yep, I'd caught it at every single minute. And there were still another ninety-eight minutes to go before Mason should be home. I'd already done the prep work for dinner, so I had eighty-eight minutes to spare before I needed to start cooking. Mason didn't like eating the minute he arrived home, needing time to wash off the ickiness of his day first. Sissy hadn't answered her phone the last time I called, so I couldn't even kill time talking to her.

I flopped sideways onto the hard couch, rolled onto my back and stared at the ceiling. I could never be a housewife. I'd lose my damn mind.

I thought about letting my mind wander into another daydream, maybe finish rubbing one out, but that didn't even sound good compared to the real thing. I wanted to be hot and achy for him. *Eighty-seven minutes*, I thought with a sigh, my groin already throbbing. Hmm ... I wondered if Mason would freak out if I made and served him dinner wearing nothing but an apron. We'd had sex in the kitchen, after all, although we'd spent an hour afterward bleaching everything. No food had been out, though, and how would he react to my naked hooha so close to his dinner?

My cell phone rang, making me jump.

"Sissy," I said, a little excitedly when I answered. "I'm so—"

"Bex," she interrupted with panic in her voice, "you need to get to the hospital immediately."

"What's wrong?"

"Mama's bad, and they're taking her in the ambulance now. Call Mason, okay?"

She hung up without another word. I shot off the couch, ran for my shoes and purse and then for the door while dialing Mason. His voicemail greeted me.

We lived only a few minutes from the hospital, and I arrived there right before the ambulance pulled into the emergency bay. When I tried to follow them inside, though, they shooed me out, telling me to go around to the front desk and start the paperwork. The middle-aged brunette at the desk handed me a clipboard at the same time Sissy came running through the doors.

"What happened?" I asked her as she threw her arms around me.

Sissy stepped back and wiped at her cheeks. "She had a rough night last night, barfin' every time she ate or drank anything, and she just kept gettin' worse today. The last couple of times she ralphed, it was blood."

"Ohmagosh." I took her hand and pulled her into the waiting room with its pale blue walls and lines of blue vinyl-covered chairs. The obligatory TV in the upper corner of the room showed the weather. We sat in the first two seats we came to—only one other person sat in the corner, his crossed arms resting on his round belly and his head lolled to the side as he snored. Hopefully the empty waiting room meant the ER wasn't overly busy inside.

"It's not the first time there's been blood," Sissy said. "It happened a few months ago, when I first started helping her? The doctors said she'd probably irritated her stomach or esophagus linin'. But, Bex ... today it was nothin' but blood. *Loads* of it, like she was a damn vampire and just sucked someone dry or somethin'. The home nurse Mason hired doesn't come today, so I was by myself. It was scary as shit."

I slid my arm over her shoulders and pulled her close to me—as close as we could get with the chair's arm between us. She tucked her face into my neck and began to shake with sobs. I stuck the clipboard between my hip and the chair and wrapped my other arm around her.

"This is bad, Bex," she said between sobs. "I feel it in my bones."

"Shh," I soothed as my hand stroked up and down her back. "No jumpin' to conclusions. Let the doctors do their thing. Mason will do whatever it takes."

She sniffled and drew in a ragged breath. "Is he here?"

"He's here at the hospital. I got his voicemail, but surely they paged him down to the ER since his patient is here."

After Sissy calmed down, I filled out the paperwork with her help and gave the clipboard back to the woman at the front desk. She wasn't able to give me any news. We waited for what could have been minutes but felt like hours ... or days. So many times I was tempted to call Mason again, but if he was busy with Mama, I didn't want to interrupt him. Finally, someone came through the double doors and called our last name. Sissy and I hurried over to the motherly woman dressed in scrubs with cartoon zombies all over them. She had a messed up sense of humor.

"We've stabilized your mother," she said, "and they're taking her to the ICU now."

"What's wrong?" I asked.

"Is she going to be okay?" Sissy asked at the same time.

"I can't tell you any more than that. Her doctors will come talk to you when they can. ICU's on the second floor."

We had a few more papers to sign, and then we hurried to the elevator and the second floor, only to find ourselves a few minutes later waiting in another room, this one called a family room. The space was much smaller than the one downstairs, pale green instead of blue, and with only a few chairs and a door to close for privacy. I couldn't help but imagine how many times a day doctors walked through that door to say, "We did everything we could." Were we the next family to hear those words? How would I react if we were? Mama's and my relationship was still rocky at best. I didn't know anymore if more time—whether days or years—would improve it. But that didn't mean I was ready to say goodbye forever, either.

When an older man with gray hair curling around his paper hat and wearing blue scrubs approached the door, my lungs froze mid-breath. Another man jogged up behind him, this one younger, probably in his late thirties. They exchanged a few words before opening the door. Where was Mason?

A few pleasantries and introductions were made, followed by the older doctor, Dr. Wilcoxson, saying, "Your mother's in serious condition, but stable. She has some internal bleeding, but we're not sure where yet. We're going to keep her in the ICU overnight for close observation. If she remains stabilized, we can discuss options tomorrow. We may have to go in for surgery."

Sissy had all kinds of questions, most of which I didn't understand and they didn't know how to answer. They just kept saying Mama needed rest and time before they'd have more definitive answers.

"Where's Mason?" I finally blurted out.

The doctors exchanged a look.

"Who?" Dr. Wilcoxson asked.

"She means Dr. Hayes, sir," Sissy said, giving me a dirty look. Shit. I could get Mason in trouble if I showed too much familiarity. "Mason Hayes?"

"Oh, of course," the younger man, Dr. Munthe, said. He obviously recognized the name, but his dark brows pushed together, he cocked his balding head and squinted his brown eyes as though confused. "Um, I haven't seen him in a long time. I guess you'd have to ask his attending. Why?"

Now Sissy and I did the look-exchanging-thing. Not at the "attending" part because I didn't know or care what that meant.

"He's Mama's doctor?" I said, unable to mask the sarcasm. "Shouldn't he be here? Shouldn't he be the one deciding what to do?"

Dr. Wilcoxson's bushy, gray brows pinched together as he looked at Dr. Munthe again.

"*We're* your mother's doctors," Dr. Wilcoxson said. "Most people prefer speaking with us than a resident, especially when the condition is this grave and surgery may be involved."

"What?" I snipped, thoroughly confused.

"Oh, I know," Sissy said, her hand going to her chest. "It's your office Mama goes to, right?"

"Yes," Dr. Wilcoxson said with a nod, his shoulders relaxing. "We've been seeing her for a few years. We'd been hoping to avoid where she is now." He shook his head, and his mouth turned downwards. "She's a sweet woman, your mother."

My eyes popped wide. He couldn't have been talking about *my* mama. Maybe that's where the whole confusion started—these guys had the wrong family.

Dr. Wilcoxson placed a hand on my shoulder. "She's confided a lot to me. You're Bethany, right?" He waited for me to answer, but I could only nod, feeling dazed. "She regrets so much, young lady. She's had a rough go at it for a while, and we've been fighting it together. I'd hoped my son-in-law here, Dr. Munthe, would be able to continue the fight with her long after I retired."

"And we will," Dr. Munthe said. "We won't let her give up."

Sissy moved closer to me and took my hand. "We won't either," she said. "Right, Bex?"

"Yeah. Right," I murmured distantly, my mind still reeling.

"We'll be back in the morning," Dr. Wilcoxson said, "and see how she's doing. You two may as well get some rest. There's nothing to do overnight but pray."

"We can't see her?" Sissy asked.

"Maybe for a few minutes after she's settled in," Dr. Munthe said. "But she really needs her rest."

The two doctors left, and Sissy plopped into a chair.

"You've never met them?" I asked as I turned toward her.

"I did in the beginning, but only for a minute when I'd taken Mama to an appointment. Dr. Wilcoxson had walked her to the waiting room. I don't remember seeing either of them here last time she was in the hospital, though. It was always Mason and a couple of other younger ones."

I dropped into the seat next to her and whipped my phone out of my purse. I dialed Mason's number, but his recorded voice answered again instead of his real one. I texted him to call me. I crossed my arms over my chest and slung one leg over the other, the top one swinging impatiently. After ten minutes had passed, I texted Mason again. Still no answer.

CHAPTER 19

Bex

THE CLOCK ON the wall ticked by as we waited on both Mason and the nurse to come get us so we could see Mama. Finally at seven-thirty, the nurse came in.

"One at a time," he said.

"You go first," Sissy said to me. "Then you can go home."

I hesitated at the doorway of the dark room where Mama lay unconscious, on a bunch of machines that filled the space with a rhythm of hisses and beeps. With a deep breath of chemical-infused hospital air, I crossed over to her bed. I didn't know what to do, so I simply stood there, holding her bony hand in mine, my gaze stuck on her bloated stomach that made her look like she had a baby bump. Her skin was yellow with jaundice, and dry and papery, like the outside of an onion, and I was afraid it'd peel off just as easily.

The nurse had given me ten minutes, and for nine of those minutes I stared at her, stray tears rolling down my cheek as flashes of memories passed through my mind, some good but most of them horrible. A more recent one of a time I'd gone to see her and Sissy came up. Sissy had made a quick run to the store, leaving us alone. I'd been okay with it when she left because Mama had been sleeping, but then she woke up.

"You know, I've been sober for a few years," she'd told me. "Straight, too. Completely off everything. Been goin' to those anonymous meetings and all."

Several thoughts had run through my mind. I was glad she'd cleaned herself up, but if she had, why didn't she come back to us? A few years ago meant she could have at least come to each of our graduations. Come to see Grams.

"It took me a long time to build up the nerve to call ya'll," she went on. "I thought ya'll were better off without me, even if I was clean. Too many hurts there between all us. I reckoned you and Sissy didn't need me struttin' back into your lives right when you were startin' 'em. My sponsor said I needed to, though." She paused for a long moment, catching her breath. I had nothing to say, because both she and her sponsor were right—we didn't need her waltzing back into our lives but that didn't mean she shouldn't have tried. "See, as part of the twelve steps, we're s'posed to apologize to the people we'd done wrong. I'd made a few calls, including to your Grams. My mama. I had to tell her how sorry I was for bein' such a mess."

She stopped again, this time tears choking her up. I had no idea she'd talked to Grams before we'd received The Call. Grams had never said anything, so I'd figured when Mama called us, it was the first time she'd heard from her, too.

"She wouldn't listen to me. Said it was ya'll, you and Sissy, who really needed to hear my apologies." Mama sniffled and blinked. "I didn't think ya'll would give me the time of day, and I was scared. I'd done you and your sister the most wrong. I didn't see how on earth ya'll could forgive me. I didn't want to see the hatred in your eyes I knew you had for me." Her voice had weakened, and her breath rattled in her chest. But she seemed determined to tell me all of this and pushed on. "When I finally got the guts to call or maybe even go see you, I learnt I was sick. I tried to get better at first, but when they said I prolly had less than a year, I realized for the first time how short life can be. You'd think I know that with your daddy and all, but we never think that applies to ourselves.

So, then I realized how little time I had left to make amends with you ... to make sure ya'll would be okay. Especially you, sugar. I didn't want hate to ruin't your life. Even if you couldn't love me again, I wanted you to know I still loved you. Always had."

Tears had been flowing down my cheeks by then. I swiped at them hard and inhaled a deep breath. Once I'd regained control, I looked over at her. Her eyes had closed, and her jaw had gone slack.

"I love you, too, Mama," I'd whispered, but I didn't think she'd heard me. I didn't know if I wanted her to hear me.

That was the last time I'd seen her awake.

Once again, I brushed tears from my cheek. Even if I forgave her, I'd never forget what she'd done to us. And that's what made standing here so hard. Part of me wanted to bolt, still thinking she deserved to die alone, but most of me couldn't do it. The nurse tapped on the glass door. My time was up. As I turned to leave, Mama's eyes fluttered open. It took her a moment to focus on me, and when she did, the corners of her mouth moved in a small smile.

"I'm here, Mama," I whispered.

"Thank you," she mouthed.

"Be strong, okay? You fight this."

She blinked once, which I didn't know whether that meant yes or no or nothing at all, but I took it as a yes.

"They won't let me stay in here any longer. It's Sissy's turn now. But I'll be back."

She blinked again, and then her eyes fell closed. The machines continued their steady sounds, so I figured she'd fallen back asleep and nothing more serious.

I waited in the family room while Sissy visited Mama for her allowed time. My phone finally rang right when she returned.

"Where the hell are you?" Mason demanded as soon as I answered, his voice angrier than I'd ever heard it. "I come home to a mess in the kitchen, no dinner, and you're gone!"

A mess? There was one covered platter with pork chops marinating in the refrigerator, and a single bowl in the sink.

"I'm at the *hospital* with my *mama*," I snapped back, my nerves worn. "If you'd answered your phone or even checked your voicemail or texts, you'd know that. Where the hell have *you* been?"

"Working! Where else?"

I snorted. "Well, I'm here, and you're not. Thought you would be since, you know, this *is* where you work."

Mason's voice fell quieter and softer. "Why are you there?"

"Like I said, my mama's here. She's in ICU."

"Oh, Bex, I'm sorry. I'm so sorry. I kind of panicked when you weren't here with no note and everything left out. I didn't think to check my messages, just to call you right away to make sure you were okay."

I pinched the bridge of my nose. He had a funny way of showing his concern.

"I'm fine. I don't know about Mama, though."

"Go home and take care of your man," Sissy said. She'd resigned herself to the idea of Mason and me as a couple when I told her I was moving in with him. About the same time she went to Ty's fight. She swore up and down they were just friends, and that made sense because he'd been her friend as long as he'd been mine, but I wondered if she wanted it to be more … if she weren't spending all her time with Mama and all. Not that she would tell me.

I covered the phone. "I want to stay here with you. You don't need to be alone."

"I'm goin' home, too. The nurse said I should. I need to get some things for Mama, and I may as well grab a few hours of sleep while I'm there. There's nothing we can do here."

"I'll be home in a few," I told Mason, then hung up. "Are you sure? I can go with you."

She gave me a weird look. "Why would you do that? I'm a big girl. I can handle picking up Mama's jammies and book. Go on.

Sounds like Mason needs you. And maybe he can tell you more about what's goin' on with Mama."

I nodded, and then gave her a hug. We held each other for a long moment before finally breaking apart and heading downstairs to our cars. I didn't know why, but part of me seriously wanted to go with Sissy, not because she needed help or even company, and definitely not because I wanted to sleep at Mama's. That part of me simply didn't want to go home.

But Mason was waiting. Maybe once I was in his arms, I'd feel better.

"What the fuck took you so long?" he demanded as soon as I walked in and closed the door, making me jump. I turned to his figure looming in the dark entranceway.

"It's only been five minutes," I said, my heart still pounding. "I came straight here. Are you okay?"

"Oh, I'm just peachy," he said as he turned back for the living room. He certainly didn't sound peachy. He sounded pissed off. And was that a slur in his voice? "Are you finally going to make me dinner?"

I stared at his back as I dropped my purse on the little table that sat in the entrance. "Are you kidding me? You want me to make you dinner *now*?"

He turned and took two long strides until he stood in front of me. Towering over me. "Yes, now, Bex," he said through a clenched jaw as he glared down his nose, his usually beautiful eyes dark and glassy. The sharp smell of alcohol lingered on his breath. "It's eight o'clock, and I'm fucking starving. You already started it and left a mess, so get your ass in there and finish it."

My mouth fell open. My fists balled at my sides. My nostrils flared.

"Is there a problem?" he asked.

"Uh, yeah. Are you too drunk to remember what I told you five minutes ago? My mama's back in the hospital. In ICU, Mason! And you're worried about your fucking *dinner*?"

His finger flew into my face, and he shook it at me while he spoke. "First of all, I stopped for two drinks after work. I had a long, shitty day and needed to unwind before I came home to your ass whining about how bored you are."

I opened my mouth, but he jabbed his finger into my chest and went on.

"Second of all, I called the ICU. Your *mama's* not going to die tonight. Someday, yeah, she is. But not tonight. Not tomorrow. Probably not the next day. So, yes, right now, I want some fucking dinner."

He grabbed my shoulder, twisted me, and practically shoved me into the kitchen. I stumbled, catching myself on the counter.

"What the hell is wrong with you?" I yelled.

"I'm hungry, in case you didn't notice." He yanked the refrigerator open with such force, the door flew out of his control and the handle banged against the wall, rattling all the jars of condiments in the door. He pulled out the container of marinating pork chops and set it hard on the counter in front of me.

I crossed my arms over my chest, tears burning the backs of my eyes. I'd never seen this side of Mason before. I'd expected to come home to his comforting embrace and soothing words, not to a monster.

"Cook me dinner, Bex," he ordered.

Was that it? Was he taking his dominant fun a little too far tonight? Well, I wasn't going to play this time. I wasn't in the mood, and he definitely wasn't in the safe zone.

"No," I said, and I turned for the living room.

His hand clamped around my upper arm, and he spun me around. "I said to make me dinner, Bex."

He shoved the platter of meat and juices into my hands. I shoved it back at him. "I said *no*. Make it yourself."

"Cook for me!" he snarled. "I've had a long fucking day. I'm hungry, and I'm tired. Do you have any idea the shit I go through every day? The stress of being a doctor? All I ask is for a nice dinner and some loving when I get home. Is that too much to ask?"

"Tonight it is," I said through clenched teeth. "Pretend like I'm not here and make your own damn food."

"After all I do for you—pay your bills and your mom's and everything—and this is the thanks I get?"

My chest heaved. Tears of anger fell no matter how hard I tried to blink them back. I clenched my jaw and said quietly, "I'm not your fucking maid or your whore."

"Are you sure about that?" he sneered, and I felt like I'd been slapped. I should have known, though, that he'd eventually throw everything back in my face.

I yanked the lid off the dish still in my hands and threw it at him.

"Make your own God damn dinner, *doctor*," I screamed, my voice sounding maniacal as I hurled a pork chop at him. It skimmed by his head but missed. "Or are you even a doctor, Mason?" I threw another, nailing him in the chest. "You've been lying to me this whole time, haven't you? Saying what you thought I wanted to hear so I'd give you some pussy!" A third chop hit his shoulder. "You lied to my mama and my sister, too, you FUCKING IMPOSTER!"

I threw the last one right at his face. When his hand flew up, I thought he meant to catch the meat before it hit him again. But rather than grabbing the chop, his fist slammed into my jaw. Stars shot across my vision. I staggered to my right as pain blossomed over my face. My hand lifted to my cheek, and my mouth fell open.

"Oh, shit, Bex," Mason said, all anger in his voice gone, replaced by panic. "Oh, my God, I'm so sorry."

I shook my head side-to-side and stared at him wide-eyed, no words coming. He reached for me. I jerked away and stumbled backwards.

"Don't you touch me!" I yelled. I spun on my heel, grabbed my purse, and ran out the door.

I flew down the stairs, surprised I didn't twist an ankle or face plant on my way down as tears blurred my vision. By the time I ran into the parking lot for my car, Mason was yelling after me, making his own flight down the steps. I ignored him, sprinting for my car, glad I'd thrown on my ballet flats rather than heels before leaving for the hospital.

"Bex, please, I'm sorry," he yelled as he crossed the parking lot. I jumped in my car and slammed the door just as he reached it. He banged his fists on the window. "Please, Bex. It was an accident."

"Leave me alone," I yelled loud enough for him to hear me through the window as I cranked over the engine.

"Don't go, please," he begged. "I'm so, so sorry."

I shook my head, put the car in gear, and gave him the finger. "Fuck you, Mason."

His face fell. His eyes darkened. "Don't leave me, precious. Please don't leave me."

I turned away from him to look out the back window as I pulled out of the parking space. I threw the car into drive. Mason ran after me in his bare feet and meat-juice-stained shirt, crossing the grassy areas as I made the turns through the parking lot. He ran in front of me, forcing me to stop. Standing in my headlights, he held up his hands. A bluish-white object was in one of them.

"At least take this," he said as he rushed for my door. "For your face."

He held up an ice pack. I rolled down my window, snatched it out of his hand, and drove off. As I glanced in the rear-view mirror, Mason fell to his knees in the middle of the lane. I told myself not to feel sorry for him.

I held the ice pack against my jaw as I drove, not sure where to go at first. I really didn't want to see Sissy. If my face was bruising as I thought it would be, she'd ask questions I didn't have the desire to answer right now or make snide remarks I didn't have the energy to deal with. But I had nowhere else to go. I knew nobody else here. Tears began streaming so quickly, I couldn't see, so I pulled into a strip mall and parked in the nearly empty lot. I leaned over the steering wheel and sobbed. My phone kept ringing and then dinging with voicemails and texts. All Mason. All ignored.

Not knowing what else to do, I followed where my heart took me, and that was back to Lake Haven. Back to home. I slowed as I passed the RV park, noticing that Leni's camper was dark. She might have been working, and I wasn't going to bother her anyway. A heavy feeling of darkness pressed down on me as I kept on driving into town, not stopping the car until I reached Elizabeth's house, but obviously nobody was home there either. In fact, the house looked empty, and a For Sale sign was stuck in the yard. She'd actually moved away. All those times she had talked about it, but I never thought she would. If I felt the eeriness of a cemetery at midnight covering the whole town, though, I could only imagine what she felt. Putting the car back into drive, I continued out of town to where my heart and soul were really pulling me.

The trees hanging over the driveway with their dripping Spanish moss blocked out the moonlight, enveloping me in near blackness as I crept the car to the cabin. My already heavy heart fell when the cabin came into view with its little yellow porch light no brighter than a firefly. Ty's truck wasn't there. The windows were all black. He obviously wasn't hanging at home, pining over me.

My chest constricted with more despair as I sat there for a while, hoping he'd come home. I pulled out my compact mirror while I waited and peeked at my cheek as best as I could in the dim light of my car's overhead lamp. Either the ice pack had worked or Mason hadn't hit me as hard as I'd thought because no bruise or swelling showed. Only a slight redness that would probably be gone by morning. Thank God and sweet baby Jesus for that.

After an hour of waiting and still no Ty, I was exhausted from the emotions of the day. Had I really been bored out of my mind only hours ago? I drove back to the trailer park, not even checking to see who was at Sullivan's. I had no energy to deal with a crowd. I'd just needed someone to talk to, maybe to hold me. Unfortunately, Leni's camper was still dark. I was grateful Uncle Troy had given me a month, after all. Not enough to thank him personally, though. I went straight to my trailer to be alone.

As I lay down on the bare mattress with only a towel from my car to wrap around me, I couldn't help but think about how my heart, maybe even my actual soul, had brought me here. When shit hit the fan, I'd been drawn here, to Ty, to Elizabeth, even to Leni, who I'd only known for a few weeks, but sometimes felt like forever. My sister and my mama, any of my family, had been the last people I'd wanted to see when I needed someone. In fact, I'd rather be completely and utterly alone like I was now than be with them. The grief of that fact, more than anything that happened today, overwhelmed me.

When the sobs slowed to only sniffles, my phone sounded off again. With a sigh, I pulled it out of my purse, rolled on my back and held the phone above me as I scrolled through Mason's text messages and then listened to his voicemails. Thirty-seven total, in a little over two hours. Pretty much the same thing over and over: "It was an accident, Bex. I'm so sorry. I didn't mean to touch you, just the stupid pork chop. Please, precious, believe me. I'd never hurt you." Desperation filled his voice. The last message ended on what sounded like a sob. "Please don't leave me, Bex. I love you and need you too much."

I dropped my arm over my face and closed my eyes as more tears seeped down my temples. The scene in the kitchen instantly replayed behind my eyelids. And damn if I couldn't be sure whether he really was grabbing for the pork chop or if he'd intentionally hit me. Either way, things had gone way too far tonight, and coming here was the right thing to do. We'd both needed cooling off. I'd thrown raw, dripping meat at him like I was a damn five-year-old, for heaven's sake. He wasn't the only one who should be apologizing, but I couldn't decide if he deserved to hear it from me. Had it been an accident? I couldn't think straight about it now, and calling him tonight would be a mistake. Hopefully, morning would bring clearer thoughts. I kept my eyes closed and tried to sleep.

I dreamt about the man who often showed up in my dreams, although he hadn't for a few months. I'd thought he'd come to life in Mason, but I could no longer be sure. The beautiful man who captivated my unconscious mind was nothing but kind and loving. I could feel his love flowing through my veins, reaching all the way to my soul. A cocoon of warmth surrounded my entire body when he embraced me with his strong arms. His features changed every time I looked up at him, but the love in his eyes never did. Nothing had ever felt so right. So complete. So much like home.

First Ty, then Mason tried to intrude on my dream. Each were full of love, too. Each began morphing into my dream man. But then he'd shake his head and become someone else entirely. Faces that seemed somewhat familiar, although I didn't know who they belonged to. And as the dream went on, his expression turned to concern. Dark shadows flew over us, closing in on us, pressing in as though to crush us. He screamed out a plea, becoming desperate and then urgent.

"Please come back to me," he called out with such grief, my heart hurt as I drifted back to consciousness. The forlorn words echoed in my head as I blinked at the bright daylight flooding into the window. And then I gasped. A monstrous figure loomed over me.

I bolted upright, the fog of the dream clearing. Mason stood next to the bed, his face almost completely blocked with the biggest bouquet of flowers I'd ever seen.

"Please come back to me," he begged.

CHAPTER 20

Leni I LAY ON my stomach in bed wearing only a cami and panties, flipping through the Book of Phoenix pages—again—instead of getting my butt up and ready for the day. Jeric had been awake for hours already and had gone to see why Ty wasn't answering his phone. I took the opportunity to once again study the Book. A thought had awoken me in the middle of the night, and the more I dwelled on it, the stronger it felt true: Jacquelena had created the Book in a past life long ago. All night I kept telling myself it was a dream, but now I didn't think so. My soul told me I created the Book for us, the Sacred Seven. Well, we weren't Seven then either, but for those of us who were on Earth at the time—Jeremicah and me, Broderick and Anastasia, and Rebethannah and Nathayden. Unfortunately, I couldn't remember any more than that—not what the Book was supposed to do for us or the clues we might have left in it.

The Book obviously could communicate with us, leaving us short, cryptic messages. But where did they come from? From the Space Between? From another world? Or from us, either from the past or the present? Had I, or all of us, somehow given the Book special ... powers?

Huh. I hadn't considered the Book as having powers—not in a paranormal way—but maybe that was exactly what we'd done to make it exceptional. Not too long ago, I would have thought any of these ideas to be a bit out there, a little too woo-woo for me, but a lot had changed in the past few months. Our lives were full of woo-woo. So thinking a book that had already given mysterious messages as being supernatural no longer exceeded the realm of possibilities in my mind. And if it had the one power of communicating with us, what else could it do?

I closed the Book and studied the cover even harder than I'd already done, running my fingers over the image embossed into the leather: a weeping willow tree with a phoenix branded into its trunk, which stood on a tiny island with a sea surrounding it and dolphins and other marine creatures swimming in the water. An image of the island over the Gate in Tampa Bay. I vaguely remember stretching the leather over the metal plate to create the embossment. The whole image was enclosed in a large circle and tiny, unfamiliar symbol-like markings surrounded the circle, so faint, they weren't even noticeable on first glance. Had I put those there, too? I couldn't remember. Were any of these clues we'd left for ourselves? If so, I hadn't the slightest idea what they meant.

Sometimes, I wanted to hurl the Book across the room or toss it into the fire. Not being able to remember anything about it was quite infuriating. But not this time. Right now, I was bound and determined to figure something out if it was the only thing I did today.

So, I opened the Book and starting from the inside cover, I reconsidered each page individually, the leaves of paper themselves rather than the words written on them. A watermark of a phoenix like the one on the front cover, which was similar to those branded on our arms, decorated the corners of each page. I saw a flash of a memory of me putting them there, but I didn't remember why. Did they mean something, or were they just for decoration? Was I supposed to do something to them? With them? On them? Memories dangled on the edge of my mind, out of reach, taunting, like when a word hovers on the tip of your tongue. I felt that the Book was to be used more than to simply write and draw in, but how? Frustration returned with each turn of the page as I found nothing to help me along.

When I reached them, the words, "You know the rest. Remember." glared brightly at me. Had they meant more than remembering that Jeric and I were Jacey and Micah? I hadn't realized it before, but I thought so now. Then came "Save Rebethannah." Scratched onto the page, like a prisoner would etch on a wall.

Theo's instructions echoed in my mind:

"Believe."

"Follow your instinct."

"Trust your intuition."

"Believe in yourself, little bird."

I rolled over onto my back and closed my eyes, listening to the words bounce around my skull. If only my instinct wasn't broken. Even when I reminded Jeric that he was supposed to follow my intuition, I couldn't believe in it myself. I didn't exactly have the best track record in understanding my gut, most recently proved by being wrong about Bex. In fact, following my soul's pull to the manor and thinking we should have listened to Theo and Mira instead of jumping out of the window our first night there had probably been the only two times my intuition had been right. Well ... and inviting Jeric to the lake with me. Trusting him ...

Besides those, I had a history of making poor decisions. Something my mama never let me forget.

I opened my eyes and stared at the ceiling as my thoughts transitioned to my mother and father and my multiple discussions with Theo about them and our familial status. I hadn't been surprised when he called our relationships temporal, as much as I didn't want to believe it. I knew deep down we hadn't been a close-knit family. In fact, I didn't tell Theo, but I'd always had an underlying suspicion that my dad cheated on my mother. During those times she'd treated me like a puppet and no more, I even fantasized about Daddy having another family and we'd run off and live with them. Since he worked so much, I always thought we'd had a good relationship, just that we didn't get to spend much time together. But reconsidering now, I saw that we'd been little more than two people who lived in the same house. Judging by my lack of reaction at the moment, I supposed I'd also known that deep down all along.

The sound of my truck's engine rumbled across the park, and my soul felt Jeric's approaching. I smiled to myself, always pleased to have him near, and rolled back over onto my stomach. As I reached for the Book to close it, my breath caught for a moment. In huge letters, "HELP HER" scrawled across the page that only a few minutes ago had been blank. "SAVE HER" scrolled across the opposite leaf. I turned to the next page, and the word "BELIEVE" repeated across the left side and "INSTINCT" filled the right.

"You're still right where I left you," Jeric said, his footsteps coming down the short hallway and into the bedroom.

I didn't know why, but I didn't want him to see the words. Maybe because I knew they were specifically for me? Or because I didn't want him to know how much I doubted myself? Either way, I slammed the Book shut, pushed it to the side of the bed, and turned to face him. "Yeah, I was just getting up."

He leaned over and placed a hand on each side of my shoulders so that his torso hovered over me, effectively trapping me with his body.

"But you're in my favorite place," he murmured before brushing his lips across mine. His bright blue eyes skimmed over my face, and then his gaze lowered over my skimpily clad body. He gave me a sexy half-smile. "And dressed perfectly."

He delivered a more proper kiss, his lips lingering on mine for a good long time before moving to my chin and jaw.

"Did you see Ty?" I asked as I rolled my head to the side, giving him better access.

"No," he said, his lips not moving away from their path down my neck.

"It's been almost a week."

"I know." His breath fluttered over my skin in a sigh. "He's a grown man, though. Not much I can do."

"I hope he's okay."

"I'm sure he is. The Lakari are still hanging around here, so they haven't gone after him."

"Unless they've already done something to him and left his body in the woods like they did Bex." I paused, my heart contracting at the thought. "I mean, Jacey's Bex."

Jeric lifted his head to look at me. "You're the one who doesn't think he's going Dark. Do you think they're after Ty now?"

I frowned. "No. I'm worried about him, though."

"He probably just needs time away from this town and its memories again, now that Bex has moved away."

"He could have at least called you. You're like his boss, aren't you?"

Jeric dropped one arm to his elbow, shifting his weight to the side of me. "More like he's my boss. If he doesn't want to fight, I can't make him. He's his own manager. He's a big boy, Leni, and probably doesn't want to feel like he has to check in with anyone. I'm definitely not his mother."

With one arm free from holding himself up now, he used that hand to play with the strap of my cami.

"Speaking of Bex, did you know she was coming home?" he asked.

I tilted my head on the pillow and gazed up at him. His eyes followed his finger as it pushed the strap over my shoulder. "I had no idea."

"I saw her car at her trailer early this morning when I went for a run. Just hers, as if she'd spent the night there. But as I was headed home a few minutes ago, I passed both her car and Mason's headed for the interstate."

I gave a little shrug, enough to move my cami to expose the rise of my breast. "She didn't call me. She probably decided to move something else down there."

Jeric lowered his head to press his lips on the skin I'd just bared, nudging the fabric down farther with his mouth. His hand moved to my waist, and his thumb slid up and down along the sensitive skin over my hip.

"I'd like to move something down there," he murmured as he pushed the waistband of my panties down.

I giggled and rolled onto my side to face him, pulling him away from my breast. I cupped my hand to his cheek and directed his mouth toward mine. Our lips parted almost immediately, and our tongues reintroduced themselves, although it always felt like the first time they met. Kissing Jeric sent chills across my skin every single time. As the kiss deepened and we explored each other's mouths, his hand slid down my thigh, over my knee and to my calf. He hitched my leg up over his hip, causing his pelvis to press against mine. His erection grew between us. His hand moved back upward, to my butt, where it stopped and squeezed and caressed, his fingers often grazing the tiny piece of material between my legs, teasing the area underneath. I moaned into his mouth and moved my hips against him.

"Damn, Leni," he gasped against my mouth. "You have no idea what hearing you moan like that does to me."

I did have an inkling of an idea, feeling it pulse against the thin fabric of his running shorts as his lips traveled over my jaw again, heading southward once more. I leaned away enough to pull the cami over my head.

"Mmm ...." I moaned, louder this time, as he trailed kisses over my breast. His thumb dug into my hip, his fingers splayed over my ass, and he squeezed at the same time his tongue traced a circle around my areola. Then he jerked me harder against him, his lower head pressing into me right as he flicked my nipple then clamped his mouth over it and sucked. I arched my back, trying to thrust my tit further into his mouth while rocking my hips so our most sensitive areas felt the friction through the clothing. "Oh, God, Jeric."

His tongue ran a circle around my nipple as he gazed up at me before he pulled away and smiled. "I like hearing that even more."

I grasped at the bottom of his shirt and yanked it upward, pulling it over his head. I reached for his nipples and pinched and tugged on the rings until he leaned out of reach. He backed up, onto his knees, his bare chest a beautiful sight to behold as it rose and fell with his heavy breaths. Slowly, my eyes lifted to his face, questioning. That smile—mischievous and daring—lingered on his lips as his blue eyes pierced me to my soul.

"You know what I love to hear more than anything?" he asked.

I propped myself up on my elbows and stared back at him. "I love you, Jeric."

His smile faltered. "Well, besides that."

"Um ..." My head fell back, though my eyes remained glued to his. He circled his hand around one of my ankles and moved my leg to other side of him, and his fingers trailed lightly over and between my breasts, down to my belly button, making my tummy quiver. "Make love to me?"

Both hands were on me now, sliding over my hips and under my panties, pushing them down. I lifted my butt up so he could continue, and the lock of our gaze broke. His eyes jumped lower, watching as I lifted one leg and then the other, allowing him to free my panties from my body. His hands clamped onto my bent knees and pushed them apart. His tongue slid over his lips as he stared hungrily at my center. I couldn't help but wriggle under his gaze. The corners of his lips tilted into that teasing smile again. His eyes traveled up my body, leaving a trail of tingles as though he'd actually touched me, and back to my face.

"I love to hear you beg," he said huskily before he crashed down on top of me, his mouth pulling on my tit and his fingers digging into my thighs.

"Please, Jeric," I said as I arched against him. "Make love to me."

He pulled my nipple between his teeth, then said, "Nuh-uh. Not like that," before diving after the other one. His hands continued squeezing and kneading my thighs as they made their way toward my butt. Toward the area that throbbed with an aching need. His thumb barely grazed me.

"Touch me," I whimpered.

He released my breast, my nipple standing hard and long, and moved his mouth downward, while his hands pushed my thighs further outward.

"That's better," he said, his breath hot on my stomach. "But not quite."

His lips and tongue left a trail as they moved around my belly button and side to side across my pelvis. He clutched my thighs, now spread wide, and his thumbs stroked and massaged an outer circle, not touching the normal sweet spot, but still sending shockwaves over me. His eyes held mine as he stretched his legs out behind him, hovering his face right over me.

"Oh, God, please, Jeric," I moaned, and I reached down and grasped his head. "Lick me, baby."

"That's more like it." He dipped down, his thumbs separated me, and his tongue swept against me. My pelvis jerked toward him, my hands fisted in his hair, and I cried out. When he didn't do it again, I looked down at him. He was staring at me, his eyes glassy but expectant.

"More, please," I whined. He licked me again, and then his tongue lingered over my clit, swirling and flicking. "Oh, yes. Don't stop."

Thankfully, he didn't. His tongue and his fingers and his lips did miraculous things over the entire area, from my pelvis to my ass, making me moan and cry out and convulse against him. He built me up and up and up until I was screaming his name, about to lose myself completely. And when I thought he had no more magic to perform, his lips wrapped around my clit, his fingers slid inside and twisted and stroked, and waves and waves of orgasm overcame me.

"I want you," I gasped as I tried to pull him upward.

He leaned back, then stood up to take his shorts off. My eyes fell to exactly what I wanted, and my tongue slipped over my lips.

"Beg, Leni," he said.

"Make love to me," I said again, my voice raspy and my chest heaving.

He shook his head, but he dropped down over me, bracing himself with his hands. His erection rubbed my belly. "*What* do you want?"

"You," I said. His eyes narrowed. "Your cock?" His lips quirked. That must have been what he wanted to hear. I lowered my voice. "Give me your cock, Jeric."

He chuckled softly. I gave him a dirty look. "That sounds a little weird from you. But I still like hearing it. Beg some more."

I slid one arm over his shoulders and reached the other one down between us, and I wrapped my palm around him, guiding him to the right spot. I tightened my grip slightly and slid my hand up and down a few times, making him moan. I pulled him closer to me, licked up the side of his jaw and wrapped my lips around his ear lobe then scraped my teeth over it.

"Fuck me, Jeric," I whispered, breathing heavily against his ear. "*Please.*"

He groaned and thrust his hips, sliding inside me. My hands went to his shoulders, and my nails dug lines down his back as he pumped in and out, and I rocked up and down to meet his every stroke. I grabbed his hard ass and lifted my hips out and up.

"That's right, baby, fuck me hard," I said, and this must have been exactly what he wanted to hear because he moved faster, going deeper, sending jolts of pleasure up my belly, over my breasts and out to my limbs. Just as I was about to come again, he pulled out.

"Turn over," he said.

I rolled onto my hands and knees. He slapped my butt cheek, then grabbed my hips and drove into me from behind.

"Oh, *yes*," I cried out. "More, Jeric. Give it to me."

He pounded harder. "Keep begging, baby."

"Fuck me. Harder. Faster. That's it. Oh, *yeeeessss*."

"Scream my name for me."

And I yelled it for the whole park to hear as he drove into me over and over, one of his hands splayed over my belly and his finger pressing and rubbing my clit, while his hips slapped against my ass, taking us all the way to the edge and beyond. With a shout from both of us, our souls exploded out of our bodies and collided into each other, heightening every sensation, until we were both screaming for the other even as our essences swirled into one.

Our bodies stayed in the moment as we slowly drifted down from our high. We hovered in the room, no need to leave, enjoying our togetherness for a while. We noticed the Book had fallen to the floor by the side of the bed, and the revelation that it could have powers passed through us, enlightening Jeric. He also learned of the new messages the Book had left. I couldn't keep anything from him when we were like this. We hoped the Book's power of communication didn't mean someone could hear us any time they wanted to. What just happened was only for us. As Jeric told me many times when I'd been a little hesitant to try a few things, what happened in our bedroom stayed in our bedroom.

Eventually we returned to our bodies and jumped into the shower, one at a time because my bathroom was so tiny. Jeric went first, needing less time than me, and after I washed, I stood under the warm water for a few minutes. The words "Believe" and "Instinct" echoed in my mind as "Save Her" and "Help Her" flashed before my eyes, but then my mind wandered back to my parents. To my father, especially. I was still thinking about him after I'd dressed and was combing my hair out, and then I remembered the newspaper page I'd taken from Bex. More specifically, the article about an international summit my dad attended every year for work. I'd wanted to read more about it and find out where it was being held this year. I thought maybe if I saw him one more time, I'd know for sure what I'd always felt but denied.

As I squatted down to retrieve the article from a drawer under the bed, my eye caught on the Book of Phoenix. Water had apparently dripped from my hair onto the cover, and everywhere there was a drop, the leather glowed a silvery blue. I picked it up, stood and studied it in the light. The drops moved across the leather, accumulating together in the parts of the cover that depicted the ocean, showing it as crystal blue. I brushed my fingers over the water, and it disappeared, returning the leather to its normal, cracked brown. But again, something danced on the edges of my mind. A memory? A thought. I had a new idea— something I thought maybe the Book could do. One of the powers I'd given it.

"Hey, Jeric, come here," I called out to the living room as I stuffed my phone in my pocket and my feet into the closest pair of shoes. He was by my side in two seconds. "I want to see something." I had a feeling I knew what would happen if we tested the bottom of the water in the image, below the island and the tree, where the Gate would be, but I wasn't ready to find out. I wanted to start small. I didn't really know what to do, but I took a guess. "I'm going to touch the phoenix, and I'm going to *believe*. If something weird happens, grab me, okay?"

"Believe in what?" he asked skeptically.

"Believe in the Book," I said, and before he asked more questions and analyzed the situation to death, I stroked my finger over the phoenix engraved into the weeping willow's trunk.

Color filled the bird's body and tail, and a ghostly image of it rose from the cover and grew. Blues, teals, peaches, pinks, and purples swirled in the shape of the phoenix, and it flew in a circle around us like colorful smoke, there but not there. As its wings rose around us, the colors in the bird's body turned into yellows, oranges, and reds, and expanded outward to its wings, head, and tail, and the phoenix burst into fire.

Jeric's arms wrapped around me, and the flames of the bird surrounded us, licking at our bodies, though we felt no heat or burns. Starting at the tips of the tail and working its way upward, black now filled in the shape of the bird. The phoenix exploded in sparks and ash, and then blackness engulfed us. And then bright light and cold air against my skin. I blinked against the brightness until shapes began to form. White capped mountains in the distance under a clear blue sky. If that wasn't enough to tell us we weren't in Florida anymore, the much cooler air was.

"What the fuck was that, and where the hell are we?" Jeric demanded as he patted himself down while eyeing me, as though making sure we were each in one piece.

"It ... it *worked*," I said breathlessly as I looked around. We were in a rundown industrial area with empty warehouses on each side of us. One gray wall displayed in faded red lettering "Juneau Shipping."

"Looks like Alaska," I said with awe. "Score one for my intuition."

"*What?*" Jeric threw his hands in the air. They landed on his hips. "Damn it, Leni, what did you do?"

I looked down at the Book still in my hands. "It brought us here."

He glanced at the Book, at me, then back down, now glaring at it. "No way. This is not happening."

"Look around you, Jeric. It's definitely happening."

"It's not real."

I reached over and pinched him hard.

"Ow!" He yanked his arm away.

"It's real," I said, and I began walking down the alley toward a road about a block away.

"Where do you think you're going?" He caught up to me and stepped in front of me, blocking my way. He jabbed a finger at the Book. "That thing needs to take us back. Right now. And how—"

"It was a guess. A theory. Something that popped in my mind, and I knew I needed to try, so I believed as hard as I could. The warehouse might be a portal, like Jacey's apartment building had been, or maybe not. Maybe the Book doesn't need a portal. I don't know how it all works, but ... here we are." I stepped around him and headed for the road.

"Babe, what are you doing?"

"I know why we're here, Jeric. Why we came to this place." I continued walking. His footsteps crunched on the road behind me as he caught up. "I've been thinking about them all morning."

He must have made the connection, because the next thing he said was, "Oh, hell, no, Leni. You can't do this. It's against the rules. You *can't* see them."

"I have to. There's a reason we're *here*. In this place. There's something I have to do. If I'm right, it won't take long, and if I'm wrong, well, we'll have other things to worry about."

His hand landed on my shoulder, stopping me again. "No. Absolutely not."

I turned around and looked him in the eyes. "You have to trust me, Jeric. You *have* to."

Our eyes locked, and we stood there in a standoff ... until I shivered. His features twisted.

"Shit, babe. Seriously?"

"Yes, seriously." I spun around, knowing he wouldn't stop me again. He knew our calling and roles for each other. I had to give him props for actually following my instinct this time without an argument and need to fully consider every possible aspect of the situation.

We made it to the road where people walked on the sidewalk with us, coming and going from the businesses lining the street. Several shot strange looks our way, both of us dressed for Florida, not Alaska, in short sleeves, shorts, and flip-flops. A sign down the street showed the temperature as forty-six. Freezing to me. I rubbed my hands up and down my arms as we came to a corner and stopped to look around. I was about to pull my phone out of my pocket to look at a map, when my eyes landed on exactly what I was looking for: the state capitol building was practically right in front of us, only a block to our right. It was a weekday and the beginning of the workday here, and my father should either be in that building or on his way.

We rounded the corner, and I crashed right into someone. When I looked up to apologize, I gasped audibly.

Tall and thin, with lighter skin than mine smudged with age spots and dark brown eyes surrounded by wrinkles, she looked like she'd aged twenty years since I'd seen her—last Christmas. I thought I'd never see her again. My mother stood right in front of me.

"Oh, I'm so sorry," she said, her voice laced with the edge I knew meant that she was not sorry at all. She stepped to her right to move around me. No recognition of me in the slightest.

"Ma—Mrs. Drago?" I said, catching her forearm with my hand. She looked down at it, then back at me.

"Do I know you?" Her tone was as sharp as ever.

"Um ..." My throat stuck to itself, making it difficult to talk or swallow or even breathe. I'd already been through this once, had basically accepted it. I thought I had, anyway. The pain of my own mother not recognizing me wracked through me again, nonetheless, making my chest tighten around my heart and lungs. Always her dutiful daughter, though, I swallowed down the tears and smiled. "Not really. I know your husband, though."

She sniffed. "You mean my ex. Or soon to be anyway. If you're looking for him, I just left him and his *assistant* at The Oxfire, a restaurant one block that way."

She pointed in the direction we'd been headed, then without another word, stalked off.

"Are you okay?" Jeric asked, his voice low as he wrapped his arms around me.

My body trembled, but I didn't know if it was from the renewed shock or simply the cold air. My soul had felt nothing from hers. No connection beyond the one we'd had of parent and child in this lifetime.

"I need to be sure about him, too," I said. I broke away from his embrace and strode down the street toward the restaurant.

I didn't need to walk inside. My father waltzed through the doors with a blonde hanging on his arm. She leaned up on her toes and whispered something in his ear, making them both laugh. I didn't miss the little nibble she gave his lobe before pulling away. My stomach clenched. The way my mother had said "assistant" with a nastiness only I could detect made sense. He and the woman glanced at us, giving us the standard look for being dressed inappropriately, but no indication of recognition. And he wasn't the only one who'd known me since I was a child. The voluptuous blonde had been my father's assistant for as long as I could remember.

"Excuse us," my father said as he looked me in the eye for a brief moment, before pushing past us, leading the way for his mistress.

"I've seen enough," I choked out to Jeric, and I ran for the alley by the warehouse since we couldn't just disappear from the middle of a busy sidewalk. I didn't think about minding my unnatural speed, though, and probably ran faster than I should have. As soon as we reached the same place we'd appeared, I grabbed Jeric's arm and wrapped it around me. I didn't know if he needed to be touching me or the Book or what, but it worked last time. I pressed my finger against the phoenix on the Book cover and believed.

The colorful, translucent bird surrounded us again, then black, then white, then my camper.

Jeric immediately drew me into a hug. "I'm sorry, babe. I don't know why you thought that would be a good idea. I mean, the teleporting or whatever we did was pretty cool, but going to see your parents, Leni? Why would you want to do that? You had to have known—"

"It's okay. I'm okay. It was something I needed to do." I stepped away from him, swiped at my moist cheeks, dragged in a jagged breath, and then straightened my back. "Now I know my instincts aren't completely broken. I was right about my daddy and that woman. Had the feeling since I was little. And that means I need to trust myself ... my intuition."

Jeric's fingers slid under my chin and lifted it. His gaze swept over my face, as though studying it. "What do you mean, babe?"

"I know what we need to do now." I only hoped I could convince everyone involved to believe in me just as strongly.

CHAPTER 21

Bex

WHAT A DIFFERENCE a night makes. And a bouquet of flowers and lots of begging and pleading for forgiveness.

As I drove back to Orlando with Mason following me, I basked in the memory of the dramatic scene in my bedroom this morning. I especially enjoyed the part where he'd begged me. He'd actually fallen to his knees with his hands clasped in front of him, his stunning eyes darkened with sorrow and regret.

"It was an accident," he'd repeated, as he had in his phone messages. "I still never should have swung, I know that now, but I honestly didn't mean to touch you. My anger was out of control, I know, and I won't make any excuses. *Please* believe me. I love you, Bex. I care for other people, making them better. How could I ever mean to hurt *you*, the one I love most?"

Sincerity had filled his tone and eyes. I'd pretty much already decided last night that he hadn't meant for his knuckles to connect with my jaw. But I enjoyed watching him squirm and beg for my mercy maybe a little too much.

"I'll make up for it, I promise," he'd continued as I sat on the edge of the bed silently. "Anything I can do for you. Just believe me that I love you. I sat with your mom all night long, partly hoping you'd show up, but also because I could when not even you or your sister can. I made sure she was okay and taken care of. I talked to her about you—we believe unconscious patients can hear us. I told her how you'd turned out to be an amazing young woman she could be proud of and that I'd always take care of you."

His eyes had shone with tears by then, making my own eyes fill.

"You know what put her in that bed in the first place, right?" I asked quietly. "Drugs and alcohol. Drunks don't exactly have a great track record with me, and you'd been drinking last night."

"I promise I never will again."

I rolled my eyes. "I don't expect that, Mason. Don't make stupid promises. But if you're an angry drunk—"

"But I'm not! Not usually. My day—" He stopped and pushed his hands through his hair, then shook his head slowly. "I said I wasn't going to make any excuses, and I'm not. I'm sorry, Bex. I sincerely am. I let my anger get out of hand, and I swung at the pork chop, but my judgment was off and you were closer than I thought. I know it's all my fault. I can't tell you enough how sorry I am."

"It's not just that," I'd said. "I'd been at the hospital, thinking my mama was going to die. And you expected me to serve you? The things you said?"

He blew out a heavy sigh. His shoulders sagged, and his chin dropped to his chest. His eyes rose to look up at me through his lashes. "I know, I know. I was cruel. You didn't deserve any of that. Your smaller than me and so fragile and—"

"I'm not fragile," I said firmly. "I'm a pretty tough cookie. But, really, Mason. You're a doctor. You've got to understand what I'm going through."

He lifted his head and placed his hands on my knees. "You're right. With everything. I was an inconsiderate ass worried only about myself and the shit I was going through with losing a patient, and never stopped to think that your day had been just as bad."

"Wait. You lost a patient yesterday?"

He nodded, and now I felt like the ass. He'd even told me he'd had a bad day, and had I ever stopped to ask him about it? No, I'd been as self-absorbed as I'd blamed him for being. With Grams and likely Mama soon, I had experience on the family side of losing someone, where you feel helpless and at everyone's mercy. I'd imagined before how hard it would be for a doctor to tell their patients' next of kin that they hadn't made it, but this morning I thought harder about being the one who couldn't save the person. Being the one who may have done all they could, but that still hadn't been enough. Being the one who everyone expected to make it all better, but you failed.

The tears spilt, and I fell off the bed to my knees in front of Mason and threw my arms around him.

"I'm so sorry," I'd said into his shoulder as he hugged me back, pulling me tightly against him.

"You have nothing to be sorry about."

"I wasn't much better, Mason. I do need to be sorry, and I am."

His hand cupped the back of my head and smoothed my hair down my back. "No, no. Last night was all my fault. I let things get out of control."

I pulled back and looked at him. "Mason. I threw raw pork chops at you."

We stared at each other for a moment before we both laughed. "Yeah, that was disgusting. Did I mention I took a scalding shower before going to the hospital?"

"I'm sorry," I said again. "I let things get out of control, too."

He pulled me back against him. "I will take all the blame. I thought I'd lost you forever because of my asshole ways. And I can't lose you, Bex. Now that I know what life's like with you, I can't imagine it without you."

Tears threatened to fall again as I recalled those words. Nobody, not even Ty, had ever said anything like that to me. And I could hear in his voice, feel in his body as his heart pounded against my chest the conviction that he believed what he said without a doubt. So here I was, driving back to Orlando with a heart full of love and hope. We'd made it through our first fight, and I thought, if anything, we might have loved each other more now than before. And that was a good sign.

As I rolled the car to a stop at the bottom of the exit ramp near home, my phone rang. Leni.

"Hey, girl, what's up?" I answered cheerfully.

"You sound happy." She sounded surprised.

"Yeah, everything's great. I mean, Mama's back in the hospital, in ICU even, but Mason thinks she'll pull through. At least for now. I'm on my way there."

"So you're back in Orlando? Jeric said he saw your car this morning."

"Um, yeah, I drove down last night for a couple of things I forgot." I wasn't about to tell her the truth. Now that Mason and I had made up, nobody needed to have their noses in our business. "I needed to get back here this morning, so sorry I didn't stop by to say hey."

"That's okay. Um ... Brock and Asia and Jeric and I are talking about coming down there. Can we meet up for drinks tonight?"

"Actually, if Mama's doing okay, Mason's taking me out to a nice dinner." One of his promises to make up for last night.

"Oh, too bad. I'd, uh ... we'd hoped to see you guys. We'll be there a few days, though, so maybe tomorrow? I at least need a coffee or something with my girl."

"Sure. Sounds good." Once we hung up, I wondered if she'd really sounded off or if that was my imagination. I still thought the girl was a little odd, even though I'd come to like that about her. But sometimes she seemed even more so than usual. Like today. I worried about her, wondering if something was wrong.

Maybe wanting to go out for drinks or coffee was an excuse to talk about something she needed to get off her chest.

I pulled into the hospital parking lot and shifted mental gears. Mason said he'd needed to go home and shower and take care of stuff before he came to the hospital, but I'd come straight here. If Mama was still doing okay and they didn't need anything from me, I'd go home and shower later to get ready for our date. I spent a few hours in the family room with Sissy, each of us taking turns to see Mama when they allowed, but she slept the entire time. Her condition hadn't worsened, but Dr. Munthe came by to let us know he couldn't yet make a decision about the surgery. By the time I headed home, Mason had never showed.

When I walked in the door and into our bedroom, though, I forgot to be mad at him. A gorgeous, fancy black dress lay on the bed, the tags still on it, and good night, it took me a week of tips back home to earn that much money.

"I love it," I told Mason as soon as he answered his phone.

"I can't wait to see it on you. Sorry I didn't get to your mom before you left. I had a couple other patients to see. I'm about to see her now, though, then I'll be home."

I took a long, luxurious shower, scrubbing and polishing every inch of my skin and removing every unwanted hair. I painted my toenails and applied my makeup carefully, following the online tutorials to create the smoky-eye look. I watched another video and tugged and twisted my hair into an up-do with half of my hair piled on my head and the rest falling in ringlets down my back. After wiggling into the body-hugging dress and strapping on my favorite platform heels, I inhaled deeply, and then stepped in front of the full-length mirror.

My eyes went directly to the dress, which couldn't have fit more perfectly if it'd been custom sewn for me. A sleeveless number with a plunging yet tasteful neckline, the swanky material pooled around my boobs, then tightened at the waistline, hugging every curve down to a few inches above my knees. Sexy as hell, but still classy. As I turned and twisted, loving how it fit my body, the light bounced off small, sparkly pieces woven into the fabric. Damn, the dress looked hot on me.

I checked out my hair and face next and loved how the black dress set off the red of my hair and made my blue eyes pop. My gaze quickly traveled down to my feet, approving the shape of my legs in those heels. I grinned widely and nearly squealed with giddiness for the night. That first time we'd gone out to the upscale steak house, I hadn't been prepared. This time I was and looking at my reflection, I appeared to belong in a fancy restaurant or even a club house as much as any high falutin' debutante.

But then my eyes couldn't help zeroing in on the tattoos on my arms and collarbone, displayed in all their glory. Or the zirconia stud in the right side of my nose, or the hoops along the ridge of my ear. My makeup suddenly looked caked on and my hair ridiculous. The dress was still beautiful, but who I was fooling? This so was not me.

My shoulders fell, my mood tumbling after. With a sigh, I bent over to undo my shoes. I couldn't go out in public like this.

"Holy shit, Bex," Mason said from the bedroom door, his voice filled with an awe I'd never heard before. I stood up and looked over my shoulder at him. "I thought that dress would look good on you, but I had no idea ..."

I tried to give him a smile. He narrowed his eyes.

"What's wrong?"

"This isn't me, Mason. I look ridiculous." I turned back to the mirror and waved my arm toward my silly reflection.

"Like hell you do." He walked up behind me, his gaze reflecting back at mine, holding it. Without breaking the lock, he dipped his head down and planted his lips on my neck. "You look phenomenal. I don't know if I can manage getting through the night before taking it off of you, though."

I turned around and draped my arms around his neck. "Let's not go out, then. Let's stay here and order in, and we can spend the night alone ... but together."

His lips tipped up slightly. "Very tempting. But I'm too proud of you and need to go out and show off my girl."

I frowned. "I look like a fake wannabe, Mason." I flicked my fingers over the tattoo on my collarbone. "I don't belong at a fancy restaurant or even in this dress."

He stared straight into my eyes. "You belong by my side, wherever that is. Don't let anyone tell you differently, especially yourself. I'm in this forever, precious. And that will mean fancy dinners and club houses, and you will be there looking every bit as hot as you do now. And you damn well do belong in that dress. I swear it was made for you." He gave me a kiss, and then said, "We're going out. I just need a quick shower."

I sighed as he pulled away, undressing as he walked for the bathroom. I was half-tempted to follow him in, but he was insistent about our plans, and I didn't want the steam to ruin my look, as fake as it was.

"Do you know the first reason I fell in love with you?" he asked a few minutes later as he came out of the bedroom, wearing black dress pants and buttoning up a light green shirt that made his eyes even more stunning than usual. "You didn't seem like the type who cared what other people think."

I turned in my place on the couch and looked up at him. "It's not that I care all that much about what other people think, especially snobby-nosed assholes. But I do know where and how I'm comfortable, and that'd be wearing a halter top, cut-off shorts and cowboy boots while whoopin' it up at a K-bomb. Not dressed like this and eating fancy food at a restaurant so dark you can't see what you're eatin' and so hoity-toity, you're afraid to even laugh out loud."

"Maybe this will make you feel a little better." He held out a small, square box in his palm. I froze. I was so not ready for this. He must have seen the panic in my eyes, because he snorted. "Don't worry. It's not that. Not yet."

He gave me a wink before sitting on the couch next to me and leveling the box in front of my chest. I reached out and lifted the top. Inside lay a pendant—a silver pair of cowboy boots with a bright pink stone at the top of each. A kind of squeal mixed with a laugh escaped my lips, and I picked it up. A silver necklace dangled from it.

"This is too much, Mason," I said, but I turned my back for him and held the necklace out. "But I love it."

He fastened the necklace and although it might have looked all wrong with the dress, it somehow made it all feel more right. Mason took me out to an amazing dinner, and after we came home, the best part of fighting began: the makeup sex.

"I don't want to do the dominance thing tonight," I said against his mouth as we kissed while making our way to the bedroom.

"Okay. Why don't you take control this time?"

So I did. And I'm pretty sure he enjoyed every single second of it.

He woke me up the next morning with breakfast in bed and cleaned the kitchen spotless by himself. Then he stepped in the shower soon after I did and made sweet, crazy love to me before tenderly washing my body. He left me standing under the warm water, rinsing off.

"What do you think about getting a puppy?" he asked from the other side of the glass door.

"A puppy?" I echoed.

"Yeah. Or are you more of a cat girl? You seem like a dog person to me."

"I've never had a pet," I admitted. "Unless you count Sissy."

"He'd keep you company during the day until you found a job."

"And then I'd have no time for him and neither do you. You're hardly home as it is."

I turned the water off, and when I opened the door, Mason stood there with a towel hanging from his waist, holding another.

"That's going to change," he said, handing me the spare towel. "I guess you heard that I was a resident?"

I stopped rubbing the terrycloth over my head and looked at him. "Yeah, about that ..."

"I'm really a doctor, Bex. I don't know what you know about the process—"

"Pretty much nothing." I nearly missed his smile as I bent over to twist the towel around my hair. When I came up, he held out another, bigger one for me, which I wrapped around my body.

"Well, as soon as you finish med school, you have a doctorate degree and are called a doctor. Then you do your residency, which is like a paid apprenticeship. By the time you're done with that, you finish the tests to get your license and go for Board certification. I just finished my residency."

I stared at him and lifted my brows. "So you're not really a doctor?"

His eyes tightened, and his nostrils flared, as though I'd accused him of lying. Maybe I had. But I was also trying to understand. He gained control over whatever anger had risen.

"Yes, I am. I'm allowed to treat patients. I've just been under supervision. I finished my residency, though, and will soon be licensed to practice on my own."

I processed this, then bounced on the balls of my feet and smiled. "That's a big thing, right? We should celebrate!"

He laughed and pulled me into his arms. "Yeah, it's kind of a big thing. But let's hold off on the celebration until my license is in hand."

"So the residency is when you have to work all those god-awful hours, right? Like they do on the TV shows?"

"Right. And I'm done with that now. Being a doctor still means I'm on call and will have some long days, but not like it's been."

"I always thought they didn't make much money. Seems like they complain about bein' poor all the time, even the characters who come from *real* poor." Like me.

"We get a salary, but nothing like when you have your practice. Most residents have hundreds of thousands in student loans, so the salary seems pretty paltry from that perspective. I'm lucky enough to have an inheritance."

"I thought you said you put yourself through school."

He gave me a blank stare for a long moment, but then nodded slowly.

"Uh, yeah, I did. I didn't get the inheritance until I finished." He didn't explain any further, even when I raised a brow. Instead, he reached behind him, and his hand came back with my phone. "Leni's been texting you all morning. Says you have a date?"

I frowned.

"Something wrong?" he asked.

Possessive much? I wanted to say, not liking the tone of his voice or the fact that he'd read my text messages. Or that something felt odd about his whole explanation.

"We were supposed to meet for coffee this morning," I said, trying to play it off. Reading my messages wasn't really a big deal, was it? He did pay for my phone and the bill ... "She's probably waitin' for me."

"Maybe you can reschedule. I'm headed to the hospital." He leaned in and kissed my forehead. "See you there?"

"Here, there, and everywhere, you are a part of me, and therefore always with me," I murmured, the phrase suddenly coming to mind.

Mason chuckled. "What?"

I blinked. "Didn't you say that to me last night?"

He rolled his eyes. "I'm not *that* cheesy."

Huh. I didn't think it cheesy at all. In fact, it kind of made my knees weak. And I could have sworn Mason had whispered it into my ear last night. Maybe it had been a dream?

Without another word, he strode out of the bathroom and into the bedroom. I hadn't even finished brushing my hair when I heard the front door open then close. After waiting a few minutes to make sure he didn't return for some forgotten item, I called Leni. For some reason I couldn't explain, I didn't want him overhearing my conversation with her.

We met at a nearby coffee shop, and I found her sitting at a table alone. When I asked where everyone else was, she said Jeric, Brock, and Asia had dropped her off before going to the mall down the street. I was surprised at that. I kind of had the feeling Jeric was a little overprotective of Leni. He'd been at Sullivan's a lot when she worked and hardly ever gave her space, like he didn't really trust her. I supposed having coffee with a girlfriend was different in his mind than working at a bar. I could sort of understand, but still thought he could lighten up.

She asked me about my mama and Sissy and squeezed my hand when I told her about Mama being in ICU. Other than that, we didn't really talk about anything important. Back home, the blue-haired ladies would call it a gossip tea, but we didn't really have anyone to gossip about. I supposed the coffee date was nice, but a little on the weird side. Sometimes I really didn't get Leni.

"Do you mind giving me a ride to the mall?" she asked when I said I needed to get to the hospital when we finished our coffee. The mall was on the way, so of course I said yes.

When she got out of my car, she leaned back in, her big purse swinging forward. "I almost forgot I'm supposed to ask you something. You haven't heard from Ty, have you? Like in the past week?"

"No. I called him the other night, but as usual, he didn't answer or return it." I didn't tell her about sitting in his driveway for an hour. She nodded and shut the door, and as I was driving away, I wondered if I should have mentioned it. Something about Ty and the way she asked didn't sit well with me.

I quickly forgot about it, though, when I arrived at the hospital. Dr. Wilcoxson and Dr. Munthe had exited ICU at the same time I rounded the corner and stood in front of the door to the family room. Sissy grabbed my hand and pulled me in, and the doctors followed. Their expressions scared me.

"Your mother's taken a turn for the worse," Dr. Wilcoxson said, his voice heavy as though he sincerely cared about her.

"You already know her liver and kidneys were failing, and her heart and lungs were weak," Dr. Munthe said when his father-in-law seemed unable to go on. "Whatever improvement they'd made is gone. She's developed pneumonia now, and she's headed for end stage renal failure. I'm sorry ..."

Sissy and I both stared at him. Sorry for what?

Dr. Wilcoxson cleared his throat. "At this point, it's probably best to contact hospice and set her up so she can rest comfortably."

"And then what?" I asked.

"Then we pray," Dr. Wilcoxson said.

I blinked. He put a hand on my shoulder and squeezed.

"Don't worry about expenses or anything. Whatever isn't covered by Medicaid has already been addressed. Apparently, your mother has a benefactor."

My heart skipped at this news. *Mason.* Had to be. How much inheritance did he have? I pressed my hand to my mouth and nodded.

"How ... long?" Sissy asked, choking on the words.

"How long does she have?" I clarified for her as I slipped my arm over her shoulders. Her body trembled against mine.

"It's hard to say. A few days, maybe a week or so," Dr. Munthe said. "We're very sorry."

The doctors left, and Sissy turned into me and cried on my shoulder. "I hate her, Bex. As much as you do. I really do. But I love her, too."

"I know, Sissy, I know," I whispered as I smoothed her hair.

We spent the next few hours filling out paperwork and talking to the hospice people. They said they needed to develop their plan of care with the doctors and would let us know if they'd be moving her tomorrow or the next day.

"I wish they could just put her down like a dog, bless her heart," I muttered as Sissy and I walked toward the parking garage.

She grabbed my hand. "I actually agree with you. Too bad it's against the law."

I drove home in a daze. When I reached to the passenger side floor for my purse, my hand landed on something else. A book? I lifted it up and tried to see it better in the dim light of sunset. It was big enough and spread open, so I didn't know how I'd missed it before, but now it was too dark to see the open pages. I pressed it against my chest, found my purse, and headed upstairs. If Mason had stopped in to see Mama, it must have been while Sissy and I were talking to the hospice people, because I never saw him. I was glad to see him home, sitting on the couch and reading. I dropped the book on the entrance table and my purse on top of it, kicked my shoes off as I walked over to him, and curled into his side. He put his magazine down and wrapped his arms around me while I cried.

Mason continued treating me like a princess—a sad and conflicted one—all night. He didn't complain about me leaving my things everywhere, and he picked up my shoes and put them away for me. He made me dinner, even though I only picked at it, and cleaned up afterward.

"You paid for everything?" I asked as we snuggled in bed. He lay on his back, and I lay on my side with my head on his chest. One of his arms was behind his head, and his free hand twisted and twirled my hair.

"It's not a problem," he said, indirectly answering me.

"Why?"

"Because I love you. I want to take care of you, and right now, that means taking care of your mother."

"You didn't have to do *that*, though."

He smoothed the hair away from my face, then gripped my chin and tilted my head back so he could look in my eyes.

"I told you. You are my life now. Your problems are my problems. I won't always be able to solve them for you, Bex. I know life doesn't work that way, but we'll figure those out. This problem, though ... this is one I can solve for you, so I did."

"I can never repay you."

His eyes flickered, and it almost looked like anger had passed through them, but then they softened. "You can repay me by loving me. That's all I need from you."

I gave him the best smile I could muster, too exhausted to argue tonight. "I think I can handle that."

When I awoke the next morning, Mason was already gone. I padded into the kitchen in my tank and panties to pour a cup of coffee. As I headed back out with a cup in hand, I noticed the book on the entranceway table, still open under my purse. I retrieved it and went back to the bedroom. I propped myself up against some pillows, pulled the covers over my legs, and set the book on my lap. Both pages it was open to were blank.

As I lifted the yellowish pages to thumb through them, I noticed for the first time that a lock hung from the edges of the covers. I sucked in my bottom lip. This was a journal. It must have been Leni's diary and fallen out of her purse yesterday. Before I could be tempted to read it, I went to close it immediately. The pages fluttered and something caught my eye, stopping me at the last moment. I stuck my hand between those pages and opened the book back up.

A face stared up at me.

A face I didn't remember ever seeing before.

But somehow, a face I knew.

CHAPTER 22

BEX THE FACE, ALTHOUGH a pencil drawing, looked a little like Mason, I thought, with darkish hair and light eyes that I could imagine being silvery green, but I guess they could have been gray or even blue. The rest of his features were like Mason's, too, only … hotter. *Lots* hotter. More rugged than Mason's pretty-boy face, but that somehow made this one more perfect. I didn't think it possible, but this picture blew Mason's reality out of the water.

I turned the page, backward. Another face. Several pages, actually, of hand-drawn faces, all male, all different, all vaguely familiar. Kind of like I was feeling déjà vu again, but different. For some weird reason, my heart ached for all of them. As if I missed them terribly, although they had obviously lived in different times, judging by their styles, so I couldn't have ever known them. I didn't even know if they'd been real people or the objects of an artist's imagination, especially since some didn't even appear to be quite human. My reaction to the drawings made no sense, but it only continued to grow, making my stomach hurt as much as my heart.

"When I hold you once more, you will know where you belong and never question it again. Together, our souls as one, is how we're meant to be."

Another swoon-worthy phrase popping into my mind like the one yesterday, making my tummy dip. This time, I knew for sure Mason hadn't said those words. But who had? And why did they suddenly pop into my head now?

I continued paging backwards, curiosity getting the best of me, until I reached pages of handwriting. I flipped to the front, where I learned this was not Leni's diary after all. It may have been her book, but the journal was claimed by a Jacey who'd written it back in 1989. As soon as I turned to the first entry, my gaze fell on a single word: Bex. And then I was a lost cause. I couldn't stop myself from reading, no matter how bad I felt for snooping. And the funny thing was the parts about this Jacey and Bex at college gave me the same feeling of recognition as the men's faces. But I had no idea why.

I finished a gut-wrenching entry about Jacey's pops dying, which reminded me of my own mama. I glanced at the clock. Oh, good heavens, how time flies. I was supposed to meet Sissy at the hospital in thirty minutes. I closed the book, sprang from the bed, took a quick shower and finished getting ready in a rush. By the time I parked my car, I was already fifteen minutes late.

A feeling of dread and hatred for this place blanketed over me as I walked down the corridor toward the ICU. I was sick of it— sick of the pale green walls, the hushed voices, the smell of bleach and disinfectant that ironically made me think of illness and disease. Sick of seeing Mama doing nothin' but lying there, practically dead already. Not too long ago, when I'd first come to see her on the fifth floor, I'd been scared of myself, that I'd kill her as soon as I saw her. Now, I almost wished I had. Instead, we'd gone through two more months of suffering alongside her. Once again, she'd be leaving us with a mess of pieces to pick up. At least she'd be leaving us alone for good this time.

Bitter thoughts I shouldn't be having. More reason I'd be going to hell.

I passed the family room we usually used, but it was empty. I'd texted Sissy to let her know I'd be late, but I didn't know if she'd received my message. I hoped she was in with Mama and hadn't left or moved on with plans without me. As I approached the nurse's desk to find out if she was inside, sounds of their whispered voices carried over to me. They weren't exactly whispering, though, but speaking in hushed tones. I stood at the desk for a long while, thinking at first their backs were to me because they were discussing something important. But they spoke loud enough for me to hear that they were gossiping. And about my man.

"Well, Dr. Hayes won't be much of a doctor now, will he?" one of the nurses said, a younger woman not much older than me, judging by her profile. "I've missed seeing that gorgeous face of his around the hospital."

The other woman, older with short, graying hair, and quite a bit plumper, grunted. "A pretty face can't make up for a temper like that. I heard it was scary as all get-out."

"Such a shame. He had so much going for him, too. I can't believe he gave up everything over that. All that school and work ..."

"From what I hear, he was just playin' doctor. He's got some huge trust fund. He wouldn't have to work a day in his life, could travel around the world fifty times, and still die a billionaire. That's just what I heard, though."

I blinked. And almost laughed. Mason had said he had an inheritance, but a billionaire? Not even. He wouldn't be living in a condo, cooking his own food, and doing his own cleaning, if that were the case.

"Must be nice," the younger one muttered. "I guess we should feel better that they kicked him out. I feel bad for whatever bimbo he picks up next, though. He seems like a catch at first glance."

I cleared my throat and both of them turned to look at me.

"Excuse me," I said, my voice sweet as honey, "were you talking about Dr. Mason Hayes?"

Both nurses' faces turned about as red as my hair.

"Oh, you shouldn't have heard that," the older one said. "Didn't realize you were standin' here."

"But I was, and I couldn't help but overhear. I'm a good friend of Dr. Hayes, and I think you have your facts messed up. You see, he won't be around as much because he finished up his residency. But he'll still be working here."

The nurses exchanged a look.

"I think you're the one who's mistaken. Dr. Hayes was fired and escorted out of the hospital by the police two weeks ago," the younger nurse said as she sauntered over to stand across from me. Her brown eyes, lined with smudged green eyeliner, watched me carefully.

I shook my head and opened my mouth to tell her that was impossible, but I hesitated. I couldn't exactly say I watched him leave every morning and come home every night dressed for work. Or that Mama wasn't his patient anymore but he still came to check on her. Or could I?

"He's been here every day to see my mama, though," I said. "Checking in on her even when she's not his patient anymore."

The older nurse's gray brows rose. "I haven't seen Dr. Hayes in weeks. It's been even longer since he's been to the ICU."

"Then he came when you weren't here," I said. She *had* to be mistaken.

She leaned her heavy arms on the counter between us, her bodacious tatas resting on the top. "Honey, we have a list to track everyone's comin's and goin's and his name hasn't been on it. He has no reason to be at the ICU even if he was still on staff. And the only souls comin' to see your mama are you and your sister."

I shook my head harder, anger growing. "Honey," I said, my voice no longer sweet as I echoed her endearment, "you're wrong. Dr. Hayes has been here every day. He sees patients. He even lost one the other day."

"Well, aren't you precious," she said, and my hand balled at my side. That was no compliment. "If you're callin' us liars, you better back yourself up. How do you know he's been here? Have you seen him with your own eyes?"

My mouth gaped open, no words spewing out as I wished they would. Because I hadn't seen him here. We'd always missed each other, crossing paths as we came and went. In fact, the last time I'd seen him here at the hospital was two months ago, when we'd first met.

"Don't you watch the news or read the paper?" the younger woman asked. "It was everywhere. He punched another doctor. Almost hit a patient. All because the poor man vomited on him. I'm pretty sure he's facing charges."

I pressed my lips together, shook my head again, and spun on my heel. My legs carried me down the hall, away from them, away from their lies. They *had* to be lying. He may have had a bit of a temper that one night after a bad day, but he took his work seriously. Always the professional. And why on earth would he pretend to come to work every day? Where did he even go if not here? Why would he ask me to move in with him if he had all that going on? He knew then he'd have to lie to me.

No, their story made no sense. This was too big for Mason to try to hide from me. And from Sissy! I didn't watch the news or read the papers—I wasn't even in Orlando two weeks ago to see—but Sissy surely would have heard something. Mama didn't have TV at her house, but still. These women made it sound like everyone in Orlando knew. Dr. Wilcoxson and Dr. Munthe didn't even know, or surely they would have said something the other day. The nurses were lying bigger than a no-legged dog. All there was to it.

That younger one probably had a crush on Mason. She'd called him gorgeous and was definitely smitten with him. That was all it was. Maybe since Mason had been coming to see Mama, they'd put two-and-two together, and she made up this crazy-ass story to run me off. I mean, really. Why would they be gossipin' like that for real when anyone could have heard them? I was no city slicker or college graduate, but anybody would know how unprofessional that was, as well as the way they'd talked to me.

"Bex, hold up." Sissy's low voice hissed after me, and she caught up with me as I turned the corner for the elevator. "Where you goin'?"

I closed my eyes and inhaled a deep breath. "I had to get away from those nurses," I said.

She snorted. "Yeah, I don't like those two either. Always tellin' stories. They're worse at gossipin' than the women's Bible study group at their Wednesday night teas, aren't they? I don't even work here, and I know half their stories are wrong."

I opened my eyes and smiled at my sister, then wrapped my arms around her. She hugged me back, but quickly pulled away.

"What was that for?"

I shrugged. "How's Mama?"

Her face fell. "The same. I haven't heard from the hospice people yet. Have you?"

"Nope. I guess she'll be here another night, then?"

"I guess. At least she's gettin' good happy drugs here." She laughed once and pressed her palm against her forehead. "Doesn't that figure? Drugs put her in here, and now they're gonna carry her out, making her oblivious to everything she's leavin' behind."

"Just like always," I muttered.

Sissy wanted to chat, but I barely paid any attention to the conversation, and she must have noticed the one-sidedness because she shooed me off. Finally free to focus on the bee in my bonnet, I hurried down to my car, dropped inside it and locked all the doors before pulling my phone out. I hardly ever used the Internet on it because I didn't want to take advantage of Mason's generosity and make him pay more, but this was an emergency. I had to be sure.

It didn't take me long to pull up the news story.

Then I drove home in a daze, thinking the news had to be wrong. They'd shown no pictures of Mason. No mug shot or anything. Just his name. Maybe there was another Dr. Mason Hayes? Here in Orlando? At this particular hospital?

By the time I reached home and walked up the stairs on autopilot, I realized things were about to change. And I begged to God and sweet baby Jesus that Mason had a really good explanation for everything. I'd fallen so hard for him, especially over the past couple of days, but if he'd been lying to me all this time, I didn't know what I would do. The heartbreak would be too much for my poor, battered heart. What Ty did to me would be nothing in comparison.

When I opened the door and found Mason cooking dinner, I didn't know what to say. Based on experience, throwing out accusations wasn't the best way to start with him. So rather than say anything, I set my purse in its usual spot in the entryway and silently walked to our bedroom, noticing that the closed and locked journal sat on the dining table, which was already set for dinner. I slipped my shoes off in our room and put them in the closet. I felt as though I walked on eggshells, pissed off that I couldn't simply say what was on my mind, but afraid of how he'd react if I did.

"You sure are quiet tonight," Mason said half-way through dinner as he poured himself a second glass of wine.

I shrugged. "Just not feeling like chatting, I guess."

Although I didn't really want it, I shoved a red potato wedge in my mouth so I wouldn't have to say any more.

"How's your mother?" he asked a few minutes later.

"Shouldn't you know?" I muttered before I caught myself.

"What was that?" A sharp edge laced his voice, as though he'd heard me clearly.

"Nothing," I said, trying to cover up my mistake. The Southern girl in me was screaming *Oh, hell, no!* and wanted to go off on his ass, but I needed to keep her in check. I still hoped

Mason could explain away what I'd learned today. "Mama's no better. I guess you didn't make it in to see her today?"

"No, I'm sorry. I wasn't at the hospital long this morning. I saw something and couldn't get it off my mind."

His eyes glanced at the diary still sitting on the table. When they came back to me, I held them with my own. "Yeah, the nurses said you hadn't been in this morning. In fact, they said—"

"I thought you didn't feel like chatting," he snapped, and I raised my brows. He let out a sharp breath. When he spoke again, his voice had softened. "Before we get into the hospital gossip mill, can you tell me what this is?"

He picked up the brown leather book from the table and handed it to me. I set it in my lap without looking at it, my gaze on him, trying to figure out what his problem was.

"Looks like an old diary to me," I said, failing at keeping the sarcasm out.

"Yours?" he demanded.

"No. Leni left it in my car yesterday."

"You saw Leni and didn't tell me?" There was that possessive tone again.

"I told you we had a coffee date."

"You told me you *missed* your coffee date. But apparently you didn't. What else are you hiding from me, Bex?"

"I could ask you the same thing!" I finally snapped.

He nodded at the book, ignoring my accusation. "Open it."

"Why?"

"I want to see what's in it. I want to know what you've been writing about me."

I snorted. "I told you, it's Leni's, not mine."

He leaned forward. Anger sparked in his eyes. "I don't believe you. You know why? Because I saw that book wide open under your purse when I left this morning. And then it was on the bed when I came home, which was left unmade, by the way. You're not the type to read someone else's journal."

I leaned forward, too, so our faces were only inches apart. "It's not mine, Mason. Get over yourself."

I placed the book on the table, stood up and grabbed my plate. Mason knocked it out of my hand, and it crashed to the floor. He shoved the journal at me.

"I said to open it, Bex. Prove it to me."

"Are you deaf? I said it's not mine! How can I open it when I don't have the key?" I grabbed the lock to show him, then shoved the book back at him. "If it's so damn important to you to know, figure out how to open it yourself."

He grabbed the book and my hand, squeezing it so hard, I thought I heard bones crunch. I cried out, but he didn't let go.

"Stop fucking lying to me and open it!" he yelled. "If I could, I would have already."

I yanked my hand out of his grip and held it close to my chest, while taking the book from him and heaving it at the front door. Then against all better judgment, I stepped right in front of him.

"Why are you so worried about what I might have to say about you?" I asked, my voice low. It rose as I spoke until I yelled the last words. "Is it little dick syndrome, Mason, or because *you're* the fucking liar?"

He stood up to his full height, towering over me, and looked down his nose at me. And before I saw it coming, his hand lashed out at me, landing against the side of my head. The force pushed me sideways, and I stumbled to catch myself, but my dinner and broken plate on the floor made me slip. I fell onto the broken glass, my heart racing against my ribs, but I could only laugh.

"Thank you for just proving them right," I said through the maniacal laughter. "You're an asshole, Mason. The lowest of the low and the biggest coward there is."

"I'm not a fucking coward," he boomed.

He lunged at me and circled his hands around my neck. He squeezed as he picked me up off the ground and slammed me into the wall. Stars shot across my vision when my head made contact. My breath flew out of me. As best as it could anyway, against my tight throat. I kicked out wildly at Mason while clawing at his hands still around my neck. My foot finally connected in the best place possible—his balls—forcefully enough that he let go of me and bent over with a grunt.

I dropped to my hands and knees, struggling to catch a breath through my painful throat while trying to crawl away from him. A vice-like grip closed around my ankle and yanked me backward. I landed on my stomach and face, and Mason pulled me across the glass-littered floor.

"Where do you think you're going?" he sneered.

"Away from you," I gasped.

He grabbed me by the waist now and flipped me over. My little body was no comparison for his much larger one, but I wasn't going to give in. I kicked at him again and squirmed, barely feeling the glass shards that dug into my back. With two large hands pressing my wrists to the ground and his full weight on my hips, he pinned me to the floor. My hand throbbed under the renewed pressure.

"You have nowhere to go, Bex. Ty won't take you back—I made sure of that. Your trailer's rented. I took care of it today. Elizabeth's gone and so are your jobs. Sissy lives in a shit-hole and won't be there much longer when your mom dies anyway. That will make you both homeless. And forget about finding somewhere else to live because you owe me so much money, you'll never be able to pay me back. You were right about that. My attorney's got all the paperwork ready for the judge if we need to go there."

I glared at him, my chest heaving with the feeling of claustrophobia, more from the meaning of his words than his heavy weight on me.

"If you leave me, I guess you and Sissy could always go back to living in your cars again. You're used to that, right?"

I arched my back and tried to buck him off but couldn't budge him, so I spit at his face. "To think I actually loved you. That I believed you loved me!"

His green eyes flickered, and his grip loosened slightly. I tried to break free, and he tightened his hold on my wrists again, but his voice came out softer. Almost cooing. "But I do love you, precious. Why do you think I've done all these things for you? So that I could never lose you. I can't stand the thought that you could leave me. I can't live without you, Bex. You're mine forever."

I stared at him in disbelief. Was he serious? Was this really the man I'd thought to be generous and kind and gentle? To be The One? If he was The One for me ...

"I'd rather die," I said, and I opened my mouth wide and screamed as loud as my lungs and sore throat would allow.

Mason's hand clamped over my mouth. I bit down as hard as I could, and the coppery taste of blood filled my mouth before he yanked it away. His hold on me loosened, and I squirmed and bucked, wriggling free.

"HELP!" I yelled.

As if in response, my phone rang. With Mason's weight still on my legs, I used my arms to pull myself toward my purse ... and the door. He shifted, and I was suddenly free, up on my hands and knees, crawling and trying to get to my feet at the same time, scrambling for my purse and phone. But he'd only moved off of me to get there first. His shoulder hit the table, knocking it over. My purse tumbled off. My phone slid out of it and skidded across the white tile floor. I made one last-ditch effort to grab it, but his hand closed around it first. And he hurled it as hard as he could at the mirror-wall, shattering both my phone and the glass.

Mason turned to me, his eyes that I'd thought so beautiful before practically glowing like the devil himself.

"You're mine, Bex. Nobody else's." His lips turned up in a snide grin that made me think of the Joker. "I told you I was a selfish bastard."

I screamed again. Someone pounded on the front door. My eyes flew wide, and I lunged forward.

"Help!" I yelled. "Help me! Call the po—"

Arms came around me. A fist pounded up into my chin, slamming my jaw shut. Knowing I couldn't bite him again, he covered my mouth before I could open it. His arms squeezed me, lifted me up. I kicked at him as he half-carried, half-dragged me into the master bedroom and then into the walk-in closet. The pounding on the door continued.

"You say one word, and I *will* kill you. And Sissy, too. Ty … all of them. Dead." He shook his finger at me. "If you be quiet, though, and let me get rid of this nosy, asshole neighbor, we can talk. You'll see that everything will be okay. I'll take good care of you, Bex, and everyone you love. Just be quiet for one minute, okay?"

Wide-eyed, my heart hammering against my ribs, all I could do was nod. He backed out of the closet and closed the door. Something scraped loudly over the tile toward the closet, and then his footsteps retreated. I sprang for the door, but it wouldn't budge. He'd pushed the dresser in front of it.

I backed up as far as I could go, until I pressed against the rear wall of the closet. I slid down to my butt, staring at the closet door, not knowing what I would do when it opened again. Mason had me trapped in every which way possible. Physically. Financially. Emotionally. Although he was a monster, would he really kill Sissy and Ty? I didn't know if he'd go that far, but I was pretty sure he wouldn't kill me. What would be the point of all this? No, he wanted me as his toy. His pet. He'd set it all up and snared me like a small animal.

Tears streamed down my face, and when I wiped at them, my hands came away red and watery. Adrenaline must have still raced through my veins because I felt only a little pain. The longer I sat there, though, shaking like a dog shitting razor blades, the more I began to feel. The more I felt, the more my heart broke, and the more I cried. I almost didn't hear the strange female voice.

"Hello? Anyone in here?"

"Me," I rasped out, even though she probably couldn't hear me.

"Oh, shit. Dude, look at this."

A minute later, the sound of more furniture scraping across the floor. Light seeped in from under the door, then filled the space as it flew open. I cringed against the wall, afraid to see Mason.

"Oh, sweetheart, what the hell's happened to you?"

Two uniformed officers stood in the closet doorway, a man and a woman, gaping at me. The woman, who was closest, slowly stepped inside, hesitating, as though I were a trapped, wild animal. She reached out a hand toward me. I lunged at her, and she caught me in her arms. Sobs wracked through me.

CHAPTER 23

Jeric "OH, NO," LENI gasped from across the motel room, where she sat at the table in front of the window. She picked up her tablet and crawled across the bed to me, where I'd been flipping through TV channels. I didn't fully understand why we were still in Orlando, in this crappy motel room that was even smaller than Leni's camper, but she'd insisted we stay another night or two. She *felt* the need to on behalf of Bex, and after our trip to Alaska, I tried my best to show that I believed in her. Brock and Asia didn't quite buy into Leni's instinct yet and had headed back to Lake Haven in case Bex wasn't the Lakari's prey, or at least, their only prey. "Look at this, Jeric."

She held the screen for me to see a headline dated a couple of weeks ago: "Orlando Doctor Attacks Colleague and Patient." Her finger tapped a Play icon, and a video newscast began.

"Damn," I said when the video finished. "Does Bex know?"

"I don't think so." She looked up at me with worry darkening her green eyes. "Jeric, she could be in danger."

She sprang from the bed, her sudden agitation rolling over me.

"We don't know the whole story," I said. "The media isn't exactly reliable."

She turned toward the table, grabbed her purse and shoved her feet into her shoes. "Come on. We need to check on her. She at least needs to know about this. And I ... I *feel* something. Something's wrong, I think."

"Leni—"

"I'm going, Jeric." Her hand grasped the doorknob. "Are you coming or not?"

Of course I wasn't letting her go alone, and she knew that. I jumped up and ran out the door after her.

"Do you even know where she lives?" I asked as Leni turned onto the main road. I knew Bex couldn't live too far away—Leni had picked the motel for a reason.

"I know the condo complex. It's across the street from the coffee shop we met at. I don't know the apartment number, though. We'll just have to look for her car and go from there."

That'll be a crap shoot in the dark, I thought, but kept to myself. I indulged my girl, proving to her that I'd always be by her side as she showed the way.

Surprisingly, we had no trouble finding Mason's place. We followed the blue flashing lights of cop cars sitting in front of one of the stairwells. Bex's car sat in a space nearby. Leni didn't even pull into a parking space. She threw the truck into park and jumped out. With a groan, I followed. She ran up to the first person she saw—a guy wearing a t-shirt and shorts with bare feet. Definitely not a cop. Although their cars were all lit up, they were apparently on the third floor in a condo with the front door open.

"What happened?" she asked.

"Don't know," the guy answered.

"Have you seen a girl, about my age, red hair?"

"Yeah, I've seen her," the guy said, the blue glow of the cop cars lighting up a smirk I didn't like. "A hot little thing. I've seen her go up to that place where the cops are. Might be who went to the hospital."

"Yeah, it was that girl," his friend said. "She didn't look too good. I think the dude she was with beat her up bad."

Leni gasped and looked at me with wide eyes full of fear.

"Come on," I said, taking her hand. I walked her to the passenger side of her truck, and once she was in, I went around to the driver's side. A pit of anger began to take form in my stomach, but I tried to remain cool. For Leni's sake, if nothing else. "You think she's at the one with the sign we always pass down the road? The one by the mall?"

"That's where her mama is. And it's the closest hospital."

Neither of us said anything else the rest of the way. My jaw ached from clenching it so hard, and if I didn't loosen my grip on the steering wheel, my new superpower strength might destroy it.

"Oh, shit," Leni whispered when we turned onto the side street that led to the hospital. She leaned forward, her head tilted up as she stared through the windshield at the dark sky. I glanced up quickly and automatically slowed. Dark souls floated and swirled in the sky above the hospital. Dozens of them.

"It's a hospital," I said as I eased down the road, my eyes darting everywhere, my body on full alert. "I'm sure they're here all the time, sucking on dying souls and waiting for new recruits."

A few dropped down into the shadows of an indent of the building. Out strode three figures dressed in black.

"Or they're here for Bex," Leni said, and before I could react, she threw her door open and jumped out. The truck was still fucking moving.

"Damn it, Leni." I slammed on the brake and threw open my door while jamming the gear stick in park.

Leni was already on the attack, her body springing into the air, one foot out, aiming for a Shadowman's head. Even before he disintegrated, though, more Lakari dropped from the sky and materialized into human shapes. I charged at them, fists swinging. We managed to destroy them all, except two that we saw running into a side door of the hospital. We chased after them. If they were after Bex, they'd lead us right to her. But when the narrow corridor we ran down dumped us into a wider hallway, the Shadowmen were nowhere to be seen. Leni and I both spun in circles looking for any trace of them.

"Bex!" Leni gasped, and she jogged down the hall toward the sign for the ER where Bex and Sissy stood at a reception desk. At least she was in her right mind this time to pay attention to her speed. I strode after, my gaze still swinging everywhere, watching for the Lakari. If they were after Bex, they weren't getting her tonight.

"Mason?" Leni asked as I strode up.

Bex nodded, and my eyes scanned over her for the first time. Came back to her face. And I nearly exploded. My fists clenched and every muscle in my body tensed. Images of my sister looking the same way—battered and bruised, and the haunted look in her eyes showing that her soul was more damaged than anything—passed through my mind. I strode out the Emergency Room double-doors before I punched something. That was the last thing Bex needed.

I stalked out to Leni's truck parked in the middle of the street and moved it to the parking area for the ER. Anger still coursed through my veins, though, and I couldn't go inside yet, so I paced several times up and down the sidewalk in front of the ER's entrance, trying to cool down. But I couldn't get the images of Bex and my sister out of my mind. My heart raced as I wished for one minute with the fucker. After a while, Leni walked out, looking for me.

"I'll fucking kill him," I said through clenched teeth.

She nodded, but placed her hands on my tight biceps pumped with adrenaline. "I want to, too, but you need to calm down. We're taking her home, and she doesn't need to see you like this right now."

Her touch and her soothing voice soaked into me like the cooling gels we used after fights. My core temperature dropped. The anger subsided. After a long moment, I nodded. We went back inside to get Bex and escorted her to the truck, leaving Sissy behind to take care of something that had come up with their mother. Bex slid in through the passenger door first and scooted to the middle, her face twisting as she did. My jaw clenched again. Leni climbed in after her, and I returned to the driver's side.

"We're taking her to Mason's to—"

"The hell we are," I said.

"She needs some clothes and things," Leni said.

"I'm right here," Bex reminded us. "And yes, I need some damn clothes. And my car."

"And then where?" I asked, trying to stay calm. I didn't have to be the girl's Twin Flame to feel the fear rolling off of her.

"We'll get our things from the motel, and you'll drive Bex back to Lake Haven in here, and I'll drive her car," Leni said.

"And if the fu—if he's there?" I asked.

"He won't be," Bex said quietly. "They arrested him. Apparently his second offense in two weeks, and he was out on bail already. Hopefully, he won't be out for a while."

"I'm so sorry, hun," Leni said. She slid her arm over Bex's shoulder and pulled the other girl to her.

"You're a better sister than Sissy," Bex said as she leaned her head on Leni's shoulder. My eyes cut sideways at them. Bex's battered face was wet with tears.

I almost wished the asshole wasn't in jail. I so wanted to kill him.

"She's being a good sister by dealing with whatever's happening with your mama so you don't have to," Leni said.

Bex sighed. "Yeah, I guess."

The way she said it, there seemed to be more to the story, but she didn't share it.

When we pulled back up to the condo building, only one cop car remained, its lights dark now. I parked in a space this time, right next to Bex's car, and escorted the girls up the stairs.

"Can I get some of my things?" Bex asked the officer at the top of the stairs, an older, balding guy whose stomach seemed too big for a cop.

"Sure can, little lady," he said with a surprising kindness as he pushed the door open for her. "They've collected all the evidence they need. Finding you barricaded in the closet looking like you did makes it a pretty cut and dry case."

My gaze shot to the cop's. He looked back at me and nodded. We didn't say a word to each other, but an exchange passed. The police and I usually didn't get along too well, but this guy and I agreed on one thing. I saw in his eyes what I knew he saw in mine: the bastard deserved to die a long, torturous death.

Leni and Bex disappeared inside as the cop and I stood silently at the door. I wondered if he wished, like I did, that Mason managed to get out of jail already and showed up.

"Is she okay?" the cop finally asked. "Physically, I mean. I know mentally ..."

"Some cuts and bruises. A couple stitches, but nothing broken," I said without tearing away my watch over the parking lot.

"I guess that's good."

"It doesn't mean she's okay."

The cop grunted. "Believe me, I know. You're going to stay with her, just in case, right? She needs someone big like you around. She needs to feel safe."

"Damn right," I said.

The girls' voices came closer, and I turned toward where they stood in the hallway. Bex had changed out of her bloodied clothes, and both girls carried overnight bags.

"Oh, here, you dropped this in my car," Bex said, shoving a book at Leni. *The* Book.

Leni's eyes sparked as her hands closed over the Book of Phoenix, and she glanced at me, but said nothing except, "Thanks. I was wondering what happened to this."

"Let's get the hell out of here," Bex said.

I took Bex's bags from her and Leni, and we left the cop at his post—why he remained, I didn't know. Maybe he *was* hoping Mason managed to come home. I tossed the overstuffed bags in the back of the truck at the same time Leni's phone rang.

"Sissy," she said, handing the phone to Bex before turning to me, gnawing on her bottom lip.

After only a few moments of silence on this end, Bex's face blanched at whatever Sissy had to say, making every cut and bruise stand out. She closed her eyes and nodded.

"Alrighty then," she said. "See you in a few." She held the phone out to Leni. "Well, doesn't that figure? This day is goin' down in the history books for the longest and shittiest day ever. I gotta go back to the hospital."

"Everything okay?" Leni asked.

Bex's lower lip quivered, but she shrugged. "My mama just died."

The words hung in the air for a long moment, and then fell flat to the pavement. Leni wrapped her arms around Bex while looking at me. I pushed my hand through my hair and nodded.

"It's alright," Bex said, shrugging Leni off. "I just need to get this done with so I can go home."

She didn't say anything else as she climbed into the truck, and we returned to the hospital with Leni in front of us, driving Bex's car. This time when we approached the building, no Lakari swarmed overhead. If they'd been after Bex tonight, they must have given up. Just in case, though, Leni and I followed the sisters from floor to floor as hospital personnel sent them to every place that needed a signature on some form or another. Neither girl cried the whole time.

The sun had already begun lightening the eastern sky by the time we headed back to Lake Haven. Bex slept almost the whole way. Or at least pretended to. I didn't know how she could really get comfortable, though, between Leni's hard seats and all the cuts and bruises on her body.

"I can't believe how stupid I am," she murmured when we were about fifteen minutes from Lake Haven. "Falling for some rich guy asshole with a history of violence. Did you know Mason Hayes is only *one* of his names? I had no idea. God, I'm fucking stupid."

I glanced at her out of the corner of my eye. Her head leaned against the window, her gaze staring out beyond, but she probably didn't see the landscape passing by in the gray morning light. She would relive the scene with Mason over and over again, just as I relived the scene of the accident with my parents and sister.

"Don't," I said, keeping my voice as soft as I could, but she still cringed into the door at the sound of it. I lowered it even more. "Don't blame yourself, Bex. This is nobody's fault but his."

"I made choices," she said. "I chose to move in with him when I really didn't know him all that well. I chose to ignore any signs that things were off with him. I—"

"Did his business card say Doctor and Cowardly Woman Beating Asshole, and you chose to be with him anyway? Did he hand you a police record that you chose to ignore? Even if you'd known about what he did at the hospital or his past, he would have found a way to explain it away. He's that kind of person. You didn't *choose* any of this, Bex."

"But I shoulda—"

"Shoulda, woulda, coulda … We all have those. If you go down that road, I should have known about the asshole who dated my sister—and beat her. I'd known him since we were six years old. If nobody saw the signs in him for over eight years, no way could you have known about Mason."

Her head turned slightly toward me. "Your sister?"

I swallowed, my throat dry. Until Leni, I hadn't talked about this with anyone since it happened. But if anyone needed to hear the story, Bex did.

"Yeah. The guy she dated in high school—the damn quarterback football star who everyone loved—he abused her. Repeatedly.

I hadn't known for months, until she finally told me. She died on the side of the highway when I was trying to get her away from him." My white knuckles caught my eye, and I loosened my grip on the steering wheel.

"I'm so sorry," Bex whispered.

"And I'm sorry you had to go through this, too. Bex, these fuckers ..." I shook my head and rolled my shoulder. "They know how to pretend like they're the greatest people you could ever meet. That's how they do it. Otherwise, they'd never reel anyone in. So don't blame yourself. *Please* don't blame yourself. Nobody deserves this, and that includes you."

She turned to look out the window again and fell silent for another mile or so. "I'm done with men. They're no good for me."

"Hey, we're not all assholes." Although, I basically had been before I met Leni.

"Yeah, well, I must be a magnet for the ones who are." She sighed. "I'd only wanted true love. Like what you and Leni have."

I couldn't say anything to that. What Leni and I had was way beyond true love or anything comprehensible. There may have been thousands or millions of Twin Flames on Earth, but only a handful of us—those in the Phoenix Guardians—actually knew what we had. Nobody else could possibly understand the timeless and penetrating connection we shared, especially after being One soul, ripped apart, and finding each other again.

"As they say, that usually happens when you're least expecting it," I finally said as I pulled onto the exit ramp. "Or even wanting it."

"Great," she muttered. "I definitely don't want it now. I think I'll get me some cats and grow old with them. Sit in my rocker on the front porch when I'm old and gray with nothing but cats to keep me company. At least you know from the start that they're assholes."

I chuckled, glad to hear she kept her sense of humor. Probably a defense mechanism, but the best one anyone could have.

"Do you want me to call Ty?" I asked. He probably wouldn't answer, but maybe a voicemail about Bex being hurt would be the kind he'd finally respond to.

She sniffed and closed her eyes before shaking her head. "Nah. That could only go one of two ways—either he doesn't care, or he'd drive down to Orlando in a fury and end up getting arrested himself. I don't think I can deal with either right now."

Leni stopped at her camper and met us over at Bex's trailer a few minutes later. I was still pulling the bags out of the back of the truck when she drove up. Sissy reached for the sheets and blankets Leni had retrieved from her place—Bex apparently hadn't left any when she moved out—and Leni took the bags from me. The girls all went inside while I stayed out and kept watch. The Dark feeling of the Lakari wasn't too far off, but not directly overhead. They were probably scattering for the shadows as the sun rose.

The sky was a light gray by the time Leni came out. She grabbed the Book from Bex's car, and we walked home, leaving her truck where it was for now. We both sank into bed, exhausted.

"You *dropped* the Book, huh?" I asked Leni later that afternoon as we sat outside, drinking our coffee. Said Book sat on the picnic table between us. "The one special thing that could have all of our answers just fell out of your purse?"

Her lips quirked. "I may have helped it along."

"And why the hell would you do that?" I demanded.

"Following my instinct, Jeric. I thought maybe her memory needed a little jogging."

I stared at her, not understanding.

"The trip to Alaska confirmed everything I'd felt in my gut about my parents and the relationships we didn't really have. Confirmed my *instinct*. So I decided I needed to trust that same instinct that told me Bex was Rebethannah. And I figured if she is, maybe she'd see something in the Book that would remind her."

"Except she wouldn't be able to open it."

Her smile grew. "That's why I left it open."

I let out a growl. She was pleased with herself. I was anything but. "And what if she's not Rebethannah and read everything in there? What if the Book fell into the wrong hands, like the Lakari's? You know how big of a risk that was for us *and* Bex?"

Leni waved me off. "If she's not a Guardian, and if she actually read it, she'd think it was a made-up story and some drawings."

I stared at her with disbelief. "Well? Did she look at it? Did she remember anything? *Is* she Rebethannah?"

Now she finally frowned. "I don't know. She didn't seem too impressed with the Book when she gave it back to me. I know she'd just been through a lot, but I'd hoped for some indication ..."

She pulled the Book closer and swiped her finger over the lock to open it. She thumbed through the pages. No evidence that Bex had even looked at it.

"Whoa. This wasn't here before," Leni said when she reached the last page of the drawings I'd done of Nathayden.

This sketch had been weird, because the vision of his face had come to me, but neither of us remembered when he'd looked like that. We still knew it was him, though, in the same way we knew the others were. And now, scrawled to the side of the drawing were the words: "I feel you close, my love. Please come back to me."

Leni and I looked at each other. She flipped through the rest of the pages, but no other messages showed up. She slammed the Book shut.

"That has to mean she's Rebethannah and Nathayden's communicating with her."

I cocked my head. "We don't know that. It could mean all kinds of things. We could be wrong that the picture is even him."

She shook her head adamantly. "I denied my instinct this whole time, thinking we were wrong. Maybe if I had listened to it and tried harder with Bex, she wouldn't be all beat up right now."

I rubbed my hand over her back. "Babe, you can't blame yourself for that. That was nobody's fault but the asshole who did it."

"I know," she muttered, "but the point is, we didn't follow my instinct and that's what we're supposed to do. I have to stop denying what I feel deep inside, and so do you."

I kissed the side of her head. "Bex is safe now. We don't have to rush into anything until we know more. Maybe figure out that damn Book."

She folded her arms on the table and leaned her forehead against them, then started mumbling to herself about instincts and believing and bullshit clues. I went inside for something to eat, and Leni's phone rattled on the counter. I glanced at the screen. A text message notification. I carried the phone outside to her, along with a box of crackers. Ghost ran up to me as I handed her the phone, and we shared some crackers while Leni read the text.

"No fucking way," she said, jumping to her feet. "And I just now got this?"

She climbed away from the picnic table, tossed the phone at me and ran inside. "Call Brock and Asia. We need to go!"

I read the message from Sissy's phone: "This is Bex. I didn't want you to worry. We had to go to Orlando to take care of funeral and other stuff. Since Mason's still in the slammer, we're going back to get as much of my stuff as we can while we're down there. We checked. He's still there. We'll be fine."

The message showed as being sent over an hour ago. Which meant they had a big head start on us.

My own phone buzzed in my pocket, and I pulled it out. I hadn't had a chance to call Brock, but he'd sent me a text: "They found Ty's truck at a dead-end road in the swamps, over by the springs of the actual Lake Haven. Doesn't look good."

Fuck. I blew out a breath. "Leni?"

She came flying out of the camper, but froze on the step.

"What the hell?" she gasped.

I followed her gaze to the Book on the table.

Smoke seeped out between the leaves of paper. I threw the Book open. The pages flipped by themselves as a plume of dark smoke curled upwards, then cleared when the pages fell still. A new message had burned into several of them:

"You KNOW, Jacquelena! SAVE HER!"

CHAPTER 24

GET IT DONE. Get it over with. Move on.

Bex The words started playing on repeat in my mind the moment Sissy and I got in the car.

"I can't believe what an ass he is," she said for the sixteenth time as she drove us to Orlando. Maybe not that many or maybe more. I wasn't really paying attention. "*Good riddance.* That's what Uncle Troy says about his own baby sister's death."

I wasn't so surprised. He'd said before if Mama were on fire, he wouldn't walk across the street to piss on her. He'd written her off long ago. Maybe if I'd had been a stubborn mule like him, I wouldn't feel like I'd been hit by a truck right now. A truck with *Mason* on the grill instead of *Mack.*

"And then to say we had to be out of our own home in three days because he'd rented it?" Sissy carried on.

I tuned her out, tears stinging my eyes as I stared at the passing green landscape. I was so sick of crying. They hadn't stopped all night. Or morning, I should say. I hadn't managed a wink of sleep. I couldn't stop thinking about where I'd made the wrong turn.

The morning after the pork chop fight? Had I been stupid to believe the accident bit and forgive him? Was I an idiot for going back to him then? It sure seemed like it now, but at the time, I don't think I could have known. He'd been so sweet, so caring and giving before then. I'd had no reason to believe anything like that would happen again.

Besides, I'd already been neck-deep in debt to him by then. He would have said the same shit he did last night, getting a damn hard-on for trapping me so completely. I had no idea what I would do if he came after me for the money for Mama's medical bills. No way in hell could I pull all of that together, and I couldn't afford two minutes with a lawyer, so I couldn't fight it. But I could never stay with him and pretend to love him either.

My stomach clenched at the thought, and a shudder ran down my spine.

What choice do you have? A small voice whispered in my head. And that's what brought me to tears every time. Because I didn't know if I really had much choice. If I did, I couldn't see it now. I could only hope he stayed in jail long enough for me to figure something out.

We went to the crematorium first, signed the last of the papers and said goodbye to Mama for good. She'd wanted to be cremated, and we had no problem with that. It was the cheapest option, and when we told the man we had absolutely no money and no reason for a service or a plot, he really cheapened it down. Probably put her in a cardboard box and pushed it into the fire right after we left. How sad to go like that, when not even your own kids care. She was my mama, but she'd been the one to put us all where we were in the first place. Broke in the bank. Broke in the heart. Broke in the soul.

If it weren't for her, I'd have never met Mason Hayes.

If it weren't for her, I'd have never been born. At the moment, I really wished I never had been.

But I couldn't blame Mama for what Mason did. She'd fallen for him like everyone else had. And it wasn't like she'd intentionally set me up with him. Like Jeric said this morning, I couldn't blame anyone but the asshole himself.

"Are you sure you wanna do this?" Sissy asked when we parked in front of the condo building.

I looked up at the third floor door, squinting through the growing darkness of twilight. I couldn't see the yellow police tape that had been there last night, and no cop stood duty anymore. With a hard swallow to wet my desert mouth and throat, I nodded.

Get it done. Get it over with. Move on.

"Clothes and photo albums. I'm not gonna worry about anything else," I said. There wasn't much else to worry about. Mason had made me put most of our belongings in some storage unit I didn't have the key to because he didn't want it cluttering up his home.

We both climbed out of the car and made our way toward the stairs.

"What about your angels?" Sissy asked.

I snorted. "Sissy, don't you know by now? There ain't no such thing as angels."

When we reached the top of the stairs and stood in front of the navy blue door to Mason's condo, I froze. I didn't want to return to the scene. I didn't want to remember it all again. It had replayed on the backs of my eyelids all morning when I was supposed to be sleeping.

Get it done. Get it over with. Move on.

But I couldn't make my arm raise the key to the hole. Sissy eventually took the keys out of my hand and unlocked the door. As soon as she twisted the knob, panic set in.

Don't go in. Don't go in. Please, for the love of us, don't go in.

I blinked and shook my head to clear it. I couldn't listen to that voice, although the sound of it had been shocking. It hadn't been mine. It had almost sounded like a man's. Regardless, I had to be strong. I could do this. I *had* to do it.

Sissy pushed the door open. My heart raced in my chest. Darkness loomed in front of us. With only a little bit of fumbling, Sissy found the switch and flipped it up. Light flooded the hallway and into the kitchen and dining area, barely touching the living room. I wiped my damp hands on the back of my jean shorts, stepped inside and reached behind me to close the door as Sissy went farther in and turned on all the lamps in the living room.

"Ohmagosh," she gasped.

The place smelled like bleach and lemons and something sweeter. I took a few more steps down the hall, the sound of my flip-flops on the tile echoing, and realized why. The condo had been cleaned. A business card for a cleaning service lay on the table in the entryway, now standing upright. All the glass and mess had been cleaned up. And the sweet smell? Dozens of bouquets of flowers sat on every flat surface in the kitchen, dining area and living room. Roses, tulips, carnations, and other flowers I didn't know the names for, all pink or white or both.

"Forgive me," Sissy read from one of the cards stuck in a bouquet. She picked another out randomly and another, reading from them. "I'm sorry. I love you. Forever mine."

Every bouquet had a delivery card from a florist. They must have arrived while the cleaning service was here.

"They all say the same—whoa." She paused at a bouquet of roses and held one stem out for me to see better. Something sparkly dangled from it. "A diamond bracelet. You think it's real?"

"No doubt it is," I muttered as my eyes swept over all the flowers. Several of them included presents that Sissy inspected— other jewelry, hot pink and black lacey lingerie, even gift certificates for spa days and massages and clothing stores. Did he really think I was so shallow? That I could be bought like this?

Of course, he did. That's what he'd been doing all along, wasn't it?

I swallowed hard against the lump in my throat. "The photo albums are in the guest room closet. I'll get my clothes packed."

"It's kind of a shame to let all this go to waste," Sissy said. "Maybe we should pack it up, too. We could sell a lot of it."

"Don't touch any of it, Sissy," I said through clenched teeth.

She sighed as she headed for the guest room. With a deep inhale and then exhale, I opened the master bedroom door, flipped on the light and walked several steps inside.

And my heart shot through the roof.

"Ohmagosh!" I gasped.

I clapped my hand to my chest, trying to stop the galloping of my heart. It hadn't really shot through the roof, after all, but I thought it might fly out of my chest now as I stared at the man sitting in the corner chair, one leg crossed over the other.

"What are you doing here?" I said with barely any force as I tried to catch my breath. I shuffled a step backward.

"Precious Bex, you didn't really think I'd give up so easily, did you? You're mine. Forever."

CHAPTER 25

Leni I'D WANTED TO jump in the truck right away and follow Bex to Orlando, but Jeric made me wait for Brock and Asia. So we sat at the picnic table, my leg bouncing with impatience, and I flipped through the Book to see how many pages showed the burnt-in words. Six, with the letters on the last page a faint brown against the tan paper. There were still no answers to my previous questions, but this was a perfect opportunity to try again. I ran inside the Airstream, found a pen and rushed back outside. Brock and Asia were ten minutes away, and we were leaving as soon as they drove up. I had a little time to try to pull some answers from Nathayden, or whoever communicated with us on the far side of the Book.

"Who are you?" I wrote, and my breath caught when letters immediately began to appear, faint at first and then darker, like the opposite of fading.

"Nathayden."

"Oh, my God," I said aloud, my leg bouncing harder with excitement now. "I was right! Jeric, come here. I was right!"

Jeric, who'd gone to the bathroom, came out of the camper and looked over my shoulder.

"Dude," he said as he sat down next to me, his voice sounding in just as much awe as I felt.

"Where are you?" I wrote, surprised my words were legible because my hand trembled so hard. The message came so quickly the first time, I'd assumed he was close. At least on this world.

"Enyxa Separated us." Pause. "We're not together." Pause. "Different worlds." The words came even slower. "She's ... with you. I'm ... here. Going Dark."

I clapped my hand over my mouth and looked at Jeric. He looked back at me with one brow lifted.

"Bex has to be her," I said quietly behind my hand. "Here's your proof."

"If this ... whoever it is ... is telling the truth," he said, "then, maybe, yeah. But how do we know? It could be Enyxa communicating with us just as easily as it could be Nathayden."

"I feel it, Jeric. In here." I moved my hand down and pressed my fist against my chest. "In my soul. Which means you feel it, too."

I stared at him, daring him to deny it. He couldn't, of course. Not anymore.

"She's hurting." The words appeared on the page. "I feel it. Going ... Dark ... soon. Fast."

Brock and Asia pulled up then. When Jeric and I didn't immediately jump in their car, they turned the engine off and climbed out.

"I thought we were in a hurry," Brock said. Jeric waved them over.

"Whoa," Asia said as she hovered over my shoulder.

"Bex is Rebethannah," I said.

"Are you sure?" Skepticism laced Asia's tone, as usual, but I felt confident this time.

"She has to be," I said. "Everything points to her. Including this." I jabbed my finger at Nathayden's messages.

"Help her, Jacquelena!" he wrote as we spoke. "SAVE HER! SAVE US!"

He filled the page with the words, so I turned to the next one. We watched and waited for more, our collective breaths held. A minute passed, then two, then several more. The clean page remained blank.

I stood up, making Asia jump back before I knocked her over. I opened the camper door to lock it and shut it again.

"We have to help Bex," I said as I picked up my purse and the Book. "And obviously, we'll be helping Rebethannah, too."

"And what?" Brock asked. "Do you think Bex is just going to say, 'Oh, yeah, you're right, I'll go to another world to be with my Twin Flame, this world sucks anyway'?"

"Considering what she's been through lately, she might," I muttered as I stood by the car door, waiting on all of them. "I don't know, Brock. We'll deal with that then, but right now, Bex could be in trouble. Forget about her being Rebethannah if you need to. A human soul needs our help, and she could be taken by the Lakari at any time. Let's GO!"

Jeric clapped his hand on Brock's shoulder. "Come on, dude, she's right. Bex's life could be in danger."

Brock and Asia exchanged a glance, but headed for the car. Jeric sat up front, and Asia and I hovered over the Book in case Nathayden wrote any more.

"So what's the emergency with Bex besides this?" Asia asked, waving her hand at the journal.

Jeric and I gave her and Brock a quick rundown of everything that happened last night, from what I found on the internet to what Bex told Jeric on the way home this morning to her text message this afternoon. I'd barely finished when new words began scrolling across the page of the open Book. Broken phrases became complete sentences and paragraphs, flowing onto other pages. I couldn't read aloud fast enough to keep up.

My name is Nathayden. I used to be One with Rebethannah, and we were known as Ra'den. We were One soul. Now we are two. Enyxa tore us in half and sent our halves to different worlds by bypassing the Space Between. Rebethannah and I have spent thousands of life cycles together. We were part of Earth's Original Seven, along with Ja'mai, An'bris, Ny'zan ... and others. I don't remember their names. I don't recall any of this myself. Enyxa has told me when she comes to see me. She comes often.

She wants me to remember the pain, but to do so, she reminds me of the joy and the love first, so that the pain cuts deeper. She forces me to relive moments with my Rebethannah, good ones and then the worst. Each time, she takes me to the end, to our Separation—from the moment of ripping us apart to stepping into the Gate with one of us in each hand to when she throws Rebethannah's piece through one opening while holding onto mine, severing our Bond completely. Each time she forces me to relive it, the agony slices through me like a double-edged blade.

I don't know how much more I can take.

I thought I was done, ready to succumb, but I saw my Rebethannah. You did something, Jacquelena. I know it was you. I have to believe it was you, because if it wasn't, then it was Enyxa playing more games. I saw my true love's beautiful face as though she stared back at me. I felt her in my soul again, if only for a brief moment. A moment of Light that has driven away the Darkness, as temporary as it may be. A moment I will treasure for as long as my soul is my own ... until it reBonds with my cherished love or until Enyxa takes it.

She waits for something. Enyxa does. For me to go Dark, I am sure. For Rebethannah to, also. She believes it will happen soon, I think. She's been growing more agitated lately. More hurtful. More excitable. So I believe she waits for something else to happen as well.

You can save us, Jacquelena. Enyxa has told me things about the Book of Phoenix. You can use it to help us. She says you know how. You and the others can keep us from going Dark. It's in your hands ...

She's coming.

Enyxa will be here soon, I'm sure, to take me as I succumb. Please, Jacquelena and Jeremicah. Broderick and Anastasia, I know you're there, too ... please help us. Please bring me my girl with the fiery hair and big eyes the color of Earth's skies. She's hurting so much. I can feel it. Hurry ... before it's too late.

Asia and I stared at the last words, waiting for more, but none came.

"You're right," Asia breathed. "Bex is Rebethannah."

"And something's seriously wrong with her," I added. "Mason was already out on bail, so he should still be in jail—"

"You said he's rich?" Brock asked.

"Loaded," Jeric replied.

"Then the rules are completely different," Asia said as her body tensed next to me. "In fact, the whole damn game is."

I looked over at her. She stared straight ahead with a hardness to her pale face that I'd never seen before. Her eyes shone like onyx marbles.

"Step on the gas, Brock," she ordered. "We have to hurry!"

The car sped up noticeably as we rocketed toward Orlando.

"But what are we going to do once we get to her?" Jeric asked. "How are we going to convince her about Nathayden? She pretty much told me she wants nothing to do with the male species right now."

Silence filled the car. We all stared out our windows, none of us having a solid answer to Jeric's questions. I tried to imagine being in Bex's shoes and how I'd feel if someone approached me with the insane ideas we would have to tell her. It would probably take a miracle to convince her of the truth, but if it were Jeric's and my souls on the verge of going Dark and the others knew how to help us, I'd hope they'd do anything in their power to bring us back together.

"Whatever it takes," I whispered, and then I lifted my voice and said it more firmly. "We'll do whatever it takes to reunite them."

CHAPTER 26

THE MAN WHO I thought had been so dreamy before flashed what I'd once believed to be a stunning smile. Now it was nothing but frightening.

He appeared calm and cool as he sat in the chair in the corner, one leg crossed over the other and his hands folded in his lap as if he posed for an ad for brandy or some other gentlemanly drink. His dark hair was combed back, his crisply ironed shirt buttoned and his dress pants creased. Two glasses and a green bottle with a gold-wrapped top in a bucket of ice sat on the nightstand to his right.

"You're supposed to be in jail," I whispered.

He stood. I slid a step backward, too scared to make a fast move. "You have no idea how sweetly money talks, do you, precious? Cops love the sound of it. So do judges. That attorney who has the paperwork for everything I've done for you? He gets the wealthy clients for a reason—he earns them."

A reminder of how he'd trapped me with his money.

"Why are you doing this?" I asked, trying to stall him as I shuffled another foot backward while looking around me for anything I could use as a weapon. Of course, there were no knickknacks, not a jewelry box to throw at him, or a letter opener in sight. Not even a lamp in reach. "You could have *anyone* you want without being like this."

His lips turned up slightly as he cocked his head. "I don't want *anyone*. I want you, Bex. Only *you*."

"And you had me. Until you went all psycho."

He shook his head slowly, his light green eyes never breaking away from my face. "Why would you say that, precious? I'm not psycho. I'm in love. And I'm just trying to show you how much I love you."

I started to move another step back, but his eyes tightened and his jaw clenched. I froze. Except for my heart, which pounded a millions miles a minute. I needed to distract him, to keep him talking and focused on my lips that he seemed to like so much rather than my feet.

"So you ... you trapped me?"

"I only took some precautions. I need to be sure you'll never leave me, Bex. I told you—I can't live without you. And I couldn't take the chance that Ty or Jeric or Brock or some other asshole would come in and try to take you away from me. I knew the moment I set my eyes on you as you leaned against the wall by your mother's hospital room that I *had* to have you. I had to make you mine. And then I had to make sure you'd *always* be mine."

The truth of why he'd picked me over the nurses and doctors who'd been falling all over him hit me. They were just as pretty as me, if not more, and had education, fancy degrees, and professional careers. Mason took one look at me and saw a poor, small-town girl with no promise of a future who was young and sexy, yet naïve. Vulnerable.

He may have thought he was in love with me at first sight, but he also saw me as an easy target.

I moved another half-step backward, feeling behind me with my hand for the doorjamb so that as soon as I reached the door, I could spin and run.

I was *not* going to be an easy target.

"Bex, don't do this," he said, his voice pleading now. He'd taken a step, too, toward me. "I don't want to fight tonight. Didn't you see all the flowers and gifts I bought for you? I want to make up for last night, not fight more." He held his arms out and open. "Come on, precious. Come back to me. Let me make love to you. Let me show you how much I love you."

I couldn't help the laugh that escaped, sounding a little on the crazy side. "Are you *serious*?"

"Bex, who ya talkin' to?" Sissy called out, her voice nearing with each word.

Shit. Mason's gaze went to a point behind me. One side of his mouth turned up in a smirk. "Mmm ... sisters. A fantasy come true."

Oh, hell no.

"Sissy, *run*!" I screamed as I spun to sprint after her. "Get out!"

She froze in the middle of the living room, a deer in headlights, as she stared behind me with eyes the size of pie plates. I ran several steps and reached my hands out to shove her into motion. Mason grabbed me from behind and threw me to the side like a ragdoll. My body slammed into the marble dining table. Something cracked, and I cried out as pain wracked through my side.

My heart raced. My breaths came in pants, each one agonizing, but I couldn't slow them down. I pressed my hand against my ribs, sure at least one was broken, and pushed myself off the table, back to my feet.

Sissy tried to run, but Mason lunged, tackling her to the ground. I grabbed a vase of flowers and threw it at him. It smashed into his back, shattering and soaking his shirt as the petals rained to the floor. I grabbed another bouquet, intending to hit his head this time, but as I pulled back for the throw, he turned around. He held Sissy with her back against his chest, one of his arms pinned across the front of her shoulders. The other held a pointed glass shard to her neck.

"Let go of her!" I screamed as I hurled the vase at him.

He ducked, taking Sissy with him. The flowers hit the wall behind them and more glass shattered to the floor. Sissy kicked backwards at Mason as he forced her back upright. Whether he'd done it on purpose or it happened during the ruckus, the glass shard had dug into my sister's skin and a small line of crimson trickled down her neck. She froze. So did I. Tears slid down her cheeks.

"See what you did, Bex?" Mason barked. "You made me hurt your sister! Don't do that again, okay? Let's not make this any worse than it already is."

I held my hands up in surrender. They shook like leaves, betraying my fear. "Okay. Just let her go. She has nothin' to do with us, with you and me. She doesn't need to be a part of this. I'll do whatever you want, Mason. Just, please, let her go."

"No," Sissy said as she stared at me with big blue eyes. "Don't give in, Bex. I had this comin'. It's all my fault to start with. I should have told you weeks ago what happened."

"What? Sissy, shut up," I said.

"Yeah, shut up," Mason growled.

"No, you need to know," Sissy persisted, determination on her face even as Mason dug the glass further into her skin. "I wanted to tell you before, wanted to warn you, but he threatened me. Said he'd kill me and Mama *and* you if I said anything to anyone."

"Told me what?"

"*Don't*," Mason warned.

"I saw him, Bethany. Watched him throw a fit and hit that doctor. I saw what he was capable of and knew what he'd do to you if—" Her voice fell silent, and her eyes widened even more. Her fingers scratched at Mason's hand, but only for a few seconds. A whole line of blood now poured from her throat, like from a second, dripping mouth he'd slashed into her neck. Her body went limp. Mason dropped her, and she fell to the floor.

"NO!" I screamed as I lunged for her.

His fist swung out and clocked me in the temple. Stars shot across my eyes. I stumbled and fell. The other side of my head hit the coffee table, and my vision went gray. I squeezed my eyes shut, trying to push the darkness away. I could *not* pass out now. No telling what Mason was fixing to do to me if I did. I opened my eyes in time to see him reaching for my upper arms. I flailed my fists and kicked my legs, landing a few blows but mostly missing.

"You *killed* her," I screeched at him as I tried scooting back, away from him, keeping my eyes on him the whole time so they wouldn't wander to Sissy's body.

"She asked for it. I warned her many times." His voice was eerily cool and calm.

"You're a fucking *monster*!" I yelled. Pain tore through my ribs with the effort. Something warm dripped into my eye.

"You did this to me, Bex. *You're* making me do this. I just wanted a quiet night alone with you, but you had to be all melodramatic about everything. So don't turn the tables on me. This is all *your* fault, not mine."

I shook my head, still crab-walking on my elbows and heels. He stood over me, letting me scoot, taking slow steps so I didn't get out of reach. I moved until I could move no more, until my back pressed against the couch. He'd known he had me trapped. Again.

He leaned over to grab me. I bucked and kicked, swinging my arms as my fists pummeled at him. His large hand caught one of my wrists and twisted. I screamed as the bone broke. My body fell still.

"Now behave, and I won't have to hurt you anymore," he said as he lifted me by a fistful of hair. When I was almost to my feet, his other hand grasped the back of my neck. He shoved me, trying to make me turn. My ankle twisted, my feet tangled, and my shin hit the end table. I went back down to my knees. Instead of trying to lift me again, Mason dragged me by the hair toward his room. I tried to grab his legs to trip him up, but my good arm couldn't reach. So I clawed at his hand twisted in my hair instead.

As we passed through the doorway, I kicked my leg out, catching it in the doorjamb. The snag surprised him, and he loosened his grip just enough that I could grab his thumb and yank, forcing his hand open. At the same time, I threw myself forward, feeling the hairs rip out of my scalp as I did. I lurched to my feet, hitting my head again on something I didn't see, and the room spun as I fought a wave of sickness. I heaved myself forward, grabbing on to dining room chairs, the table, anything I could to hold myself up as I stumbled for the door. Vases of flowers tumbled to the floor, sending glass skittering across the tiles. The dark shape of Sissy's body lay in a heap to my left. Tears streaked down my face.

"I told you, precious, I can't let you leave me."

Something big and hard, like a cinder block but probably Mason's fist, slammed into my cheek. I screamed as I went down hard on my face, my broken arm unable to catch me and the other caught on a chair. As it bounced to the floor, my palm landed on something sharp. I wrapped my hand around it, and then I blacked out.

I didn't know how long I was out, but it couldn't have been more than a few minutes. I awoke with blood still seeping from all kinds of cuts on my hands, arms, and legs, and judging by the wetness tickling the outside corner of my eye and the taste of salty copper in my mouth, blood dripped down my face, too. I was on Mason's bed in a kind of slumped over sitting position, propped up by pillows and my legs sprawled out in front of me.

Music suddenly began playing—You Are Mine by Mutemath—from somewhere in the room. Pain shot down my spine and across my shoulders as I lifted my head to look around. Rope and duct tape were on the nightstand to my left, next to the champagne and glasses. Mason stood at the side of the bed, looming over me, looking barely hurt at all. The sight of him had my heart galloping again and my hands balling into fists. Something dug into my right palm, slicing into my skin.

"Oh, good, you're awake," he said. He fingered the rope and tape. "I thought we might have some bondage fun in a bit. But first, we must celebrate."

He picked up the green bottle and began peeling the gold foil away, while I stared at him silently. He'd overpowered me so many times already, I knew I needed to be able to catch him by surprise if I had any hope of getting out of here alive.

He looked at me expectantly. I said nothing, and he rolled his eyes.

"What are we celebrating?" he asked with an air of annoyance because I hadn't. He dropped the foil on the nightstand and paused his fingers over the wire cage. "Let's see. There's my freedom to start with. Of course, there's always our love, too. I know you'll forgive me by the end of the night, Bex. We love each other too much for you not to. And then we can celebrate when you say *yes.*"

What the hell? The man was off his fucking rocker.

He twisted the wire on the bottle and the cork popped, the sound making me jump. Mason sat down on the bed beside me, stroking my thigh with one hand as if to soothe me while pouring the bubbly liquid with the other. Every muscle tensed at his touch and my stomach rolled. My whole body remained rigid when he reached for the glasses and turned to me.

"I got the good stuff, precious. Only the best for my girl." One hand moved toward me, and I fought the urge to flinch. He held the glass to me, waiting for me to take it.

Gritting my teeth through the pain, I smacked the glass out of his hand with my bad arm while swinging my good one up, aiming my hand for his throat. The glass shard in my fist sliced down his ear and neck before he jumped up and knocked it out of my hand.

"God damn it, Bex!" he roared. "Why do you have to be so fucking difficult?"

He looked down at his champagne-soaked button-down and ripped it off, leaving him in an undershirt. He pressed his shirt to his ear. I tried to scramble off the bed, but he swung his arm at me, knocking me back down. I lay on my back, my legs dangling over the side of the bed as he towered over me.

"You're fucking soaked, too," he growled, and his hand shot out, fisted in my collar and jerked down, tearing the front of my shirt down the middle.

With only one good hand, I tried to pull the two halves together and scoot away from him, but he smacked my hand away and pinned his knee against my thigh. He dropped his bloodstained shirt and wrapped his fingers over my throat, ensuring I couldn't move, and then reached for the front clasp at the center of my bra. I hit and shoved at his arm, and I thought I'd succeeded because his hand landed on the bed next to me. But only for a second. Long enough to grab the glass shard with both of our blood mixing on it. With a flick of his wrist, my bra sprang open. I tried to cover myself, but when he jabbed at my hand again, the glass sliced from my thumb to my forearm. What had been my good arm fell limp to the bed.

With one hand still on my throat with enough pressure that I could barely breathe, Mason used the tip of the glass to lift the pieces of my shirt and bra to the sides. My eyes widened and my chest heaved as he traced the point of the shard lightly over my breastbone and then down to circle each breast like he was drawing the infinity symbol across my boobs in blood. His eyes never left my face as he did so.

"Are you ready to cooperate now?" he asked. "Ready to tell me you love me and forgive me?"

His green eyes stared into mine, and I held his gaze, locked it into place as I searched into his eyes and found nothing but a dangerous darkness. The man of my dreams, the one I thought I knew and loved as my soul mate, was nowhere in there. I didn't know if he ever really existed or if everything had been a charade since the beginning, acted out by this heartless, soulless nightmare hovering over me. What was left of my broken heart crumbled to pieces. My soul shattered into fragments.

But I would not cry. I would not give him the pleasure of seeing that he'd destroyed me. Very slowly, I slid my tongue over my swollen bottom lip, tasting more blood. His pupils dilated slightly, and his head lifted in a nod. And then I rasped out against the razor blades in my throat, "*Never.*"

He frowned.

"Not the answer I was expecting," he said with a sigh, and then with a slow twist of his wrist, he carved a circle around my areola, nearly taking it off. I watched in horror as blood flooded over my nipple and down the curve of my boob.

With a delayed reaction, sharp pain rocketed through my breast, and I screamed. My back arched, and I kicked my free leg out, connecting with something. More glass broke. Mason looked down at his feet. He looked back at me with annoyance, but then smirked as he leaned down, reaching for the floor. His hand still gripped my throat as he pulled me slightly off the bed while he bent down, and my breast felt like it was on fire. Then he stood and pressed me into the mattress while lifting his free hand. The edges of my vision blurred with tears and blood and lack of air, but I could clearly see what he held: the broken neck of the champagne bottle.

"If I can't have you, Bex, then no one can." He pushed my legs apart with his knees, tightened his hand on my throat and at the same time thrust the jagged end of the bottleneck in between my thighs.

I blacked out with the rush of pain.

CHAPTER 27

Jeric "JERIC, DUDE, THIS isn't good," Brock said as we entered the parking lot and drove toward Mason's building.

I stared up through the windshield at all of the Lakari swarmed over the roof like vultures waiting for their meal to finally die.

"Shit," Asia said under her breath.

"Bex," Leni gasped.

As soon as Brock pulled to a stop, Leni was pushing impatiently on my seat. I threw open the door and was barely on my feet when she jumped out and ran past me. She took the stairs three at a time, soaring upward like a gazelle more than climbing the steps like a human. I rushed after her, arriving at the door only a split second later. Leni didn't bother knocking. Didn't need to when we heard glass breaking and a girl screaming. She threw open the door, and we both bolted inside.

Glass, green stems, and flower petals littered the white tiles, and we skidded in puddles of water. A body lay huddled on the floor in a pool of blood. Leni fell to her knees next to the girl and gently turned her head to the side. Sissy.

Movement out of the corner of my eye caught my attention. I gave a warning look to Leni, telling her to stay by Sissy, before rushing over to a bedroom door hanging halfway open. The scene sent my stomach to the floor and my blood rushing through my veins.

Bex lay on her back, her eyes closed, her head tilted to the side, her face swollen and covered in blood. Her shirt hung open, exposing everything to her hips, including blood pouring from where her left nipple should have been. Her jean shorts were still on, but the denim was shredded and soaked in blood. On the bed next to her was a bloodied piece of glass that looked like the neck of a wine bottle.

And standing over her with his hand jerking his dick was Mason Hayes.

Rage overcame me. My vision tunneled. And with a beastly roar, I charged.

I rammed into him with my shoulder, and we crashed into the nightstand. He tried to push me off, but I shoved my body weight into him again until we fell to the floor. I sat on top of him, pinned his arms with my knees, held his throat with one hand and pummeled my fist into his face over and over and over again.

"How do you fucking like it, asshole?" I spat at him as I continued to punch him. "How do you like being the weaker one? How do you like being the girl? You fucking coward."

His cheek shattered under my fist. Then his nose broke and blood spurted. His skin turned red and purple, looking more like raw meat than human flesh.

"Jeric," Leni said quietly from behind me.

"Let's get Bex," Brock said, also close. He didn't try to stop me while I continued pounding the sack of shit underneath me. If he did, it would only be so he could have a turn. Real men didn't hit girls. No matter what. Real men had a code for those limp-dick sick fucks who did: Make sure they never forgot what a real man's fist felt like just as the girl they hit would never forget. Brock was a real man. The cop last night probably was, too.

Just as I'd always been in the cage, I became hyper-aware of everything around me. Leni and Asia covering Bex up, then Brock lifting her into his arms. The smell of roses and sweet alcohol mixed with coppery blood. Pieces of glass all over the floor. The wet bedding stained with blood. Mason's body jerking and twitching under me. Music playing lyrics that said, "You are mine."

"You *are* mine, asshole," I snarled.

Brock left with the girls. I rocked back to my feet and fisted my hand into Mason's wife beater. How appropriate. I pulled him up with me and slammed him into the wall a few times, then punched him again for good measure. His body fell limp, slid down the wall and collapsed into a heap. I spit on him, but that wasn't enough. I wanted more than anything to kill the fucker. I gave him a few kicks to the side, hearing the toe of my boot crunch into his ribs.

"*Enough!*" Leni's voice rang in my head, the first time I'd heard it like that since before we were Forged. My anger must have been overwhelming her. Her fear and concern for me rolled through me.

"Jeric, let's go," Brock called from the doorway.

"Sirens are coming," Asia said as she came running into the room.

She halted next to me, and we both stared at the cocksucker in front of us for another moment. Asia looked around the room, and her gaze landed on the bed ... and the bottleneck. I froze, riveted, as she stepped over to the bed and grabbed the glass. Then she squatted in front of Mason, grabbed a fistful of his hair and yanked his head back. His eyes rolled up at her, barely visible through the swelling.

"Since we have to let you live," she said, "you don't deserve these."

She slammed the pointed glass into his balls and twisted. He grunted and mewled like the animal he was, and blood blossomed immediately around the bottleneck as it stuck out of his crotch. The stink of human shit filled the air.

"Asia! Jeric!" Brock yelled. "Move it!"

Asia backed away from Mason's slumped form slowly at first, until she reached me. Without a word or a glance my way, she spun and took off, and I jogged after her for the door, down the stairs and to the car. Before Brock and I could jump in, though, three Lakari dropped from the sky, taking human form as soon as they hit the ground. They always landed dressed in black pants and black hoodies with the hoods up, covering their heads and putting their faces in shadow. Only their inky black eyes could be seen against pale skin. Brock and I went after them.

Still hyped on adrenaline, I swung fast and violently, punching one in the head and the other in the throat. Brock attacked the third. The tallest one kicked me in the gut while the other one I'd hit went after Brock. I elbowed the Shadowman in the ribs, then shoved the heel of my hand upwards into his chin. He disintegrated into smoke. I spun on one of the guys on Brock and kicked him in the lower back. As I threw my fist into his face, making him shatter, more Shadowmen dropped down.

And the sirens came louder and closer.

"Fuck 'em," Brock said as he ran for the car. "We gotta go."

I jumped in the passenger's seat and was still pulling the door shut when Brock peeled away. Expecting them to follow, I watched the Shadowmen in the side mirror. They all ran upstairs for Mason's condo, not a single one wanting anything to do with us. I let out a breath of relief. As we turned onto the main road, cop cars came from the other way and turned into the condo parking lot.

"A little damn late for Sissy and Bex," Asia muttered.

"Let's hope they're too late for him," Brock said.

"Pretty sure they are," I answered under my breath, probably feeling more satisfied than I should about what the Lakari were doing to him now. "Was Sissy dead?"

"I hadn't been able to find a pulse," Leni said quietly, and her grief rocked through me. "And Bex isn't going to make it, either."

I turned in my seat. Bex was draped across the back seat, wrapped in a sheet, her head in Leni's lap and her legs on Asia's thighs. Blood soaked through the white sheet almost everywhere it touched her body. Renewed anger surged through me.

"We're almost to the hospital," Brock said.

"No." Leni stroked back Bex's hair that was matted to her face. "We take her to the Gate."

"She won't make it," I said.

"She might, but if she doesn't, that's exactly why we have to take her," Leni said.

Asia nodded. "She's right. We have to try to get her to the Gate so at least her soul can be saved before the Lakari get it."

"We have to try to get her to Nathayden," Leni corrected. "So they both can be saved."

I glared at her. "She needs help *now*, not two hours from now. She won't make it that long."

"Dude, I can get us there in less than in an hour," Brock said.

"And what are we going to say at the hospital anyway? The police will come, and it'll get real messy real fast," Asia pointed out. "You'll get arrested, Jeric."

Our gazes locked for a long moment, both of us acknowledging that she'd said *I'd* get arrested, not *we* would. She didn't want Brock to know what she'd done. I wondered if he even knew about whatever had happened to her—there had to be something that filled her with so much rage that would drive her to do such a thing. As if understanding my unspoken question, her head shook slightly. Brock needed to know. She frowned and broke our locked gaze to look out the window.

I turned back in my seat to face forward. "I don't care. He fucking deserved it."

My fingers dug into my thighs. I couldn't believe we were arguing over this.

"But we don't have time for that!" Asia snapped. "Bex— Rebethannah—needs us to do what we're supposed to do."

"She'll bleed out!"

"Most of her bleeding has stopped," Leni said, her voice calm and cool although I could feel the mess of emotions swirling through her. "It's just her ... her breast."

"Cocksucker," Brock muttered.

"And her crotch?" I asked through a clenched jaw.

"I checked when they went back upstairs to get you," Leni said, her voice quieter than it had been a moment ago. "It's not good, but all surface wounds. Thank God she was wearing denim. She has lots of other injuries, though. He ... he practically murdered her, too. And in a lot worse way than he did Sissy."

"Mother *fucking* cocksucker," Brock said. "I hope you killed him."

I stared out the window, rubbing my chin, not sure if I could agree. Sure, one part of me hoped he'd bled out nice and slowly with my face and my fists as his last memory. Or of Asia's face as she did what she did. My balls tightened again at the thought. But death was quick. Easy. He didn't deserve that. He deserved to live long at the state pen with the mangled parts that used to be his jewels and the memory of what he'd done replaying every time he tried to get a hard-on but couldn't.

Brock slowed down as we approached the hospital and cut his eyes sideways to me. "What do you want to do?"

"Can we use the Book to get her to the Gate?" I asked Leni. "At least closer?"

"I don't know. We couldn't open it until we were together, remember?" Leni said. "She hasn't found her Twin Flame, so the teleporting bit might not work with her. And we don't want to disappear and leave her here alone."

Probably a dumb idea anyway, since we didn't know how the Book really worked with that stuff. If it dumped us at a nearby portal, we could still be miles away from the Gate with no transportation. I doubted the Book would bring the car with us.

"I have no idea what you're talking about," Brock said, "but I need a decision, dude."

He was asking me to be the leader I was supposed to be and to choose. To decide between Bex's life and Rebethannah's soul. Between being human and being a Phoenix. Between my life as Jeric and my role as Jeremicah, leader of the Guardians, Twin Flame to Jacquelena, who was to light my way.

And she'd lit the path we were supposed to take. I only had to choose to follow it. I just hoped we were both right.

"Let's take her to the Gate."

CHAPTER 28

TOTAL BLACKNESS. **G**ARBLED voices from far away. A swooshing in my ears. Wetness all around me. I tried to inhale. Searing pain in my throat and lungs. Searing pain *everywhere*.

"Bex," a voice called, sounding like we were under water. I couldn't even be sure I heard the correct word. "Bex?"

Where was I? Movement under me. A light rumbling. A car. So we weren't under water. Why did it sound like we were?

"Bex, sweetie." The female voice came clearer. The watery sound came from my head, along with the feeling of drills piercing my skull. "Bex, are you awake?"

I tried to open my eyes. A little bit of lightness compared to the complete darkness behind my lids, but I could see nothing. Something blocked my view. A blurred shape moved in front of me. My head spun. My stomach lurched. Agony shot through every nerve in my body. But I couldn't scream. Only whimper.

"Is she okay?" A deep voice. A man's voice.

My heart and my lungs stopped. Every muscle tensed, making the pain worse, but I didn't care, because I had to get away, I had to escape, I had to get out of here before he killed me, he was a monster, evil, horrid, he already killed Sissy, oh, Sissy, my sister—

"Shh, shh, it's okay, Bex. You're safe." The female voice again. Familiar.

"Sissy?" I tried to say, but the sound was nothing more than a hiss.

"It's me, Leni. Asia is here and Jeric and Brock. You're okay, Bex. We're going to make you okay."

Not Mas— I couldn't even think his name without being overcome by horror.

Something soft and warm brushed across my forehead. Leni. I knew Leni and the others. Had they saved me?

"Calm down, sweetie," Leni said. "Relax. Just try to stay awake, okay? Stay with us. We're going to get you help. We're going to make you okay. We're taking you to Nathayden. Do you remember—"

"No," I croaked. Flames licked my throat as I tried to speak. "No ... no more men."

"It's okay, sweetie," she said. "Nathayden's not just another man. He's what your soul *needs.*"

"Leni, the Book." Another female voice. Asia? "What's it doing?"

A gasp.

"Hand it here," Leni said, the softness in her voice now urgent.

My legs moved. The worst kind of pain shot through my hooha. I tried to scream. I sounded like a dying cat.

"Oh, my God, I'm so sorry, Bex." Yes, that sounded like Asia, but I couldn't see her. What was in front of my damn eyes? Were my cheeks that swollen? My eyelids? Had to have been. A warm wetness seeped through, and the saltiness burned down my raw face.

Blackness again. My body drifted in it. Maybe I should have been scared, but at least there was no pain.

"*Rebethannah.*" A male voice, but not frightening. The opposite actually. Kind. Low and a little gritty but in a warm way, like sand on a beach. "*Rebethannah ...*"

He said my name like it was a song. But wait. That wasn't my name.

"*Come to me, love.*"

And even though I'd just told Leni no more men, I wanted to go to this voice, I *so* wanted to. But I didn't know how.

"Bex? Are you still with us?" Leni again. Reality again. I didn't want reality. It hurt too damn much. "Do you remember Nathayden? He's your true mate, Bex. You're other half. The one you've always been looking for. We're taking you to him. You're his Rebethannah. Do you remember that name? That's you." A small, warm hand wrapped around mine. Moved my arm. More pain. More whimpering. "I'm sorry, sweetie. I'm so sorry. But I need you to understand. To remember. Maybe this will help."

She let go of my hand. It rested on something smooth and cooler. Papery?

I drifted off again.

"*Rebethannah,*" sang the voice of summer, of warmth, of goodness and love. He had an accent. Australian, maybe? "It's me, Nathayden. I'm here, my love. I'm waiting for you. Come back to me."

A vision of heaven floated behind my eyelids. No, not heaven. A face. The face of my dreams. The man of my dreams. Gray eyes, light brown hair, chiseled features. Was he an angel? He looked like a god. How could I have thought that asshole looked anything like this man? I must have been blinded by stupidity. The biggest difference was in the eyes. Not the color, but the soul that shone behind them.

I felt like I knew it more than I knew myself.

"You do know me," he said. "I am part of you, and you are part of me. Our souls have been together forever. They *were.* They even became One soul at one time, but we've been

Separated for a while, my love. Too long. We need to find each other, Rebethannah, before it's too late."

Warmth traveled through my icy hand and up my cold arm. His warmth. I could feel him over me, around me, trying to soak into me. And something within me responded, knew I needed to let him in. I suddenly wanted nothing more than to do so.

I knew it was right. He was right. We belonged together. We needed each other. Not in a co-dependent, unhealthy way that made people stupid. Not the "I can't live without you" bullshit Mason pulled on me, or in the superficial way most people said they needed someone else. No, this need went deep, real deep, all the way down to the soul. We were literally incomplete without the other, and the more this truth settled in, the more my heart and soul ached for him. The more urgent my need to be with him grew.

"Where are you?" I asked. "How do I find you?"

"I'm in the Beyond. Come to me, my love." His voice faded, drifting away. I wanted to reach out for him, pull him close, never let him go. "*Come be mine forever again.*"

A chill ran through me at these last words that floated from nowhere. *No*, I wanted to scream. Memories. Bad memories. My mind was playing tricks on me. There was no other half. No soul mate for me. I didn't belong with anyone. Love was a joke played on the lonely. And I would always be lonely.

The warmth disappeared.

The pain returned.

"Bex, hun, you with us?"

No. I didn't want to be with them. I didn't want to be with anyone. Not anymore. I wanted to be alone. I belonged alone. I embraced the loneliness that was my destiny.

Blackness came again.

Then cold.

So cold, it burned at first, like plunging a hand into a cooler of ice water. No, like sinking my whole body in a tub of it.

Freezing my skin and flesh and bones, down to my heart ... to my soul. Cold everywhere.

And then numbness. Ohmagosh, sweet, heavenly numbness. No more cold. No more pain. No more anything.

And even though there was no light and I couldn't see anything, a Darkness blacker than black pulled at me. Slipped under and around me, carried me, promised more numbness, an emptiness so complete, I'd never feel anything again. And I wanted that more than I'd ever wanted anything in my entire life.

To never feel again.

Because feeling meant caring, and caring turned into loving, and loving led to broken hearts and shattered souls, with the pieces scattering in the wind because nobody could ever put them back together again.

Loving led to mamas abandoning you, sisters betraying you, and lovers leaving you behind ... or carving you up like a piece of fucking meat.

Loving led to pain, another feeling.

And I didn't want to feel ever again.

I chose the Darkness.

CHAPTER 29

"BEX?" I SAID, my hand on her shoulder, squeezing ever so gently. I didn't want to hurt her any more than she already was by shaking her, but her losing consciousness wasn't good either. "Bex, hun, you with us?"

A lump filled my throat when she didn't answer.

"Stay with us, Bex," I pleaded with her. "I need you to stay awake. Stay here with us."

Still nothing. I leaned over to hover my cheek over her mouth. Her breath came light and cold. And very slow.

"We're losing her," I said, my voice calm and quiet although panic gripped my heart. I looked around outside, but only saw car lights and green highway signs. "Where are we? Are we close?"

"We just passed 75," Brock said. "We have to cross Tampa. We'll be there soon."

"Not soon enough!" I snapped. I looked down at Bex. Gave her shoulder another squeeze. "Come on, Bex. Don't leave us yet. We're taking you to your Nathayden. Just hang in there a little longer."

No response. Her body felt softer and heavier in my arms and across my lap. Asia tapped reflexive points, but Bex's muscles didn't jump. Then she reached out for her hand, looking at me for approval. Bex's arm was obviously broken, and if Asia moved it, the pain would be excruciating. Maybe what she needed to wake up. I gave Asia a slight nod. No scream, no reaction at all from Bex. Twisting my arm awkwardly under Bex's head, I pressed my fingers to the pulse point on her throat. She wasn't gone. Yet.

"Brock, pull over," I ordered as my own pulse sped. He only looked at me in the rearview mirror. "Pull over, damn it! Now!"

"What—"

"We're out of time!" I said. "We have to try the Book or we'll never make it, and we'll lose them both."

"There's an exit a mile up here," Jeric said.

"No! Now! Pull over so we can leave the damn car."

Bex's body flinched in my arms, but I didn't know if she could hear me yelling, or if her muscles twitched while she remained unconscious.

"What's going on?" Brock asked as he steered the car over to the shoulder and stopped.

"This is a bad place—" Jeric started. He had good reason for not wanting to stop on shoulders, but if someone slammed into us, we wouldn't be here.

"Don't worry," I snapped at him, "we're not staying long." I wiggled my left arm free and closed the Book. "I don't know how this works, but I think you have to be touching the Book or me or whoever does the ... thing."

"What thing? What are you talking about?" Brock demanded.

"Do you know what the hell you're doing?" Asia sounded like she thought I'd lost my mind.

"No, but we don't have a choice. Just do it," I said.

Asia and Brock exchanged a confused glance, but Jeric nodded at them. She put a hand on my shoulder, and Jeric reached around the seat to put a hand on my knee. Brock grasped the edge of the Book, holding it over Bex's body in the center of all of us. I held on tightly to Bex, touched the phoenix on the cover and believed with every thread of my soul that we would *all* arrive at the Gate.

The ghostly phoenix rose and flew a tight circle around us in the confines of the car. The colors turned fiery. Sparks flew. The flames engulfed us. Asia and Brock both gasped.

When the phoenix settled to ash and the whiteness faded, we were sitting on our butts on a grassy area close to the water's edge. The manor stood behind us, the Gate in the water in front of us. Bex lay on my lap. It had worked.

"How'd you know to do that?" Brock asked with awe.

"Instinct," I muttered as I looked upwards.

Lakari darkened the sky, so many of them, they blotted out all the stars and the moonlight. With screams that sounded like nails on a chalkboard, they began dropping out of the air, landing as human figures.

Their target was clear.

Bex—Rebethannah—had made it here, and the Lakari wanted her.

Guardians poured out of the manor. I sensed several projecting their souls. Brock, Asia, and Jeric jumped to their feet to fight, while I sat with Bex in my arms, trying to figure out what to do.

"We need to get her to the Gate," I yelled over the sounds of Guardians and Lakari fighting.

"How?" Jeric asked right before swinging at a Shadowman.

Good question. We went to the Gate by projecting our souls, because our bodies would drown at the bottom of the bay. But how could I get Bex to project? Was I really going to have to cut her soul out like Theo and Mira had done to Jacey and Micah? My eyes fell to Bex's limp body. Could I do that to her? What if it didn't work?

My gaze slid to the Book lying on her stomach, and my spine tingled. Another gut feeling. *Follow my instinct.* Intuition provided the theory of what would happen if I touched the Gate area of the image on the cover in the same way I touched the phoenix. We'd be transported, but not within this world, as the phoenix symbolized. I'd felt this instinct before I'd taken Jeric to Alaska, and it came stronger now.

"Jeric, come here," I called to him. His fist smashed into a Shadowman's face, making the Lakari explode into pieces that flew high into the sky to regroup. I propped Bex against my shoulder awkwardly, and as soon as Jeric was close enough, I reached out to grab his leg while stretching my hand to touch the Book cover where the Gate would be under the island.

Nothing happened.

I swiped my fingers everywhere in the water part of the image. Still nothing. Maybe my instinct had been wrong.

"We need to get her out of here," Brock shouted as he ran over to us while Jeric spun to kick a Shadowman.

"Take her, Brock," Jeric yelled. "I'll cover you."

Brock slid his arms under Bex's body and gently lifted her. A small sound escaped her throat. It was the best sign of life I could hope for. I jumped to my feet, just in time to slam my fist into a Shadowman's head. I spun and kicked him in the ribs, then landed a few punches in the right places to make him disappear. More swarmed us. Asia ran over, helping Jeric and me protect Brock and Bex.

"We have to take her to the Gate," I said.

"Through the water?" Brock asked with disbelief.

"I don't know any other way, do you?" I asked as another black-hooded figure headed toward us. More began swarming in our direction. Dark shapes swooped and screeched overhead. There were too many for the Guardians. Where were they all coming from? It's like they were gathering for some purpose. Were they not here for Rebethannah after all? "It's that or cut her soul out."

"How?" Asia yelled while fighting off a Shadowman. Guardians ran toward us to stave off the onslaught of Darkness.

"Take her into the water, Brock," I said. "Maybe her soul will leave on its own when it gets close to the Gate."

"No, Leni," Jeric yelled. "Let's take her inside."

"We don't have time!" I yelled back at him.

Brock had already started for the water's edge with Bex in his arms, and I swooped down to grab the Book then ran to catch up to him.

"Leni!" Jeric yelled.

"Come on!" I replied.

Brock and I were already several yards ahead of Asia and Jeric who fought more Lakari. We waded into the water that wasn't much cooler than a bath. As the bottom of the bay sloped downward, the water rose to my knees and then my thighs. When it reached my hips, I looked over my shoulder. Jeric and Asia were still at the water's edge, fighting.

"Jeric, come on," I called out to him. "We have to go!"

"I don't think—"

"I don't care what the fuck you think," I yelled at him, my patience gone. "This is what we have to do! Now come with me, damn it."

He turned and locked eyes with me. He must have seen I wasn't giving in. He had to feel what I felt—that taking Bex into the water might not have been the normal way to get her to the Gate, but it somehow felt like the right way. He knew what we had to do—we had to save Rebethannah. He only had to make the decision. Give the command.

But still, he lingered. Without breaking the lock we held with our eyes, I walked backward until I was even with Brock. We were out far enough for the water to reach Bex's back, butt, and legs, and she let out a moan.

"She'll hate it, but the brackish water will be good for her wounds," I said, not knowing if the condition of her body mattered longer than the next few minutes or not, but if anything, maybe the sting would bring her to full consciousness.

Brock dropped to his knees to immerse her body up to her neck. Bex groaned louder, and her body jerked and convulsed.

"Are you coming or not?" I asked Jeric. "We need to hurry!"

One more heartbeat passed.

Then he gave me a sharp nod.

"Come on, Asia," he finally ordered. "The rest of you, cover us!"

I gave him a small smile. Told him *I love you* with my eyes and my soul. My Jeremicah finally sounded like a real leader. A warrior leader. His lips tilted up in response.

"Aye!" the Guardians yelled out in unison, and they went on the offensive while Jeric and Asia fought off Shadowmen as they made their way into the bay.

I turned and pushed through the water alongside Brock, splashing it around me. Several drops landed on the Book's cover. It glowed a silvery blue everywhere the water touched. I dipped my hand in the water and spread more over the cover. The entire area of the image that depicted the sea lit up.

And I knew what was coming. My soul knew.

"Jeric! Asia! *Hurry!*" I bellowed.

Jeric punched the last Shadowman on their tails in the face and looked at me with wide eyes.

"No, Leni!" he yelled when he saw what was happening. A bright light was already rising from the bottom of the bay. "Get back here!"

"Hurry, Jeric!" I screamed as I reached out to touch Bex's shoulder. He and Asia were several yards behind us. Too far behind us. The light of the Gate rose higher, surrounding only Brock, Bex, and me. Panic made my heart pound in my chest. "Asia! *Jeric!* NOW!"

The Shadowmen behind them stopped fighting the Guardians and stared, their inky black eyes, usually expressionless, sparking with excitement at the sight of the Gate. Everyone's faces reflected the bright light.

"Come on!" I screamed even as Jeric and Asia ran for us.

But it was too late.

The light of the Gate shot skyward and solidified around Brock, Bex, and me. The water drained from under our feet. Brock and I stared at each other in horror. Bex moaned, the sound vibrating through my hand.

"We *have* to," I whispered, and then said with all the conviction I could muster, "We *believe* we'll join Nathayden."

The light around us grew blindingly white. Brock dropped his head and squeezed his eyes tightly shut. I lifted my arm to shield mine, squinting against the brightness. I turned in place, watching for any changes.

A pinprick of a hole. It widened like a camera shutter, slowly at first and then yawning widely.

"Brock!" I yelled.

He looked up, and his eyes widened. Without warning, the hole at sucked us, and right before I passed through, the Book jerked out of my hands. The Gate expelled us violently just like it had Asia and me last time. Since we hadn't entered through an official, permanent Gate, we must not have exited through one either. We fell for several seconds before splashing into a shallow body of water. The jolt through my spine as I hit the bottom didn't compare in the slightest to the agony in my core—in my soul. My heart felt like it'd been ripped out of my chest, leaving a gaping hole. My soul felt like it'd been torn in half again, Separated from Jeremicah, from my Twin Flame.

We were no longer on the same world.

I rose to my feet, into the dark night, gasping for air that I didn't think I'd ever get enough of until we were reunited. Brock stood, too, his ashen face twisted in the same pain I felt. Bex's body floated on the water, face up. Pushing through the agony, we each grabbed an upper arm and towed her the several feet to the water's edge.

"Where's the Book?" Brock asked. "We need to get back as soon as possible."

I shook my head at him, and my bottom lip quivered. "I ... I don't have it. It didn't come with me."

He closed his eyes and breathed deeply, his chest hitching on the inhale. When his lids opened, his eyes were full of the same pain and grief I felt.

"Jeric and Asia will figure it out then," he said. "They'll come and get us and take us back."

I nodded. "Of course they will. Or there must be a Gate somewhere on this world."

"We'll get back to them, Leni. I prom—"

"What the hell?" a male voice called out as it came running toward us.

Brock and I instantly dropped into fighting stances to protect Bex, not knowing what to expect. I squinted at the figure in the darkness. Tall, one head, two eyes, a nose, and a mouth. A torso with broad shoulders, a narrow waist, two muscular arms, and two thick legs, clad in a grimy, dark-colored, long-sleeved shirt and grimier, ripped-up jeans. The air smelled and tasted a little off compared to Florida, but not terribly different. From what I could see in the darkness, the landscape had no otherworldly features. I glanced up at the sky, and there seemed to be millions more stars than I'd ever seen, but there were also no nearby city lights obliterating any of them.

Were we still on Earth?

The pain in my ragged-edged soul told me no.

The man stopped in front of us, and his gaze immediately fell on Bex's body. I tensed, hoping I could fight when I felt like I could barely breathe.

"Rebethannah!" he rasped as he rushed over and fell to his knees beside her. Brock and I both relaxed. "My love, my Rebethannah."

The guy scooped his arms under her and pulled her into his lap, his eyes never leaving her face. Brock and I fell to the ground, too, both of our hands pressed to our chests, though no actual wounds existed.

"Nathayden?" I croaked.

He finally looked at me with breathtaking, light-colored eyes, then at Brock. He studied our faces closely before returning his attention to Bex. Enough light hit the guy's face to show its familiarity: he looked like the last drawing Jeric had made of Nathayden. The one we hadn't recognized before.

We'd done it. We'd brought Rebethannah and Nathayden back together.

"She's hurt," he said, his voice full of grief and worry. "What happened to her?"

"We'll explain later," I said.

"You need to Bond," Brock finished. "It's the only way to save her."

Nathayden frowned at us. "How do I do that?"

Brock and I exchanged a look. Bex was in no shape or form to Bond the way most first times went—during orgasm.

"Your souls need to combine," I said. "You have to figure it out, or she'll die. Both of you will."

He looked down at her again, and then nodded. With Bex in his arms, he rose to his feet with little effort.

"It's not safe out here," he said. I noticed for the first time that he had an unusual accent. He obviously spoke English, and sounded a lot like an Australian, but the lilt was a little different. "Come with me. I'm guessing ... Jacquelena? And judging by the pain on your faces, you're not Jeremicah, so you must be Broderick."

"I go by Leni this time," I said as I pushed myself to my feet.

"You can call me Brock." He struggled to stand, and we set off across the small beach surrounding the pond we'd landed in.

"Call me Hayden." He didn't slow for us, so we rushed to keep up with him. "I feel like I know you, but I really don't."

"It's normal," Brock said. "As long as you know her, that's all that's important."

"I felt her arrive before you even splashed into the pond. I didn't know if you'd make it here."

"Where is here?" I asked, panting. Every step felt like a huge effort, and I didn't think it was because of the different atmosphere. The heaviness came from within.

"We call it Erde. According to that bitch Enyxa, it's a Darker version of Earth. Practically its duplicate, except she's already claimed the souls here. I guess she hasn't accomplished that on Earth yet? She says this is a lower world."

I paused mid-stride. "Everyone here is Dark?"

He looked over his shoulder. "No, not everyone. But a good majority, and the rest are headed that way. Come on. We need to hurry before we get caught."

"Is there a Gate close by?" Brock asked. "We only came to bring you Rebethannah, but we need to return to our own mates."

"The only gates are into the cities, and you do *not* want to go there."

Brock's eyes cut over to me. "I mean a Gate to go Beyond, to the other worlds."

Hayden stopped and turned toward us, his light eyes piercing us. "I have no idea what the hell you're talking about, but if you have a way off this world, we're going with you. So first, we need to help her."

We had no Book and no idea if a Gate existed anywhere nearby or where to begin searching, so Brock and I had no choice but to follow Hayden. We didn't go far before traveling up the side of a hill, but each step made my feet feel pounds heavier than the last. Finally, he led us into a cave, through a tunneled passageway, and into a room where burning coals from a dying fire provided the only light. A large backpack like hikers used and another sack sat on the ground next to it. Otherwise, the cavern was bare.

"I don't have a home," Hayden said as he knelt beside the bags. Still holding Bex in one arm with her legs draped across his lap, he pulled a blanket out of one of the bags and tossed it our way. "This is the best I have to offer for the night. Make yourselves comfortable."

Brock and I both collapsed to the floor, neither of us able to remain upright. I lay on my side and pulled my knees to my chest, curling into a ball, as though I could protect or somehow fill the hole in my soul. Brock tossed the blanket over me before he took the fetal position, too. We'd never be comfortable again until we were with our other halves.

CHAPTER 30

Bex THE DARKNESS PULLED me further, and I tried to follow it, wanting nothing more than the eternal numbness it promised. But only my soul could go, not my body, and they remained stubbornly attached to each other. Every time my soul tried to free itself and drift away, something physical would jerk it back. The feeling of acid burning into my flesh brought me back one time, and then, a blinding light pushed away the Darkness. A hard jolt followed and wracked enough pain through my body that it finally felt ready to let go. Or I felt ready to let go of it. The Darkness gathered again, and I welcomed it. Would have offered it some sweet tea and biscuits if I had any, as long as it gave me the numbness I sought, not just in my body, but in my soul.

As I was about to drift off and I thought my body and soul were finally ready to say their goodbyes to each other, a new sensation surrounded me—the soul part of me. Something I never felt before. A Light chased the Darkness away, which annoyed me for a moment, but with it came a pleasurable warmth that settled into me, filling all the tiny spaces of my soul that I hadn't known had been empty until now. A new energy swirled through me, mixing within my soul, becoming a part of me. The feeling was so perfectly sensual, I forgot about the Darkness.

"Rebethannah." I felt the word more than heard it, and my soul responded, acknowledging the name as mine. Rebethannah. That was my true name, my soul's name. But I'd also been known as Ra'den, when I was One with ...

"Nathayden?" I whispered, and a deep pleasure blasted throughout my soul, filling me with a joy I hadn't felt since ... since we were One.

"We're together, my love. Together again."

My soul wept with sobs of happiness. True happiness. True love. And I knew it was true this time because I'd experienced it before. Many times. Images flashed through my mind of past lives with Nathayden and when we were together as Ra'den. Short glimpses of memories that were fleeting but confirmed what I felt throughout every fiber of my soul.

"I've been waiting for you for what feels like forever," Nathayden's soul said into mine. "Lifetimes of heartache and despair, but I never lost hope. I believed we would find each other again. Our love, our connection, is too strong to be overcome by space and time and even evil. Our love prevails, Rebethannah. Always believe that."

"I do believe. I'd forgotten ... I don't know why ... but I remember now. I know who you are to me and who I am to you."

"Twin Flames. Two halves made whole again."

His words sparked another memory, a recent one. "*When I hold you once more, you will know where you belong and never question it again. Together, our souls as one, is how we're meant to be.* That was you who said it, wasn't it?"

"That was me," he confirmed.

Our souls knitted more tightly together, and we paused in the moment, taking each other in, taking our love in, fortifying ourselves after being apart for so long. The memories of evil herself, Enyxa, destroying our soul came clearer than any others.

We'd been on a world with a sky the color of the natural springs back home, a beautiful greenish blue, and with hot pink trees across the land. Was that why it'd been my favorite color? I loved those trees, I remembered now. Their pink leaves smelled sweeter than any flower on Earth. We'd sit on the highest limbs and keep our watch from there. That's where Enyxa had found us.

After her icy Darkness reached into our physical body, tore our soul out and ripped it in two, she tried to leave me like a piece of trash as she carried Nathayden away. I followed her, needing my Twin Flame. She picked my soul up and heaved it through the portal she'd come in, laughing maniacally, sending me past the Space Between and directly to Earth. I hadn't remembered a bit of this until now.

"She personally brought me here," Nathayden said. "She somehow made it so our souls could only return to the same world we'd left every time we died—so you always went to Earth and I came here, ensuring we'd never find each other. She's been waiting for us to come to her side."

"I almost did just now," I admitted.

I felt him try to bring us together even closer, like a soul hug. "I almost did many times. But then I'd only remind myself that I couldn't, for your sake. If I went Dark, so would you, and I could never allow that to happen. I couldn't allow for your soul to be forever extinguished. I couldn't imagine the universe without your light."

His feelings soaked into me, and I felt every word he said, including the deepness of their meaning that couldn't be expressed verbally.

After a long while of simply existing as a single unit again, I became more focused on what was around us than what was within us. We were in a dark room, hovering near the top of it, which I only realized when I saw bodies on the floor below us. And one of them was mine. I lay on my back, my head turned toward a man who lay on his side as close to me as possible without touching me. Except his hand, which held mine.

"Whoa," I breathed. "Where are we? What's going on?"

"*We*, the soul parts, are projected from our bodies. I sort of figured it out not too long ago, but it's never been like this. When Broderick and Jacquelena said our souls needed to Bond, I gave it a try and found yours already out." He didn't say what we both knew—that I'd been trying to leave. He didn't need to. Now that I found him and understood what had been wrong with me all this time, I had no reason to leave again.

As I studied Nathayden's face, I recognized it as one of the pictures that had been drawn in Leni's book. I didn't know how that could be, but there he was in the flesh. His physical self had never been what I loved—it changed life to life. It had always been his soul. *Our* soul. But, oh, my, goodness. How did I get so damn lucky? Nathayden was flippin' hot! The beautiful man of my dreams.

"You're pretty damn hot yourself," he whispered. If I'd had flesh and blood, I'd be flaming red right now. I'd forgotten for a moment that he could feel everything I felt and sense my thoughts. "You've always been beautiful to me."

But not right now. Not with my beaten body.

"Yes, now more than ever."

I pulled us downward to hover closer, taking in the damage, and cringed. My soul broke into fresh sobs.

"I'm so sorry, my love," Nathayden said. "I wish I could have been there to prevent this. You didn't deserve it. You deserve only love and kindness. I promise that's all I'll ever give you."

"I'm afraid I'm too broken for you now."

"Oh, my love, you have no idea everything we've been through. You don't remember it all, but I do. You're not broken. I'll help you heal, inside and out, just like we've always done for each other." His soul tightened around mine again. "We're together now, and that's all that matters. We'll get through everything else."

I let him soothe my soul, and I did the same for his, which I realized was just as battered and beaten as my own. The intermingling of our souls as we shared our eternal feelings for each other felt like nothing I'd ever experienced before. Not in this lifetime anyway. The gentle bumps and light touches that I thought of as soul-kisses, the soft caresses against each other as we learned and remembered more about the other and our connection, the pure high of being together that would make my belly quiver and my thighs clench if I were in my body ... This was what I would call truly making love. We lifted each other up, shared our love, twisted and swirled, stroked and collided again and again until we combined and exploded together in what I could only call a soul orgasm.

And then we drifted down in the most perfect peace.

I didn't want to, but eventually, I pulled away from Nathayden, testing myself apart from him. I still felt him in me, which brought me more joy than I'd ever felt in my life. I went as far as across the cave to where Leni and Brock slept. Both of their faces looked scrunched and pinched, as though they grieved. I vowed to Nathayden that we'd do whatever we could to help them, and he agreed. After all, we didn't just owe these lives to them. We owed them the full existences of our souls.

"I don't know how much time has passed," Nathayden said, "but as much as I hate to say it, we can't stay like this forever. This world is a dangerous one. We must figure out our plans."

I slid back into him, and we mixed together for a bit longer before reluctantly slipping back into our bodies.

"I love you, Rebethannah," Nathayden's soul whispered to mine right before we did.

"I love you, Nathayden," I replied.

Excruciating pain zinged through every part of my body as soon as I returned to it. Sharp jolts in my muscles and organs, dull aches in my bones, burning and stinging across my skin. I hadn't moved a hair yet, but even the simple act of breathing brought agony.

But that was okay. I didn't want to be numb anymore. Because if I could feel pain, that meant I could feel love, too, and I had someone who loved me very much. I'd always had him. I'd just needed to find him again.

I tried to pry my eyes open as much as possible against the swelling. I could see better than I could in the car, which gave me hope. Especially when I focused in on the most breathtaking face I'd ever seen. I mean, he seriously took my breath away, and I realized I'd never really known what true beauty was until now. I saw it in the silver eyes staring back at me—no, I saw it in the soul behind those eyes. He smiled as he gazed at me with utter adoration, and if my body didn't ache so much, it probably would have melted.

"Hi. I'm Hayden," he said, his warm but gritty voice sending a charge straight to my soul.

I gave him the best smile my tight and aching face could muster. "Hey. I'm Bex. And I belong to you. Forever."

His grin grew, and his hand gently cupped the side of my face. Then ever so softly, he brushed his lips against mine. And I knew I'd never stated anything more true in my life. *All* my lives.

Hayden whispered against my lips, "And I'm yours. Always."

CHAPTER 31

I'D CLOSED MY eyes but never fell asleep. I didn't see how I could with the pain in my soul. Would I ever be able to sleep again? Or was that how I would go Dark?

My body trembled, and I opened my eyes. The cavern was just as dark as it had been when we arrived with a faint orange glow on the walls, but a freezing cold had set in. I shivered again, as much against the agony as the cold. Brock's eyes opened. He probably hadn't slept either. Bex had never awoken, and Hayden lay with her. I hoped they were Bonding.

"You okay?" Brock whispered.

I gnawed on my lip, and tears stung my eyes.

"They'll come for us, right? Jeric and Asia?" I asked, doubt already darkening my hopes. Why hadn't they come already?

"Of course," Brock said through gritted teeth. "They probably don't know what you did with the Book and are trying to figure it out."

I pressed my lips together and nodded. "Until then, we keep each other alive. Okay? We can't let each other go Dark."

"You have my word, Leni."

We held each other's gazes for a moment, then I nodded again and closed my eyes, squeezing them against the tears. I envisioned the current face of my Twin Flame—his royal blue eyes, the ring in his eyebrow, his full lips and the dimples in his cheeks. With every bit of my heart and soul, I tried to reach across the worlds to him, believing as hard as I could.

I love you, Jeric. Come find me, babe.

CHAPTER 32

Jeric I SAT ON the sand near the water's edge, my knees bent and my arms hanging on them. My eyes stared out into the water where I'd last seen Leni, but I didn't see the scene as it was now. I knew the sky had lightened with the pastel shades of dawn and the water rippled with an unusual calm, but my vision saw this place several hours ago. The pain of my shredded soul wouldn't let my mind stop replaying the scene on a damn loop.

Brock had been carrying Bex toward the Gate with Leni walking next to them, and Asia and I had just entered the water after I accepted that I'd needed to trust Leni and her instincts. Stupid. I'd been so stupid, arguing with her instead of trusting her. Once again, I'd majorly fucked up. And then what happened next baffled the shit out of me, which was probably why I kept returning to it—because I needed to figure it out. The Gate had somehow *moved*, as if it had come to Brock, Bex, and Leni instead of them going to it. Was that something our instincts had never discovered? Our souls had never remembered? That the Gate would come to a Broken soul if it was close enough?

I mentally kicked myself in the ass for the thousandth time for not considering this possibility before. If we had known, Leni and Brock would still be here right now. Or, at the very least, Asia and I would be with them. Of course, if I had listened to Leni sooner, we wouldn't be in this position either. But since Asia and I hadn't been close enough to them, the Gate had blocked us out. I'd charged at it, but the light had become a solid wall stronger than steel between us. And then it simply disappeared, taking Leni, Brock, and Bex with it.

I'd been watching for its return ever since. Waiting for it to spit Brock and Leni back out, like it had done before. Asia remained glued to this spot, as well.

"It feels like they're waiting on something," Asia whispered from her place by my side, where she sat in nearly the same position as I did.

I didn't dare tear my eyes from their focus point, but I didn't have to look at her to know who she meant. Hundreds of the Dark souls of the Lakari floated in lazy circles overhead, more like a circling cloud of mist than individual souls, as though they'd gathered for something. As soon as Leni, Brock, and Bex disappeared and the Gate did, too, the Shadowmen had all returned to their spirit forms and their domain in the sky, unseen to the rest of the world.

Several Guardians projected, trying to drive them out, but they returned as soon as the Light of the Phoenix souls had moved far enough away. They didn't attack, though. They waited. Like us.

Asia sighed. "What's taking so damn long?"

"I wish I knew," I muttered.

Other Guardian souls had projected and gone to the normal site of the Gate to try to open it for Leni and Brock to return. That was hours ago, and we hadn't seen or heard from them since. Without our Twin Flames, Asia and I couldn't project. This fact, combined with the pain of our missing halves weighing us down, made us pretty fucking useless.

I blew out a frustrated breath at the same time the ground trembled underneath my ass. Asia sprang to her feet.

"What was that?" she asked.

Another, more violent rumble had me jumping up, too. The water that had been so calm before wrinkled with waves. A third shake nearly knocked us off our feet, and the waves grew higher, forcing us to hop backward to avoid getting wet. The Lakari overhead became suddenly excited, swooping and screeching like crows.

"They've opened the Gate," I said. I didn't know this for sure, but that was my guess, and as if in confirmation, the island out in the water lit up. My heart took off in a gallop.

"They're coming back to us!" Asia squealed with the same hope swelling my chest.

But the light on the water blacked out. Even from here we could see the movement. More Lakari souls were rising from the water like a fountain of Darkness.

"Oh, shit," Asia murmured, her hope deflated.

"No kidding," I said, bracing myself for the fight.

The outpouring of Lakari from the Gate stopped almost as quickly as it had started. The chaos above us heightened, but then settled, and then the Darkness over us thinned.

Asia looked at me with those big, dark eyes of hers threatening to spill tears. "What happened? I don't feel Brock."

I shook my head. The pain in my chest resurged. "I don't feel Leni, either."

A few minutes later, a voice called from behind us. "Jeric, Asia."

We both turned around. Kel came running out of the manor toward us. He and Mat had been at the Gate, I'd thought. Kel stopped in front of us, and his face twisted. "I'm sorry, man."

"What's wrong?" I asked.

He shook his head. "We tried to open the Gate, but the Lakari poured through it. *Masses* of them. We had to shut it down. For good."

"*What?*" Asia shrieked.

Kel threw his hands in the air. "We didn't have a choice. It's like they were waiting for us to open it." He put a hand on each of our shoulders. "Don't worry, though. There are six other Gates on this planet. They'll get back."

Mat came running up behind him, with Melinda and Uri on his tail. They frowned when they looked at us.

"I'm afraid you're wrong," Melinda said, her voice thick. "All of the Gates had opened at the same time. Phoenix around the world were trying to help Leni and Brock. But the Lakari swarmed them all. They—" She paused, as if she couldn't finish.

"They had to seal the Gates," Uri finished for her. "Every single one."

Asia and I glared at him.

"What do you mean?" Asia asked, her words slow and heavy.

"No soul enters or leaves Earth," Melinda answered, "except in physical death."

Asia and Mat both gasped.

"For how long?" I demanded.

Uri looked at his feet before bringing his gaze up to mine. "Forever, maybe. We don't know right now."

I shook my head. "No. We have to get Leni and Brock out of there ... wherever they are. We have to get them back."

"I'm sorry," Uri whispered. "We don't have a choice."

"*NO!*" Asia screamed, tears spilling down her cheeks. She threw herself at me, the only one who could understand her pain, and I caught her in my arms. "We're trapped, Jeric. *They're* trapped. We're here, and they're stuck in the Beyond, and there's nothing we can do!"

She sobbed the tears that wouldn't come for me. Only a deep, lasting despair came, filling my heart and weighing my soul down like a lead stone.

Because not being able to rejoin with our Twin Flames meant all four of us would go Dark and not in another lifetime or two. This way that we'd been Separated—by the Gate itself—

we'd go quickly. In the present. It was only a matter of time and not a lot of it.

As this reality set in, I couldn't bring myself to care, at the moment, about Brock and Asia, or about myself. Only one thought hung in my mind, and its five-ton weight crushed my soul:

The Light that was my Leni would be snuffed out forever.

A NOTE FROM KRISTIE

ALTHOUGH *THE SPACE Beyond* is a paranormal story, it deals with real-life demons that unfortunately affect us all, either directly or on a societal level. The facts are real. According to the U.S. Center for Disease Control, 24 people per minute are victims of rape, physical violence or stalking by an intimate partner in the United States—more than 12 million women and men over the course of a year. 1 in 4 women (24.3%) and 1 in 7 men (13.8%) aged 18 and older in the United States have been the victim of severe physical violence by an intimate partner in their lifetime.

The situations depicted in this book are fictitious, but were inspired by memories of scenes I witnessed as a child and stories I've heard from close friends and family members who are survivors. My heart aches for the people who go through similar experiences every day, and I pray that they find a way out.

If you or a loved one needs help to escape an abusive relationship, please don't wait another day. There are so many resources available to you. Please contact one of the numbers below to start to heal. And if you are fortunate enough to be able to help, I pray that you'll find it in your heart to support these organizations. A $5 donation can ensure the phone is answered that could save a life.

Domestic Violence Help
USA
The National Domestic Violence Hotline
1-800-799-7233

UK
National Domestic Violence Freephone Helpline
0808-2000-247

Australia
1800Respect
1-800-737-732

Another real-life demon haunting the pages of this book is drug and alcohol abuse, which has permeated today's society. Sadly, everybody can tell their own personal story of how alcohol and drugs have torn lives and families apart. If you or someone you love needs help, please reach out for it. You can't do it alone, and you don't have to.

ABOUT THE AUTHOR

KRISTIE COOK IS a lifelong, award-winning writer in various genres, from marketing communications to fantasy fiction. She continues to write the Soul Savers Series, a New Adult paranormal romance / contemporary fantasy, with *Promise, Purpose, Devotion, Power,* and the latest release, *Wrath,* book five, available now. She's also written a companion novella, *Genesis: A Soul Savers Novella,* which details the compelling history of her Soul Savers mythology. Over 300,000 Soul Savers books have been sold, with *Promise* peaking at #54 on the Amazon Top 100 Paid list and at #1 in the Amazon Fantasy category.

Kristie's second series, The Book of Phoenix, is a New Adult paranormal trilogy. *The Space Between* and *The Space Beyond* are currently available, and *The Space Within* will be available Summer 2014.

Besides writing, Kristie enjoys reading, cooking, traveling and riding on the back of a motorcycle. She has lived in ten states, but currently calls Southwest Florida home with her husband, three sons, a beagle, and a puggle.

CONNECT WITH ME ONLINE

I love to hear from and connect with readers.
Please don't be shy.

Email: kristie@kristiecook.com
Author's Website & Blog: http://www.KristieCook.com
UK Fan Site: http://www.kristiecookfansite.co.uk
Soul Saver Series Website: http://www.SoulSaversSeries.com
Facebook: http://www.facebook.com/AuthorKristieCook
Twitter: http://twitter.com/kristiecookauth

If you'd like to get an automatic email when my next book is
released, sign up here:
https://www.facebook.com/AuthorKristieCook/app_16630360
3381066. Your email address will not be shared and you can
unsubscribe at any time!

Word of mouth is very important for any author. If you
enjoyed the book, please consider leaving a review, even if it's
only a sentence or two.

WHEN DARKNESS
THREATENS, WHAT
MATTERS MOST LIES IN
THE SPACE WITHIN

THE SPACE WITHIN

BESTSELLING AUTHOR
OF THE *SOUL SAVERS* SERIES

KRISTIE COOK

PART THREE IN THE BOOK OF PHOENIX

THE SPACE WITHIN

Part Three in The Book of Phoenix series
Author: Kristie Cook
Release Date: July 14, 2014
Where: Amazon, B&N, iBooks, Kobo (all countries)

When Darkness threatens, what matters most lies in The Space Within

Completing a mission that reunites Guardian Twin Flames turns devastating when the Book of Phoenix throws Leni and Brock into a Dark world, leaving Jeric and Asia behind. They count on their other halves to rescue them, but when that doesn't happen, they must fight through the Darkness and find a Gate that will take them home.

Except all of Earth's Gates are sealed.

Enyxa, ruler of Darkness, and her horde of Dark souls storm the Gates to push their way through to Earth. While Leni and Brock fight Enyxa on their side, Jeric and Asia must figure out how to save their Twin Flames without jeopardizing all of Earth's souls. Through it all—and with a little help from Enyxa—Brock and Asia begin questioning their relationship and whether they're truly meant to be together...or if they're two Lost souls forced to become one.

If the Broken dyads don't find each other fast, they'll be lost to the Dark forever. But to reunite means choosing themselves over all of Earth's souls. Can Jeric make that decision? And will Brock and Asia find the love they both desperately crave? Or are they all doomed to perpetual Darkness?

Discover how it all ends in *The Space Within*, the explosive conclusion to The Book of Phoenix trilogy.